Who comes to your side...

others ca

A grea.

who causes the deepest pain?

Someone lying..., close.

LYING CLOSE

Frank F. Weber

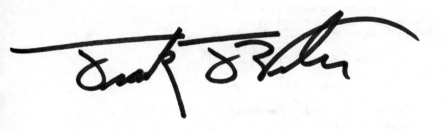

For press inquiries, contact the author at frankweberauthor.com

First Edition August 2020

Published in partnership with BookBaby, 7905 N. Crescent Blvd., Pennsauken, NJ 08110.

Published by Moon Finder, 500 Park Avenue, P.O. Box 496, Pierz, MN 56364

ISBN: 978-1-64970-207-4
EISBN: 978-1-64970-205-0

LYING CLOSE

DEDICATION

I would like to dedicate this book to the amazing people at CORE Professional Services, who are committed to making the world better. People who offer help to those of all histories, predominantly in poverty, and guide them successfully into meaningful, moral lives. Where there's meaning, there's happiness!

Thank you to my editor, Tiffany (Lundgren) Madson for your brilliance and willingness to work around the clock like I do, to meet deadlines. I appreciate that we can respectfully disagree and still work effectively together. Tiffany is also a colleague in my forensic work which gives her a unique understanding of forensic cases.

A special thanks to Krista Rolfzen Soukup, Literary Publicist and Blue Cottage Agency for your guidance in this writing and publishing venture.

And finally, and most importantly, thank you Brenda for yesterday, today and tomorrow—all better, together... K Love (A reference to science theories. In math, K = constant and refers to entities that rise and fall uniformly together.)

PROLOGUE

JON FREDERICK
6:00 PM, MONDAY, OCTOBER 5, 2020 BEAVER ISLAND
BREWING COMPANY, ST. CLOUD

I'M SURROUNDED BY the walls of a log cabin while a chilled glass of nitro coffee lager is being poured in front of me as a full glass of foam. I give the bartender a questioning eye about what appears to be a badly poured glass. Curt advises me to be patient. I reflect on the murder of Todd Hartford, which I, as an investigator for the Bureau of Criminal Apprehension, recently closed.

One of the trysts exposed in this murder book is a romance between a Christian man and a Muslim woman. This mystery is not intended to be a judgment on Christianity or Islam; it's based on a true crime, and is simply what happened. Jesus expressed the same concerns I have when he warned us not to turn his house of prayer into a robber's den. With that said, the vast majority of violent offenders I work with have no religious beliefs. There are problems to be resolved in every religion, but religion isn't the problem. Believe what you believe, just treat others with a kind and tender heart.

My glass of bubbles wondrously morphs into a full glass of beer. I have never seen anything like it. Have I just experienced a miracle? The 1917 Code of Canon Law would require at least one more miracle to qualify me for sainthood, but the lovable Pope Francis was canonizing Blessed John XXIII "after a legitimate relaxation of current law." So, one miracle might give me a shot. A cold beer and a legitimate period of relaxation sounds perfect, following a case that ultimately cost me my job.

This case will be presented in chronological order, from the perspective of the most relevant person at each stage of the story. To the reader, then, pay attention to the name at the top of each chapter. I added physics and science theories at the beginning of each chapter. The theories are not essential to solving the mystery, so ignore them if you find them getting in the way of the story. They're simply fodder for other science geeks.

LYING CLOSE

1

CHAOS THEORY =
*A small change in the initial conditions can create
a significantly different outcome.*

Edward Lorenz Mathematician & Meteorologist
Proposer of Chaos Theory and the Butterfly Effect Massachusetts
Institute of Technology (MIT), 1963

JASPER ROSS
5:25 PM FRIDAY, FEBRUARY 1, 2019
CHIPMUNK ROAD, GREY EAGLE

AFTER WORKING AS a financial analyst for Ore-Ida's parent company for four years, I took a cut in pay to live in God's country and work for the First State Bank of Swanville. The endless and obnoxious potato-head jokes were not my primary reasons for leaving. I was simply one of the ninety percent of people who left their jobs because of difficulties with a coworker.

My wife, Brenna, and I had moved into a rural home by Grey Eagle with our four-year-old son, Zack. As a bank loan officer, I felt the place was a great buy. And for God's sake, the house was on Chipmunk Road. Nothing bad could happen there. Brenna wanted to hold out for something better, but finally acquiesced. She said as long as we were together, she'd be happy. Despite our difficulty getting this old house warm through the bitter windchills of this past winter, Brenna made the best of it. It was her nature. Maybe God was getting even with me for not being the husband I should have been. Regardless, I was trying to be that man now.

My thirty-one-year-old wife was a couple years older than I. She was also a fit cross- contry skier who taught environmental biology at Upsala High School. We weren't resort skiers, but rather the couple who bought skis at a good price and made trails through the forest. Brenna lovingly shared her wisdom of nature with us as we traipsed with Zack through the woods. Last night, we learned that pine trees have female cones that produce seeds, and male cones that drop pollen.

My guilt over buying this money pit was further compounded by our paranoid neighbor, Owen Warner, who, like a stalker in a horror flick, silently observed us. Owen was crusty and mean. He was always on alert for any shenanigans going on in the area. He had this insane fear that the only reason a young person would buy a place in the woods was to make meth. He'd run out of the house, shameless in his blue union suit, just to videotape us when we harmlessly explored our land. His VHS recorder was the size of a camera you'd expect to be perched on the shoulder of a cam-eraman from an investigative news team. With Brenna's naïve heart, she'd kindly suggested we get to know Owen, but I felt the less she interacted with that crazy old fool, the better.

Our Friday routine involved Brenna coming home to rest, exhausted after a week of teaching. Her parents usually picked up Zack, while I worked late. But tonight, I was starting family night. I left work at 4:00, picked up my son, and we were going to eat nachos and watch Disney's original Pete's Dragon all nestled together on the couch.

I was frying hatch peppers a work colleague brought me from Texas and my young assistant was kneeling on a chair at the kitchen table, eating cheese directly out of the bag—the cheese he was supposed to be sprinkling on chips.

We were in for the evening, so Brenna had slipped into her pajamas and thick stockings.

As she entered the kitchen, Zack farted and giggled.

Brenna kissed him and said, "It's so cold in here, I think I saw snowflakes come out!"

Zack laughed harder. "I tooted snowflakes!" For a moment, life was perfect.

As I checked the peppers the kitchen suddenly became eerily quiet behind me.

When I turned back, there was a burly man with Pacific Islander features standing by Brenna and Zack. I flashed on the totem of the Kú—the Hawiian god of war—the taker. The man's grimace was as threatening as the face carved into that totem. I froze, trying to process what was going on. I thought I'd locked the door.

The intruder looked as surprised to see me as I was to see him. The amped-up Hawaiian had short, dark hair, large shoulders, and tree-stump biceps. His hooded eyes were menacing, and I didn't like the way they slid lazily from Brenna's thick socks up to her breasts, braless under her pajama top. He slid a hunting knife from its leather sheath on his belt, revealing a violent-looking steel talon at the tip of the blade.

Brenna immediately crossed her arms over her chest and I felt my hand slowly cover my neck. This couldn't be happening—not tonight. Brenna and I had finally, fully reconciled.

As we stood frozen, Kú took out a cell phone and ordered, "Get in here. We've got a problem."

I searched for words to get this psychopath to leave, but my mouth went dry and my mind was blank.

A gargantuan, Paul Bunyan–looking man, with wild red hair and a full beard, barreled through the door, holding a handgun. He clearly wasn't happy. The gun seemed unnecessary, as I could picture this guy snapping trees in half with his bare hands.

Bunyan asked Kú, "Now what?"

Emotionless, Kú told him, "Nothing's changed."

Still holding the spatula, I pointed with it and impotently stammered, "My billfold's in the drawer—you can have all my money. That's all we have."

"Take the kid upstairs," Bunyan ordered.

Brenna stepped toward Zack, but Kú shoved her hard into Zack's toys, which had been neatly stacked against the wall. She landed hard in a crumpled heap of Transformers and Legos.

He hooked my son around the waist with his bulging arm and headed upstairs.

Zack's eyes pleaded with me as they escalated out of sight.

I begged, "Don't hurt him." I took half a step toward Bunyan, but with the mammoth of a man pointing a gun directly at me, I stopped in my tracks. Handguns could be more lethal than high-powered weapons, because the bullets bounced off bone, tearing up your insides instead of passing through.

Brenna clumsily knocked toys aside as she made her way back to her feet.

I wanted to be a man who'd die rather than let someone take my child away, or harm my love, but at the moment, Brenna once again stood statuesque, while I was scared stiff. The high-pitched blare of our smoke alarm jolted me out of my trance, and I realized the peppers were burning.

Bunyan barked, "Shut the burner off!"

I turned and did as I was told. I took the frying pan by the handle and considered tossing the burned peppers into his face, but I didn't. I was afraid he'd unload that gun on me. I slid the pan off the burner and turned back, like a damn coward.

"Make that alarm stop," Bunyan yelled at Brenna. Without hesitation, Brenna gracefully stepped on top of a chair and, with trembling hands, knocked out the battery, ending the piercing screech.

Kú returned down the stairs, alone.

I asked frantically, "Where's Zack?"

Kú threatened, "He's fine, but he isn't going to stay fine unless—"

Bunyan cut him off. "Unless you come up with some serious cash. That's all we're looking for. You can keep your jewelry and credit cards."

Fumbling, I opened the kitchen drawer and took out my billfold. There was a knife next to it. I tried to will myself to grab it. I couldn't muster the courage. I simply retrieved my billfold. Another opportunity squandered. Brenna's silent disappointment weighed on me. That knife was our last chance.

When I handed my wallet to Bunyan, I implored, "Here's all the cash we have. Brenna's tapped out. You can have it. We won't call anyone. Please—just leave us alone."

Bunyan appeared to be weighing his options. He finally directed me, "Let's find some duct tape, just to guarantee you won't call the cops when we walk out the door."

I led him to the garage. My eyes darted from the hammer, to the screwdrivers, to the drywall blade.

Aware of my deliberation, Bunyan warned, "Right now, thinking is your worst enemy." When we returned with the tape, Kú sneered as he ordered, "Kneel on the floor."

I always wondered why people allowed themselves to be executed. I had two reasons: The first was shame. I deserved this for my past infidelity. The second: I was scared to death. I had some insane hope that this would all pass and we'd be okay—an Avenger would burst in at the last second and save us.

Because of the pinecones and acorns, I could typically hear
a car approaching on our gravel road from a mile away. But
tonight, Chipmunk Road was painfully silent. Like a lamb to
the slaughter, my wrists were duct-taped tightly behind my
back and my feet were taped together. My little Zack had to
be terrified, and I was sick over how this could end for Brenna.
I had considered what he might to do to her, yet I had done
nothing to stop it. I had failed the people I loved most.

Ogling Brenna, Kú made his intentions clear to Bunyan.
"You've got to let me do this—keep your partners happy."
He took Brenna by the arm and started to escort her out of
the kitchen.

I begged desperately, "No!"

Bunyan didn't appear necessarily okay with it, but he
wasn't stopping it, either.

In a last-ditch effort, I tried jerking myself to my feet, but
Bunyan cracked my skull with the butt of the gun and I fell
back to the floor. I curled into myself, trying to blink the stars
out of my vision.

Bunyan was angry, like somehow it was my fault Brenna
was going to be assaulted. He roared, "It's a little too late
now, don't you think? Unless you're going to tell us where we
can find some real money, I don't want to hear another word
from you." He squatted down, filling my vision with his oversized frame, and ground the barrel of the gun hard into my
temple to emphasize his point.

I squeezed my eyes shut in equal parts of fear and self-hatred.

Then Brenna, in a barely audible voice, offered, "I can take
you to some money, but you have to guarantee my family's
safety." She seemed to be gaining composure as steadily as it
drained from me.

"Too late," Kú snarled.

Bunyan looked at Kú sideways, in part exasperation and in part derision. He ordered over him, "Talk."

Brenna countered, "First, I need to see my son."

With a tight grip around her bicep, Kú jerked her to his side and they disappeared up the stairs.

It was dead quiet at first, and then I heard a scuffle. With the gun still pressed to my head, I pled with my eyes for Bunyan to intervene.

Bunyan muttered under his breath, "Fucking Cocaine." He shook his head in disgust, pulled the gun away, and yelled, "Money first!"

When they returned, it was clear by Brenna's expression Kú had groped her. Her eyes had gone flat, and there was tension in her lips and nostrils. Her cheeks were bright and burning. She was never one to be overly dramatic, but I had come to know her tells of distress.

Flustered, but fighting for composure, Brenna stuttered, "We had—had a fundraiser at school yesterday. There's money—$18,000 in cash donations, locked in the school's office. I had planned to take it to the bank on Monday. But the room is secure, and has an alarm that requires my eye recognition to open it."

"Looks like we hit the jackpot," Bunyan said, grinning.

My thin, brave Brenna pointed at me. "Jasper can't call anyone all tied up like that, and he wouldn't anyway, knowing my life is at stake."

Bunyan seriously considered this.

Kú's lecherous eyes continued to ogle Brenna as he spoke to Bunyan. "Let me do her here, first." His black eyes cast the emptiness of his soul.

Gaining confidence, Brenna insisted, "If you want me to get the money for you, nothing happens here. My family has to live here. I won't have my boy hear that."

I begged, "No, Brenna."

Kú sneered at me, "I'll be gentle." He rubbed her cheek with the back of his hand.

Brenna jerked away as if he had scalded her.

"Money first," Bunyan repeated.

As the pair of outlaws were about to leave with Brenna, Bunyan's phone buzzed. He quickly answered it, then swore and said, "Okay, we're coming." He yelled, "Let her go! We've gotta run."

Kú argued, "No way!"

Bunyan threw my billfold at me and directed his partner, "Unless you want to spend the rest your life in prison, we gotta go. There's a man out there filming us. He may have already called the police." The two men vanished as fast as they had appeared.

Our crazy neighbor, Owen Warner, had saved us. Real-life Avengers may not be as handsome and spry as the movie versions, but they were just as effective.

Brenna quickly removed the knife from the drawer and cut my ties.

I was right on her heels as we ran upstairs to Zack. When I opened the bedroom door, there he lay, sound asleep on the floor. Confused, I looked to Brenna for an explanation.

She knelt down and kissed him, then looked up at me. "He's fear-frozen. It happens with small animals and small children. When they're terrified, their system gets overwhelmed and they just fall asleep."

I knelt down next to her. "I didn't know the Upsala school had that kind of security."

"They don't," she said, laughing sadly. "And we didn't have a fundraiser. They do have an office door that will bring law enforcement if you don't shut off the silent alarm. My plan was to let the signal go off, and find a way to stay alive until the police arrived."

Thoroughly humiliated over my cowardice, I covered my face to hide my tears. "I love you so much and I didn't do a damn thing. I keep letting you down. I understand if you leave me. I couldn't think."

"This isn't your fault." She held me tightly. "It's okay. I love you." Brenna kissed my tears. "I didn't marry you because I expected you to kill an intruder. I married you because you are this sweet. I love you."

I clung to her. If this ever happened again, I would lay down my life without hesitation. I could never live with the shame I was feeling now. As a man who calculated risk for a living, I knew the odds of this happening again were pretty slim.

As we caressed and carefully woke Zack, Brenna shared, "We need to thank Owen."

I softly told my precious superhero, "I'll call the police and, if you want to pack, we'll stay at your parents'. I'm not asking you to spend another night in this damn house."

2

VIOLENCE AND HATE THEORY =
*The ultimate weakness of violence is that it is a descending spiral,
creating the very thing it seeks to destroy. Instead of diminishing
evil, it multiplies it. Through violence, you may murder the liar, but
you cannot murder the lie, nor establish the truth . . . adding deeper
darkness to a night already devoid of stars. Darkness cannot drive
out darkness; only light can do that.
Hate cannot drive out hate; only love can do that.*

*Martin Luther King Jr.
Christian Minister & Civil Rights Activist, 1968*

JON FREDERICK
4:30 PM, MONDAY, MAY 20, 2019
DOUBLE R BAR, STATE STREET, GREY EAGLE

IN MAY OF 2019, I drove to Grey Eagle to see if the Ross home break-in, in February, was related to a case I was working. Brenna Ross had played it out perfectly. If you can't prevent the assault, postpone it for as long as possible, and pray for intervention. Even though Paynesville and Grey Eagle are in separate counties, the two incidents occurred only thirty miles apart. The Stearns and Todd County investigators didn't feel the cases were related, but both remained unsolved, and I wanted to form my own opinion.

I was sent here to investigate a hunting fatality. In November of 2018, Todd Hartford was discovered slouched over the steering column of his own car, in his driveway. He had suffered a gunshot to his chest while deer hunting, but had managed to make it to his car before dying. His rifle was found in the woods, where the blood trail started, suggesting he dropped it after he was shot. I'd spoken to Todd's friends and coworkers, and everyone described him as a quiet man who steered away from trouble. People used terms such as, "great father," "dependable," "soft spoken," and "no enemies." My task was to find justice for people who no longer had a voice.

Every year in Minnesota, there is at least one report of someone being killed by a careless shooter. Just a few years ago, a twelve-year-old girl from Pillager, playing clarinet in her bedroom, watched her instrument explode after it was struck by an errant hunter's bullet. The shot reportedly came through her bedroom wall; fortunately, she wasn't injured.

Everyone handles loss differently. Todd's widow, Leda, had already been involved in two romantic relationships since her husband's death just six months ago. To paraphrase Hamlet, "She was ready to move on before the meat was cold at her husband's funeral." In typical rural Minnesota fashion, his friends offered no opinion of Leda. If you don't have anything nice to say . . .

One of the problems with the case was that no one, other than Todd, hunted close to his property. Todd had told his brother stories of a magnificent, but elusive, buck on his land, but no one else had seen such a prize. As a quiet family man, he hunted alone. Todd had been a little depressed lately but, on the night of his death, his rifle hadn't been fired.

Since Leda wasn't available until this evening, I opted to meet with Brenna Ross first.

I sat next to Brenna at the end of a sleek wooden counter at the Double R Bar. I noticed right away there was a depth in her hazel eyes that expressed pensive wisdom. She had agreed to meet with me after her school day to discuss the home invasion her family had experienced earlier this spring. A gift bag sat on the empty stool between us.

Brenna sipped a Starry Eyed Brewing Company Blood Orange IPA as she told me, "Jasper's still embarrassed. They never arrested anyone. It's hard to get police to make it a priority, after you tell them no one was seriously injured and nothing was taken." She smacked her glass on the bar. "If it wasn't for my neighbor, that Hawaiian guy would've raped me."

"Could you identify them in a lineup?"

Brenna smiled. "Remembering faces is part of my job as a teacher. I can tell you exactly what they look like." She sipped again, and added, "Jasper and I refer to the really nasty one—the Hawaiian—as Kú. We toured Hawaii." She shrugged. "An attempt to rekindle. Anyway, we stopped at the totem of Kú, the taker. I feel like that devil put hands on me."

She pursed her thin lips. "The big one was in his early twenties and smarter. Jasper said the big guy referred to Kú as," she added air quotes, "'Cocaine.' Kú was the smaller of the two. He was scary—black eyes. They seemed surprised to see us home and they only wanted cash. Why? The big money is in the bank cards and credit cards, right?"

"I'd bet they're still in the area. They can't use credit cards, because they're afraid someone might recognize the names."

Brenna leaned back on her barstool. "The gargantuan guy stands out like a sore thumb. I've asked around—nobody's seen him. A couple folks have claimed to have seen the Hawaiian guy, but then referred to farms with Mexican laborers. He wasn't Mexican."

"You could steal from a lot of homes without being reported," I shared, "if you only took cash. People might just blame family members who had access to the home." Curiosity got the better of me, so I finally asked, "What's in the bag?"

Brenna handed it to me. "A present for you. It's the night-shirt I was wearing when those dirtballs violated my home. I followed all of the news reports by your friend, Jada Anderson, on the I-94 murders. She said you had an apparatus that can pull fingerprints off fabric. It didn't help solve those murders, because the perp wore gloves, but Kú didn't, and he grabbed my breasts, hard, over my pajama top. As angry as I was, I remember thinking, 'now we've got your fingerprints, jerkoff.' But the county investigator just left it with me and said, 'You watch too much CSI.'"

"Some of the county investigators are better than our BCA agents, some aren't. It depends who you get." I took the bag.

"Kú's going to rape somebody. My gut feeling is he already has. I still believed somebody would want this shirt."

Brenna became quiet and I respected her need to shake her-self out of the memory. Eventually, she slid her glass away and said, "If one more fool says, 'Nothing bad is going to happen, it's Chipmunk Road,' I think I'll punch him."

"You can tell them that's what they said about Elm Street."

Brenna graciously offered, "Thanks for looking into it."

I finished my Dr. Pepper and thanked her for the information.

Brenna smirked as she slung her purse over her shoulder. "It finally registered—A Nightmare on Elm Street . . ."

I drove Chipmunk Road past the old Ross residence and up a hill to the wooden cabin owned by their neighbor, Owen

Warner. A wooden-peg cribbage board sat ready for players on a weathered whiskey barrel on the porch.

Owen was in his early seventies, but was as fit as a much younger man. The deep lines in his face and hard expression suggested this was no one to cross. He scrutinized my BCA badge under overgrown eyebrows. When he looked up at me, I felt the intensity Jasper had described and made a mental note of it. He took one of my cards and called the number to verify my credentials before finally inviting me in.

Owen scowled as he gave me a full once-over. "Jon Frederick—that's a German name. You're not one of those fourteen eighty-eight pecker-woods who think somehow the Nazis and the confederacy should sleep together, are you?"

I laughed. "I am not. My ancestors were some of the poor Catholics who came from Germany; they were targeted by the KKK." The man understood his history. The number 1488 was a secret code used by white supremacists to identify sympathy for their beliefs. The "14" came from a fourteen-word statement issued by white supremacist leader and murderer David Lane: "We must secure the existence of our people and a future for white children." The "88" came from "H" being the eighth letter of the alphabet, so "HH" was taken to mean "Heil Hitler."

"Those mother-kluckers hate the blacks, Catholics, the Irish, Jews, gays, and basically everyone who doesn't fit into their cone-head hats. No respect for character."

Owen directed me to a ladder-back chair that creaked on the old wooden floor as I sat. A grimy window overlooked the woods outside Owen's home.

"On February 1, 2019, you recorded a video of a vehicle outside your neighbor's house."

Owen nodded and said, "I reckon you want the tape." A closet just off his kitchen had a wall full of VHS tapes, and a large

VHS recorder rested on the floor. After several minutes of rifling through the shelves, Owen pulled out a tape. "Do you want to take a gander at it?"

"Sure."

The recording was dark and blurry. We watched a figure exit the back seat of a car and walk toward the Ross home. The car was indistinguishable in the dark, beyond having lower headlights than a truck. The figure—who appeared to be a male—walked around the house, looking in the dark windows before heading to the back of the home.

"That boy has some gumption," Owen muttered. "People think the problem is all those migrants walking across the borders. Well, they bust their asses workin'. No country has ever been hurt by hard work. The problem is this generation's snowflake, yuppie-ass punks, who think having money is more important than how they got it."

I wasn't fond of the terminology, but understood his point. I smiled and said, "You're preaching to the choir."

We watched the blurry landscape shake as Owen was obviously running. He finally stopped and held the camera still.

Owen interjected, "I didn't catch it on camera, but I did see the sawed-off guy walk in front of the car light. I can't say for sure, but I think he was Métis."

Métis was a century-old term used to refer to someone who was half white and half Native American. In the 1800s, there was a Métis nation along the Red River Valley in northwestern Minnesota.

Owen spoke as I watched the video. "Few people know Minnesota history anymore. The Métis pulled oxcarts from St. Vincent to St. Paul, camping on the banks of the Mississippi in St. Cloud, to restock the food supply and make repairs. They used almost no metal, because it was too expensive. Imagine building an oxcart with wooden pegs and leather straps, designed to float across a river. If that wasn't enough, they got grief because the new settlers were anti-Métis and anti-Catholic. Finally, Canada passed the Manitoba Act, in 1870, which allowed for separate schools for the Métis and protected the practice of Catholicism. Canada seized land from the Hudson Bay Company across the Minnesota border in Manitoba, and the Métis settled there." Owen cracked, "Back when men were men, and so were women."

The porch light enabled us to watch a man, below average in height, hunch in front of the back door. He tapped on the knob with an object. As an investigator, I was familiar with this mode of breaking into a home. The burglar had a blunt key. Blunt keys could be purchased for almost every type of home lock. When you tapped them into the lock, the key opened all of the tumblers, which opened the door. Jasper Ross thought he locked the door. Apparently, he had.

The man disappeared into the home.

Shortly after, a large, lumberjack-looking man exited the passenger side of the vehicle and ran to the back door.

All was still for about ten minutes, then the camera made its way back to the car, until it was directly facing the car's headlights. Owen had apparently stepped in front of the car.

"That was gutsy," I said.

Owen nodded with a grin. "I reckon, but what's an old man armed with a camera going to do? I needed them to git before someone got gutted. The driver never left the car, so I decided to put him on camera—give him incentive to leave. But I'm no fool. Once I made my presence clear, I skedaddled. It's only a hop, skip, and a jump, as the crow flies. But when I returned with the widow-maker," Owen picked up the Winchester rifle leaning in the corner and lovingly caressed it, "they were already down the road."

"You started filming immediately. How did you know they were a threat?" Owen smiled and looked at the rows of videotape.

I realized, "You videotape everybody."

"This is rural Minnesota, man. These yuppie snowflakes are trying to make it meth country.

But I'm not having it. So I scare them away before they set up." "Have you ever seen these guys here before?"

"No."

"You're certain?"

"Yeah." He rewound the tape. "Look at the headlights on that car—kind of an unnatural distance apart. And they flashed twice after the guys got out. That's a foreign jobber. I would have remembered it."

The headlights didn't look particularly unusual to me, but I wasn't a car expert. I'd have the lab look at it.

"I'm going to need the tape."

Owen pulled it out and handed it to me. "Proud to serve my country."

3

THEORY OF HISTORY =
*History, despite its wrenching pain, cannot be unlived, but if faced
with courage, need not be lived again.*

Maya Angelou
Civil Rights Activist & Writer, 2012

MIA STROCK
8:45 AM, TUESDAY, MAY 21, 2019 BUREAU OF
CRIMINAL APPREHENSION MARYLAND AVENUE EAST, ST.
PAUL

I NEEDED TO GET my internship transferred to St. Cloud.
I was working part-time in Albany for the summer. Grandpa
promised me an internship close to home and I knew Investigator
Jon Frederick was working in the area. While I'd never met Jon
or Serena Frederick, recent stories of their crime-solving were
renowned at the BCA.

My grandfather, Maurice Strock, was the former
Superintendent of the Bureau of Criminal Apprehension. It
was an odd title for a man who led the most powerful investigative force in Minnesota. Grandpa had been considering
retirement; the heat he had taken over the BCA's investigation
of Mohamed Noor demanded it. Justine Ruszczyk had called
to report a sexual assault of a woman in the West Fifty-First

Street alley, between Washburn and Xerxes Avenues in south
Minneapolis. Noor was a Somali police officer who, in the
dark, mistook Justine, an Australian yoga instructor, for a
threat. She died, only weeks after another police officer was
acquitted for mistakenly killing African American Philando
Castile. At the time of his death, Phil had been a nutrition-
ist for thirteen years in the St. Paul public school system. The
officer who shot Phil was actually Chicano, even though many
online news stories described him as white. I guess that made
the story a little more sensational. I wasn't white, or black, or
Chicano, but I would have loved racial harmony. Grandpa
was accused of being too "police-friendly" in the BCA's investigations of officer-involved shootings.

Part of Grandpa's unwritten retirement agreement was that
I would get this internship. Interning with the BCA wasn't an
easy mission, with my social anxiety, but my partner encouraged me. Hong seemed to always know what was best for me.

Like a minion, I waited in the entry of the St. Paul BCA
headquarters for my next meaningless grunt task. Sawyer
Koep, an old high school acquaintance, came strolling in. His
slick, clean-cut features reminded me of a JCPenney model.
Sawyer wore a pristine white polo shirt, embossed with
"Kleinfeld and Pritchard Attorneys" in gold lettering, just left
of where one would expect a heart to be. Back in high school,
Sawyer was a senior heartthrob who drove a Bimmer, when
I was an awkward sophomore who rode the bus. One morning, he approached me and asked if I was enjoying school.
Sawyer put his arm around me as we spoke, sending my heart
fluttering. Much to my chagrin, I later discovered that, during
his gesture, he had placed tape over "White" on my White
Bear Lake jacket. I am an Asian adoptee into Grandpa Strock's
family. I walked around school wearing it all day, without a
single friend letting me in on the joke. This clarified for me

that I was a "Bear Lake" resident, but not a White Bear Lake resident.

I guess I shouldn't have complained, as there were two Asian American students for every one African American at that school. My effort at retaliation enraged everyone. I dumped a large caramel latte in that shiny BMW, only to find out it was the wrong car. The car I hit belonged to an African American student, who had just transferred in to play hockey, of all things. I was accused of being a racist. When confronted by the principal, I panicked and was speechless. I ended up paying to have his car detailed and got a long lecture from Grandpa. Proud of turning the tables on me, Sawyer taunted me, slyly uttering, "Blackface," whenever we met in the halls.

Hoping Sawyer had matured since high school, and having a desire to be in everyone's good graces, I went out of my way to kindly greet him at our office. "Sawyer Koep! How are you?" It wasn't fair for me to hate Sawyer simply because he was from Kenwood, the richest neighborhood in the state. I planned on having a lot of money myself, someday.

Sawyer glanced around to make sure no one was in earshot as he smugly retorted, "Blackface. A little bit of nepotism going on here?"

He was such a dick!

Making reference to Grandpa's support of Mohamed Noor, Sawyer added, "I thought your
grandpa would get you a job over at the Jambo Kitchen on the West Bank."

The West Bank neighborhood on the Mississippi, in Minneapolis, has a large Somali population. While I stood red-faced and silent, Sawyer calmly delivered a subpoena to one of the agents and departed.

The new BCA supervisor, Sean Reynolds, had apparently observed the interaction through his office window. Seeing it upset me, he called me into his office and I poured my heart out. I woefully reflected on my past. "At that point in my life, I felt like I had no value—an empty vat resting on a shelf of shame. I cried to Grandpa and he came up with the money so I could transfer to Breck High School when the year ended." I wasn't sure why I felt the need to tell this story to Sean—perhaps for some egocentric, vicarious redemption from a black person, which suddenly seemed pretty pathetic.

Sean heard me out with patience before rendering his cocksure judgment. "You would've been better off if Maurice hadn't bailed you out. It basically kept you from working through it. I know some great people from White Bear Lake, and there's a Sawyer in every school."

"I'm not a racist," I said, "but trying to help Noor got Grandpa in trouble and no Somali ever thanked him for it."

Sean remarked, "Every time someone starts a sentence with, 'I'm not racist, but,' you can count on them saying something racist. If it was the right thing, shouldn't we all be thankful?"

I held his gaze as he spoke, then quickly looked away when his words hit home. He was

right.

"Have you ever spent time in the Cedar-Riverside neighborhood?" "No. Absolutely not."

Deadpan, Sean suggested, "Visit Riverside. The Jambo Kitchen has an amazing grilled steak sandwich, and they put half of their profits back into West Bank community programs."

Ugh! I didn't need another multicultural program. I needed to get out of town. I inquired, "Is there any possibility that I could have my internship transferred to the St. Cloud office? It's what Grandpa promised." I needed to be closer to Hong. He was my rock. It didn't help to read the data on social anxiety: you were less likely to get married and, if you did marry, it was more likely to end badly. Basically, you were scared to death and the data verified you were, indeed, screwed.

Sean stood up, put his hands in the pockets of his black slacks, and surveyed the streets of St. Paul, the wheels in his head spinning down a path I couldn't foresee. He turned to me. "I have an investigator who works in central Minnesota you could work with, Jon Frederick. When he's at work, his brain is always investigating, even about things you'd consider irrelevant. Jon's a little obsessive and he comes up with odd problem-solving strategies, but he's effective." He then asked, "Do you know Jada Anderson?"

I was a bit thrown by the change in subject, but clarified, "The Eyewitness News reporter?" I feigned ignorance to knowing Sean and Jada were now lovers. Jada was a past lover of Jon Frederick. Where was he going with this?

Still avoiding eye contact, Sean said, "You can transfer to working with Jon Frederick immediately, provided you let me know of any contact between Jada and Jon. And this is a directive. You report only to me . . ."

2:30 PM
TODD AND LEDA HARTFORD'S HOME BRIAR CREEK ROAD, PAYNESVILLE, MINNESOTA

I packed as quickly as possible and drove to Paynesville. I met Investigator Jon Frederick on the gravel of Briar Creek Road. Jon was strong and slender, six feet tall, in his early thirties, and had dark hair and boyish blue eyes. His untucked forest green shirt had "Compassion" and "Hope" embroidered in metallic copper that seemed to glow in the warm sun. A spring green canopy of trees and overgrown brush enveloped the gravel path. Show time!

I tried to shake Jon's hand strong, even though I felt a little sweaty.

"We're here to investigate the shooting of Todd Hartford," he shared somberly. "I've already spoken to his family, friends, and coworkers, and everyone has the same story. Todd was a quiet, unassuming man who steered clear of trouble. His daughter was his world. He had no enemies."

I felt terrible for Todd and his daughter.

He studied me and said, "You're stepping right into a case with me, so it would help me to know a little about you."

I knew the look from Grandpa's friends. "You're wondering how my very white grandfather has a Chinese granddaughter. Maurice knew my mom wasn't able to take care of me, so he helped his son adopt me. It was none too soon, as my mom was killed by her boyfriend three months later. I graduated from Breck High and I'm a senior at Macalester College."

Jon commented, "Private schools." I wasn't exactly sure what he meant by the comment.

He glanced down at my shiny, black, floral-decorated shoes. "What are those?"

"I bought them a week ago, at Schuler Shoes." Proud of them, I stuck my foot out and added, "Danskos."

"My wife would love them. Is that an acid stain on the side?"

I inspected the blemish. "Mm-hmm," I said, nodding. There was a white spot, less than a quarter inch in diameter. I hadn't even noticed it. "I'm working a couple days a week at Kraft, in Albany, this summer. It's sorbic acid." I chastised myself—Stop over-explaining!

"If you're going to work with me," he pointed at my shoes, "you'll need shoes you can run in."

Jon was wearing solid black Nike VaporMax tennis shoes.

My sweat felt like pins and needles. Flustered, I challenged him to find something wrong with my conservative clothing. "Any other suggestions?" I opened my hands over my faded sunflower tunic and black jeans.

He gave my clothing only a brief glance. "Your style is appropriate."

Appropriate? Don't talk to me like it's my first day of school, you Patagonia-wearing farm boy. I hated my insecurities. Take a deep breath. He's not trying to be condescending—don't take it that way. "Anything else?"

"Do you have access to any exercise equipment?"

Now what? I'm fat, too? I forced out, "Yes."

"I want you to lift weights three days a week and either run or go on the elliptical for forty

minutes, three times a week. You're going right into the field so I need you to be smart and strong."

"Okay." Think positive. I'd been waiting for the right motivation to exercise. It had arrived. "Is there something magical about the number three?"

"It takes forty-eight hours for muscles to regenerate, so three times a week is enough."

Jon studied Todd Hartford's rural yard as he spoke. "Two last requests. I need you to listen when I'm with others and ask questions when we're alone. Everything I do at work has a direction and I can't have you interfering. You know who asks me the most questions?"

"No idea."

"Sean Reynolds—and he's the best investigator we have. You know who asks the fewest questions?"

Anticipating a complaint about Grandpa, I offered in resignation, "Maurice?"

"No," he sighed. "I know you hear grumbling about Maurice, but he worked hard, long hours and staunchly supported people he cared about. People got all worked up after Maurice asked the BCA staff to all turn in a DNA sample. It allows us to rule out any DNA that could've been accidentally left by an investigator at the scene."

His defense of Grandpa warmed my heart. "That just seems to make sense."

"People felt it was an invasion of privacy. I think if we expect the rest of the world to trust the security of our lab, we need to trust it, too. Do you have any reason to question his integrity?" "No. I thought Grandpa was a rock star until I started my internship." The harsh comments were unrelenting.

"Remember, it's the unbalanced parts in the machine that make the most noise."

I smiled appreciatively as he continued. "Interns ask the fewest questions. They're afraid of looking like fools and don't want to embarrass themselves. Get the information you need, regardless of embarrassment."

Jon's expressive eyes searched mine and he offered a friendly smile. "Look, I'm sorry for being so damn intense. I'm all about getting the job done right, so I'm very direct. My phone conversations are short and to the point. Don't take it personally—it's just how I work."

I needed that. The anxiety that seemed to be whistling out of every pore in my body was gone, for the moment. I relaxed and said, "Thank you."

It was hard to believe my mother started her career as a professional pianist—a performer— and I was so anxious. I guess she also ended her career as a performer, of sorts.

The empty Stearns County squad car in the driveway indicated a deputy was inside the house, talking to Todd Hartford's widow. I sat in Jon's car and read through the police report and the autopsy, while Jon walked the road in front of the

Hartfords' long, dirt driveway. Todd was reportedly shot in a hunting accident, only thirty yards to the right of the path, by a hunter who was believed to be standing close Briar Creek Road. The bullet pierced his right lung and nicked his spine, but hadn't been found. I found myself sympathetically touching the photo of an attractive, fit young man, hunched over in his car. Todd had a bullet hole through the right side of his chest and a stream of blood on his clothes ran straight down from it. This poor man died, right here, about a hundred feet from me.

Jon beckoned me to join him at the end of the driveway. I shared what I had read. "So, Todd was apparently in a rather odd position when he was shot, leaning back and to his right against a tree." I pictured the handsome country boy, with a piece of wheat between his teeth, enjoying the beauty of a nice fall day.

Jon responded with skepticism, "Apparently." "You don't believe that?"

"No. I think they started with the theory that Todd was accidentally shot by a hunter and then tried to make the evidence fit. The exit wound is above the entrance wound, so they had Todd leaning back. And there's no bullet in the tree behind him so, based on his footprints, he had to be leaning against the tree to his right, in order for the bullet to just miss the tree behind him. But Todd was standing straight up."

"How do you know?"

"Did you see the picture of him?"

I nodded, gesturing to the file in my hand.

"What direction was the blood running down his shirt?"

After some hesitation, I said, "Straight down, I believe."

"If Todd would've been leaning to the right, the blood would initially have run down his body at the exact angle he was leaning, and would've straightened as he stood up. You get an L- shaped blood stream if a person changes position after being shot. The blood stream was straight, which suggests he remained straight."

"But it still could have been an accident."

To our left was the Hartfords' farmhouse. The right side of the driveway was bordered by a forest. A small, four-foot-by-four-foot wooden school bus shelter sat at the end of the driveway in front of us. The door was facing the drive and had an opening opposite, allowing a child a clear view of the bus coming down the road. On a glorious, sunny day like today, that opening would allow wisps of breeze to enter, making it comfortable to play in.

Jon said, "I'm going to ask you the same question Tony Shileto asked me on my first day on the job. What do you think when you look at the scene here?"

I studied our surroundings. "The hunter must not have seen the house." Jon patiently waited for me to continue. Knowing he didn't waste time, he had to be testing me. I had to come up with something. "The report said he sat in his car. Why didn't he go in the house? Was Leda the shooter?"

"Good question. The car was a little closer and people don't always behave logically after they're shot—but it's worth exploring."

He was clearly seeing something that eluded me. Frustrated, I asked, "What am I missing?

Something about the scene bothers you."

He pointed to the bus shelter. "Do you remember how cold it was last winter?"

The memory brought a shiver down my spine. "Yes—thirty-nine below zero last January. It was colder in Minnesota one weekend than at either the north or south poles."

Jon raised an approving eyebrow at me. He gestured toward the shelter. "Follow me." We walked to the structure, which resembled a large dollhouse.

"Where's the window?" he asked. "Nor'easters swirl east as they bring cold winds down from the Arctic. It's too cold to have an opening this size on the west side of the shelter." He pointed toward the woods. "I walked down the road and found where the shot was supposed to have come from. The trees surrounding Todd were all maple, poplar, and birch, so they were all barren of leaves during hunting season. Even now, I can see a little of the house in the background. An avid hunter would never fire that shot and an inexperienced hunter wouldn't randomly stop here—it's a difficult place to find."

We both peered through the opening of the shelter and saw broken glass scattered inside.

Jon continued, "The investigators couldn't find anyone, other than Todd, who hunts around here."

"You don't think it was an accident?"

He didn't seem to feel a response was necessary. Okay, it was a stupid question.

After a moment, I opened the shelter door and asked, "Why would he kick in the window? The door doesn't lock."

"So he could rest the barrel of his rifle on the edge and stabilize his shot. Since the shelter is made for a child, an adult would have to be on a knee. It would be difficult to kick in the window from the inside." With an outstretched hand, Jon cautioned, "Don't step inside."

I wished I knew what he was thinking. "The report said the Stearns County investigator thought it was an accident. Del Walker wrote in his report that the shot had to come from over by the road, in order to miss the tree behind Todd."

"The bullet went through his right lung and then nicked his back vertebrae," he explained, "before it exited. It's possible the bullet lost enough velocity that hitting the vertebrae altered its direction."

I nodded nervously, with the realization I was in way over my head. The only thought I had to contribute was that hunters shot through the lung, but I was too nervous to say it.

Jon retrieved a large reel tape measure and a yellow ribbon from the car. He knelt by the shed and measured up from the ground.

He calculated out loud, "The window base is thirty inches off the ground. It's safe to assume the barrel of the rifle was two inches above it. The bullet went through Todd's heart at forty-eight inches from the ground."

He handed me the reel and I stood holding it outside the shelter's window, while he walked the tape to where Todd was reported to have been standing when he was shot.

"Ninety-two feet," he shouted.

I scrambled for a pen and started jotting notes in the file. That would be an easy shot for a hunter with a stabilized rifle.

Jon tore the yellow ribbon in half and tied one piece around the tree. He waved me over. "The ribbon is tied at the height Todd was shot. Part of the reason they didn't find the bullet is because they assumed the shooter was standing. Del's explanation for the higher exit wound was that Todd was leaning back. I believe the shooter was on one knee, which meant the bullet was rising when it hit Todd and that changed the trajectory. Del was right about one thing—the bullet would've hit the tree behind Todd, if the trajectory hadn't been altered. But if it was altered, even slightly, it could have missed the tree."

I watched Jon use the compass on his phone to deduce the angle the bullet would need to take to barely miss the tree and continue on its way into the woods.

He pointed to a small poplar tree close to the direct path. "You can use that tree as a reference point." He left me in the dust as he ran to the poplar and tied the other half of the ribbon to the bough. He then jogged back. I was beginning to understand his directive about sensible shoes. "I want you to download a coordinates app, like Compass, to your phone, so you can make note of that exact location."

I had my phone in hand immediately and searched the app store till I found it. As the app loaded, he shared, "After you get that window put together tomorrow, I'm going to have you walk at eighty-two degrees, for about a mile, from that tree. I'll explain when we leave."

Feeling overwhelmed, I did my best to register his instructions.

Picking up on my confusion, he directed, "I'm going to the house to question Leda Hartford. You're going to put gloves on, get an evidence bag, and collect every small piece of glass you can find. You'll have to reach carefully through the window from the outside to pick up the pieces. You can't step on any of them. And tomorrow, instead of starting the day with me, you're going to spend the morning at our St. Cloud office, reassembling that window. We're looking for a shoe print, so don't, whatever you do, wash the glass."

4

COLOR THEORY =
*There are three primary colors on the color wheel, and the wheel is
divided into a warm and cool side. Red is a hot color; blue is a cool
color. (The color wheel, created by Newton, remains a tradition in
all forms of art, including makeup artistry.)*

Sir Isaac Newton
Physicist & Theologian University of Cambridge, 1666

JON FREDERICK
3:35 PM, TUESDAY, MAY 21, 2019
BRIAR CREEK ROAD, PAYNESVILLE, MINNESOTA

L EDA HARTFORD HAD thick, chestnut-colored hair
cropped to her shoulders and teardrop- shaped, electric
blue eyes. Her full lips looked sticky with gloss, such that her
makeup gave her doll-like features. In light of my being here
to investigate her husband's questionable death, her cuteness
didn't sit right with me.

An older Stearns County deputy, with weathered skin
resembling sand-blasted wood, sat next to her at the kitchen
table. The deputy, Del Walker, had broken blood vessels on his
nose, referred to as "gin blossoms"—the tattoos of alcoholism.
He was teasing a slim little girl seated with them about having
boyfriends in school. She didn't look particularly amused.

The girl's wild red hair and dirty fingernails made it look
like she'd been living in a thicket with animals in the wild. Her

31

lightly freckled face was streaked with a smudge of dirt, as was her too-big Monson Lumber t-shirt. I assumed this must be Todd and Leda's nine-year-old daughter, Giselle. When I entered the kitchen, she looked me over skeptically with wise, big blue eyes.

I introduced myself, offering my hand. "Hello, I'm Jon. You must be Giselle." "No one calls me Giselle. I'm Zelly." She took my hand timidly.

"Noted." She smiled slightly.

I declined Leda's offer of coffee. As she poured herself a cup, she asked me, "Do you think this lipstick's too red?" She gestured to the last empty chair at the table.

"No." I sat down. I thought it was the exact color it was intended to be.

Leda set a cup of coffee in front of the deputy and rested her hand on his shoulder, as if to gain strength from him for the interview. I was curious about that gesture of solidarity.

"Thank God for Del. Since Todd's death, he's been willing to spend some nights here, to keep me safe."

Del cleared his throat. "In my squad car. In the driveway." A bird thumped into the window, startling all of us.

Leda pursed her lips. "I told Todd not to put the feeder so close to the house." "Don't move it, Mom," Zelly pleaded. Then I can't see the birds."

Leda turned to Zelly. "Could you do me a big favor and vacuum the living room? The vacuum's all ready to go."

Clearly wanting to stay in the room, Zelly pouted. "The only reason you had me was to have a slave."

Leda tiredly responded, "Yeah, about a decade ago, I thought, what if my living room carpet gets dirty nine years from now? I decided the easiest solution was to have a baby."

Still glowering, Zelly left to vacuum. The whine of the machine ensured she was not hearing our conversation.

Leda nervously rubbed her hands on her jeans at the mention of Todd's name. She quickly explained her alibi. "Zelly and I were shopping at Crossroads Mall in St. Cloud. Sometimes," she mused, "I think about going completely with that cowgirl, tough look. RCC Western–style. But I'd still prefer to spend any extra money on soft, comfortable PINK pajamas."

Del cut in, "Leda's on video at the mall."

After about five minutes of vacuuming, Zelly stormed by and slammed her bedroom door behind her.

"Let me check on her," Leda sighed and pursued her daughter.

Del looked out the kitchen window and laughed. "I see you got that poor little dolly of the Asian persuasion out there contorting her body through the window, retrieving the glass. More power to her. Even though Leda didn't know when that window was broken, I told her not to use it until you State guys rule it out. We knew you guys were coming. Ever since the heat we've taken over the Wetterling investigation, the State has to check on us, right?" He sadly reminisced, "That boy was taken thirty years ago, and it still feels like yesterday." Pulling himself back to the moment, he turned on me. "Now, you BCA boys are holding the hot potato with the Noor case. You put the cop car back into circulation the next day, when you still needed lab work. What the hell were you thinking?"

"I didn't work the case. The agent asked the officers if Justine had struck the vehicle. Neither cop initially acknowledged this, so he assumed the car offered no evidence and put it back to use. After the car returned to circulation, Noor used the slap on the car as his defense, and then we had a problem."

Del shook his head derisively.

Returning to the task at hand, I asked, "Are you aware that a couple of guys tried to rob a home a few miles from here, in rural Todd County?"

"Yeah. It's out of my jurisdiction, so I heard about it, but never investigated it. I'm not even sure the motive was robbery. Nothin' was taken." Del studied me. "You suspect Leda, here. Like she's sugar and spite and everything white, right?"

Owen had referred to the driver as a man, but no one actually saw the driver.

Del was still chuckling at his rhyme. "You're wrong. I know her and her family. Leda wouldn't intentionally hurt anybody."

"Does Leda have any female friends?" Typically, when a BCA investigator makes a pre- planned visit with a woman, there's a friend supporting her.

Del methodically searched the recesses of his brain before an answer. "No. I think she views women as competition. And, when it comes to men, the word 'no' just isn't in her vocabulary."

Keeping my voice soft enough so only Del could hear, I quietly confronted him. "Did you sleep with Leda?"

Del spat back, "How derelict do you think I am? No! Do you think I'd be talking about it if I had?"

I wanted to point out that he hadn't brought it up—Leda had—but Leda was returning, so I put it on the back burner.

Leda's posture was rigid with tension when she sat. "I don't know what I can tell you that I haven't already told Del. Todd was a good man and a good husband. I loved him. If it was up to me, he would be with me right now."

I appreciated what she was saying, but the words fell flat. She was either on something or holding back. I asked, "Do you mind if I talk to your daughter for a little bit? I have a young daughter myself; I'd like to make sure she's doing okay."

She granted me permission and brought me into Zelly's bedroom to speak to her. "I'd prefer to talk to her alone."

Leda fussed with Zelly's frizzy hair, smoothing it into a ponytail, telling her, "You play so hard, girl." She reluctantly left us.

I thought of my own daughter and considered how this girl was a precious angel to Todd.

Zelly initially ignored me as I spoke, but finally responded when I said, "Giselle and Leda are both pretty names. Hundreds of years ago, there was a very famous woman named Leda. She had a pretty daughter, like you. They called her Helen of Troy. Leda's daughter was believed to be the most beautiful woman in the world." I didn't bother to add that she was also referred to as "the face the launched a thousand ships," as men competed for her affection.

Zelly held a boy and girl doll in each hand, moving them as if they were walking across the blanket on her bed. She made it clear her thoughts were devoted to her father when she asked, "What was the girl's dad's name?"

"Her dad was a great man. They didn't have the name Todd back then, so they called him Zeus. Do your dolls have names?"

Her gaze remained transfixed on the dolls as she shared, "Zelly and Todd. We're walking through the woods looking for deer tracks." She had the boy doll say, "When you see the complete heel in the track that means it's a big deer."

She stopped the dolls and the girl doll exclaimed, "Oh, I see some. They're going this way..." The dolls changed direction. Her face was so expressive; it was obvious Zelly loved and grieved for her father.

"Who walks through the woods with you now?"

The motion of the dolls froze. "No one—my dad's dead." The sadness that came over her was a tangible force I wished I could have thrown out of the room.

"I bet your dad looks down at you and hopes you're still having some fun."

She smiled then leaned into me, wrapped her spindly arms around me, and hugged me tight. Her voice stuttered as she asked, "Could—could you walk through the woods with me?"

This tender heart needed help. I only had to observe Leda for a couple minutes to be cognizant of her self-absorption. "If it's okay with your mom, let's go."

Still wearing her latex gloves, Mia studied Zelly curiously as we approached the bus stop.

Zelly told me, "Mom doesn't want me going in that house anymore. The cold busted the glass out and it's all over the floor."

Mia smiled at us and said, "Almost done."

The weather didn't break that window. It took a force from outside to land all of the glass inside the structure.

Zelly asked Mia, "Can I help you?"

Mia kindly offered, "There's nothing I'd love more."

I cut in, "No, but you can help me." I needed to gain Zelly's trust, and I was afraid Mia would unwittingly dominate the conversation. Mia seemed a little overzealous, so I needed to make sure she didn't take on too much. Her grandfather, Maurice, wasn't easy to work with, but I was no picnic, either, so I wasn't about to complain.

I took Zelly by her hand as we walked into the woods, avoiding the area where her father was shot.

Mia quickly wrapped up her work and came trotting toward us. "I have all the pieces in an evidence bag in the car."

"Thank you! Zelly is going to show us where we can find deer tracks." Zelly grinned and led us on our way.

After I returned Zelly to the house, we made our way back to our cars.

I asked Mia, "Would you mind driving my car? We're going to visit Todd's brother and I need to do some math on the way."

I appreciated that Mia didn't waste any time getting in the driver's seat. I put Marc Hartford's address into my navigation system and we were on our way.

"After you're done reassembling the window," I told her, "I'm going to have you come back out here and look for the bullet. I'll make sure to get you a knife and a metal detector. The two ribbons outline the path."

"Why the knife?"

"You'll have to dig the bullet out if it's lodged in a tree. If it comes to that, be careful not to scratch the bullet."

I took my notebook out and thought out loud. "The bullet was fired at thirty-two inches above the ground and, at ninety-two feet away, was sixteen inches higher when it hit Todd." I scratched some notes. "Assuming the bullet was traveling at 2,500 feet per second, it was moving at an angle of .86 degrees."

Mia interrupted. "Sean suggested you have a thing with numbers. Does talking about numbers calm you?"

"When they provide answers. The exit wound in Todd's back is .86 degrees higher than the entrance wound." I paused. "Passing through the body slowed the bullet down considerably. A full metal jacket bullet fired from a standard deer rifle could travel two miles, but substantially less after passing through a body." I wrote a little more. "I'd bet this bullet is about 468 feet from the first tree."

"That's pretty exact."

"Search in a pretty wide range around it, just in case. But I don't want you in those woods unless either I'm with you or a Stearns County deputy is out here. It's the edge of a forest and we don't know what's out there yet. After you find the bullet, I'm going to have you go through Owen Warner's videotapes, to see if you can find anything useful."

"What if I don't find the bullet?"

We needed that bullet, so I didn't want to offer the option of giving up. "It's going to be a long summer for you."

HIGHWAY 23, PAYNESVILLE

I took Mia with me two miles north, to meet with Todd Hartford's brother. Marc Hartford had a nice, one-story home in a wooded area. It was unrelated, but, since Del had brought it up, I couldn't help thinking this wasn't far from where Jacob Wetterling's body was discovered on September 1, 2016. My heart still sank when I thought of the tragic death of that innocent, eleven- year-old boy, and the years of trauma his caring family experienced. When I held Jackson and Nora, I thought of how Jacob was once held and loved in the same manner by his parents. The aftermath of those thoughts was that Jacob was part of the reason I performed my work with wholehearted intensity. The Paynesville community had been traumatized years earlier, by Jacob's killer, and still had a lot of resentment about the manner in which the investigation was handled. This, combined with the recent criticism of the BCA, could complicate my efforts to get people to cooperate.

The three of us sat by a table on his rustic wood porch, discussing the loss of his brother.

Fortunately, Marc was eager to help. He shared, "A lot of people in the community want me to be mad at the county, but they're trying. Some hunter randomly wanders on my brother's land, hears some movement, and shoots him. What do you do with that? It's not like the city. There are no witnesses, no cameras, nothing. My brother probably didn't even see the guy." He took a large swallow of lemonade. "Think about all of the damage one killer does—to the victims, the community, everybody. The cases here have ruined Del Walker. He was a respected lawman and now he's treated like a joke, just because some terrible person hurt someone and he couldn't stop it. I went to school with Del's daughter, Katie. She's a good-hearted, decent person. She watched her dad dedicate his life to law enforcement, only to lose his sobriety, his marriage, and now the respect he once had from his community."

Investigators worked for victims and their families so, when we didn't deliver, it was heartbreaking. "Can you tell me a little about your sister-in-law, Leda? What's she like?"

With some sadness, Marc commented, "Shallow streams are noisy." He glanced out at his well-groomed yard. "Even though Leda hasn't really dealt with Todd's death, I know she didn't do it. She's never fired a rifle and the story is she was in St. Cloud with Zelly at the time."

I found it interesting that he questioned her alibi. I said, "You don't trust her."

"Leda loves to be the center of attention and Todd was attracted to her because he was quiet and unassuming. Shy guys are easy for a flirt. She gave him the attention he couldn't get on his own—but she was just too much. She couldn't shut it off, even when Todd wasn't around. I don't think he was happy in the end."

I considered this. "Did Leda ever hit on you?" "She knew better." He laughed.

Mia cleared her throat and stated, "You don't believe that Leda was shopping in St. Cloud when Todd was shot."

I had planned on coming back to his "the story is" comment, so I didn't mind Mia's statement.

Marc shared, "A friend of mine said he met her car headed north on County Road 1 that morning, when she was supposed to be shopping with Zelly. But that doesn't make sense. It was an hour before Todd was shot. She'd have to be headed south of Highway 94 to go where Todd was shot, but she was headed north. And Del verified her alibi. He said she was at the RCC Western store in the St. Cloud mall. My friend must've been mistaken."

"That store isn't even open anymore," Mia interjected. "And if Leda lied about where she was, what else is she lying about?"

Marc remained steadfast. "I don't know. I was in the Boundary Waters at the time."

I held my hand up toward Mia to get her to stop interfering, as I asked, "With whom?"

"By myself. I make the trip every year to clear my head."

I continued, "I know it's been months since you've talked to investigators. Tell me what's gone through your thoughts since then. I'm not recording this, just brainstorming, so feel free to say whatever comes to mind. This case is getting cold, and I'm trying to stoke the fire."

He studied the slowly melting ice in his glass, a man wrestling with his thoughts. "A couple weeks after Todd was killed, Leda asked me to look at the million-dollar insurance policy he had through work. After I looked at it, I explained to her it wasn't an insurance policy for Todd. It was liability for the company."

Perception was more important than reality, at times. If Leda thought it was an insurance policy, that may have been all that mattered. It was something, but not enough to support a warrant. "Is there anything else?"

Marc nodded. "This isn't about Leda, but Todd told me, about a week before he was killed, that he was almost shot while hunting on his land. A bullet whizzed by his head, swaying a branch right in front of his face. He had no idea where the shot came from. It could have been more than a football field away. People need to be more careful."

Mia's ever-so-subtle gasp suggested she understood the gravity of that information. It was too much of a coincidence to be an accident.

"Why didn't you share that with investigators?"

"They were grilling me and I was overwhelmed with my brother's death. It didn't occur to me until weeks later. How would it help them? I don't even know where he was hunting at the time."

"Marc, I need you to spend time with Giselle. Leda is too wrapped up in her own misery to see the pain her child is going through. Zelly seems to be suffering the most, and I don't know yet if Leda has any trustworthy friends."

Marc understood the seriousness of my concern and readily accepted the request. "Absolutely."

Even though prosecution was based on evidence, hunches typically guided investigations. With little said, Marc appeared genuinely concerned for Zelly's well-being and that moved him down on the suspect list for me. Still, I reminded myself that initial impressions weren't always accurate.

Once we were on the road, Mia swept her straight black hair off her forehead and said, "I'd bet once Del watched a clip of Leda and Zelly walking into the Crossroads Mall, he never bothered to verify that Leda stayed there. If you'll give me permission, I'll look into it. I don't trust her."

"I appreciate your exuberance, but put the window together and find the bullet first. I'll look into it."

After I dropped Mia off at her car, my phone buzzed and I answered through the hands- free speaker as I headed toward home.

It took a moment before we could hear each other, the result of rural Minnesota phone coverage. I finally heard Sean Reynolds clearly. "We had a case settle, which freed up the lab crew, so Brenna Ross's nightshirt was tested in the VMD."

The vacuum metal deposition system looked like a large glass aquarium. We placed the clothing inside and melted less than a dollar's worth of gold. The gold, now in gas form, adhered to oil left from fingerprints on the fabric. We then melted zinc, which turned the gold black, revealing the prints.

Sean continued, "The vacuum revealed clear prints on the chest area of Brenna's pajama top, just has you suspected."

"Did you get a chance to run the prints through AFIS?" The FBI has an Automated Fingerprint Identification System we could use to detect if prints came from anyone who'd been arrested in the United States.

Sean casually answered, "I did."

He knew I wasn't particularly patient and enjoyed making me wait. I calmly asked, "What did you find?"

"They belong to a fugitive named Kaiko Kane. Kane was facing a pending sexual assault charge and two charges for possession of a methamphetamine when he left California in early 2017. He has no charges in Minnesota. Clean-cut, muscle builder. Looks half white, half Pacific Islander. I'll send you the mug shot. He was raised in Hawaii. His last known address was Eureka, California."

I postulated, "Isn't that in the Emerald Triangle?" The Emerald Triangle included Humboldt, Mendocino, and Trinity Counties, where most of the employment since the 1960s had been in large-scale marijuana production. Significant environmental damage had been done by illegally damming rivers and diverting streams, clear-cutting forests, and heavy use of pesticides to increase production, which was degrading wildlife habitats and killing their salmon fishing. Sixty percent of the weed used in the United States was grown in Humboldt County. "What's he doing in rural Minnesota?"

Sean remarked, "Probably nothing related to the Todd Hartford shooting." "Brenna Ross believes he's a serial rapist."

"I give you your assignments, not Brenna," he warned. "Give Kaiko Kane's name to the Todd County investigators and be done with him."

I didn't respond. Sean had only recently been promoted to supervisor, so he was still pretty raw to people questioning his authority. Sometimes, it was more effective not to argue with intelligent people. Sean had a good heart. I just needed to give him some space to consider what he'd do if he was in my shoes.

After some quiet consideration, Sean acquiesced. "I'll give you a little latitude with this, but the focus of your work needs to be the Hartford case."

When the call ended, I ruminated over the fact that Todd's shooting had sat stagnant since deer hunting ended last fall. Del was either covering for Leda, or he never considered her a legitimate suspect. Could Del or someone else close to the investigation be leaking information? I gave Kaiko's name to the investigators working the Ross home break-in, as my boss instructed. I had the ability to investigate throughout the state, but county investigators could be hampered by jurisdiction issues. Grey Eagle is in Todd County, but on the border of Morrison and Stearns, and close to Benton and Kandiyohi Counties. Kaiko's name and picture might not be shared with other counties.

5

THEORY OF REFLECTION =
Light travels in a straight line and reflects at the exact same angle at which it hit.

Euclid
Greek Mathmetician, 300

JON FREDERICK
10:30 PM, OCTOBER 5, 2020 PIERZ

I T'S ESSENTIAL I share information from "Kú's" past, for you to get a context of Kaiko Kane's behavior at MudFest 2019. In my extensive search for Kaiko, I subpoenaed the recordings of his juvenile therapy sessions. I discovered Kaiko, being the narcissist he is, left a detailed diary of his oppositional thoughts to spite his therapist.

It quickly became apparent that identifying Kaiko was the easy part. The challenge lay in finding him and that could only be achieved by discovering who was hiding him.

6

THEORY OF NATURAL SELECTION =
*Individuals with traits that enable them to adapt to environmental
pressures reproduce and endure.*

Charles Darwin
Geological Society of London, 1854

KAIKO KANE
2:30 PM, WEDNESDAY, MARCH 15, 2007
HAWAII ISLAND RECOVERY
JUVENILE CHEMICAL DEPENDENCY TREATMENT
PROGRAM HUALALAI ROAD, KAILUA, HAWAII

MY ADOLESCENCE IS caught in a loop of behavior and consequences that will only end when I turn eighteen and get out of the juvenile system.

The counselor asks, "Do you have any idea how violated people feel when you break into their homes?"

I really don't care, but I say nothing. The last time I was honest, they accused me of not taking treatment seriously. At age seventeen, I've been in ten foster homes, done stints with five relatives, and been in and out of juvenile detention more times than I can count. When people leave their homes for a night out, I step in and take what I want. Eventually, I get caught and go to juvie. After a couple weeks in lockup, they see drugs among the repossessed stolen items. So, they send me to CD treatment. Their mistaken assumption is that I possess drugs because I enjoy using them. Drugs are a means to an end for me. Once I turn eighteen, I'm buying a ticket to California and finding my way to Humboldt County, California. I'm going big-time. I'll start out as a "trimmigrant," a guy who comes to town to trim weed and learn the business. As long as they don't legalize it, I'll learn firsthand how to develop an effective model for marketing drugs.

My group counselor asks me directly, "Cocaine, how much of your addiction is related to being abandoned by your addict mother?"

"Did you the get that nickname from my wombling peers?"

"Wombling?"

"Street term for aimless. Didn't they teach that in doctorate school?" I add, "I hate the nickname 'Cocaine.'" It's a stupid play on my name—Kaiko Kane. I use drugs only because that's how you sell them. Plus, I'm more of a meth guy. Everyone can afford meth. One thing I can't afford is to tell Doc off again. Each time I do, they send me back to lockup. It's better here. In lockup, I'm a "scourge to society," but in CD treatment, I'm a "victim." "It's not your fault—it's the addiction," they say. Can you be a victim of circumstances you created?

Doc apologizes. "I'm sorry, Kaiko. Do you ever wonder what your life would be like if your mom hadn't abandoned you?"

Instead of honestly telling them I'd have been better off if Mom would have abandoned me the day I was born, I say, "I need to think about that." This passes the baton on to the burnout sitting next to me. It's funny they never mention my dad. It's okay, my dad never mentions me, either. His driver's license should be tagged, "Orgasm donor."

I hate sitting in these stupid groups and listening to everyone mourn about their drunk-a- logs. You got wasted and bad things happened. Well, cry me a river! What the hell did you think was going to happen—you'd graduate with honors or win the Heisman Trophy? Half of my delinquent counterparts are here because of meth. More people die in Hawaii from drug overdoses than car accidents, and more than twice as many die from overdoses than from guns. If you think we're different than the rest of the nation, you're wrong. But I'll survive. I'm not making any attachments here. Half these people will be dead in a decade. Why bother? I get what I need and move on. Right now, I need a place to stay until I'm old enough to get a plane ticket off this rock. Just four more months!

Skinny platinum blonde, candy red, and royal blue–haired girls make up half the group members today. The counselor thinks I'm an astronaut—taking up space—but I'm learning. Why are there so many girls with dyed hair in this program? Because we're all on probation, and you can't drug test bleached hair.

Platinum Blonde is embarrassed over all of the sexual things she did for drugs. I could listen
to her all day.

Candy Red interrupts my fantasy to tell a story of how she was raped at a party after she was done tweaking and crashed.

Royal Blue says, "Me, too."

Platinum Blonde takes the talisman back, proclaiming, "Me, too."

I ask, "Did any of you call the police?"

They shake their heads no, no, no.

"I couldn't afford to risk another drug charge," Royal Blue explains.

Now, that's useful information. Trying to stay out of juvie a little longer this time, I force myself to share, "I dated a girl who got raped by her meth dealer."

The bleach babies wait for me to continue. Candy Red finally asks, "So, what did you do?"

With a confident smirk, I reply, "Slammed the door and dumped the whore." Everyone gasps.

Dumbfounded, I ask, "What?"

Platinum Blonde feels powerful in this "safe space"; I might have to help her reevaluate that, once we're both on the streets again. She puffs up and says, "It's not her fault. She didn't ask to be raped. No one has the right to touch another person without their consent, no matter what state they're in. You can't blame her for what some terrible guy did to her!"

Time for me to shut up. When you use a drug, you abandon your brain, so you're giving away access to your body, and giving free access to every child you're caring for.

7

KAIKO KANE
PRESENT DAY
9:40 PM, SATURDAY, MAY 25, 2019 MUDFEST, 113TH
STREET, HILLMAN

THE OVERCAST NIGHT sky curtains any light the stars have to offer, forcing me to follow a narrow path of headlights into an overgrown field of opaque blackness. I park and make my way across the cool, dew-drenched grass to the artificial lights beaming down on the revving trucks. I try to contain my frenzy over the opportunity to choose from the wasted women here in the wilderness of northern Minnesota. I just need to find a weak and impaired filly straying from the herd.

Upwards of 3,000 people attend MudFest in eastern Morrison County annually to watch jacked-up four-wheel-drive trucks power through the mud. Modified engines roar and the smell of exhaust cuts through the cool night air. I love the total experience of man versus nature. It's raw mechanical ingenuity at work. This year, some of the runs have been cancelled due to the ponds of water around us. I'm told it's been the wettest spring in Minnesota history.

The crowd cheers and yells as a truck buries itself in the mud lake. I circle the perimeter like a wolf on the prowl. I think I'll make it easy and find myself a bleach baby.

Cherry red–haired Merida has a boyfriend who's too focused on her. She's cute, but there has to be a less-risky option. I slowly make my way through the crowd. Let's see what else we have. I have a purple-haired Ursula, standing alone, and a parakeet green–haired Tinker Bell, tweaking. Ursula isn't as fat as Tinker Bell is skinny; her purple hair, thick, emo eyeliner, and the gold amulet on a black cord around her neck give her that Ursula feel. She is scratching her arms and Tinker Bell is aggressively scratching her legs, typical of coming down from meth. Ursula's caked-on makeup is likely covering her meth-induced sores. Tinker Bell's gaunt cheeks are her giveaway. So, do I take the tramp that's easy to overpower, or go with more cushion for the pushin'? Ursula is more appealing, but she's stronger and presents more of a risk.

I'm thinkin' Tink. She's with a guy, but it looks like he's on the verge of ditching her. I drift over until I'm standing close enough to overhear the conversation with her trucker boyfriend. Her tweaking is coming to an end and she's starting to crash. She leans more and more into him in the cool night air, until he's basically holding her up. Understandably, Trucker is annoyed. He grips her arm tight, tells a friend he'll be right back, and walks her to the dark, open field they call a parking lot.

They're easy enough to follow, but there's a lot of security here. I just need a window of opportunity. I fade into the darkness as I walk along the parked cars.

This dude is pissed and, even though she can barely walk, he's asking her, "Why did you come along? You're going to spend the whole night sleeping in the truck. This is the last damn time . . ." He roughly heaves her up into his Ram truck and she makes herself comfortable, lying across the bench seat.

And that's when I see she's wearing a Department of Corrections–issued ankle bracelet. Tink had to seriously lie to someone to get permission to be out tonight, and that means she won't report a word. I grin. She can't afford to be drug tested tonight. Free ride.

Trucker locks the truck and looks around.

I duck behind a car and Trucker heads back to the event.

Once he's gone, I step up onto the running board and knock on the window. Comin', Tinker Bell.

She weakly raises a hand, shooing me away.

I look around. No one. I slip the Slim Jim between the window and the weather stripping and, after a few minutes, the door is unlocked.

A security officer turns this way in the distance, so I slide the Slim Jim up my sleeve and start walking toward the crowd. I'll never be able to do her here and Morrison County deputies are waiting just outside the gate. Ursula might be easier.

I catch Ursula standing by herself and suggest to the millennial, "I've got a little rocket fuel if you're interested."

An amicable smile lights up her face and, in a friendly gesture, she taps my bicep. "Trey is the absolute unit, but he may need the whole rocket to get through this swamp."

Ursula doesn't grasp that I'm talking about meth. I read her wrong. She's just a friendly hipster with purple hair who overdoes it with the makeup.

She reaches into her jacket and itches her arms, grumbling, "This damn wool coat." Ursula slowly bats her gooped-up eyelashes. "You're looking for somethin' beyond throwin' shade."

"Throwing shade?"

"Yeah talkin' smack. No cap."

"No cap?"

"No BS. You want a thot, thot boi."

I may need a translator. "I'm not interested in guys."

Ursala busts out laughing. "Don't get salty. Come on—you're not that old. A thot boi is a promiscuous fool. Thot is 'that hoe over there.'" She nudges me. "It's not me, but how about VSCO girl, there? She seems nice enough."

Ursala nods toward a plain woman in an oversized Nike sweatshirt. Her hydro-bottle has me thinking about how meth users pound down their water, but the thick-maned blonde with the metallic blue scrunchie in her hair is too athletic. I don't want to mess with her. "Not my type." I point to a sad brunette in her early thirties. "Tell me about her."

"Swerve. Tea girl. Literally, spilling the tea."

Picking up on my blank response, she adds, "OMG. She's a gossip. 'Let's talk about it over tea.' Do you want to be talked about?"

I feel like I've landed on the wrong planet.

Ursula tugs at my jacket, surreptitiously teasing, "Basic. You need to get with it, boy. Tell me one internet slang term."

The best I can do is, "YOLO. You only live once—right?"

Her head bobs with pure joy at my effort, as she chastises me, "That's so 2013." She sighs dramatically. "The struggle is real."

I can't take another second of this conversation. Tink's my ticket. I make my way back to the darkness of the parking lot.

Tink's head is leaning against the door panel.

I retrieve my truck—well, honestly, it's Chad's GMC Sierra. I pull up next to the green pixie, debating whether she's worth the trouble. My partners would go Saints Row on me if they knew what I was about to do, but they don't have to know. I get out and rub mud from the saturated ground over my license plate, making it impossible to read. My CD counselor would have said, "You're too far into your cycle to go back now." I never really saw it as a cycle—simply a straight line. Nothing triggers it. It's there all the time. Morality, to me, is just a lack of opportunity.

I yank the truck door open and Tinker Bell's head drops down. She groans, but is too incoherent to resist. I shake her until she can at least partially balance, guide her into my truck, and close the doors. Security's coming, so I quickly lean her up against me, like we're lovers. I wrap a seatbelt around her, to help her hold her upright, and she moans tiredly.

"Come on, girl, you can do this. You've only got to be upright for a little bit."

A security guard is eyeing me, but I'm just a sober guy giving a smashed girl a ride home.

The guard steps in front of my vehicle. What the hell is this Longmire-looking cowboy thinking?

Longmire gives me a skeptical once-over. With his boot, he scrapes the mud off my license plate. He waves for me to lower my window and yells to Tink, "Are you okay?"

If she mutters a word, I'm done in by some rural-ass cowboy. This is the last time I'm putting one of these meth whores in my vehicle. I unsnap the sheath on my belt, giving me swift access to the blade.

Eyes closed, she half-moans something unintelligible.

What's he doing, eyeballing me? What the hell is this, an inquest? He has no reason to stop me. My hand sweats on the grip of my knife as I contemplate cutting his throat.

Longmire mutters, "Nice date," and makes me wait. Finally, the cowboy slaps the side of my truck. "Get her home safe."

We cruise out the gate slowly, past the deputies. Once I'm beyond their sight, I turn onto the first dark and desolate road I can find.

Tinker Bell finally wakes up, all drugged out and groggy, "Where are we going?" She finally gets me in focus and fearfully asks, "Who are you?"

I am so amped! I pull over and set a small bag of the rock salt–looking meth on the dash. "I'm your savior, honey."

Disoriented, Tink asks, "Where did you find me?"

"You came to my truck. Said you needed a real man. I'm delivering."

"I can't see myself saying that." She goes rigid and yells, "Take me back!"

I put some bass in my voice now as I threaten, "I'm not taking you back if you're going to act like a crazy bitch."

She finally catches a glimpse of my guns, and softly begs, "Please, just take me back."

Despite her pleading, she can't take her eyes off the bag of crystals.

"I will." I take out a glass pipe. "We're just going to have a little fun first. You're going to take your clothes off and I'm gonna have you." I shake the bag, "I have some meth to share."

Fearful, she offers, "I don't really want to. I'm sorry, but I'm okay with just going back."

I squeeze her chin in my hand. "Now, you see? Right there's your problem. You're assuming I asked. My friends all saw you coming on to me."

She swallows several times in succession, trying to remember, before finally giving up. "I swear, I didn't know what I was saying."

"This isn't a negotiation. Strip or start fighting. If you choose the latter, just know it might be your last day on this earth." Tink doesn't realize how good she has it. I had to fend for myself because my mom—a drug whore just like Tink— was too wasted to protect me. I growl, "Due process, bitch. If you try me and lose, the consequences are more severe. I'm offering you a plea bargain. Your call."

Her next swallow comes hard. For the first time, she registers that her life is in my hands. She has no idea where she is and she's starting to get a clue of what I'm capable of.

I continue, "Or, you could take a hit of meth and just enjoy the ride."

Tinker Bell glances out into the eerie darkness. There is no light—no hope—for her. "What if a car comes? I have a boy- friend. He gets jealous." Her pathetic arguments were almost cute.

"I'll kill him. This isn't my first rodeo."

Conceding defeat, she says mournfully, "Let's get spun out and get it over with."

Tink didn't put up much of a fight after accepting the meth, but now she has lots of shame. She did attempt to push me off, but that just makes it more arousing for me—fight to the finish. She's crying as I order her to get dressed. Struggling with her jeans, I have to lean over and yank them hard up her emaciated, pasty legs. Why do skinny women have to wear their jeans so tight? I can't leave her undressed—someone will call the cops. If she's dressed, people will assume anything that happened to her was by her own choice.

Fully dressed, she curls into a ball and leans against the passenger side door, sniveling.

Pathetic! Now, what the hell am I going to do with her? I usually just leave them in the bedroom at the party or in the alley. She's so pitiful. The cops are still close enough to hear a gunshot. I could drag her into the brush and cut her throat, but I'd still have a problem—that damn security guard. And I'd have to cut the ankle bracelet off and toss it somewhere to buy some time. Too much blood and too much work.

Tink picks up on my uncertainty and whines, "Please, take me back. I promise I won't tell anyone." She slumps down in the seat.

I order, "Sit up!"

She struggles into an upright position. She's eyeing me like a nervous cat and I fight the urge to backhand her.

I reach across her into the glove compartment and she peers to see what I'm after, probably expecting a gun. I take out Chad's insurance form and a pen. I give her a firm directive. "Write, 'I love you,' add your phone number, and sign it."

Aware that she could be moments from death, she's sobering up quickly. Tink scratches out letters and numbers with a shaking hand.

She's about to learn the consequences of lying to me. I order, "Hand me your phone."

As a sign of absolute concession, she hands it to me. Using my own phone, I thumb in the number she's written. What do you know? It's hers. She might have just saved her life. Tink is good for her word. I notice an unread text from just minutes ago.

It reads, "Where the hell are you?" I show it to her.

In full compliance, now, she asks, "What should I say? If he finds out—"

I text back, "Went for a walk. Be right back. Sorry."

I hand her phone back and she accepts it with shaky hands.

As I drive back toward MudFest, I pat myself on the back for a successful mission. I'd do her again, and at the right moment, she'd let me. I stop close enough to hear the engines, but far enough away where the truck can't be identified. I order, "Get out and walk the rest of the way."

She opens the door, but thinking better of the long journey, asks, "Could you take me a little closer?"

I lift my feet up on the seat and use both to give her a hard push, sending her tumbling out onto the tar.

Stupid bitch—I'm not a taxi service. If she gets hit by a car, there'll be no rape investigation. I gun it and thunder down the road, reveling in the power of the V8 engine. In my rearview mirror, I can see Tinker Bell awkwardly managing her way to her feet. Head down, she does the walk of shame back. She's not telling anybody, but I need to find myself a regular . . .

8

LOOP QUANTUM GRAVITY THEORY =
*Reality is just a complex network of events onto which
we project sequences. If time is perceived as a loop, it
suggests we are capable of re-experiencing the past.*

Carlo Rovelli
Italian Theoretical Physicist, 2014

JON FREDERICK
8:30 PM, SATURDAY, OCTOBER 4, 2020 REDS AUTO,
104 MAIN STREET NORTH, PIERZ

I'm stepping out of order with this story for a moment.

HANI EGAL NOW enters the murder book. A series of encounters gradually bends the course of our lives in intriguing, and sometimes devastating, ways. This incident is the impetus that sets Hani on a crash course toward Kaiko Kane. I'll let Clay Roberts explain. If it doesn't seem relevant, that's just how conversations with Clay can be. This one becomes relevant. After this next chapter, you will have met all the players in this story.

People wonder how I can be friends with Clay, knowing I can't trust him farther than I can throw him. We have a bond that was forged in childhood trauma, which makes it almost unbreakable. Both Clay and I had physically abusive fathers.

I'm not whining about being spanked. I'm talking about beatings with a three-foot-by-one-inch stick that left shameful bruises on the body you hid from others. We knew the extent of our misery, because we went swimming in the creek together. Clay's father was worse than mine; I fared better, because I didn't have a mom telling me to forgive him. The abuse ended in my family when Mom told Dad if he ever hit me again, she was taking me and leaving. The abuse ended in Clay's family when his mom left without him, and his dad stopped coming home until after the bar closed. Clay always defended his heartbroken father; I hated mine. I knew I was hit because my dad was tormented over financial pressures and losing the family farm. It wasn't about my behavior—I was a good kid. I got distracted and didn't get my work done as fast as I should have, or I wasn't watching my mentally ill brother close enough and he damaged something. My dad and I eventually worked through this and I love him. Even though he dotes on my kids, I still never leave them alone with him. I'm not sure if that's just wise or an unwillingness to completely let go of it. We try to remember, and we try to forget, our past. So many children, women, and men have it worse. I hate talking about it, but maybe doing so will help it make more sense.

9

THEORY OF RELATIVITY = E=MC2
Energy = Mass x Speed of Light (Squared)

Albert Einstein
Great American Theoretical Physicist Prussian Academy of
Sciences, 1905

CLAY ROBERTS
4:30 PM, MONDAY, MAY 27, 2019 WILSON AVENUE
NORTHEAST, ST. CLOUD

I BOUGHT A HOME to repair and sell in an area of St. Cloud known as Somaliville. I brought Victor Frederick with me to work on the remodel, more for entertainment than labor. Vic is Jon's schizophrenic brother and I've been friends with the Frederick brothers since I was a kid. Neither of them hunted, turned a monkey wrench, or made repairs worth a damn, but they somehow managed to remain my closest friends.

I was struggling with framing an upstairs window and barked over my shoulder, "C'mon, Vic, are you bringing that level or waiting for it to turn into a monarch butterfly and fly to me on its own?"

I sat on the window sill and allowed the summer breeze to give me some relief from the stifling heat of the un-air-conditioned home.

Vic was moving slower than usual today, which sometimes happened with his mental illness. He wandered over with the level. Vic's t-shirt read, "Surely, not everyone was Kung Fu fighting."

"Put the pedal to the metal," I told him. "Hard work eventually pays off."

Vic dolefully responded, "Laziness pays off right now. Maybe I should go to Mass more.

Einstein postulated that energy is related to mass—and the speed of light."

"Well, right now you're moving at the speed of mud."

"Can I crank up the music? That might help." "Have at it."

Vic loved his classic rock, and shouted, "Turn it up!" as he played "Sweet Home Alabama."

He danced around like a stork struggling through a seizure, until I finally busted out laughing. "What the hell is that? You look like you're being attacked with paintballs."

Vic stopped and asked in all seriousness, "Do deaf people think people who dance are crazy?"

Not sure if he was serious, I didn't respond. Looking out the window again, I watched a Somali Muslim woman walking down the street and waved Vic over. I jutted my chin toward her and said, "Maybe you can get her to dance with you."

Victor peered out the window over my shoulder. "Why do Muslim women dress like that?" "Dean Martin."

Vic said, "Dean was the epitome of substance abuse—had a drink and a cigarette in his hands all the time. Did you know that, during the height of the Beatles, Dean Martin was the highest-paid entertainer in the world?"

"I did not." Vic, like Jon, would sometimes fill you with unnecessary trivia at the mention of a word or a name.

Vic questioned, "But it doesn't really explain why she's wearing all of her bedding."

"I had this conversation with your brother a while back. Jon told me that Muslims initially dressed this way to keep out the blowing sand. But when a Muslim man was invited to a Christian dance, back in the 1940s, he saw couples dancing together and mandated Muslim women always dress this way."

"You're shittin' me. Let me look this up." After a moment of intently swiping across the surface of his cell phone, Vic began reading, "Sayyid Qutb was an Egyptian educator. He moved to Greeley, Colorado, which at the time was a small, religiously conservative town that prohibited alcohol. He was invited to a church social to welcome him to the community. When he saw people dancing to the then-popular song, 'Baby, It's Cold Outside,' and saw dancers cozying up to their partners, he became enraged. Qutb described the women's bare arms and their long dresses, with bare ankles, as seductive. He complained that 'arms circled waists, lips met lips, chests met chests, and the atmosphere was full of passion.'" Vic read the last part with a dramatic flair. He paused and looked up at me. "Sounds like a good time to me." He returned to his phone. "Qutb is known as the father of modern Islamist fundamentalism. He used what he witnessed that evening to profess women should remain fully covered and be separate from men."

I wasn't getting it. "So, this Qutb guy is pissed that people show affection for each other, and suggests we completely cover women—make them disappear. Isn't it convenient that men weren't given a dress code?"

Vic continued, "The Washington Post described Qutb as a racist, a bigot, a misogynist, and an anti-Semite."

I walked over and picked up the baseball hat sitting by my tools, which read, "Premium Concrete, for Those Who Like it Hard," and asked, "What's he got against cement? Not hard and cold enough for him?"

"Not cement. Semite—anti-Jewish. And that hat should say 'For Those Who Like it Soft for Hours Before it Gets Hard.'"

We watched a car pull up next to the Muslim woman, which contained a couple of vixens who looked to be itching for a fight. Both the black teen driving and the white teen passenger glared repulsively at the Muslim. The white teen taunted her, "Hey, Haji."

"That's military slang for followers of the Muslim faith," Vic translated. "It's an ignorant insult. In Muslim terminology, it's a compliment to people who made the trip to Mecca."

The woman gave a half-smile but continued to look straight ahead. The teen added, "I'm talking to you, Balija."

Vic narrated, "Now that's an insult. It means an illiterate and unwanted Turkish Muslim."

"How do you know this shit?"

"Cousins in the military."

The Muslim woman shot back, "Wrong country."

The black teen yelled from the driver's side, "You Majoo fucks killed my cousin in San Bernadino. She was at a holiday party, never hurt anyone. She was only twenty-seven."

Vic continued to interpret, "'Majoo' refers to a fire worshipper. Sunni Muslims use the word to insult Muslims from Iran."

This was getting interesting. As they say in the boxing arena, 'Lets have a good clean fight'.

The woman yelled back, "Look, Creeping Jesus. Buy a map and learn some history."

Vic was also feeling the situation heat up. He was practically on my back when he whispered, "'Creeping Jesus' refers to hypocritical Roman Catholics."

"You mean like us?" I nudged him back with my shoulder a bit. "My relatives would say, 'heepin Mick.' Basically meaning Irish Christian prick."

The teen's car swerved abruptly to the side and the arrogant shits jumped out and took off after the young woman. There was no way she was going to outrun those kids in that dress.

I reluctantly told Vic, "Stay here," as I removed my tool belt.

I heard him yelling as I took the stairs two at a time, "Just leave your shirt on. You always have to take your damn shirt off."

The Somali woman had gathered the bottom of her dress in her hands and was running in fear. The femme fatales were close behind her. She tried cutting through a nearby yard, but was thwarted by the chain-link daycare fence. This forced her to turn back and face the music, harsh as it would be. Her Islamophobe attackers quickly caught up with her and threw her to the ground.

I yelled as I rounded into the yard, "Hey!"

Ignoring me, they tore off her headdress. The white teen punched her and the black teen ripped a slit down the front of her dress.

I grabbed them both by the hair, one in each hand, and yanked them off of her, throwing them aside. Surprised by my intervention, they both cowered away.

"What the hell is wrong with you? You're going to beat up an African woman because your cousin was killed by an American? You're the problem, here. I ought to kick both of your asses." I turned to the battered woman, crumpled on the ground. "Are you okay?"

Her eyes were on fire as she nodded affirmatively and sat up. Her nose bled and tears of helplessness streamed down her cheeks. Her voice was thick when she said, "Just let them go."

The teens took off running.

The woman gripped the fabric of her dress tightly, holding it together as I helped her to her feet.

Me being me, I couldn't help but appreciate her smooth skin and thick, dark hair. She shouldn't cover any of that. "I'm Clay. I was working on the house across the street. And by the way, I'm a Creepin' Jesus, too, if my help somehow offends you."

Trying to be gracious, she said, "I shouldn't have said that; I just get so sick of it." Her eyes danced about in fright and embarrassment. I'm Hani."

Hani didn't seem to be aware of the blood smeared on her face. I looked back toward Vic, who was watching from the window across the street, and removed my t-shirt. He threw his hands in the air in exasperation. I worked out regularly and was proud of my abs. I didn't see anything wrong with letting others know I took care of myself. I found a clean spot and used it to wipe the blood off her face. Maybe I was trying to impress her, but I was really concerned about her. Shut up, Vic.

She was uncomfortable, but appreciative. Her guard finally fell away and tears of frustration took the form of jagged gasps in her breathing. Her tensed shoulders shook as she sobbed. I waited uncomfortably. This was never my strong suit.

Hani eventually said, "Thank you. You didn't have to do that." As her gaze traveled over my shirtless body, I gave her my million-dollar smile. Hani was still rattled. She placed her hand on my chest to balance, then snatched it back in horror. She quickly apologized, "I'm sorry."

"You have nothing to be sorry about. Come on, I'll walk you home—or wherever you're going."

Embarrassed, she countered, "You don't have to. I'll be okay."

"I don't have to do anything, but I'd like to—I feel like I need to. What are you going to do if they come back? Walk home naked? If it's about being seen with a Christian, I don't go to church very often, if that makes you feel any better."

"It's not that—" she stopped. "Fine, but please, put your shirt on. My family will have no sympathy for me if they see me walking with a shirtless Brad Pitt."

"Ah, come on—Brad's a fossil." I took my shirt from her and put it back on. She seemed to have cleaned most of the blood off her face. A little part of me hoped she wasn't carrying any diseases, since I was about to put my shirt, with her blood on it, against my skin. I wondered for a second what this concern said about me.

Hani apologized, "I meant it as a compliment." She pointed her thin, long index finger at my shirt. "I'm sorry about the blood. How can I make it up to you?"

I smiled. "Have dinner with me?"

10

INTERPERSONAL DECEPTION THEORY =
Lying is a social process in which the deception both meets the
immediate needs of the liar and the desired perception of the deceived.

Judee Burgoon
Professor of Communication & Family Studies
Arizona University, 1996

JON FREDERICK
8:30 AM, MONDAY, MAY 27, 2019
BCA EVIDENCE PROCESSING FACILITY, 11TH AVENUE
NORTH, ST. CLOUD

DEL WALKER FORWARDED the partial footprint the Stearns County investigators had taken from inside the bus shelter. I gave Del credit for carefully collecting this evidence, even though it didn't seem relevant to him. He was abrasive, but I had to admit most of the evidence Del gathered was recorded in a professional, nonjudgmental manner.

Mia had carefully reassembled the window. She proudly showed me the puzzle, but pointed out her efforts were futile as there was no visible evidence on it. We carefully placed the window in a chamber, poured out some super glue, and set it inside. The fumes slowly revealed a blackened, partial footprint on some of the shards of glass. The wavy treads on this print revealed we were dealing with a unique shoe.

Mia pointed out, "The print is appearing on all of the pieces that were piled under other pieces of glass. The pieces sitting on top were washed clean by the snow."

"But the combination of the print Del collected and the print we have here will give us a full shoe print. There's a program called SoleMate we can run this through. SoleMate will tell us the exact brand and size of any shoe."

It wasn't a name brand, but still, within an hour, we knew the shoe was a handmade, size eleven work boot, created by shoemaker Amara Hark Weber in her workshop in St. Paul. Only one pair was made to perfectly fit the owner's feet at a price tag of $1,200. For a moment, I was elated, believing I simply needed to track down the owner. My initial excitement dissipated when I discovered the boots were stolen from a home in Minneapolis on the corner of Fifty-First Street and Xerxes Avenue back in 2017. There were a series of break-ins in the area at the time that were never solved. Still, not all was lost. The nature of the home burglaries was consistent with a thief who resided in the area.

I told Mia in frustration, "I'd like the name of everyone who lived within a three-block area of those home break-ins."

She asked, "What makes you think the robber was local?"

"The robberies didn't all happen on the same day and they always occurred when the homeowner wasn't home. Someone in the neighborhood would be familiar with the occupants' routines."

"I'd love to work on this!" she eagerly offered. "I took a class in environmental criminology and I found it fascinating that people typically commit crimes close to home."

"The FBI has become so adept at geographical profiling of serial rapists, they can often tell you, within a two-mile area, where he lives. You can help, as soon as you find me that bullet."

2:10 PM
BRIAR CREEK ROAD, PAYNESVILLE

Mia and I returned to Leda Hartford's home. I wanted Mia to understand some of the purpose to my madness, so she'd stay motivated to work. With heartfelt honesty, I told her, "I've heard dozens of great stories about you from Maurice. My favorite is that, since you first became part of his family, you always thanked kids for playing with you. I want you to know I care about you, but at work, I'm candid. Most of the time, I hope to be working together, but there are tasks, like finding this bullet, I'll ask you to do on your own. The work I'm giving you is important. I'm going to spend the morning playing with Zelly. She may be our best source of honest information. I don't know how you felt about it, but without saying it, I think Marc believed Leda was having an affair."

"That's the sense I got, too." Mia smiled in appreciation. "I understand. You want that bullet as soon as possible. I can also help you come up with a list of people who lived close to Xerxes Avenue at the time of those burglaries. I have relatives living in that area who could assist me."

Mia headed to the woods with the metal detector and knife, while Zelly and I looked for deer tracks once again.

Forlorn, Zelly stopped and showed me some apple trees she planted with her father. She shared, "Last year was the first year they had apples."

I put my hand on her shoulder to comfort her. I took a leaf off of the tree and rubbed it between my fingers to enjoy the sweet smell and she did the same. I asked, "What does it smell like?"

Zelly wrinkled her nose. "I thought it would smell like apple, but it just smells like grass." I loved the enjoyment Zelly received from exploring. Fruit trees were particularly susceptible to the destruction of harsh winters, so I didn't want Zelly to be devastated if they didn't survive. I told her, "You and your dad gave these fruit-bearing trees life. Those seeds will always be part of life, somewhere, even after the trees are gone."

Zelly hugged me around my waist.

"Do you know why you should never eat apples off the ground?" She shook her head. "No."

"Deer love apples, but if deer have pooped in the area that apple landed, you could get salmonella poisoning, which will make you very sick."

"Oooh, yuck." Zelly said, "Dad and I went looking for deer tracks in another place, too, but I don't know where it was. Dad said, 'I think the deer are bigger at home,' and we didn't go back."

"Tell me about the place."

With a slow turn, she gazed at the panorama of trees and brush. "They all kind of look the same. I just remember that we drove there."

"Zelly, anything you can remember could be very helpful."

"There wasn't as many trees. It wasn't too far away. I just started a game on Dad's phone and I had to stop right away, because we were there."

"When you say there weren't many trees, do you mean a farmer's field?" She scrunched up her freckled face, recalling. "Yeah, I guess it was." "How big were the plants?"

Zelly held her hands knee high. "The plants were kind of sharp and they smelled moldy." "What were the leaves shaped like?"

Giving up, she turned her palms up. "I don't remember." "Were the leaves big or small?"

"Small."

Small leaves; moldy smell in the fall; sharp to walk on. "Do you remember if your dad called it alfalfa?" Fresh alfalfa smelled like a sunny spring morning, but as it aged, the smell turned musty.

"I don't remember." She shrugged in frustration. "I'm sorry."

I bent down and looked in her eyes. "You've already helped me a bunch. Thank you!"

Suddenly excited, Zelly blurted, "Oh—there was something written on a tree up high. Dad said it was probably written by one of those big flaxen-haired women who lived there." Zelly proudly asked, "Do you know what flaxen means?"

"What?"

"Blonde hair. Dad taught me that."

Unfortunately, that didn't narrow my search considerably, as there was a deluge of Scandinavian communities close to Paynesville. Ironically, most Scandinavians didn't have flaxen hair, contrary to the myth. Most had dark hair, but blond hair is more prominent in Scandinavian countries than the rest of the world. A theory is that genetic mutations occurred with hair in this area, due to the lack of sunlight. The Vikings spread the passage of flaxen hair, beginning in the eighth century. This may have lent some credibility to the Kensington Runestone found in Solem Township in Minnesota, which suggested the Viking explorers arrived in Minnesota in 1362. I dismissed the trivia that raced through my brain and refocused on Zelly.

"Do you remember what the sign said?"

Her freckled nose scrunched up, uncertain. "I think it was a bad word. My dad told me it wasn't a bad word, but Mom said it was. Mom said we all have different standards and when it comes to words, I should go by hers."

"What was the word?"

She hesitated and said, "Fricken. Dad said it was just a casket. But Mom said it was one of those words people say that makes them seem not very smart."

I thought for a moment before asking, "Is it possible the sign said 'firken'? A firken is a cask, or something that holds wine or beer."

Zelly grinned gleefully. "Yeah, that's what it was—a cask. So, it isn't a bad word?" "No."

She looked up at the sky with a smile, as if to say, Dad, I never should have doubted you.

As Zelly and I continued our venture through the woods, I remembered how Leda had sent Zelly out of the room when she gave me her alibi, so I said, "I've heard that your mom wasn't with you the whole time when the two of you went shopping in St. Cloud. It's important you're honest with me about this."

Zelly's face reddened, embarrassed at being tangled in her mother's lie. "Well, Mom wasn't exactly with me. She left me with Grandma while she did our Christmas shopping."

"So, you didn't see her until the end of the day?"

"No."

"Did your mom have a pile of gifts?"

"No, she put them in the trunk so I wouldn't see them." Even Zelly was questioning the veracity of that claim.

I gave her a minute before I continued. "Before your dad died, did Mom have friends visit sometimes?"

"Grandma would come sometimes, and Uncle Marc." "Anyone else?"

She twisted her body back and forth, as if she was debating if she could tell me. Zelly looked down as she shamefully revealed, "A guy named Dan would visit her at night, when Dad wasn't home." Her face fell in anguish. "Dad did a lot for Mom and she didn't even notice. And now my dad's dead. If Mom's boyfriend killed Dad, I will never love her again."

It was heartbreaking to see this waif of a girl in so much pain. As self-centered as Leda was, I believed she loved her daughter, and Zelly needed her. I comforted Zelly, "Now, no one is saying that happened. Loving your mom seems like the right thing to do now." Innocent until proven guilty, right?

Zelly teared up and threw herself into me, hugging me hard. This poor kiddo was clearly starved for affection; I wanted to take her home. I called Marc and he agreed to pick Zelly up tonight.

10:15 PM, PIERZ

I asked my one-year-old son, Jackson, for a kiss goodnight. As usual, he tipped his head down and waited for me to kiss him. The gesture reminded me of a prince, but it was cute, so I let it slide.

Tucking in my daughter, Nora, was a treat, although, at age four, she often presented me with an invented crisis—the theme being I had better stay home tomorrow. Tonight, she told me, "Jackson's starting to say bad words."

"What did he say?"

Not anticipating the question, Nora searched for a response. She finally offered, "Words so bad nobody's ever heard them before."

Challenging her, I asked, "Can you give me an example?"

My curly-haired girl was good. She'd come up with something. With an impish grin, Nora said, "Shloogle."

"That is bad," I feigned concern. "I wish I could stay home tomorrow and help you and Mom deal with it, but I have to go to work. What do you think we should do?"

Nora rubbed her brunette curls back. "Hmmm. We could not feed him."

"That seems a little harsh. When I was one, I said and did the wrong things all the time.

When your mom was one, she did, too—maybe even worse. And you know who else did?"

She grinned in eager anticipation. I tickled her and said, "You! But we still fed you. Your mom and I could really use some help teaching Jackson the right words. Could you help us?"

"Sure."

Serena peeked in the room. "Time for all little angels to rest." She knew how easily Nora could manipulate me into long conversations at night. I hugged and kissed her goodnight and Serena joined us for a nighttime prayer.

Serena and I sat on the couch in front of the fireplace while I massaged her legs and feet. My petite bride had long, dark curls and heartwarming, alexandrite green eyes. Like Serena, alexandrite was one of the rarest gems.

She held up a chip and said, "Potato chips. Friend or foe?"

"An addict I worked with told me it was harder to quit potato chips than cocaine."

Serena's grin set her viridescent eyes ablaze. "I believe him. I think it's the crunch." She popped the chip in her mouth and chewed it with a show of mock ecstasy. After savoring, she said, "Vic told me Clay is spending a lot of time with a Muslim woman. I have to give Clay credit for being open-minded."

Clay was like rain. At times, useful and desirable, but also seeped into the cracks and destroyed—in Clay's case—people and relationships.

Serena asked, "Did you see Mohamed Noor got twelve and a half years in prison for shooting that Good Samaritan? Jon, this is what scares me about your work. He was just trying to help."

"I'm tired of thinking about it," I groaned. "It's terrible for Justine's family; it's terrible for Noor's family. Everything about this case is messed up."

She picked up my reticence. "Of all people, they interviewed Agnes Schraut. Agnes evidently lives on Washburn in
Minneapolis now."

Agnes Shraut was formerly from Pierz. She was a cantan-
kerous elderly woman with a diabolical personality. I tried
to give her the benefit of a doubt. She was born during the
Depression and raised in a backwoods home, with no running water or electricity. When she was in her twenties, Agnes
suffered burns in a house fire that resulted from a build-up of
creosote in her wood-burning stove. The story was she was
bitter over being unable to have children, but truth be told, the
old-timers say she was irascible long before then.

Serena continued as I massaged her feet, "Agnes just spat
out, 'Old news! Why don't you arrest one of these hedge
whores?' She pointed to a group of white teenagers in distressed jeans, and added, 'Walking around with their pants
half torn off.' The girls giggled at her craziness and strode on."
Serena closed her eyes for a moment. "I first spoke to Agnes at
age ten. My mom brought me along to help her, after Agnes
poured salt over a wound. She always did figuratively, but this
time she literally did, and needed it washed off. She had to be
in excruciating pain. When Mom stepped out of the room,
Agnes asked me how fast I could run. I told her I was one of
the fastest kids in my class, and she said, 'That might keep you
a virgin until you're fourteen.'"

I smiled. "That's as close as you're going get to a compliment from Agnes."

"How so? It doesn't say much for my virtue."

"It was her way of saying you were pretty."

As I rubbed the lotion into her legs, Serena asked me about
the case I was working. I shared, "I'm worried the deputy I'm
working with is leaking information about the investigation.
I'm nervous for Zelly's sake, even to talk to her."

Serena's brows furrowed, "He could get her killed."

I let out an infuriating, guttural moan. "I know. I spoke to Del about it. He denied it, and then told me, 'Don't tell me how to do my job.'"

"Shhh," she warned, "don't wake up the kids." She kissed my forehead, "You're a good man. Say something kind about him."

She pushed me to be better than I was. "How's this? He's kind of a prick."

11

NEWTON'S THIRD LAW OF MOTION =
*When one body exerts a force on a second body, the second body
exerts a force equal in magnitude and opposite in direction. (In
other words, a single isolated force doesn't exist. There is always a
reaction.)*

Sir Isaac Newton
Physicist & Theologian University of Cambridge, 1686

KAIKO KANE
8:30 PM, WEDNESDAY, JUNE 5, 2019 DIVISION AND 7TH
STREET, LAKE GEORGE, ST. CLOUD

JUSTIN PLOOF AND the Throwbacks are rockin' the outdoor stage by Lake George, to introduce the Summertime by George events in downtown St. Cloud. It's seventy degrees now, and the temperatures are expected to be hot this weekend. The music is great and thousands of people have hauled their lawn chairs here to celebrate a glimpse of sunlight after a dreary spring. I'm going to find a vulnerable tweaker here.

After an hour of possibilities eliminated—she's with too many people; there's a sober person keeping an eye on her; she looks like she's going to throw up—I've found my mark. A white woman with straight pink hair has made the same lap five times. At first, I thought she was an exercise freak, but she stops at the same places in her circle and makes the same odd gestures— she's not autistic. These are normal gestures, but repetitive. Growing up in CD treatment has taught me she is in the throes of "the shoulder." Meth users know the repetitive behavior can last for hours. I follow her to the most remote part of her circle. Then I patiently sit back on a bench, waiting for her to circle back my way one more time.

As my pink-haired, Billie Eilish–type approaches, I hold out a hand full of crystals, for her eyes only. "Do you want to recapture the rush?"

She steps by, ignoring me, until I add, "It's on me."

She stops, glances back and, with that addict brain working overtime, she can only imagine the potential pleasure. She simpers, "Hi, I'm Kimmy."

I love addicts!

I follow her to the Cloverleaf Trailer Park, just off of Highway 10—the prototype of American poverty. It's filled with people either trying to fight their way out of poverty, or people like Kimmy, who've descended into it. Kimmy leads me through the dented door of her crusty- looking unit and down the hall, to a small bedroom that smells like sweat. The pungent smell triggers me, as it smells like my mom's slovenly cot. Kimmy shrugs and smiles. "It's just temporary."

It is. She'll eventually be dead.

Kimmy paws at my pockets for the meth and I tell her, "There's something I need from you first."

She giggles and begs playfully, "Don't make me wait. I'm not in the mood. Just give it to me."

"This isn't a free trip." I pull the straps down on her tank top.

Kimmy squeezes her shirt to her chest like a whining child. "Noooo. Just give me it. I don't even like guys. They're disgusting."

Her response infuriates me. What makes her think a weak, WASP woman has the right, or power, to deny me? I'm not a religious guy, but I'll vote for all those religious fanatics who want to take us back a couple hundred years, to a time when women had to do what men demanded, with no recourse. And I don't believe in anything. The message is clear, as far as I'm concerned. Just shut up and do what I say and you might live.

I push her onto her back, on a twin bed with a bunched-up afghan someone's grandma made a hundred years ago. I pin her down and hold her still, until her panicked eyes meet mine. Take a good look, bitch. I love this part. "You're about to be driven with the force of a train. Go ahead and fight; a little pain just makes it better for me."

I immediately experience a lightning bolt of hurt in my ear and roll off the bed. I look up to see a barefoot, African American woman wielding the handle of a broom like a bo staff. She's wearing a sweat-stained tank top and tattered jean shorts that cling to a muscular, no-nonsense body. I absolutely would have avoided her when picking out my playmates.

Her whisper of a voice offers, "How're you likin' pain now, you bachi bastard? Better?

You're gonna be lookin' up at dirt!"

Kimmy stammers, apologizing to her, "I promise, this was the last time. I was so stupid."

Ninja chick chops the staff down on me and I block the blow with my arm to keep her from splitting my skull. Son of a—the crack of wood on my ulna was less than humorous.

I bull-rush her to keep her from striking again. She manages to step aside and sends me flailing head-first out the bedroom door. I get up and don't look back.

I need to find me a regular . . .

12

NEWTON'S LAW OF ATTRACTION =
FORCE = MASS X ACCELERATION
*The force of an attraction is inversely proportional to the
distance separating the core of each object's center.*

Sir Isaac Newton
English Physicist & Theologian University of Cambridge, 1704

CLAY ROBERTS
3:30 PM, THURSDAY, JUNE 6, 2019 WILSON AVENUE
NORTHEAST, ST. CLOUD

THE HOME I was repairing when I first met Hani was just north of the Somali Café and Halal Grocery in Somaliville. This area was once known as Upper Town St. Cloud. It was just a couple blocks west of the train yard, making it a tough area of town long before the Somalis arrived. Like most poor immigrants, the Somalis settled in an area where the rent was cheap. My own poor German and Irish Catholic ancestors had settled in this same part of town before them. Few St. Cloud residents realized that, before the Catholics became the majority in this neighborhood, there were even worse-off Africans living here.

I had a rough time in school, but Civil War history was always my jam. In 1850, Kentucky general Sylvanus Lowry moved—slaves and all—to Upper Town St. Cloud, along with a bunch of other southern slave owners. Lowry became the first mayor of St. Cloud in 1856. People in the area who opposed slavery got a voice when a young newspaper editor migrated from Pittsburgh to St. Cloud. Jane Grey Swisshelm repeatedly attacked Lowry's slave practices and his treatment of the Winnebago Tribe in print. Lowry responded by organizing a "Committee of Vigilance" that broke into Swisshelm's newspaper office and threw her press into the Mississippi River. But it didn't shut her up.

The southerners and their slaves moved back south when the Civil War broke out. Jane headed east and worked as a nurse for the Union during the war. She published support for Abraham Lincoln. Jane was hired for government press after the war, but was fired for publicly criticizing Andrew Johnson. It was Johnson who allowed the Jim Crow laws to emerge—like vagrancy laws that enabled southern slave owners to arrest Africans for being unemployed, and then force them to work as slaves to pay off their debt to society. But the movement for equal rights for African Americans grew in St. Cloud. The only Minnesota governor from St. Cloud, Stephen Miller, took office at the end of the Civil War, and was an active abolitionist.

Jane, where are you today? I'd marry you in a heartbeat! Jane's paper, the St. Cloud Visitor, was changed to the Central Minnesota Catholic in December of 2018.

The first thing I repaired in my sell-for-profit home was the plumbing, so I could clean up after a hard day's work. My Somali friend, Hani Egal, walked over after my workday ended, and I'd take her somewhere for a bite to eat. She waited outside the house until I was ready to leave, out of fear her family might see her enter my home with me. But after we ate and walked around Munsinger Gardens or, on a crappy day, the mall, I'd drive my truck into the garage and we'd sit and talk. Hani considered the garage a safe area that was technically not in my house. I didn't bother to tell her that her last name, Egal, a common Somali surname, meant "whatever" in German—exactly my thoughts about being in the house or garage.

I couldn't stop thinking of Hani, like "a song I can't unlearn." A conversation with her felt like sinking into a warm, soft pillow. I wanted to put my feet up, let go of my worries, and rest there. I found myself looking out the window in anticipation of her arrival every day. Was love a gift, or a curse that tormented you until you couldn't think straight? We weren't the same religion. We weren't the same race. We weren't even from the same country. I guess if I really needed things to be the same, I'd be with the same sex. What I wanted was compatibility—a perfect fit to my jagged edges. Could it be Hani?

Tonight, I asked Jon to stop over as I wanted to surprise Hani with a picnic. Considering I knew little about cooking, I had to ask, "Jon, do you honestly think the two of us can create a decent meal?"

Jon had no doubt. "It's like building a house—just a matter of putting in the right things at the right time. I cook as often as I can."

"Well, I cook as little as I can. I have no problem paying others to make my meals." Jon began emptying the grocery bags as he bantered, "Is Clay Roberts in love?"

I almost said, "unfortunately," but decided to smile and only give him, "I don't know." "Well," he said, "if you want to force the attraction, just accelerate your attendance to Mass."

"What?"

"Just paraphrasing Isaac Newton."

"My mom would have a cow if she knew I was dating a Muslim woman—not a calf, not even a heifer—a cow."

Jon sardonically added, "The poor woman. She's already given birth to one disgusting large mammal." He took out a salmon steak and set it on the counter with onions, peppers, mangos, avocados, cucumbers, radishes, and some spices.

I was immediately overwhelmed. "That's a lot of food."

"If I'm going to help you make a meal, I'm going to bring enough home for my family, too." He turned the oven on and put me to work.

As I chopped the salmon into half-inch chunks, Jon commented, "You're thirty-two years old and you're still hiding your dates from your mom."

"She's going to hate Hani. She hates the Christians I date."

"I like Hani. But be prepared for a Romeo and Juliet scenario," he suggested. "Neither set of parents is going to approve and you don't want the same ending."

"I'm not killing myself over a woman. As I've always said, 'I have an undying love.'" "That is what you've always said, but I don't remember you ever preparing a meal for a woman. You're potentially giving up the relationship you've only recently developed with your mom. If things go awry, you'll get desperate—maybe undo all the good you've done in the last year."

"Not happenin'."

Jon peeled a mango as he spoke. "Hani's giving up a lot to be with you, too. Christians are much more tolerant of people dating outside their faith than Muslims. And Islam is more tolerant of Muslim men than Muslim women being with Christians."

That wasn't my fault. I pointed out, "I'm giving up my share, too. No pork chops, Italian sausage, pepperoni, and for God's sake, no Thielen's bacon."

"I can have Serena make you an 'I love you more than bacon' sign." "Yeah, I don't know that it would mean a lot in Hani's culture."

I wanted this meal to be perfect. What was happening to me? I was nervous about saying the wrong thing when I was with Hani, and constantly worried her family would convince her to dump me. It was crazy that Hani and I could be so kind and respectful to each other, yet people insisted we shouldn't be together because of the categories they imposed on us.

Jon could read me like a book. He tortured me, "It doesn't surprise me that you love her." "I never said I loved her."

"You love strong women. I like that about you. Your problem is there's no bottom to your 'settle-for' column."

"Ouch. That's cruel. I stay away from married women." "It only counts if it's by choice."

I had no idea what he was talking about. He probably heard one of the many rumors about me. I never did half the things I did. I countered, "I can't believe Serena puts up with you and all your . . ." I couldn't think of the right word.

"Idiosyncrasies?"

"If the root word is 'idiot,' that might be right. What are you cutting up a mango for? You know I don't like fruit on my meat."

"The mango, avocado, cucumber, radishes, and green pepper are all part of the salad. They're all uncooked. We'll drizzle some lemon and lime juice on it, and the salad's good to go."

"No lettuce?"

"You don't need lettuce for it to be a salad."

"If you say so." I had finished chopping up the red peppers, onions, and the salmon. "Now what?"

"First, put a little salt and pepper on the red peppers, rub a pan with olive oil, and we'll roast them in the oven. We'll fry the onions in butter. Put the salmon in a bowl and sprinkle some of that Penzeys fish seasoning on it. Spray it with some lemon and lime juice and mix two eggs into it."

"So we're big on the lemon and lime juice? If life gives you lemons, you just need to find someone that life has given gin, and make a Tom Collins."

Jon looked at me deadpan. "A drink named after a lame joke." I avoided his need to offer me useless trivia. He took the hint.

"I like the taste of lemon and lime will help keep the fish fresh and the avocado green. Do you know that the acid in lime will cook fish, even without heat?"

"I'm not eating uncooked fish." People died from eating uncooked food.

He pointed out, "You'd have to soak it overnight in lime juice. We're frying the salmon, after we get the roasted pepper and fried onions mixed in. There's some siebenfelder bread from Pete and Joy's Bakery in the bag. We'll slice that up, spread some butter on it, put it in the oven until it's crisp, then place the salmon patties on it." He looked at me like a dad. "If you can work hard, with discipline, you can cook."

While neither of us were iron chefs, we both knew how to work, so it wasn't long before we had the meal put together and the kitchen cleaned up. Jon pulled a straw picnic basket out of a paper bag. "Serena suggested you use this."

"Okay." I picked it up by the handle and swung it like Jack and Jill might have, while I gave Jon my best what the hell look.

Jon teased, "Not because it offers that cuteness I know you love—" I cracked, "Go to hell."

"A cooler seals in the moisture, so the bread will get soggy. The basket allows it to stay crisp."

"You think she's going to like this?"

"She's going to love it. Even if it sucks, she'll appreciate the work you put into trying to make her happy. Plus, I make an awesome salmon patty and mango salad."

"Okay. Now get out of here. I want full credit for this."

Hani and I enjoyed our picnic in Wilson Park, sitting on a blanket on the bank of the Mississippi River. She loved the meal. The only downside was that she suggested I cook more often.

When we stood up, she pulled me into a strong hug. I never imagined holding a woman in full Muslim gear. This was the closest we'd gotten, physically, and I could only guess what she was feeling. At that moment, pressed against her body, all worldly worries vanished. All the time we'd spent alone, hidden away from the world in my garage, we hadn't been intimate in any physical way. That's not to say I wasn't fighting the urge to touch, and kiss, and feel her, but whatever power she had over me, I held back; I didn't want to push her. Now, I breathed in her unbridled tenderness. Her hands gently rubbing across my back stirred familiar, yet unfamiliar senses in me. I felt a little light-headed in the moment. She was as reluctant to let go as I was and, finally, after we realized people were watching us, we both started laughing.

Before we got too far apart, Hani put a soft hand on my cheek and looked so intensely into my eyes, I stopped breathing. The watchers disappeared from my vision again. Hani showed some hesitance and then leaned toward me. She kissed me so lightly, for the first time, I almost wondered if I'd imagined it. Before I could think, I cupped a hand at the back of her neck and kissed her again, with a little more urgency. We pulled apart and stared at each other, almost like we were afraid the earth would crumble around us. Because this was impossible, wasn't it? The air practically crackled with electricity and both of us were breathing harder. Hani then broke our gaze and awkwardly suggested we should pack up our picnic and be on our way.

When we got back to my house, I pulled into the garage, as always. I had barely turned the ignition off and hit the button to close the garage door, and we were back in each other's arms— the kiss this time was much more heated and promised amazing things to come. The old familiar ache was back, but for once, that wasn't my entire focus. Eventually, Hani disengaged from me and smoothed her clothes. She looked almost ashamed, and then, with nothing more said, she asked me to walk her home.

I felt so off-balance, walking with her. I wasn't sure what just happened. As we neared her home, she turned to me and searched my face. She said, "That was . . ."

I said, "Incredible."

She smiled and nodded, then made her way home as I watched over her from a safe distance.

13

THEORY OF RACE, CRIME, AND URBAN INEQUALITY = *Racial disparities in violent crime are attributed to the movement of well- paying manufacturing jobs and upwardly mobile families out of African American communities. The ultimate causes of crime are similar to all races.*

Robert Sampson
Sociologist Harvard University, 2004

JON FREDERICK
12:15 PM, FRIDAY, JUNE 7, 2019
JIMMY'S POUR HOUSE, 2ND AVENUE NORTH, SAUK
RAPIDS

I MET JADA ANDERSON in Sauk Rapids for lunch. Jada was an attractive former lover who worked as a reporter when I began my work with the BCA. She exuded elegance and poise. Her black hair was pulled back into a ponytail, exposing her swanlike neck. Jada's dark, smooth skin contrasted well with her white blouse.

We were the toast of the Twin Cities as a young interracial couple, half a decade ago. We had since gone our own ways. Jada has a child with my boss, Sean Reynolds. As his feelings for Jada intensified, Sean was becoming wary of even mentioning Jada's name in my presence. Jealousy was an evil monster and I hoped it didn't consume him. I tried to avoid Jada, but there were times she had information useful to my work. Jada was now an investigative reporter for KSTP Eyewitness News. She was recognizable to many in Minnesota, as she occasionally filled in as a news anchor and hosted a variety of events.

The comfort Jada and I once shared had abandoned us, and had been replaced with the awkward uneasiness that settles between former lovers.

I asked, "Does Sean know you're here?"

Jada countered, "Have I ever felt I needed to get approval from a man?"

"I don't want to give the appearance we're having clandestine get-togethers. Serena's aware."

"Serena can handle it," she said reluctantly. "I screwed up— not intentionally. I may have said your name when we were making love—Sean—Jon. I wasn't thinking of you. I had a little wine and slurred a little. Now I know why you preferred not talking during sex."

I elected not to respond. It wasn't that I was worried about saying the wrong name. I felt nothing I said could be better than the act of making love.

Jada continued, "I'm not here to talk about Sean."

Our Amish-looking waitress, Sarah, arrived, and was clearly intimidated by the casual confidence that emanated from Jada. When I ordered the fried chicken, Sarah asked, "White or—" she nervously hesitated and finally whispered, "dark meat?"

Jada's classy smile flashed across her face as she awaited my response.

I found it humorous when people made situations unnecessarily uncomfortable. We had serious racial issues to deal with in the US, but ordering chicken shouldn't have been one of them. I said, "I would like a thigh—dark meat."

Jada winked at me and pressed our server, "Now, that surprises me. Doesn't he seem more like a white breast man?"

Sarah flushed scarlet and murmured, "I don't know what a white breast man looks like." Jada patted her arm, "Well, good for you! I can appreciate an open-minded woman."

I changed my mind. "Just give me the fried chicken sandwich."

The skittish Mennonite said, "That meat is neither white nor dark." I smiled and responded, "The census bureau would say 'undetermined.'" Sarah was ready to crawl into a rabbit hole.

Jada's gentle touch of her arm seemed to comfort her. "You're doing fine. As long as you don't start yelling racial slurs, you're good with us."

I apologized, too. "I'm sorry. Are you okay?" Sarah gulped down a hard breath.

"We all need to keep talking to each other," I shared softly, "and it gets easier. The next time you see either of us, we'll laugh about this. And I promise to leave you a generous tip for the grief."

Relief washed over Sarah as she finished our order.

When she left, I asked Jada, "So, what happened to dating the guy who bounces a ball for a living?"

"He bounces a ball for six million dollars a year. You can't tell me you wouldn't play in the NBA if you had a shot."

"His friend tried to kill me. I have reasons not to like the guy."

Jada had offered me a sincere apology, months ago, for inadvertently setting in motion an attempt on my life last year. There was no point in rehashing it.

Jada shared, "I'm sorry. With the exception of Isaiah, I'd love to do 2018 over again." She sipped her tea. "Sean and I are a thing now, but we've exchanged some words on his involvement in the gang drug busts in Minneapolis. The whole history of our war on drugs bothers me. Nixon vilified hippies and African Americans to get the vote of poor white people, and every president since Reagan has told America our biggest problem is inner-city drugs, and rewarded police departments for hammering away at inner-city youth. The biggest drug gang problem in Minnesota is white supremacists distributing meth."

"Sean was doing the job he was asked to do," I pointed out. "Every Vice Lord he arrested was guilty of dealing drugs. The only innocents harmed in the investigation were harmed by the Vice Lords—and this is why we shut them down."

Jada suggested, "I think Sean was assigned to that bust because the administrators wanted to see if he'd play ball, going after inner-city African Americans, before he was promoted."

This accusation must have infuriated Sean. It was certainly possible, as there was significant federal funding awarded to departments for making inner-city drug arrests, despite the fact that the drug problem was basically the same everywhere. Studies consistently showed that suburban white illegal drug use was the same as metro black use, but we didn't raid those homes. Deciding not to be pulled into a quarrel between my boss and my ex-lover, I responded, "Sean was the best candidate for the supervisor position and that raid was going to happen even if he stepped aside."

"How politically correct of you," she chided. "I find it interesting that you seem to stay out of the metro drug busts."

"I'm more of a violent crime type of guy." Jada gave that just be honest look.

She had a way of being so expressive without words. I acquiesced, "The truth is, we all get dragged into drug problems, because they're so prevalent. I wish the war was on poverty. If so, maybe we'd have better success. The best measure of who's using drugs is emergency hospital visits for overdoses, and seventy-five percent of those are white people." I didn't need to tell Jada that seventy-five percent of people incarcerated in prison on drug charges were African America or Chicano. I added, "I never volunteer for undercover drug busts. You end up having to use drugs or sleep with somebody, just to keep your head from getting blown off. I have no desire to be part of an investigation that's as immoral as the people we're trying to arrest. I respect my marriage."

"You're a good man, Jon." She smiled warmly.

"I was expecting to hear more from the African American community, after Mohamed Noor was the first police officer convicted of murder."

Jada dismissed this. "After years of complaining that police aren't getting consequences for killing innocents, it would be a little hypocritical to complain that someone was finally punished, wouldn't it? But believe me, the fact that the victim was white this time hasn't gone unnoticed."

"In Minnesota, the recent shooters have been rookies. Too many young cops are placed in critical situations too soon. I know this is no consolation to families burying loved ones, but understanding it may help with developing a solution. Like a lot of people in law enforcement, I feel shaming guilt when a cop shoots an innocent—like I owe everyone an apology. It's always heart- wrenching for me."

She quietly considered this.

I turned my hand open. "So what did you need to see me about today?"

"I've been helping a seventeen-year-old girl, who goes by the name of Raven, get out of life as a sex worker. She's in trouble. She's a tough kid, but she needs help. These homeless kids are an easy target for creeps. This is from last night." She took a recorder from her bag and set it on the table between us. "It's quiet—you'll need to lean in to hear it."

When Jada started the recording, a frantic young voice, presumably Raven's, filled the space across the table.

Raven: "Jada, you've got to help me, please. This guy is scary." Jada: "Where are you?"

Raven: "I don't know; we drove at least an hour into the sticks and stopped at a hotel." Jada: "Are you alone?"

Raven: "Cocaine just stepped out, but he's coming back." Jada: "Tell me what you see out the window."

Raven: "A high school across the street. He's already made me have sex with four guys today, including him. I don't feel good . . ."

The line went dead.

I instinctively sat straight up and reached for my car keys. I told Jada, "She's in Paynesville." Here was this name, Cocaine, coming up again, just a half hour from the home break-in.

"By the time I figured it out, Raven was gone." Jada sighed in frustration. "How did you know?"

"Anyone who has driven from St. Cloud to Marshall, before 2013, has driven between the school and the hotel. It's an odd combination. Highway 23 was rerouted in 2012."

Jada placed the recorder back in her bag. "It makes me sick. Almost half of all sex workers in Minnesota are under eighteen. They come from broken families, and some guy flirts with them online or at the mall. He gets them to join him and soon these girls are selling their souls for survival."

"The demand is disheartening," I agreed. "When we put out a sting, advertising an underage female looking to be an escort for an adult male, the offers pour in within minutes. Backpage was making over five million dollars a month on sex trafficking before it was finally shut down in 2018."

Jada looked troubled. "I haven't heard from my girl since she called last night. I'm worried. Sean said you're working a case in Paynesville. Even if Raven's disappearance isn't connected, maybe you'll hear something."

I'd had the case for less than a month and I now had three separate crimes to look into. All three were unusual, and the fact they all happened in a thirty-mile stretch of rural Minnesota may have suggested they were all symptoms of a larger problem in the area.

"What does she look like?"

"Your typical emaciated, oily-haired, teenaged sex worker. Black hair, dyed blue on the ends. Her name is Raven Lee."

"What race?"

"White—pale white. Dabbled in drugs, but she has never really been an addict. More ADHD and manic, with neglectful parents."

"That's a bad combination."

"Her stepdad accessed a lot of online porn. She found it open at age eight and has looked at it regularly since then. She did a lot of sexting online in her early teens. She got in trouble at school for being boy crazy and an easy mark for horny boys. I started talking to her after she was picked up during a raid at the Metro Inn Motel off Lyndale Avenue South in Minneapolis. I got her a job working for a wonderful woman, but Raven told her off and ended up back at the shelter. And, once again, some slimeball's found her."

14

THEORY OF COMBUSTION =
*When a match is struck, the friction generates heat and creates a
chemical reaction, producing more heat than can escape into the
air, so it burns with a flame.*

Johann Becher
German Physician & Alchemist
Vienna, 1670

CLAY ROBERTS
9:45 PM, FRIDAY, JUNE 7, 2019 WILSON AVENUE
NORTHEAST, ST. CLOUD

I NEVER KNEW WHERE I stood with Hani. On nights where I wouldn't initiate a kiss, she'd ask, "Aren't you forgetting something?" She would then hug me, sometimes incredibly tightly, but then pulled away, as if in shame, and I'd walk her home.

I spoke briefly to Jon and Serena before heading back home. Sometimes, I wondered if Jon didn't want me to be happy. Jon claimed we were always juggling our intimate relationships with our work, our families, and our hobbies. He said the only ball I hadn't dropped was Hani. He reminded me I wasn't working enough to pay my bills and I'd avoided family since I met her. Serena's advice was to love with all your heart.

Hani and I were once again nestled together in the garage, in the cab of my Chevy Silverado, but tonight felt different.

Smiling warmly, Hani searched my face. "What are you thinking?"

I teased, "Honestly, I want you to take that dishtowel off your head." She bumped my shoulder. "It's a hijab. Why?"

"I've seen your hair. I feel like we've dated long enough, I deserve to see your hair again." Seeing her hair, that had to be about halfway to first base—or maybe not even out of the batter's box.

Hani coyly responded, "We don't really date in Islam."

I thought, then what do you call what we're doing? But I said, "I don't like what the hat symbolizes."

"Beauty should be found within."

"I can buy that. But personality can be expressed by a t-shirt, or shoes, or the way you wear your hair. You're a gift to the world—I don't want to cover you up. I want everyone to see how amazing you are." I tried another angle. "We can enjoy time together, because you're not a crazy Muslim and I'm not a crazy Christian. We're two people who believe in God and are kind to each other. And we're—" She got me so flustered I couldn't think. "Ah, come on, now I can't think of the word for it. Like we're not the same, but we're right together."

Hani offered, "Complementary."

"Yeah, we compliment each other a lot, too."

She giggled softly and looked me over, like I was part of an absurd Saturday Night Live skit. "You have no clue how far out of bounds you are? My friends wouldn't even consider what you ask of me."

"And still you sought me out," I reminded her, "and here we are."

"Touché. But Clay, I hope you understand I'm not a charity project. I don't need to be saved. I am comfortable as an American

Muslim. We're not the enemy here. Do you know how many people were killed in the US last year by Muslim terrorists?"

I guessed, "I don't know—maybe thirty."

Hani held up a finger. "One person. Do you know how many were killed by white

supremacist groups?"

I just waited this time. She'd tell me.

"Thirty-eight. There are far more white-terrorist than Muslim-terrorist killings here. And I'm not defending Muslim terrorists. Fundamentalist Islam is as representative of Islam as the KKK is representative of Christianity."

"I can buy that. You and I—we're right together. We're kind to others and far more tolerant and caring than our super-religious families. And that's why I don't like that hat." I pointed to her hijab. "It's what your crazy father wants and you don't want to disappoint your family. And I guess I don't know what to do with that."

"Is there something wrong with pleasing your family? I know you can do what you want, regardless of what your family believes, but I don't know that I can."

"What if your dad insisted you wore a dog collar to prove your ebullience?"

Hani paused, trying to make sense of my question. "I think you mean subservience, and it's not a dog collar."

"It symbolizes slavery to me. If it's so damn important, why don't men wear them?" Deep in thought, she remained silent.

I tried another approach. "What would you think if I wore the cone-head Klan hat?"

"I'd be offended," she conceded. "But why would you wear a capirote? Catholics wear them in Spain to publicly display they're serving penance. The Ku Klux Klan wears them to make fun of Catholics. It's hardly the same."

"How do you know this—" I cut myself off before swearing.

She smiled and said, "It's important to me to be a good American, so I study American

history."

"The way I see it, both Muslims and Christians believe in one God, right?" "Yes. Monotheistic."

Mono—what? I didn't know about the disease part, but I forged ahead. "So, when you and I pray, we're praying to the same God. We're just praying in different ways. And if we're decent people, I can't believe God minds. I believe in a great, kind, and loving God."

"So do I." She leaned in to kiss my cheek.

I turned my lips to meet hers. My heart pounded when we simply kissed. Hani pulled away and asked, "Have you ever been married?"

"No. I've only met one woman I'd ever considering marrying—and she's married." "You, my man, just said the right thing. But please don't assume all Muslims, or Somalis for that matter, are like me. I'm just a young woman who likes a young man. You are full of surprises, Clay, and I'm very attracted to you." She sensuously beamed. "So you're okay with this, with your religion and all?"

"I think it's fair to say I wouldn't be the first pick on the Christian team. Here's my only Catholic joke: What do you call a young woman who uses the rhythm method for birth control?"

Hani raised an eyebrow. "What?"

"Mom." The resulting crickets told me I'd missed the mark. I must have been the only one who found that joke funny.

She sat silent, and then carefully unraveled her hajib. I found the leisurely process oddly seductive.

I took her in my arms and we kissed.

She started unbuttoning my shirt; I finished for her and removed it.

Hani kissed my chest and asked, "Are the garage doors locked?"

"Yes."

Hani asked, "Abaya off, too?"

I wasn't sure what she meant, but I liked the idea of less, so I just said, "Yep."

She reached down to her ankles and, with a quick swoop, her dress was over her head and on the floor.

My adrenaline raced and I tamped down my excitement. She didn't say a word when I removed my jeans, and soon we were down to bare skin. After kissing, night after night, through clothing, the soft touch of her skin against mine was lush. We explored each other with heightened boldness, until she took my hand and held it away from her sex.

Hani gasped, "Be tender and let me control the pace." Works for me! I just nodded and followed her lead.

My seat leaned back as far as it could and, with tearful elation, she snuggled against me. I didn't want her to go away, ever, but my curiosity got the best of me. With my lips by her ear, I tenderly asked, "Was I your first?"

Hani grinned as her shimmering, coffee-colored eyes gazed into mine. "Do you mean
today?"

My body shook in silent laughter.

"I'm sorry." She shook her head. "That was such a bad joke."

"I thought it was pretty damn funny. I didn't know you could joke about sex."

"I do have a sense of humor, and I enjoy intimacy. Keep in mind, Muslims are as different in their views as Christians. But no, you were not my first." She then asked seriously, "Does that change things for you?"

"No. Hell, no. Believe it or not, you weren't my first, either."

She kissed my shoulder. "After your question, I wondered if maybe you saw me as a challenge."

"You're a challenge, all right, but it doesn't have anything to do with virginity."

"I assumed you knew I was married," she said casually.

I pushed her off, "You're married?"

Hani avoided looking at me as she started dressing. "I should have known. Heepin' Mick."

Appalled, I grabbed her arm and she swung loose of my grip. I quickly raised my hands in the air in retreat, "Stop for a minute. I need clarification. If you're married, we're done. If you're divorced, that's something else."

Hani finished dressing, and then took my hand as if she was pleading, "I'm married—" I shook my head. "Get the fuck out of my truck."

15

SOCIAL EXCHANGE THEORY OF INFIDELITY =
Unfaithfulness occurs as result of three factors:
Expectations are not being met in current relationship;
An alternative becomes available;
Willingness to risk unrecoverable investment
(children, friends, loss of love & trust).

George Homans
Sociologist Harvard University, 1978

MIA STROCK
9:00 PM, SATURDAY, JUNE 8, 2019
QUEEN BEE'S BAR & GRILL, JAMES STREET WEST,
PAYNESVILLE

JON FREDERICK HAD us all working the weekend. He was clearly frustrated with our lack of progress, as his first words to me were an exasperated umbrage. "I asked you to send Owen Warner's video to our St. Paul office, so they could tell us the exact car that was driven to the Ross home."

I could feel anxiety bubbling in my chest as I offered, "I did. Certified mail, just as you requested. I even made sure they received it."

"The video is blank, Mia. There is nothing on it." Skittish, I stepped back. "That's impossible."

Jon aggressively directed, "Tell me your exact process of delivering the videotape to the post office. I handed it to you, and then?"

I thought it over. "I put it in my bag and drove it to the post office." I then recalled, "Well, I stopped at work to pick up my check. No one else touched my bag."

"Did you set your bag down anywhere?"

"By the packaging, but it was in my sight all the time. No one else handled it. I chatted with a coworker for a bit and then went right to the post office."

"Does Kraft apply a magnetic coating to the boxes to seal them?" "Yeah, so?"

"You can't put a VHS tape by magnets. It erases them."

"Well, how would I know that? Who has VHS tapes?" I felt backed in a corner.

Jon explained, "In the future, when you are asked to directly deliver evidence, you need to directly deliver it."

"I'm sorry."

The agitation in Jon's voice was unnerving. He asked, "Did you get anything from reviewing Owen Warner's tapes?"

He wasn't going to like this. "Nothing. I even asked to see recordings from previous Fridays, to see if they'd cased the place, but it turns out on most Fridays, Owen's at the fish fry at the Double R Bar. He said he told you he'd never seen the car before."

Jon was sullen and silent.

After an extra-long workday and a week of following leads that didn't pan out, Jon insisted we stop with three local law enforcement officers at Queen Bee's Bar in Paynesville, to wind down. The friction between Jon and Stearns County Deputy Delbert Walker was now palpable. Del was at Leda Hartford's home while I was searching for the bullet today, and he was making insulting jabs at the BCA all day. I anticipated stopping at a bar would only antagonize the tension further.

We seated ourselves at a long, oval bar, which circled around the bartenders. The guys all ordered the seven-dollar special, which included a pound of wings and a sixteen-ounce glass of tap beer. I knew enough to stay sober when men are angry.

Del sneered with sarcasm, "This case is so much clearer now that the BCA has sent one of their top guys to help out. Let's see, what do we have that we didn't have before? Oh, yeah. Nothing." He taunted Jon, "I tell you what—why don't you and your friends in St. Paul have a meeting about it?"

Jon smiled slightly, but his eyes were flat as he let Del's remark slide.

I wanted Jon to point out that I found the bullet after Del left. I was proud of finding a Core-Lokt soft-point bullet, even though Jon gave me wrong ballistics. It had been fired from a Remington Model 783 bolt-action rifle. The bullet hadn't traveled as far as Jon anticipated, since the soft point mushroomed out after hitting Todd.

Del continued with his diatribe, raising his glass and sloshing beer over the side of it. "Let's have a toast to the way the BCA handled the Noor case."

Jon's anger finally poured out. "This is the last conversation I'm having with you about that case. Have you ever considered what it's like for Mohamed Noor? He came from one of the poorest countries in the world and made a life for his family in Minnesota. He is a caring father. You know as I well as I that we need cops—black cops in particular—so Mohamed was fast- tracked. He ended up in a situation he wasn't prepared for. He was scared and killed a wonderful, caring woman who was trying to stop a sexual assault. Justine's dead. Mohamed is serving over twelve years in prison. A child loses a father."

Del's expression was unreadable, but the earlier smirk had at least straightened itself out. Jon wasn't finished. "And taxpayers dished out twenty million dollars that left the state for Australia—money that could have been used to help the six thousand homeless children in Minnesota. Who do you think is paying that twenty million? Rich people aren't. You and I are. And then you have people asking, is Justine worth seven times as much as Philando Castile? Phil's family got two million; another million went to their attorneys. And if all this isn't bad enough, no one investigated the sexual assault Justine called in. The entire situation infuriates me. But I'm telling you, for the last time, this wasn't my case, so back off. There is nothing I can do about any of it."

I remained as quiet as a church mouse. My orders were to listen and learn. Even I appreciated the interruption when a heavily made-up woman with red lips, a periwinkle sundress, and impractical heels clicked by us on the tiled floor and disappeared into the restroom. Her dark, wavy hair and bronzed skin were reminiscent of a young Salma Hayek.

After the momentary halt in conversation, Jon thanked everyone for their efforts and offered to buy one more.

The bartender asked Jon, "Another Alaskan Amber?"

"No, thank you—but it was good; almost too good." He slid her a generous tip.

Del took another Grain Belt Nordeast and remarked to Jon, "Are you too good to drink with us, now?"

The woman stepped out of the bathroom, stopped, and looked directly at Jon. He was doing that I see you but am pretending I don't thing. Oh, he saw her. She was hard to miss.

Del tapped on the bar to recapture Jon's attention. He chided, "By the way, I hear you're looking for someone called Dan. Leda doesn't know a Dan and I can't connect any Dans in Paynesville to her."

Preoccupied with the woman, Jon dismissed Del. "Pardon me, but I have some business to take care of."

What happened next would torment me.

Jon tried to inconspicuously remove two one-hundred dollar bills from his billfold, but both Del and I saw what he was doing. He walked over to the woman and tucked them into her hand, then she left with him.

Del turned to me, incredulous. "Did you see that? Nice fuckin' boss."

There were few things more repulsive to me than sex trafficking. My mother was once a talented jazz piano player. Then she became an addict and eventually sold herself for drugs. Maurice Strock rescued me from her when I was four years old and soon became my adoptive grandfather. It wasn't long before my mother's body was discovered, as broken and shattered as her dreams of being a noteworthy musician. I have since learned her long and graceful pianist's fingers, ones I can still feel against my cheek, were crushed, as if they had been stomped in rage. No arrests were made, but it was presumed her latest boyfriend attacked her in his own greedy, drug-addled frenzy. That woman in heels Jon left with could be a mom, like mine.

Del's phone buzzed. He tore his eyes away from the door Jon and the sultry woman had exited and read the text to me. "I'll be damned. That was from Leda Hartford. It says, 'Sorry I lied. Dan Moene from Freeport. It's over now.' But I guess Jon Frederick," he sneered saying Jon's name, "has more important things to do at this moment than to check out leads."

I tried to defend my new boss. "I'm sure it's not what it looked like."

Grandpa Maurice told me, "Heroes will always disappoint you. Admire actions, not people." Both Grandpa and Sean Reynolds told me I'd learn a lot from Jon. Sean took it so far as to say, "You're in it for the long game, so support him even when it doesn't feel right."

I followed Jon and his lady friend out of the bar and watched Jon crawl into the back seat of his Explorer with the woman. His vehicle had tinted windows in the back, so you couldn't see inside from the sides or back of the vehicle. In Minnesota, it was illegal to have tinted windows in front, so if I really wanted to see inside, I could have.

Del was suddenly standing right behind me, a little too close, so my back end bumped into him when I turned.

He slithered against me as he stepped forward. "Let's check it out."

I shook my head. "I'm tired. I'm going home." I needed this internship. Disheartened, I got into my Toyota Corolla and headed back to St. Cloud.

I was almost home when I received a call from Del. "I walked around to the front of the Explorer and looked in. I could only see her bare back, but she was riding him like a wild mustang. After about twenty minutes, she hopped out, straightened her dress, and her pimp picked her up."

"How do you know it was her pimp?"

"A black man, driving a 1972 Plymouth Sebring, in mint condition, in a part of the state that isn't exactly overpopulated with African Americans? I was born at night, but not last night."

I hung up. Del hated Jon, but I couldn't defend him. I couldn't believe it. We were all frustrated, but it didn't justify Jon's behavior.

I immediately called Sean Reynolds.

Sean's baritone voice asked, "How are you doing?"

All I managed to say was, "Okay." My anxiety constricted my throat and I couldn't get the words out.

He asked, "Is there something I can help you with?"

I wanted to tell him, but I couldn't get myself to say it. They all thought so highly of Jon. Who am I?

Sean said, "Tell me about Jon's contact with Jada. The deal was you'd report to me and you haven't given me anything."

"I don't think any contact occurred."

"Well, I know it has." Finally, he said, "Look, I'm kind of in the middle of something right now, so if it's not an immediate crisis, I'd prefer you'd call me tomorrow."

"Okay."

He hung up.

I pulled myself together. Take deep breaths, hold them, and then blow out, slowly, in long exhales. Okay. It didn't matter what anyone thought of Jon. I would not tolerate sex trafficking from anyone. I called Sean right back, but this time there was no answer. Crap! I should have just told him right away. Now I had to stew on this.

I still wonder, at times, if my life would be different had Sean answered that second call.

16

MIA STROCK
8:15 AM, SUNDAY, JUNE 9, 2019 COUNTY ROAD 11, FREEPORT

JON PICKED ME up and we headed to a small community north of Paynesville called Freeport. He looked disheartened and he should have, after his infidelity. I didn't try to call Sean Reynolds again. I had spoken to my partner, Hong, last night, and he settled my troubled thoughts. Hong Fa reminded me to focus on my job. I really didn't see anything, other than what may have been an exchange of money. Del was the one who said they had sex and Del hated Jon. This internship was an important part of my future. I wasn't losing it over Jon's stupid behavior.

Jon pretended he and Sean had this great relationship, but Sean seemed to have some underlying animosity toward him. By Jon's tone this morning, it felt like it was being dumped on me. He said, "Sean told me you've traveled to Minneapolis to help come up with the list of people who lived within three blocks of where our boots were stolen. Who do you know that lived on Xerxes Avenue?"

Embarrassed, I explained, "The people I knew lived in St. Paul, not Minneapolis. I was mistaken."

"Xerxes Avenue runs north and south in Minneapolis. It doesn't run into St. Paul."

"They lived in Xerxes Apartments." Okay, I didn't know anyone who lived there. I simply wanted that assignment. "I'm working with the metro BCA agents, going door to door, compiling a list of people who lived in that area in 2017. We're each taking blocks, and we have to keep returning to the homes until we've compiled the complete list. Did I do something wrong?" Jon made me feel guilty. He was the one who should be ashamed. I added, "Sean was okay with it."

He was digging deep for patience. "You should tell me when you're performing work related to my case."

Changing the topic, I asked, "Why do men cheat?"

The question seemed to break his train of thought. He silently continued with his internal struggle before finally answering. "I think a lot of guys feel their partner is a lot more likable than they are, and they're afraid she doesn't need him. So, they develop a friend on the side as a safety net, in case she leaves. It's counterintuitive, because eventually the partner discovers his safety net and it destroys their relationship. When she leaves, the guy assumes she never truly loved him, and repeats the whole process in his next relationship."

"Self-sabotaging." I let that sink in. "Why would they cheat with a hooker? Is the sex better?"

"No. Then why?" He hesitated. "If I did, it would be because I'd completely given up hope. Some guys do it when they're angry, as some sort of hateful revenge." He switched things up. "Are you in a relationship?"

"Yeah, with Hong. He's smart, but we're struggling." I had no desire to reveal Hong had been with another woman. First, he denied it, now he was saying it didn't mean anything. Men are asses.

Jon remarked wryly, "Oh, sure. Hong."

"Do you know him?" How would Jon know Hong Fa?

With a sly grin, he said, "Just teasing. Hong is one of the most popular names in the world.

Does he spell it H-O-N-G or X-I-O-N-G?" "He uses the letters H-O-N-G."

We were greeted by Freeport's silver, smiley-faced water tower. A billboard featuring a child feeding a giraffe advertised Hemker Park and Zoo. I commented, "This town has a zoo? Only 666 people live here." I paused. "That's a creepy population number. I hope it isn't an omen."

"Superstition is for those who lack faith."

I asked, "So you don't believe in psychics?"

"Absolutely not. There's only been one case of a psychic solving a murder, and that was because she committed the murder."

I watched the little town go by. "This is clean community. It looks like a Norman Rockwell painting."

"It was the basis for the Lake Wobegon tales," Jon said, "where all the women are strong, all the men are good-looking, and all the children are above average."

We drove to a home on County Road 11, just north of the city limits.

Changing gears, Jon tried to prepare me. "We're going to pay Dan Moene a visit."

I couldn't admit Del and I knew last night that Dan was Leda's lover so, feigning ignorance, I asked, "Who's Dan Moene?"

"I believe this is the Dan who was visiting Zelly's mother."

"I thought Leda said she didn't know anyone named Dan."

"Everyone knows a Dan. I went through Leda's phone records last night. She called Dan almost daily before Todd's death—sporadically since. I'm curious to see what Dan has to say."

"Why didn't Del go through her phone records?" Jon didn't respond.

We parked on the edge of a dirt driveway behind Del's Stearns County squad car. Standing in the doorway, Del met us outside. He told us, "It's a mess. Dan ate his gun.

Read his letter—Dan was Todd's killer. But I couldn't find a Remington rifle. My gut feeling is the Remington was stolen and is now rusting in the sludge at the bottom of Uhlenkolts Lake."

My stomach churned. I prayed to God Del wouldn't say anything about that text.

As they spoke, Jon turned to me. "There's a spray bottle in the box in my back seat that's labeled, 'Amido Black.' Would you mind grabbing it for me?"

When I returned, I followed Jon into the kitchen and saw an image I would never be able to erase. The shower of blood and brain matter, combined with a gut-wrenching, rotten smell, was overwhelming. Everything smelled like copper; I felt like I was gagging on pennies. A lifeless body, sans a chunk of his head, was slouched in a black leather recliner, milky eyes pointed in my direction. I turned and sprinted out of the house and down the driveway, racing past where we'd parked our car. I fell to my knees and my body jerked forward as I heaved out my breakfast. I had hunted with my grandpa in the past, but hunting was nothing like seeing the back of a skull blown off a man staring straight at you.

I eventually made my way back to Jon's car, curled up in the front seat, and closed my eyes. I was in over my head.

After a couple hours, Jon came out to check on me. "Are you okay?"

I felt so weak. "I'm sorry. I'll be okay. I just didn't expect it." I tried to straighten out in the seat. "Do you need me?"

"No, it's okay." Jon kindly offered me his canteen of water. I asked, "What did you need the spray for?"

"Amido Black can make shoe prints in blood visible." "Did you find anything?"

Jon hesitated as he looked back toward the house. "We have the same size eleven hiking boot here, even though Dan's a size eight. It does appear Dan shot himself, but someone else was here with him. That boot stepped in the blood after Dan was shot."

"I'm sorry I couldn't handle it." I was thoroughly embarrassed.

"A scene like this should be heartbreaking. I'm going to stay in Paynesville tonight. Del will give you a ride back to St. Cloud."

"Do you think it's odd that Del's the only one here?"

Jon glanced back toward the house. "Do you want me to arrange another ride for you?" I had already inconvenienced Jon enough. I forced out, "I'll be okay."

Del was as abrasive as forty-grit sandpaper. With breath that smelled like rotten tomatoes, he asked, "Did you tell Jon about Dan Moene last night?"

"No, I assumed you would." I watched a red-tailed hawk circling its prey over a field as I admitted, "Honestly,

I pretended I'd never heard of Dan. Jon already doesn't trust you and I didn't want to get him mad at either of us."

"Thanks, but you don't need to lie for me." He sighed with regret. "I should've come here last night, but your boss's behavior just threw me off. This is how I found Dan when I arrived this morning."

"Were you the first on the scene?"

"Yeah." Del hawked bile from his throat, rolled down the window, and spit it out.

I wondered if Dan's death would end the investigation into Todd's murder. I was ready to be done. "Do you think he killed Todd?"

"I think so. Dan left a note for Leda, stating he couldn't take her rejection. Dumbass. Screws another man's wife, and then blows his brains out once he realizes she can't be trusted. What the hell did he expect?"

The chicken hawk descended and disappeared for a moment, then reappeared with a rodent pierced in its talons.

After a peaceful silence, Del asked, "Am I saying your name right? I don't want to be insulting. It's Nia, like 'neon'?"

"No. Mia, with an M." "Oh, M like lamp."

"Um, yeah, I guess." I was too tired to follow his thinking.

"So, like a lamp, not great in bed, but fine bent over a desk." Del heaved a guttural laugh.

I wondered how much time he spent setting that one up. I gave him nothing in return.

Del couldn't know how deeply that comment cut me. Before Hong, I had a platonic relationship with a man at Kraft. We flirted and I volunteered to perform minor errands for him, every day, just to make his life easier. I found myself fantasizing about our first kiss, and making love with him by a campfire on a lake shore. One particular Friday, I wore a dress that pushed our professional attire code. I felt naked, and he ignored me all day. After everybody left, I entered his office to check if he needed anything. He stepped behind me. I could feel his warm breath on the back of my neck. My heart pounded as I thought, Just ask, and I'll kiss you like you've never been kissed by a lover. After an anxious minute of anticipation, he yanked down my underwear, bent me over his desk, and pleasured himself in me. When he finished, he hurriedly left without saying a word. And that was the end of it.

When we arrived at my home, Del asked, "Do you want to take a ride? You look like you've got a lot on your mind."

"No." What had I done to make him think I might be interested? Just what I needed—one more dumbass guy who has the stereotype fantasy of an Asian sex slave.

He lightly grasped my forearm, "Why do you think Jon's staying at the Paynesville Inn & Suites tonight?"

I pulled away, half-heartedly, and he tightened his grip. "I don't know. Maybe he's found a connection between Todd's murder and someone who stayed at the hotel."

Del let go and chortled in raucous laughter. "His hooker's still in the area. Ride with me— I bet we'll find Jon with his concubine again."

Are you kidding me? I'd spent the morning puking my guts out. I pulled further back and looked down at my shirt, "No. I'm a mess."

He leaned across the console and seized my arm again. This was getting old. "C'mon, I don't give a damn how you look. I'm going to report him and I need a witness."

"No." I weakly shook my head, trying to pull my arm free from his clutches. Del got angry and spat his foul breath in my face. "Do your job!"

I turned my face away from his gross mouth, but kept my eyes on his. As I clawed his fingers from around my bicep, I calmly reminded him, "I'm not your intern, and you're touching me without my consent."

I wasn't sure what was going to happen next. Even though he was damn near sixty, he was mean and strong. Lucky for him, I'd dropped out of karate after one class. Jon was right about one thing: I needed to get strong.

Del suddenly softened and let go of my arm. He leaned back in his seat, palms raised in supplication. "I'm a bitter old man trying to do the right thing. But I have no credibility, so I need a witness."

I quickly exited the car without looking back. I needed to start lifting weights.

17

ATTACHMENT THEORY OF INFIDELITY = ATTACHMENT
IS A DEEP AND ENDURING EMOTIONAL BOND.
*Individuals who have failed to develop secure attachments
fail to engage in relationship-strengthening behavior, and struggle
with commitment to a partner.*

Mary Ainsworth
Canadian Psychologist
University of Johns Hopkins, Virginia, 1965

JON FREDERICK
2:30 PM, SATURDAY, JUNE 8, 2019 BRIAR CREEK ROAD,
PAYNESVILLE

I SAT WITH LEDA Hartford on her front steps, looking over a copy I'd made of Dan's suicide note:

Dearest Leda,

I'm so very sorry for everything. I love you immensely, and thought once Todd was gone, we could live happily ever after. I never intended to hurt you. I can't justify behaving so foolishly. I can't live without you. I, willingly, am falling on the sword for you.

Faithfully,
Dan

Leda was a weeping mess. She shed crocodile tears through puffy eyes, and I could envision her melting like the Wicked Witch of the West. However, knowing Leda, she'd morph into a cute, pastel wax candle on the floor that some unfortunate guy would pick up and cherish.

"What are your thoughts on Dan's proclamation of love for you?"

Leda placed her hand on my arm, "I'm sorry for lying. I am so sorry for everything. You've got to believe me—I loved Todd."

Two men were dead for having known Leda, so I was a little annoyed by her touch. I glanced flatly at her hand, then back at her. She quickly removed it.

"What did he mean by falling on the sword for you?"

"I have no idea." Leda vehemently shook her head back and forth. "If he honestly was, why would he write it down for everyone to read?"

That was a legitimate point. "How did you meet Dan Moene?"

"At a party. Todd was drunk and Dan helped me walk Todd to the car. I was mad that he got so damn drunk and I wasn't ready to go home. So, I stayed." She blubbered, "Do you think Dan killed Todd?" She reached toward me again, but at least had the wherewithal to stop herself. Leda clasped her hands together, as if she was trying to keep them in check. It was clear she resorted to feminine wiles whenever backed into a corner.

"I had planned on having this conversation with Dan this morning, but now I'm having it with you. You were with Dan the morning Todd was killed. You were seen driving to his home, and you still had time to drive to Paynesville to kill Todd."

Leda flushed as she stuttered, "I—I didn't kill Todd."

"The one thing we know—with certainty—is that you've been lying this whole time." I read her the Miranda warning and asked her to stand and put her hands behind her back.

Shocked, Leda stiffened in her chair and pled, "Please believe me! Okay, I left Zelly at the mall and drove to Freeport to be with Dan. But I went right back to the mall. Boot Barn—I know I said RCC Western before. I forgot they changed the name."

I didn't respond. Leda couldn't handle silence. I had the sense that if I just kept my mouth shut, she'd eventually tell me everything.

Her anxious chatter soon filled the empty void. "I would go to Dan's or he would sneak over if Todd had a night of dart league. Dan was like a forbidden high school crush. But I never intended to leave Todd. The fun was in getting away with it."

"It obviously meant more to Dan. He left his fiancée."

"I wasn't the reason they separated." Leda nervously stared at her hands, nearly white- knuckled at this point, as she considered how much she should share. "Dan was using meth." This downtrodden woman was ready to let it all out. "He gave me some because I was so sad."

I asked, "Where was he getting the meth?"

Leda breathed deeply; sorrow rattled in the back of her throat. "I don't know. And even though this could get me in trouble, I'm going to be honest with you. I've seen Dan since Todd's death." Before I could respond, she interjected righteously, "We haven't had sex. I'd run into him at Casey's and he'd give me a pick-me-up." She attempted to assure me, "I'm not an addict. It was just a pick-me-up. I don't let it impact my parenting." Her jittery hands unclasped and she started fiddling with her hair.

I considered the warped morality that enabled her to take pride in the fact that she stopped cheating on her husband after he died. "Zelly can get meth in her system from just touching you, because your body pushes the poison out through your skin. You need to get clean, Leda. Your use affects your parenting. It was obvious the first day we met. Zelly needs you and you're zoned out."

She hung her head. "I promise to look into outpatient treatment. I will."

I let her sit with that. After a bit, I asked, "Did you tell Dan that Todd had a million-dollar insurance policy?"

She sat up straighter. "No. No! He didn't have a million-dollar insurance policy." "But you thought he did."

"I only found it after Todd's death. And it turned out it was worthless, anyway. God, please don't tell me Dan killed Todd."

"Looking back, is there anything you said to Dan that might have suggested you wanted Todd dead? My wife and I have disagreements and I have certainly said things I regret."

"No. Well, we said things like, 'I'll love you forever,' during our nights together. But it was just in the heat of passion." Leda confessed, "I lose myself in the moment, but then later, think, 'crap—I actually said that.'"

"Do you feel like you lose yourself with men, in general?" I was looking at a very broken woman, who had somehow come to the conclusion that her only saving grace could be found through a man.

Her uneasy sniggering grated on me. "All the time. I want everyone to like me. I regretted cheating on Todd, every time. I just can't be alone. I get so down." She scraped old polish off one of her ragged fingernails.

"My parents were great people," I shared. "But while I was growing up, we lost our farm, despite the fact they were working day and night, and I had a mentally ill brother who demanded their attention. For years, I felt like an empty vat for affection—I could never get enough. And it carried over into dating for me. I needed to remind myself that every little thing my partner does for me, even making me a cup of mocha, is love. Eventually, I stopped feeling alone." It was mostly true; still, no matter where I was in the state, I drove home to sleep with Serena at night. Otherwise, I was lying awake all night, in a hotel room, lonely.

Leda appreciated the comfort. "I want you to like me."

"I'm trying to decide if I should arrest you. It's not at all about liking or disliking you." "Please, don't arrest me."

"Then be honest with me."

Leda was panicky, gushing out, "Can I say one thing about the letter? I never said Dan had to live without me. We both agreed that he shouldn't come over after Todd was shot. There were nights he wanted to and I just told him not yet. I needed more time. I never said we wouldn't be together. I didn't know! I've gone out with a couple guys since Todd died, just to get out of the house, but it was nothing."

I had a photo printed of the man who'd been at the hotel with Raven. This man matched the description of Kaiko Kane, one of the men who broke into Jasper and Brenna Ross's home. I set the black-and-white picture of a stocky man with Pacific Islander features on the table. "Have you ever seen this man? He may go by the name Cocaine."

Leda seemed to shiver a little, but said with defiance, "No." I waited a moment. "What's going on, Leda?"

"Just looking at him gives me the chills. Look how dark and cold his eyes are . . ."

18

THEORY OF THERMODYNAMICS = FIRST LAW:
Energy cannot be created in an isolated system.

Rudolf Clausius German Physicist
Federal Institute of Technology Zurich, Switzerland, 1850

KAIKO KANE
11:30 PM, SATURDAY, JUNE 8, 2019
RED CARPET NIGHTCLUB, 5TH AVENUE SOUTH, ST.
CLOUD

I PICKED UP MY girl, Raven, to bring a little life to our isolated shack. When I got back to the lab today and found Chad in bed with her, I could have beaten them both to death. I found her. I determine who she has sex with. Raven just signed her own death warrant. I don't care if Chad is big as a mountain; she should have let him beat her to the edge of life, rather than fuck a man without my permission.

You don't bite the hand that feeds you. I'm no chemist, so I need Chad, but Raven is just white trash. Whores like her are a dime a dozen. There are thousands of homeless teens in the Twin Cities on any given night. Most are of color, and half have a kid with them, but there's enough to offer a selection.

How should I kill that two-timing twat? I want to give Chad a lesson to never mess with me, or my property, again.

121

Of the three of us, Chad's the weakest at heart, so anything that offers Raven hope, and then shatters it, would be heartbreaking for him. Chad's always whining, "We don't need to hurt anybody." Wake up, Chad—we're making meth. We are killing people.

Maybe I'll let Raven think I trust her to freely walk around town and, when she's casually strolling down easy street, I'll take her life.

I'm too angry to deal with Raven tonight, so I'm taking a night out on the town. She's a mission that needs to be carried out mistake-free.

The Arcanes rock the main stage at the Red Carpet tonight, while I sit at the bar to the side of the dance floor, prospecting. Except for the lights on the band and an occasional strobe light scanning the crowd, the bar is dimly lit.

I've heard Jon Frederick is passing my picture around in northwestern Stearns County and southern Todd County. No one will be looking for me here on the eastern edge of Stearns. The Red Carpet is a shadowy labyrinth of stairs and bars, which allows me ample escape options, if necessary.

A petite brunette with long curls flowing down her back dances in perfect synchrony with the music. She's wearing a blouse exposing her bare shoulders and jeans that fit perfectly. She dances with a small group of women who are enjoying the evening. I ask the bartender, "Who's the brunette?"

He grabs a bottle of peach schnapps and begins mixing a Sex on the Beach in front of me as he grumbles, "Trouble."

"Why do you say that?"

"Ever heard of Jon Frederick?" I feign disinterest. "Nah."

The bartender chuckles and says, "He's the detective who caught the I-94 killer a couple years ago. That's his wife."

Concerned, I scan the room, asking, "Is Frederick here?"

"No. It must be a women's night out." "Is she a regular?"

"No, she came with friends to see the band. I only know who she is because I carded the whole group. When I asked if she was any relation to the famous detective, she flashed her wedding band. Serena is the group's sober driver. It's funny, 'cause she's not the most beautiful woman in this place, but there's something about her, isn't there? As Def Leppard would say, 'She's got it!'"

I add, "But are you getting it?"

He laughs. "Armageddon it." He then selects some bottles and asks, "So, where do you stand on Mohamed Noor going to prison for shooting yoga gal?"

Why does everybody have to say she's a yoga teacher? Is there a shortage? I remark, "That black cop saved my ass once." Not wanting to explain further, I point out, "Peach schnapps, vodka, orange juice—there's a lot of sugar in that concoction."

He wryly comments, "Yeah, but I don't think it's sugar ruining that gal's teeth." He juts his chin toward the end of the bar.

My ears perk up and I follow his delivery of that drink to a thin woman in frayed, white jean shorts, and a long-sleeved black-and-red flannel shirt. Her wiry blonde hair looks torn off at the ends.

She must not get a lot of stalkers these days, as the Janis Joplin–like character seems to approve of my wandering eyes. She peeks around her man and gives me a flirtatious smile, revealing decaying brown teeth. She's got "summer teeth." Some 'er there, some 'er not. I have my gal. I just need to get rid of the tattooed baboon hovering over her.

Her scruffy guy is wearing a black "Addictive" t-shirt featuring a buxom, smoking Catrina. I'm not sure how the artist figured a skeleton could maintain large breasts, but I'm no Dennis Vanderpool, so who am I to judge? I kinda like the way

Catrinas symbolize laughing at death. I'm on board with that. Not in the mood to fight a domineering redneck, I need to find another way to discard him.

I wait for him to hit the head. I use the urinal next to him, and stare straight ahead, as men do.

I finish and stand in front of the mirror, pretending to check my nose for rim-riders. As he starts washing his hands, I tell him, "You've got a fan out on the dance floor."

He smirks with arrogance as he yanks too many paper towels out of the dispenser. "Oh yeah?"

"Did you notice the brunette out there in the shirt with the open shoulders?" "Everybody has."

"She asked me if I knew you. I told her I didn't." I half shrug. "She said if I talk to you, I should tell you she's interested."

He gives me a sidelong glance, questioning why I never turned the water on. "My mom taught me to wash my hands when I'm done pissin'."

"Well my mom taught me not to piss on mine." He swears at me as he exits the bathroom.

"Sayonara, Catrina boy." I follow the arrogant prick out and watch him find his way to the dance floor. He's careful to avoid the attention of his flannel-clad, popcorn-toothed blonde friend. I go right to her and point him out. "It seems your man's found a new friend on the dance floor."

She huffs an embittered breath.

I introduce myself. "They call me Cocaine."

"I'm Desire." She steams as her man strikes up a conversation with the detective's wife. Desire takes some pleasure in watching Serena kindly turning him down.

I place my hand on her leg. Desire doesn't shy away, so I whisper, "I've got a little rocket fuel—we could smoke it like that Catrina on your Casanova's t-shirt."

Her guy isn't giving up easy. Casanova continues to pester Frederick's wife on the dance floor, even after she turns away. She waves goodbye to him and focuses on dancing with her friends.

I ask Desire, "So are you the settle-for babe?"

Casanova puts his hand on Serena's shoulder, but she brushes it off. He says something to her, looks about the bar and points toward me.

At that moment, a strobe light flashes across my face and Serena looks directly at me a little too long. Does she recognize me? Time for me to vamoose.

Desire clutches my arm. "Get me out of here . . ."

We walk a couple blocks to the Mississippi River bridge. The temperature reached eighty- eight today and it's still a warm seventy degrees. Desire takes my hand and we walk beneath the concrete bridge. She giggles nervously as we wander down the bank, through the brush, with a blanket and an eight-ball of meth, to enjoy the warm summer night by the river.

3:30 AM
MISSISSIPPI BRIDGE, 1ST STREET NORTH, ST. CLOUD

It had all been freakishly copasetic with Desire. I wanted to take my anger out on her, but as I became more aggressive, she flashed me a bizarre smile. I had to lighten up to get rid of her goofy smirk. What the hell is wrong with her? Desire now has wildflowers in her hair and, like a sixties hippie, is walking topless along the river bank, talking a hundred miles an hour. Her meth- induced mania—along with the mosquitos—are pushing me to my limit. I've only stayed with her this long because there's been a flurry of activity on the street above us for the last couple hours. One more stupid question, Desire, and I'm killing you. I can finally hear cars starting to clear out, so I now feel safe clearing out of this hellhole.

She asks, "Would you rather lick all the make-up off of a clown's face, or lick your entire refrigerator completely clean?"

I've had it.

I look around; there's no one in sight. I walk directly at her, while she mindlessly sings Miley Cyrus's, "I came in like a wrecking ball . . . all you ever did was break me."

"Overplayed." A strong push sends her flailing into the ravine of the Mississippi. With a deluge of rainfall, the river has been surging and carving away at the banks all summer. "Sayonara Desire . . ." I chuckle a little—I think La Catrina would, too.

19

CONTAINMENT THEORY =
Deviant behavior is not caused by outside stimuli. It is caused by what a person wants most at any given time. But deviant behavior can be contained by outside stimuli. External social factors can effectively insulate an individual from criminal involvement.
Subsequently,
weaker social systems result in more deviant behavior.

Walter Reckless Criminologist
Ohio State University, 1973

JON FREDERICK
3:40 AM, SUNDAY, JUNE 9, 2019
MISSISSIPPI RIVER BRIDGE, EAST ST. GERMAIN, ST.
CLOUD

FRANTIC, SERENA CALLED and told me she spotted a man who looked exactly like the picture I'd shown her of Kaiko Kane. I called the St. Cloud police and they immediately sealed off the streets in a three-block perimeter around the Red Carpet. The bar was only two blocks away from the St. Cloud police station, which gave us an incredible response time. Unfortunately, despite scouring the restaurants, hotels, and parking garages, we never found him, or the woman with whom he left the bar. It didn't seem like he should have been able to escape the sealed perimeter this quickly, but we were now sending officers home.

I walked across the tar parking lot behind the River's Edge Convention Center, realizing that, if Kaiko headed to the brush along the river, we wouldn't find him. With all the rain we'd had, the brush was wildly overgrown; the banks were high and the river was deep.

Then I heard the gargled scream for help from the river.

I sprinted around the bridge corner and down the bank of the Mississippi. A woman was flailing her arms as the turbulent water pulled her along its mighty freeway.

I called for backup while sprinting alongside the bank. I hurdled over a downed tree to catch up to her. I took one last large step on the edge of the bank and jumped to her, honing in on her closest appendage. I fiercely squeezed her cold, fish-like arm so she wouldn't slide away. As I feared, the water was over my head. It wasn't easy swimming in clothes, but I pulled and swam, with all my power, toward the shore.

She croaked desperately, "I can't breathe!"

And then she did something that was the fodder for nightmares. As I dragged her to the shore, she jerked forward and grabbed hold of my hair. Fearing she was drowning, she hoisted her body above the water by forcing mine beneath hers. I had heard the stories of Good Samaritans drowning while trying to save someone, because the victim panicked. I imagined it could happen so easily—now, I knew how easily.

I could see bubbles rising above me in the frigid, dark brown water as I swam with all my power to find that elusive surface, but I couldn't overcome her downward force. My lungs were forcefully compressed by the liquid monster that surrounded me. Sometimes, life only gave us two bad options. I could either break free from this woman, and seal her fate, or drown. But instead of letting go, I recklessly fought for both of us—to no avail.

Suddenly, I took a crushing blow to my ribs, purging any remaining oxygen from my lungs. The woman was gone. I spat out water to save myself. I had been swept into a tree, which had fallen from the bank as the land eroded beneath it.

The woman's weight was mercifully off of me and I forced my head above the water. I used my free hand to grab branches and pull my way up the trunk, gasping for air.

My guilt for failing to save the drowning woman was soon lifted.

A police officer had risked his life by walking the trunk of that fallen tree into the river, with the hope of saving us. He had taken a firm grasp of the woman and now asked me, "Are you okay?"

Once I was done heaving out water, I gulped air deeply and, hand over hand on branches, followed him along the fallen pine to the shore. I wasn't able to relax until I was finally lying on the grass in the dirt and scrub. I looked up through eyes that were finally starting to refocus at the officer. "Robbie?"

He smiled. "Yeah. Don't expect me to always be out there going on a limb for you." "Ha," I said weakly. "Thank you! I thought you worked in Crow Wing County."

"I work some weekends in St. Cloud for extra cash."

A St. Cloud Times reporter was quickly on the scene, as she had heard we had cordoned off the area in search of a predator. I pointed to Robbie as I dragged myself to my feet. "Here's your hero. I need to find some dry clothes."

As I made my way back up to the bridge, I passed a second officer who cynically retorted, "Why bother? I've Narcaned that woman out of overdoses twice. You're just postponing the inevitable."

"Well, I'm a big fan of postponing the inevitable."

In the mayhem, Kaiko Kane had managed to escape.

20

THEORY OF PRESSURE =
*A significant amount of force applied to a single unit will yield
destructive pressure.*
Pressure = Force/Unit Area

Blaise Pascal
French Mathematician, Physicist, & Catholic Theologian, 1658

CLAY ROBERTS
6:45 PM, SUNDAY, JUNE 9, 2019 WILSON AVENUE
NORTHEAST, ST. CLOUD

I'D BEEN WORKING late since my fallout with Hani. You tried to give people the benefit of the doubt, and they just lied to you. Jon told me I needed to learn to trust women. Why? So I could be periodically torched? Like a gas station hotdog, I'd rather just slowly blister in frustration with women all day than haphazardly detonate.

I used to enjoy being alone but lately, each failed relationship cuts a little deeper. Hani was unlike anyone I'd ever dated. She didn't drag me around to show me off to friends like a show dog. She didn't expect me to buy her things. Hani just wanted to come home to me, and I missed her. Her kind heart was refreshing. Even though I generally respected Sundays as the Lord's day, I worked today, in a failed effort to avoid thinking about her.

I had finally cleaned up for the day and was ready to go grab some food. When I entered the garage, there was Hani, sitting in my truck. Now what? There were some things talking couldn't fix. I hated talking when it was pointless.

She pushed open the driver's side door and softly said, "Please. Just give me five minutes." Her hijab was off her head and being squeezed in her hands, as if she was wringing out her anxiety. It was going to take a lot more than that concession. I stared straight ahead and nodded for her to continue.

Hani appealed, "You can't even look at me? If I'm that disgusting, why do you care how I dress?"

I slowly turned toward her. "Make it quick."

"Okay. I was married when I was sixteen. Half of Somali girls are married before they're eighteen. Eight percent are married before they're fifteen. Almost every girl has experienced genital mutilation."

I found myself leaning into the open door. I drifted to her sad eyes and she looked down, gesturing to her lap as she said, "Every Somali girl I know has."

My anger completely evaporated. I crawled up into the truck and took her hand. "I'm sorry."

She exhaled a long, frustrated breath. "Not as sorry as I am. God gave us the gift of blissful elation with our soulmate and man took it away from me. Never knowing is the worst."

I didn't know what to say. It was horrible. How could anyone, of any religion, justify this? "We made it to the US safely," she continued, "but then my father arranged a marriage for
me and sent me back to Mogadishu. I found out later that the nights Father claimed he was working late were nights spent at the casino trying to find a quick way to get American rich. My father received a dowry from a forty-eight-year-old

man, which paid off his gambling debt, in exchange for offering me up to marriage."

Could this story have gotten any worse?

"My husband's other wife was older and she hated me. I wanted to tell her if I could be anywhere else on earth, I'd be there. But complaining would have gotten me killed. I wasn't entitled to an opinion. If I looked in the face of another man, I'd be beaten. I'm sure you've heard of the honor killings perpetrated by fundamentalist Islamic men who felt their wives stepped out of line. Have you ever seen Black Hawk Down?"

"Yeah—it's a great flick about special forces trapped in the Moge."

"Not so great for those of use living the nightmare. That's where my married life occurred—Mogadishu, Somalia. I was there in 2011, when an Al-Shabaab suicide bomber killed a hundred students and parents who were waiting for news on scholarships. Al-Shabaab and ISIS are the KKK of Islam."

Al-Shabaab? It reminded me of the cartoon horse who hit bad guys over the head with a guitar—El Kabong. I liked the old days when men had the balls to fight someone, rather than slither around like snakes and kill innocent people. Hell, even Loretta Lynn threatened to take a woman to "fist city" when a woman hit on her man. I could respect that. "How did you get out?"

"My mother was with me in Mogadishu when the explosion occurred. She worked as a translator for the US military, which is a bit ironic, since my dad preached that women shouldn't work. He needed money, though, so Mother apparently was the exception. I don't even know how fundamentalist Islam developed the idea that women shouldn't work. The prophet, Muhammad, was employed by his merchant wife, Khadijah."

Hani had been folding and refolding her hijab as she explained her history to me. It was obviously hard to discuss.

She shook the fabric hard in frustration and continued. "Anyway, my mother and I were shopping when the blast shook the whole city. We weren't hurt, but I began crying and told her I wished I would have been killed. She held me, and then said, 'It's gone far enough.' That's when I learned I was sold to pay off a debt. Mom cut on her body until she was bloody, and then went to my husband and told him I was killed in the explosion."

"What did he say?"

"He told her, 'I'm not paying for the funeral.' Mother said she'd take care of it, and brought me back to the US. So, yes, I'm married. I'm not divorced because my husband thinks I'm dead."

She raised her hands to put the hajib back on. "Thanks for hearing me out."

I was officially a dick. I pushed the hajib back into her lap. "Holy crap." I apologized, "I didn't mean any religious insult by saying that. I'm sorry for kicking you out of my truck." I wrapped my arm around her and she melded into me.

Her tears wet my shirt and I murmured into her glossy hair, "It's okay."

"Nothing about it is okay," she said sadly. "Everyone in this neighborhood knows I'm married. It's embarrassing, but when you said the only woman you'd consider marrying was already married, I thought maybe you meant me. I guess I thought you knew."

"I haven't exactly been privy to your life story. Beyond saying 'hi' to passers-by, the only one I talk to here, other than you, is Vic. And believe me, my conversations with Vic are not very deep. There's a plaque on the wall that says, 'I cried because I had no shoes, until I met a man who had no feet.' Vic read it and said, 'I get it. The guy was happy because the footless guy might have some shoes he's not using.'"

Hani laughed through her tears.

I had a lot to think about. But tonight, I was just holding her and walking her home. I thought about the pressure placed on Hani, by her father, culture, faith, husband, the poverty of Somalia, and now me. It was a miracle she survived.

21

EVOLUTIONARY THEORY OF FEMALE ORGASMS =
*Studies of earlier mammals indicate the clitoris was part of the
vagina, guaranteeing that intercourse stimulated
the organ and kick-started ovulation. Over time, the clitoris has
moved further from the vagina, even out of reach of the penis. With
the evolution of spontaneous ovulation, orgasm was freed for a
new role.*

*Mihaela PavliĐev
Professor of Theoretical Biology University of Cincinnati Medical
School, 2016*

MIA STROCK
6:30 AM, MONDAY, JUNE 10, 2019 MIDLAND AVENUE, ALBANY

DEL WALKER SHOWED up at my home at an unholy hour and, before I could even blink the sleep out of my eyes, he insisted I walk out to his squad car to watch a video on his laptop.

Wrapped in one of Hong's huge flannel shirts, I stumbled behind him as he crowed, "Jon isn't smart enough to rent a room under a false name, so he was easy to find. I installed a hidden camera and have the recording. So, now it's not just my word against his. Watch this."

He perched his laptop on the hood of his car, hit play, and I watched Jon enter the room with the same dark-haired woman who met him in the bar. She wore a slinky white dress this time, and they passionately kissed as they held each other tight. She put on a show of being so into him for a moment, I forgot she was just his whore. She undressed Jon and he backed up until eventually, our camera view became Jon's bare ass. I looked away.

Del added, "I thought you'd enjoy this much more than me. The boy's in good shape." "Okay, you have a video of Jon's butt." I didn't dare say it out loud, but Jon should really wear tighter clothes.

Del seemed to read my mind. He gave a lecherous smile and turned up the audio. Jon was telling her how to pleasure him.

I told him, "You can turn it back down."

Del fast-forwarded until we could see the woman, now holding her dress against her chest, as she entered the bathroom. Del fast-forwarded again. She came out of the bathroom wearing an oversized, bronze-colored t-shirt that covered her like a mini-dress. She thanked him for the soft factory-worn material and crawled under the covers. Del fast-forwarded some more, and we watched them romping in triple time, engaging in missionary sex under the covers. There was a moment at the end when the woman almost seemed embarrassed, but I didn't ask Del to slow the video down. It was more than a cash encounter for her. It made me wonder if Mom ever had feelings for her clients. Crestfallen, I looked down, trying to avoid seeing any more.

Del followed my gaze and thought I was staring at his feet. Clearly insecure, he said, "You know it's not true what they say about men with small feet."

I wanted to shoot him. Did he understand that he was making that comment in the midst of accusing another man of inappropriate sexual behavior? I was thinking his small feet didn't leave our boot print. He is familiar with investigations. He could have misled us by wearing larger boots. So, did I keep staring down and risk more insecure comments, or return to staring at bare buttocks? I focused back on the video.

The woman was exiting the bathroom again, now dressed. Jon handed her cash.

Del said, "Now, listen to this."

The woman straightened her shoulders and said, "I can't do this anymore." Jon was irritated. "I'm not driving down to the metro for sex."

Undaunted, she shrugged and put her coat on.

Jon added, "Well, I guess I'll just have to find someone else."

She pulled the t-shirt out of her bag and threw it at him. "I guess you'll have to," she said, slamming the door as she departed.

He made no effort to stop her. Jon picked up the shirt and sat on the edge of the bed. He looked truly troubled.

I asked Del, "What are you going to do with this?" Minnesota law stated it was illegal to record someone where a reasonable person would have an expectation of privacy. A hotel room fell under this umbrella, so its value was primarily as blackmail.

"Not sure yet. I think I'm going to hang onto it until Jon gives us a little more on Todd Hartford's death. Like him or not, the son of a bitch is good. He found Dan Moene. Jon was a day late and a dollar short, but he found him. I think I'll give him a little more rope before I rein him in. I want to end my career without disgrace."

Del grinned and held up a case for the movie . . . And
Justice for All. He laughed as he inserted the DVD from the
hotel into it and placed into his glove compartment. "This
seems to be as good a place to save this as any."

22

BAND THEORY =
*When the spacing between energy levels is so minute, the levels
essentially merge into a band.
(A quantum-mechanical treatment of bonding in solids.)*

Felix Bloch S
wiss-American Physicist Stanford University, 1928

JON FREDERICK
9:55 PM, MONDAY, JUNE 10, 2019 PIERZ

I NEEDED TO APOLOGIZE to Serena. The kids were in
bed and, as was our nightly ritual, I was rubbing her feet
and legs in front of the fireplace. As she purred to the warm
lotion being rubbed into her skin, I told her, "I'm sorry for
asking you to roleplay with me for work. I get an idea in my
head and it seems like the only path."

"Have you thought of another way to get in contact with
Raven?"

"We have a Craigslist ad for a man in Paynseville looking
for a young adult escort. We've had responses, but nobody's
brought Raven. I think whoever has Raven is smart enough
to know the ad is a sting operation. You hear about that type
of sting every week." I lifted her leg and kissed just above her
knee. "I don't care if an old detective like Del saw me naked.
Guys deal with this in the locker room all the time—it's a

139

non-issue. Even though you were covered, I shouldn't have asked you to make love to me for my work. I'm sorry." I had located the hidden camera in the hotel room with an RF signal detector and placed my bare butt right in front of it, as a kiss my ass message to Del.

Serena leaned in and kissed me. "I'd do anything for you. I thought roleplaying a sex worker with you would be fun when I agreed to it, but when I got in the real situation, it was nerve-racking." She shuddered. "Your best sense is telling you that someone's going to offer you Raven after this rumor gets out, and I believe you. I'd like to get her out of sex trafficking, too." Serena stopped my hands and looked me hard in the eyes with concern. "But you're really trashing your reputation among law enforcement. Is it worth it?"

I reflected. "A bad reputation for saving a girl's life . . . that's an easy trade."

Serena's intensity softened. "After a couple more years of being home with the babes, I'd love for us to do some private investigative work together, so I want to help wherever I can."

I went back to kneading the tight muscles in the backs of her legs, and she hummed, "Mmmm, that is so good." She stopped herself. "By the way, if you ever get the chance to destroy that recording, please do. You told me to just look into your eyes and focus on us, so I did." She blushed. "And I ended up enjoying it a little more than I intended."

"I enjoyed it exactly as I intended."

Serena smiled in agreement. "Yeah, but it's different." "I'm just a slimeball guy."

"Sure, that's you, love—such a slimeball," she teased, and kissed me again.

"We had to make it seem real, and you did. I promise to destroy it. Del will confront me with it eventually and I'll point out his recording was illegal. And when I tell him he took a video of me with my wife, he's not going to want to risk being charged with nonconsensual dissemination of private sexual images."

"Is it still a charge if he doesn't send it to anyone?" "Yes— he never had consent to possess the video.

After some silence, Serena changed the subject. Perplexed, she said, "I was looking over your copy of Dan Moene's suicide letter. It has a lot of adverbs for being written by a man." Recognizing my confusion, she explained, "Women use adverbs more than men. The letter used adverbs of degree, such as 'very' and 'immensely,' and adverbs of manner, like 'foolishly,' 'faithfully,' 'happily,' and 'willingly.' That's a lot of adverbs for five sentences."

It would've been far easier for me if Dan had, indeed, killed Todd, but Serena had fueled my harboring doubts. "I'll try to find a sample of Dan's handwriting for you to scrutinize. That's good; thank you. If you think Dan's writing isn't consistent with this letter, the FBI has a program called ALIAS I can use. It stands for Automated Linguistic Identification Authorship System. We've used it before to prove someone was forced to write a suicide letter."

"How does it work?"

"It breaks sentences down to words and examines how the person uses words, in relation to each other. It takes a look at a person's use of simple and complex phrases—their use of conjunctions, adverbs, and adjectives. Just as people have a unique way of speaking, they also have a unique way of writing. We can go far beyond handwriting analysis."

I cupped her feet between both my hands and smoothed her soles with lotion as I shared, "There's a quantum-mechanics theory that states the space between two entities can become so minute that the two merge."

Serena tenderly caressed my shoulder against her body as she whispered, "This lotion is the perfect bonding agent . . ."

23

CIRCLE OF CONFUSION THEORY =
*When we view a situation, only a small part
of the image is in perfect resolution. The remainder is known as
the circle of confusion. The circle of confusion can be used to
determine the portion that is exceptionally clear.*

Henry Coddington
Royal Astronomical Society, Trinity College, 1829

JON FREDERICK
6:30 PM, TUESDAY, JUNE 11, 2019
OLDE BRICK HOUSE, 102 6TH AVENUE SOUTH, ST.
CLOUD

M Y PERCEPTION OF Del Walker was gradually changing. Lacking corroboration for my concerns about
him, I began considering what my prodding had failed to
elucidate. There were no past reports of Del leaking information on investigations. There were rumors of inappropriate
comments to female peers, but no formal complaints. Del
had collected and recorded evidence in a professional manner. It was time for me to set aside my personal feelings and
begin using him as a resource. Del was like a satellite drifting
through space, oblivious to the view he presented to those at
the eyepiece of the telescope. My task was to lasso and guide
him back into orbit.

I called Del and shared that the same unique boot print that busted the window at the Hartfords' was found in Dan's home. He and I scrutinized the list of suspects my BCA colleagues had formed from their list of Minneapolis residents who lived in the neighborhood where the boots were stolen. We both felt the man we were looking for was not on the list.

Del kvetched, "I'm not trying to be insulting, but all of my work, plus all of your efforts, equal nothing."

I offered to call my boss to see if he could help us out. "Sean, could we have BCA agents go through the Xerxes neighborhood one more time," I asked when I reached him, "to make sure we didn't miss anybody?"

Sean grumbled, "Are you kidding me? We can't dedicate any more resources to this. I gave you Mia, and she's proven to be a star. If she hadn't spent some nights here helping, we never would've compiled the list the first time. Your cases aren't the only crimes we're dealing with. Don't call me unless you have something for me."

Del insisted we stop at the Olde Brick House in St. Cloud to blow off some steam. I needed to learn to work more effectively with him, but I could turn into an alcoholic if I worked with Del every day. Del knew Stearns County far better than I, though, and I needed his help.

This Irish pub served one of my favorite tap beers, Kilkenny. It was first brewed at St. Francis Abbey in Kilkenny, Ireland. It was labeled as a cream ale, but I'd have described it as a red ale, even a step up from Dos Equis Ambar, which was very good. I loved the butterscotch smoothness of this roasted malt beer. It would go well with the fish and chips I ordered.

Del ordered a glass of Harp, but no food. He had chosen a private table away from other customers so we could discuss work. He asked, "Have you ever considered that Marc Hartford may have had an affair with Leda?"

"I did, before I met him. He loved his brother and he reminds me of the descriptions I've heard of Todd—no malice in his heart." I shared, "The lab sprayed ninhydrin on Dan's suicide note." People who write suicide notes tend to perspire and ninhydrin identifies amino acids that come from sweat. "Their conclusion was Dan wrote the note."

Del scratched his unshaven cheek. "Honestly, it closes the case for me. I'm agreeing with you, here. Marc loved his brother, but everyone has their breaking point. Let's say your boot thief knows the boots are expensive, but they don't fit, so he sells them and eventually the boots end up in Marc Hartford's hands. They're his size. Marc stops over at his brother's one night and realizes Leda is with Dan. Pissed, Marc walks to the end of the driveway and kicks in the window of the bus shelter. I'm thinking that window had nothing to do with Todd being shot. Marc puts two and two together and realizes Dan killed his brother. He wants justice, so he visits Dan and pushes him over the edge. Marc didn't really commit a crime—Dan shot himself."

"I read your interview with Marc. He denied kicking in the window, right? It's a pretty minor behavior to deny."

Del dismissively looked away.

I surged ahead. "I keep coming back to Kaiko Kane. What's this drug dealer doing in the area and where the hell is he staying? Why is he robbing a home in Grey Eagle? Who's the big guy who stepped in to help him out? And perhaps most importantly, who was the driver? I keep thinking that's the person who is saving the other two from detection."

He leaned back. "Whoa—you suspect an insider. Has anybody directed you away from relevant information?"

Sean had asked me to leave the Ross home invasion investigation to Todd County. But Sean also was the one who got the BCA involved.

Del interrupted my train of thought. "I don't believe Kane had anything to do with Todd. I'm not sure the Ross home break-in was initially intended to be a robbery. From what I've read on Kane, he's a drug-dealing sex offender. Somehow, Brenna Ross is unfortunate enough to cross his path and he follows her home to rape her. It's another crime in another county."

It was exactly what Sean had said, and I repeated my response. "Only thirty miles away." I opened my hands as a sign of giving up. "Something connects all of this and I just can't see it. I was hoping you could give me some insight. That boot print should've been a home run, but we've got nothing from it. Mia erased the tape of the home invasion."

Del disagreed. "Now, don't go hating on Mia. She found the bullet. She directed us to re- examine Leda and that brought you to Dan. Mia's given us the only pieces we didn't have before you arrived, so, from where I'm standing, she's a gem."

I hadn't told Del that I got Dan's name from Zelly. "Be professionally respectful to Mia." Surprised, he protested, "I just said she's a gem. Has she suggested I've harassed her?" "No. I'm just reminding you." I had sensed her antipathy for him. Having made my point,

I said, "Del. Something evil is here, right now. I can feel it—hidden somewhere in Stearns, Todd, or Kandiyohi County. And while we're dancing around in this circle of confusion, some poor soul's going to get caught in the crosshairs."

He took a large swallow of Harp. "Any particular reason you included Kandiyohi? We have an attempted robbery in Todd County and a shooting in Stearns."

"Both occurred close to Kandiyohi County." I wanted to test his reaction to a theory I'd kept to myself. "Maybe these guys know enough about law enforcement to understand jurisdiction, so they're not committing crimes in the county they're based in."

"That's good," he said, bobbing his head. "I'll talk to the deputies in Kandiyohi and see what they have." Del's demeanor visibly slipped out of business mode. "Now, drink up! I'm almost done and you're just starting."

"When this glass is empty, I'm leaving."

He squinted. "You order a beer a man could drink twenty of, and you only drink one."

"I could drink twenty—that's why I only drink one. I'm trying to exercise some discipline. Maybe it's why I'm still Catholic, despite the fact that some terrible priests damn near buried the religion. Catholicism is about getting up and doing the right thing every day, no matter how mundane it gets."

Del smirked behind his beer glass. Before taking the next gulp, he jibed, "Oh, what a tangled web we weave, when first we practice to deceive."

"Most people attribute that quote to Shakespeare. It's actually from Sir Walter Scott." Changing direction, I asked, "What happened to make you so cynical?"

He was daring me to bring up my night at the hotel, but I wasn't biting. I didn't like wasting time when gathering information, so I just put it out there. "Del, you're an impressive investigator, but you're as bitter as a glass of Stone IPA and as grumpy as the devil on the bottle. Tell me your horror story."

"We all have them, don't we?" He chuckled dryly, gulped the backwash from the bottom of his beer, and waved toward our server. "The 2012 killing of Officer Tom Decker, in Cold Spring, was a heartbreaker. I honestly don't think I can live through another cop killing. There's no accountability on the news for the guys who attack officers."

His beer arrived and Del shuffled bills across the table, dismissing the bar matron with a flick of his stubby fingers. He waited until she was out of earshot. "My worst moment happened in Somaliville, in St. Cloud, over at the apartments by the Mississippi bridge. I was working the night shift and had cruised into St. Cloud to grab a bite to eat. At two thirty in the morning, a man calls and reports he heard his female neighbor in the next apartment scream for help. I'm close by, so I rush over and talk to the man in the hallway. Around us, people start coming out from their apartments. Pretty soon, I've got three people recording me on cell phones. I pound on the door identifying myself, but no response. The guy who called in then changes his story and tells me he's not sure if the scream came from the apartment or outside. That changes everything, because now I can't bust open the door. I ask, 'Do you have any concerns about her using drugs?'"

Officers can break into an apartment without a warrant if drug use is suspected.

"The man says, 'No, she's clean.' I ask, 'How about pot?' I'm doing everything I can to find a reason to get in and check on this woman. He repeats again, 'She doesn't do drugs.' And everybody's standing around waiting for the white cop to break into an apartment without clear cause. So I tell them, 'I won't enter. I can't.' If I break in, and it's not an emergency, it will be all over the internet: 'White cop doesn't respect the rights of minorities.' I'm trying to do the right thing, but I finally have to give up and leave. Then I find out the next day, a young woman was raped in that apartment after I left. The rapist was inside keeping her quiet while we were standing outside. Online, they report the rape, with a clip of me saying, 'I won't enter,' that loops over and over. I'm a joke. There is not a single dirtball I've arrested who is more universally hated than I am. But what they think isn't near as bad what's going on in my head. I should have forced open that frickin' door. My gut instinct told me to, but those damn cameras . . ."

"That's a hard one to live with." It would have been ideal if Del would have had another officer to confide in, but county deputies work alone.

He challenged me, "What would you have done?"

I wanted to offer a solution for next time, without directly telling him. "It's much easier reflecting when adrenaline isn't pumping through your veins a hundred miles an hour." I questioned, "I wonder if anyone else had a key for that apartment?"

"No. I asked."

I waited patiently for him to discover the answer.

He finally shared an afterthought. "I guess I could have asked the manager." I didn't need
to say any more. He'd consider it next time.

"It tears me up to have anyone think I didn't want to help that young woman. I would have given my life for her. I blame myself. My job was to protect her and I backed off. I tried going back to explain, but she wouldn't talk to me." A veil of sadness descended over Del's face. He wrestled his tired body off the chair. "I'm headed to where all the dicks hang out."

I watched him labor toward the restroom, working out the kinks in his aching bones and painfully rubbing his chest.

When he returned to the table, Del solemnly swirled the dregs of his beer around the bottom of his glass, having almost downed his second in the time I drank half of mine. "I know I'm not easy to work with. They say, 'Don't argue with a dead man. He already knows how it all ends.'"

"What's that supposed to mean?"

"I've got stage four COPD. I'm prescribed steroids to help me breathe, so I can work, but I'm looking at less than a year."

"Why are you still working?"

"I need a win here, Frederick. I've got a daughter who's always supported me. And she's got my teenaged grandsons who've heard all the crap about me. I need to end my career with solving a case, for their sakes. I thought you could help me, but I don't know if you can." Del glanced from his beer toward the bar, contemplating a third. He picked up the cardboard coaster and tapped it on the table in thought. "You find a tape of a car in Todd County, but it's erased before we can use it. You managed to figure out the right path of the bullet, but you were damned lucky Mia knew something about hunting. Even though you gave her the distance a full metal jacket bullet would travel, she considered that more likely, a softpoint bullet was used."

I didn't know how to respond to that. Instead, I asked, "Would you be able to spend some time with Leda tomorrow? Maybe she'll tell you something she wouldn't share with me." I gave him a picture of Kaiko Kane. There had to be a connection between Kaiko and the Hartfords.

He took the picture. "I'll ask about Eurasian man, here, and be nicer to yer Asian intern."

I slapped some bills on the table and left, not wanting to watch this broken man drink away his angst. I'd never been a big fan of poetry, but thoughts of Del Walker and Sir Walter Scott emerged from somewhere in the recesses of my brain. On my way home, the ending of the Scott poem,

The Lay of the Last Minstrel, ran through my head:

Despite those titles, power, and pelf, The wretch,
concentred all in self, Living, shall forfeit fair renown,
And, doubly dying, shall go down

To the vile dust, from whence he sprung, Unwept,
unhonour'd, and unsung.

10:16 PM, PIERZ

Even though it appeared Dan wrote the suicide letter, I brought home examples of his writing, as promised, to Serena.

After she finished reading the samples, Serena's eyebrows were firmed by frustrated creases. "Dan may have physically written the letter, but these are not his words."

I appreciated her insight, but I couldn't do anything with it until I knew who authored the letter.

After I finished sharing my day's work with Serena, she asked, "Whatever happened to the guy who killed Mia's mother?"

"He shot himself before charges were filed. He was dying of prostrate cancer." She corrected me, "Prostate."

"He was laying down when he got it."

Serena smiled. "Aren't we funny tonight? Has Mia ever shared that she's an expert marksman?"

"No—although it shouldn't surprise me. Maurice has always been an avid hunter. In all fairness, I guess I've never shared with her that I'm a comedian."

Serena handed me her tablet, which had the cover of a magazine titled North American Whitetail on the screen. A headline read, "Way Weird Whitetails." I remarked, "So, when did you start looking at porn?"

She squeezed my bicep as she grinned and said, "That sounds like something Clay would say. If the buck on the cover isn't a clue, it's a deer hunting magazine. This issue is from 2013. Scroll to page thirty-two."

There was a picture of a sixteen-year-old Mia Strock with a rifle across her lap. The caption below read: "Golden Bullseye Award Winner for Minnesota Youth Female Hunter of the

Year." I set the tablet back down and rubbed at the tension in my forehead.

Serena studied me. "Please get that video from Del as soon as you get the chance." Like me, her thoughts on this case were bouncing all over the place.

"I promise to. I've been waiting for some news on Raven."

"You look so troubled." She took my face in her hands. "What's going on?"

I tried to explain my torment. "There's despair in my heart and I don't know why. I feel like I'm standing at the edge of a precipice, but I can't see what's below. This case is slipping out of control. I feel that, at any moment, Pandora's box is going to bust open and all hell's going to break loose."

Serena kissed me gently. "There are a couple good reasons to make love. The usual is we're excited and we can't get close enough to each other." Her soft, warm breath on my neck felt incredibly erotic as she continued. "But sometimes, I need you to make love to me because I feel afraid and anxious and I just need to feel loved. Correct me if I'm wrong, but I'm getting the sense you need me—us—tonight."

Even if she was wrong, I wouldn't correct her. If the door opens to heaven, I'm walking in, whether I should be there or not.

24

Formula for a Black Hole R =
2GM/C Squared The Horizon (R) = Gravitational constant x 2 x
Mass of the black hole ÷ the speed of light squared (A space having
a gravitational field so intense that nothing of matter can escape.)

Albert Einstein
German American Theoretical Physicist
Prussian Academy of Sciences, 1916

Clay Roberts
10:05 Pm, Tuesday, June 12, 2019 Wilson Avenue
Northeast, St. Cloud

HANI AND I were once again in my Chevy truck, parked in the garage. She was wearing a hint of makeup and had loosened her headdress when I'd arrived. She had the we need to talk look, which I hated. Talking is overrated.

I said, "What?"

"Clay, I love being with you, but you've turned our relationship into a black hole. All the joy has been swallowed and replaced with sterile politeness." Hani clutched at my hand. "I love your raw, unadulterated passion, and now you're handling me with kid gloves. You don't take me to see your friends. You stopped trying to make love to me. Pity doesn't help me."

I tried to explain, "It doesn't exactly come natural, but I'm trying to be considerate. I'm finally getting it. Islam is very important to you and after everything you've been through, you need it. I care about you too much to disrespect your beliefs. For me, religion is a way of life—it's not something I attend. Jesus told us, 'Love one another as I have loved you.' It's that simple for me. I know it's more complicated for you." My voice trailed off. "I have no desire to be a decision you regret."

Hani's compassionate eyes made me want to hold her as she said, "I love you! There are a hundred reasons why I shouldn't, but I do. I'm in an abyss with my religion. I believe in Allah, but I'm married, and can't divorce. Please don't pull away. I need you now more than ever." She lamented, "Let me figure this out, with you."

"I'd love to have you meet my friends, but I don't want you to wear the hijab or the dress.

And then I think it's not fair for me to ask that of you, so I put off the whole deal."

Hani's posture hardened in contrast with the soft lines of her face. "You're the one who is always telling me I shouldn't be taking orders from men, but here you are giving me a directive."

I rubbed my face. Hell with it, I'd just tell her the truth. "You can't be the woman I want to be with, in that dress. I love the outdoors. Minnesota has over 10,000 lakes and you're dressed for a desert. I would love to hike Gooseberry Falls with you and fish, and swim, but you can't do it in a dress. Of everything you have told me, this is what I struggle with the most. The head thing has to go, too. Because when I see it, I feel like you've accepted being subliminal to men, despite all the horror your faith has put you through."

"I think subordinate is the word you're looking for." She looked caught between laughing and crying, but softened. "What happened to my body wasn't true Muslim faith. It's like Hitler claiming to be Christian. There are crazy, brutal people in every faith, who twist religion to support their hatred of others."

"Don't stick us with Hitler. Hitler loathed Christianity. He had planned to kidnap and murder the pope, because the pontiff was one person who was publicly critical of him. His own officers thwarted the plan by warning the Vatican." Okay, she didn't need a lecture. Getting back to my concerns, I said, "Your clothing doesn't work for our terrain and it symbolizes disrespect to both individuality and women."

Hani clutched at the folds of her long dress and shook it at me. "You think I like putting on this bedspread when it's ninety degrees and humid, and I'd rather be in shorts and a tank top? There are days I feel like I'm breathing in hot soup. Of course it isn't always comfortable, or even practical, here. But what it is, is a symbol of support for our faith, even at the risk of subjugation and ridicule. The Quran initially advised that women dress similarly so men wouldn't be able to single out the slaves and attack them at night. It was about protecting those less fortunate." She prodded, "So, it's my garments and that's it? Here's your chance to unburden it all."

She asked for it. Maybe I should have said all of this in my head first, but instead, I blurted, "I don't know what to do with the sex thing. I've never considered committing to a woman who doesn't enjoy sex."

Her deep intake of breath confirmed I'd just stuck my Red Wing boot in my big mouth. I could see right away the comment cut her to the core. In my mind, I took that boot out and kicked my own ass with it. Seeing the pain in her eyes was heartbreaking. I so wished I could've taken it back.

Crestfallen, she forced out, "Why do you think I don't enjoy sex? I enjoy making love with you. I love being close to you and the feel of your skin against mine. And that you let me be in control. Pleasing your body becomes pleasing my body."

I liked the sound of that. Backtracking as fast as possible, I said, "I just assumed . . . I'm sorry. If you start with the assumption that I'm an idiot, it will be easier to understand me."

Hani continued to pry. "How about my marriage? You told me that was a deal breaker." "I hope you don't mind that I spoke to my friend, Jon, about this. I needed to sort it out. A guy's got to have a line he doesn't cross. Otherwise, he's just a life support system for an erection. Was your ex married to his other wife first?"

Hani curiously studied me. "Yes, years before. Why?"

"Then you're not married in my religion and you're not legally married in the US. Once he married, he can't legally marry again, according to our laws."

I sat quietly as she seemed to wrestle through the demons in her head. She'd been through a lot and didn't need me telling her what to do. At the same time, it was only fair that I told her what I needed. I was trying to be a better man.

Hani finally said, "The Quran states that a woman's way of dress should be based on custom and function. Respecting the Quran, would you be okay if I wear the hijab and abaya here in my community, even when we're together, and I dress in jeans and a blouse when I'm in your community?"

"Works for me." I leaned into her and kissed her. The softness of her lips and warmth of her mouth heightened my desire for her.

"I'm happiest when I'm with you." Her voice thickened with emotion. "I feel we could accomplish so much together. We're what the world needs."

"While you might be the next Gandhi, I will never be what the world needs." She chuckled. "Gandhi was Hindu."

"That just drives home my point."

Hani cautiously unraveled her hijab, revealing she had cut her hair short. "I hope this is okay."

I kissed her. "You're beautiful." Seeing her without the hijab gave me the same feeling I had when I got my first car. It was all about freedom.

Hani lifted the hem of her dress until it gathered around her hips, displaying dark, shapely legs. She unbuttoned my shirt and kissed her way down my chest.

As General Lee used to say, I was happy as a clam in high water. I relaxed and threw my head back when, out of the corner of my eye, I saw a young Somali man, wearing a 1970s-style silk shirt, peering in the passenger side window.

He pounded on the door and yelled, "Sharmuuto!"

Never one to walk away from a challenge, I hopped out of the truck. The man took off running out the side garage door.

Hani lifted her hips as she shuffled her dress over her legs and scrambled to put on her hijab. "You didn't lock the door," she hissed fearfully.

I told her, "I didn't know you'd be here. Who was that?" As a former linebacker, I itched to run him down, but I was torn. I didn't dare leave Hani.

"My brother, Maxamed. He just called me a whore." She got out of the truck and paced. "There's going to be a firefight at home tonight. My family has asked me about you and I told them you were a friend. Why come to America if we're only going to talk to Somalis, right?"

"I agree. You're about the only Somali I talk to." Hani didn't appreciate my attempt to lighten the mood. Resigned to staying put, I tried to shake the adrenaline out of my limbs. I leaned against the truck, going for cool. Both of us jacked up would get us nowhere.

I grabbed her as she stalked by and held her until her racing heart began to calm. She half-heartedly attempted to push against me, but I wasn't letting go. I eventually felt the muscles in her back and shoulders sag in resignation.

I held her away from me and took her face in my hands until she looked at me. "You didn't do anything wrong."

Her eyes were bright with tears. "I don't know if that's true."

"Please." I held her gaze. "Let me give you a ride home. I want to be able to help you if it gets crazy." Her father's need to be admired seemed to always take priority over Hani's self-esteem. I didn't want to see him destroy her again. She didn't deserve it. Hani agreed to the ride, but she looked pretty worried about it.

When we arrived at her parents' home, clothes were strewn about the front lawn. Neighbors stood in their doorways observing the fiasco. Her father, Axmed, was standing at the door, squawking, "You are not my daughter! You are not welcome here!"

Axmed fixed his rage on me and started walking directly at me. I stepped toward him, ready. Try me, jerk-off! You know how little I think of a man who would sell his daughter to pay off his debts? I would love to stomp you into the ground. Keep coming.

Hani put her hand on my chest and begged, "Please don't do anything." Her mother peeked out timidly, her body tucked behind the doorframe.

After serious consideration of my physique and my own anger, Axmed stopped in his tracks and weighed his options. His face reddened, but he stayed silent in his seething fury.

Maxamed came to his rescue, emerging out of the darkness with a gang of pals ready to defend his father's honor. I made note of the white-hot hate in their eyes.

Bring it on! I glanced from the brother to the father and, without looking at her, told Hani, "Throw your clothes in my truck. You can stay with me."

Maxamed yelled, "Gaadhi dhillo. Whoring for rent."

I was ready to hit him so hard his clothes might be back in style by the time he landed.

Max had pushed his luck to within swinging distance. My mind began calculating who presented the biggest threat. My feet spread into a solid stance, electricity flowing directly from my rage into my limbs.

Hani ran between us and took control of the situation.

"No!" She pushed against me, but I wasn't moving. She turned to her brother and kissed him on the cheek.

I had never seen a mob of angry men de-escalated so quickly. I wasn't so slow to chill out, but understood there would be no punches thrown tonight.

Hani whispered to her brother, "Jeclahay. Wankujeclahay. There's been enough hurt. I don't know where I will stay, but I will go peacefully. Waan ka xumahay." She held a hand to his cheek. "Max, I am no longer welcome here. There's nothing to fight about." She softly added, "Hate always finds me, doesn't it? Take care."

Tears streamed down Hani's cheeks as we drove away. Her expression was flat—no hysterics for this woman. She stared straight ahead and explained that she told her brother she was leaving because of love. Every streetlight we passed bounced off her tears, flashing on her pain like a strobe light.

I probably should have said, "I love you," but I didn't. Instead, I took her hand and kissed it. I told her, "Hani, you're a rock star. You were so awesome!"

Frustrated, Hani asked, "Do you know what that word means? Did I really inspire awe?" "No and yes. I didn't know exactly what it meant, but now that you've explained it, awesome is perfect."

And that's how Hani came to live with me.

25

GENERAL ADAPTATION SYNDROME THEORY =
"Every stress leaves an indelible scar, and the person pays for its survival by becoming a little older." GAS theory indicates that people respond to stress first with alarm (fight or flight), resistance (fighting the body's natural desire to calm down), and finally exhaustion.

Hans Selye
Hungarian-Canadian Endocrinologist, 1956

GISELLE HARTFORD
4:15 PM, WEDNESDAY, JUNE 12, 2019 BRIAR CREEK
ROAD, PAYNESVILLE

MOM AND I just got home from Dan's wake. We weren't there very long. Dan's mom called my mom names and his dad said, "Just leave." I don't know why we even went. My friend told me everybody thinks Dan killed my dad and then killed himself.

When we got home, I just went to my room. I didn't want to talk to Mom or anybody, really. Why did she even make me go? I pulled out my dolls. Nothing was fun anymore. I was tired of people being mad. I loved my dad. But even Mom and Dad argued a lot before he died. Dad used to yell at Mom for not playing with me. I shook the boy doll at the girl doll. It was okay if Mom didn't want to play with me—I just didn't want them to yell about it. Mom just got sad, sometimes. I laid the girl doll down at the edge of my bed. I didn't know if I could ever love Mom again if it was her fault Dad was dead. I pushed the girl doll on the floor. Then I felt bad, so picked her back up. Mom was all I had left. Maybe I'd feel better if she rubbed my back.

I opened my door and was about to go find her when I saw a man sitting in the kitchen with Mom. The man had tight, tanned skin, and had just a crease where lips should be. Mom looked scared. Where did she find these guys? Other than Dad, Mom was a magnet for losers. This one had big arms like a gorilla. I didn't know him, but I didn't like him. His voice was soft, but every word felt dangerous—mean and tense. I missed Dad. Mom was crying. It wasn't a sad crying. She was really scared. My tummy felt queasy.

I kept my bedroom door open a crack so I could watch them. Mom was shaking. Why is everybody mad at Mom? My mom never tried to hurt anybody. She just never seemed to care how the things she did made me and Dad feel. The gorilla was trying to make her write something, but she kept saying she couldn't.

I pulled my door closed to just a little crack. I watched him take a bag of pills out of his pocket and set them on the table in front of her. He whispered something in her ear.

She closed her eyes at first and then nodded. Mom took a pill out of the bag and swallowed it. That didn't seem right. It was just a sandwich bag, not like the medications we got at the NuCara pharmacy. Uncle Marc wanted me to live with him. I felt so scared right now, I had to remind myself to breathe. With Mom doing this stuff, maybe I would go to Marc's—for a little while, anyway.

The man got up and pulled Mom to her feet and pushed her toward her bedroom. Mom didn't see me, but yelled, "Giselle, I'm going to take a nap. Don't bother me."

When her door closed, I snuck out. A dull black rifle with a scope rested on the kitchen table. It looked like all the shine had been rubbed off. I touched it and it felt like construction paper. It said "Remington" on the side.

I quietly made my way to Mom's bedroom door. I could hear the bed squeaking like a rusty teeter-totter. It made me sad. He was calling her names, but other than a few moans of pain, Mom wasn't saying anything. From what I'd learned on the bus, I figured this must be what sex sounds like.

And then I heard my dad's voice telling me, This is the killer. I should've left, but I wanted to know if he was going to admit it. If he did, I'd call Jon. Investigator Frederick's card was still on my nightstand.

It made me even more sad when I realized this creep probably wasn't going to admit it. This wasn't a cop show. It was real life and in real life, nobody takes responsibility for anything. Mom never once told me she was sorry. She'll pretend she never cheated on Dad, and I'll pretend I never knew. And that lie would stand like a door we were both afraid to open, between us, forever.

As if in a trance, I found myself going back to the Remington. I picked it up just like my dad would and aimed it—like a hunter—at Mom's bedroom door. My grandpa told me the Bible says, "An eye for an eye." He told me, "You don't take crap from anybody, girl." I clicked the safety off. They could both die for all I cared. It was my turn to be angry.

Dad told me Jesus said, "You've heard it said, an eye for an eye, but I want you to turn the other cheek." But I didn't want to. I wanted someone to hurt for killing Dad.

Just then, a bird banged into the window again. My dad's voice thundered in my head, NO! NO! NO! Dad, I wish I could just talk to you, even just one more time. I suddenly felt dark, empty, and shameful. I didn't like how I was thinking. I quietly set the rifle back down. Dad had drilled into my head, "Don't you dare pick up a rifle until you're twelve years old. Shooting is only a small part of hunting." Sorry, Dad. I won't pick it up again.

The squeaking in the bedroom stopped and I could finally think again.

Mom's voice sounded panicky. She was asking him, "Where are you going? What are you going to do?"

He said, "I've got to take care of some business. Then I'm coming back and you're signing that letter."

In the back of my head, my dad's voice was saying, Run! so that's exactly what I did. I headed out the door and bolted into the woods as fast as I could. When I heard the door slam behind me, I looked back.

The man was raising the rifle to his eye, pointed toward me. He yelled, "Giselle!" I quick ducked behind a tree. He didn't fire.

When he started running, I took off again. Dad told me the deer know these woods better than we do, so that's why we couldn't always find them. Well, I knew these woods better than this guy. Dad said there was a big buck around, but he could never find him when he needed to, because that buck knew when to run and when to sit. Getting up and running was what got deer caught. I zigged and zagged until I found a dark spot. I hid behind a tree under some brush. I could hear dried leaves crunching as he got closer. He wanted to kill me. Why? I didn't even know him. My Dad's voice told me, Not here.

I slid out of the brush and ran again. Then something made me turn to the right. I slipped down into a small dip in the ground and the leaves fell over me. I lay there dead still. I couldn't afford to rustle these leaves. And then, I felt his warm body next to me. I couldn't breathe—until I realized it wasn't the man. It was the buck. Through the leaves, I saw his dark brown eyes look down on me. I wasn't sure if he felt I was as harmless as a fly, or if he was telling me to stay put. His warmth was the closest thing I had to Dad, so I stayed.

The man kept coming toward me, yelling, "Giselle! You might as well come out. I heard you—I know you're here."

He was only a few feet away now and my heart was pounding. His foot crunched the leaves inches from me. One more step and he'd be on me.

All of a sudden, the buck bolted to his feet and, like a thrashing machine, plowed through the brush.

Gorilla man fell backwards and then laughed and said, "Shit." The buck galloped off into the woods. The man shook his head at the deer and turned and walked back to the house.

I waited a long time before moving. I finally heard my mom calling me. I wanted to run to her, but I didn't. She yelled, "Giselle! Gi-selle!" again and again. Her voice told me she was shaken up. My uncle Marc told me Mom loved me, but I couldn't trust her. Mom pleaded, "Just come home."

Uncle Marc was wrong. I could trust my mom. Mom told me that Jon thought Dad's death wasn't an accident, and she was afraid. She said, "If I ever call you 'Giselle,' you should never come to me." She was telling me to stay away. It was our secret code.

But I worried about Mom. That man was scary. What would he do to her if I didn't come out?

I carefully made my way to her voice. When I got to the edge of the woods, I hid behind a tree and looked at our house. Mom was kneeling on the ground, crying. Gorilla man was standing right behind her, with the rifle aimed at the back of her head. Dad's voice was telling me, Sit quiet.

The mean man racked the slide of his rifle, sending a bullet flying to the ground while chambering the next round. I think he did it to remind Mom she was a moment away from death, like it was her last warning. He leaned in close to her ear, but said loud, "Call Giselle one more time."

Mom bent over forward, wailing, "No. No more. Just do it."

At that moment, I knew Mom loved me more than life. I had never been more scared. My dad was gone and I was seconds away from losing my mom. I didn't care if she was ever honest with me about any of those stupid boyfriends. I just wanted her to live. I needed her.

The gorilla ruffled her hair like she was a kid. "Not yet, honey."

Like Dad taught me, I silently snuck to the side, careful not to make a sound. They couldn't see me, but I could see them. I wanted to help Mom, but she didn't want me to come. Should I listen or did she need me to save her? With the patience of a hunter, I sat and waited. Finally, gorilla man got up and picked up the discharged bullet. My heart sank when he started walking toward me. Had he heard me?

He then made a sudden turn and walked, all mad-like, toward our driveway. I heard a car start in the front yard and pull away.

I ran to Mom. My mom was willing to die for me and I loved her. She was crying so hard and loud when she hugged me.

I helped her to the house and we called Uncle Marc. I trusted Mom, but she couldn't protect me. I didn't know why, but it felt like she was in more danger when I was here.

26

BEHAVIOR-BASED SAFETY THEORY (HEINRICH'S LAW) =
*For every accident that causes a major injury, there are 29 accidents
that cause minor injuries, and 300 accidents that cause no injuries.
Ultimately, the reporting of close calls saves lives.*

Herbert Heinrich Engineer, 1931

JON FREDERICK
5:30 PM, WEDNESDAY, JUNE 12, 2019
CENTRACARE CLINIC—RIVER CAMPUS, 6TH AVENUE
NORTH, ST. CLOUD

I HAD TAKEN MY schizophrenic brother, Victor, to a psychiatric consultation in St. Cloud today. The gunmetal sky was overcast and the humidity was thick as goulash, the slightest movement evoking perspiration. I blasted the air conditioning to keep the windows from fogging up.

I asked Vic, "So, tell me what's going on in your life."

Vic put his earbuds in and stated casually, "I don't really feel like talking."

He wasn't upset. Vic was just blatantly honest. I loved him, but he would never love me the same. The expectation that I would look out for my older brother, since I was eight years old, left him with resentments I'd never completely understand. I told him, "That's fine," and he turned up his music.

I called Serena to process my thoughts on the case.

Serena was watching the radar on AccuWeather app, after her phone chirped alerting her bad weather was on the way. "Jon, this looks like a pretty big storm coming. They're saying golf ball-sized hail and high winds. How long are you going to be out there?"

"Every week, we're told we're getting the storm of the century. I'll take my chances."

"Well, please just be careful. Looks like it's going to hit where you are in the next few
hours."

After I assured her I'd take precautions, I began working out my angst. "Yesterday, Kaiko Kane tried to get Leda Hartford to write a suicide note. I think he had planned to kill her daughter, Zelly, and blame Leda for it. Once he killed Zelly, he thought he could get Leda to kill herself."

Serena asked, "Would Leda have killed herself?"

"Yes. Her exact words were, 'If he killed Zelly, I had no reason to live.' Assuming Kaiko Kane is this man referring to himself as 'Cocaine,' we have him trying to rob the Ross home, picking up a meth addict at the Red Carpet, and selling Raven for sex. He needs cash and his sexuality is out of control. Sounds like he's in the meth game."

"Did Leda know him?"

"She claims she's never seen him before, but he knew she'd take a meth handout."

Serena contemplated, "Did he want to kill Zelly so Leda would kill herself? Or is there another reason he needed to kill Zelly?"

A call came in and, seeing it was Marc Hartford, I told Serena I had to go. After shared "I love yous," we disconnected.

Marc sounded frantic. "Leda just called and said that same man returned. She ran and hid in the woods until he left."

"Have you called the police?" "I'm calling you."

I headed to Paynesville. "Is Zelly safe?

"She's with me and she's not going back. Leda wanted to come and stay with me, too, but that's not happening. I've had enough of her crazy boyfriends. Intentionally or not, she got Todd killed."

"I'm going directly to Leda's."

I disconnected with Marc and immediately called Del. "Kaiko Kane returned to Leda's today. Where the hell were you?"

Del sounded hungover. "She sent me home. I'll get out there."

I called Mia, who volunteered to leave work and to head straight to Paynesville to sit with Leda until I arrived. I couldn't waste time driving Victor home, so we drove to the Hartfords' home. Mia's Corolla was already in the driveway when we pulled up.

Leda came running out and threw herself theatrically against me. "Thank God you're here!" She wrapped trembling arms around my waist.

"Are you okay?" "Yeah," she breathed. "Was Del here?"

I felt her nodding against my chest. "Last night. He was three sheets to the wind, so I told him to go home. I'm trying to get clean. I don't need to babysit a drunk."

"Where's Mia?"

"She wandered into the woods."

I patted Leda's back carefully, then gently disengaged from her clutches. My distrust of Del had resulted in giving Mia Strock too much responsibility. Mia would be in a world of hurt if she confronted this predator.

I could hear the shrill sirens of squad cars closing in from the distance. I asked Leda, "Are you going to be okay if I go find Mia?"

Leda nodded absently, shivering despite the early evening warmth. She wiped at the black veins of makeup trailing down her face and looked up at the ominous sky, unfocused. I could see she wasn't right, but had no time to address it.

I left Vic standing by the car with Leda and ran to the woods, shouting, "Mia! Mia!" Branches, bright with vibrant green leaves of summer, slapped at my arms and face as I darted through the woods. I was instantly slick with sweat and various insects swarmed around me as fast as I batted them away.

I found her sitting on the trunk of a fallen oak. She gave me an odd but casual smile and wearily said, "I'm okay. There's nothing here to find. If you want to search, have at it." She gestured dramatically to the woods behind her.

I was relieved to see she was safe, but cautioned her, "Mia. I asked you not to walk through the woods alone. If you fail to follow my directions again, we're done. I can't spend my time worrying about keeping you safe." I studied her, "How can you be so relaxed?"

"I'm relaxed now," she chuckled with sarcasm. "I had to pull over and puke on the way here. When you called, you didn't make it clear that Zelly was still alive. I was afraid I'd be the first on the scene to find her body."

Thinking back, she was right.

Mia stared off into the woods as if her thoughts occupied another world. I asked, "Are you really okay?"

Mia ridiculed me, her tone flirting with hysteria. "Am I okay? Maybe you could define 'okay' for me." She threw up some air quotes to make her point. "A child was almost murdered here. This isn't okay by my definition! Zelly is barely eluding death—and I mean barely. Leda's frantic. Del's drinking himself to death. Your marriage has gone to hell. My relationship is hanging by a thread." She maniacally waved away gnats and slapped at the mosquitos puncturing her bare arms. "Damn! These frickin' bugs!"

I sat next to her on the downed tree, processing the multiple concerns she threw out within seconds. I offered what I could. "This work isn't for the light-hearted and it's hard on relationships." I clapped a fatherly hand on her shoulder. "Take a couple days off; we can see where you're at then. Get together with some friends. Forget about this for a bit. I'll make sure Zelly's safe. I need you to take care of yourself or you're going to get seriously hurt."

We sat in silence for a bit. I asked her, "Have you ever seen a chain snap when they're pulling a truck out of the ditch?"

Mia shook her head no.

"If the truck's jammed in too deep, it takes a lot of power to pull it out. Sometimes, the force yielded by the rescuer is more than the connection can bear. The chain tightens and when it snaps, it can kill a passenger in either vehicle or any innocent bystanders." I paused for effect. "With this case, the chain has tightened, and we're either solving this, or the chain's snapping. You need to be alert and ready. Your head's not where it needs to be right now."

Mia stared intently at the ground in front of us. "I had an affair with a guy at work last summer. I thought he was funny and sweet. I hung on every word he said. I would've done anything for him. He flirted. We kissed. I imagined a variety of passionate, romantic trysts where we would finally make love." She stopped and her tone became dire. "I had made him my knight in shining armor, but in reality, he was just a coward. He used me, and that was the end of that." She finally looked up at me, gauging my reaction.

"Do you still work with him?"

"No, he quit. Last I heard he was involved with a married woman." I considered everything she had said. "Did you shoot him?"

Dumbfounded, she responded, "No! What? I loved him!" With a sad laugh she admitted, "Despite it all, I still loved him. I wanted to see him suffer a little, sure, but I wouldn't do anything to him. And then Hong came along and saved me. He made me realize I deserved so much more. But now, even he is slipping away." She shook her head, as if she was erasing a slate. "I'm sorry. I shouldn't have said any of that. I know your relationship is as much of a mess as mine." Any distress she had felt now evaporated into the humid air.

"I'm sorry it played out like that for you. You have to be kind of glad you're done with your ex-coworker, looking back. They say if you lend twenty bucks to a friend and never see him again, it's a good investment." I paused at my ineptness. "I'm sorry. I wish I had some wisdom to share that could make you feel better. I'm a mess when my relationship's stressed. That's when I need to be careful of my choices and constantly ask myself how a man of honor would handle this. Following that guide seems to get me through it."

When Mia and I returned to the house, Leda and Victor were sitting together on the steps. Leda was talking a hundred miles an hour and Victor was listening attentively. He could be a great listener and she obviously needed to talk. Deputies were inside, going through the house. Mia was emotionally exhausted, so I led her to her car and then stepped in to talk to the deputies.

Del had shown up while I was out scouting for Mia. He looked better than he had sounded earlier. After Mia was tucked away in her car, we compared notes. He shared, "Leda said this guy came in a truck yesterday and on a motorcycle today. She told me she heard him heading west toward Highway 23. We had speed traps set up north and south of here on 23 today, but nobody's seen him. Maybe he's still close."

"Would you mind getting a group of volunteers together and walking through these woods?" I asked. "My supervisor's already torqued at me for using excessive BCA man hours to create a list of everyone who lived in the area of where those boots were stolen. And Sean's right— it should have solved my case, but I have nothing to show for it."

Del chewed it over. I was expecting resistance, or at least an insult, but instead he said, "I'll see what I can do. They're gonna have to get here fast, though. If we get the rain they're predicting, all evidence is going to be washed away."

For the first time, we were finally working together.

"I've got to drive my brother home, but call me if you find anything."

On the way home, Victor began tearing open an envelope. I couldn't remember Vic possessing an envelope all day.

Picking up on my curiosity, Vic commented, "What? If you got something to say to me, I'm all ears." He stopped and pursed his lips. "Well, actually I only have two ears—but I'll listen."

I asked, "Where did you get that?"

"It was on the floor of your car." He turned it over. "Whoops. I guess it's for you." I pulled over, took the note and read it:

A friend suggested you could use some company. I'll be at the bar in the Paynesville Inn & Suites tonight, in a lace burgundy top, at 9:00.

There was a drawing of a raven in the right-hand corner. I asked Victor, "Did you see who put this in my car?" "No, but I wasn't really paying attention . . ."

A jagged shot of lightning cracked across the sky in the distance. In my mind, I began counting the seconds until the rumble of thunder followed it. By my count, the storm was still a good twenty miles away. Still, the heavy clouds robbed us of daylight earlier than usual. My headlights were triggered and came on as darkness descended too early, as flummoxed as I was about what was to come.

8:45 PM PAYNESVILLE INN & SUITES
700 DIECKMAN DRIVE, PAYNESVILLE

Del's search beat the rain, but yielded nothing, so I dismissed him for the night.

I reserved a room at the Paynesville Inn & Suites. Someone close was bleeding out details of this investigation, so I decided to run tonight's operation with three colleagues I trusted completely. My Brainerd colleague, Paula Fineday, assisted behind the counter at the hotel lobby to help detain Raven's ride, if he entered.

I had an undercover officer in a van, circling the blocks around the hotel, waiting for someone to drop off Raven Lee. My good friend, and former law enforcement officer, Tony Shileto, sat in his wheelchair in the back of the van. He scoured the streets of Paynesville for Raven. Tony was the perfect BOLO— or "be on the lookout"—investigator, since his driver didn't need to look at the suspect and he was hidden behind dark-tinted windows.

Tony called and said, "I've just spotted a young woman with short black hair with blue tips on the ends. Plaid miniskirt, burgundy blouse, too-high heels. Meets the description of Raven Lee you gave me. A biker on a Triumph dropped her off, turned around, and headed back toward Cemetery Road. She's walking east, on the shoulder of Veterans Drive."

"Let her keep walking to the hotel. Call if anyone seems to be following her."

27

THEORY OF UNIFORM ACCELERATION =
*In mechanics, acceleration is the rate of change in the velocity of an
object with respect to time. Galileo hypothesized that falling objects
experience uniform acceleration (due to gravity).*

Galileo Galilei
Italian Astronomer, Physicist, & Engineer, 1610

TONY SHILETO
8:50 PM, WEDNESDAY, JUNE 12, 2019 VETERANS DRIVE,
PAYNESVILLE

M Y WHEELCHAIR-ACCESSIBLE VAN was in takeoff
position in the south parking lot by McDonald's. This
allowed me and my driver to spot vehicles approaching the
Paynesville Inn & Suites on Veterans Drive, from both the east
and west.

I recruited my roommate—twenty-eight-year-old Vicki
Ament—to drive, after an old friend canceled at the last minute. Vicki and I shared a house in Pierz and often bickered
like an old married couple, but we'd never been lovers. I was
old enough to be her father. I allowed Vicki, a former meth
addict, to live with me because I wanted her seven-year-old
daughter, Hannah, to be safe. Hannah and I were buds. We
read together and I told her stories every night. I lost my ability

to walk, but gained a chance to be a father again—a chance to be unlike the man who was always at work when my son was working his way toward adulthood. I didn't know that I'd trade the two. While I had no control over what I'd lost, I did have control over what I'd gained.

Vicki sat in the driver's seat with the window rolled down, nonchalantly glancing over the top of her sunglasses, checking out a teen strolling by us down Veterans Drive. "She walks like an addict."

"I didn't know they had a walk."

Vicki glanced back with those bewitching blue eyes, "Come on, Tony, I know you've checked me out."

"Only because your walk is like a siren going off—it can't be ignored. But it does nothing for me." I added, "Still, it's not fair for me to criticize. I'm an old man and, if you hadn't noticed, I am a paraplegic."

She rolled her eyes dramatically at me, having heard this before. "I've kind of settled into the single life, with you and Hannah." Vicki beamed and said, "We're a family now."

Vicki, Hannah, and I were the misfit toys. Vicki's mom was an addict living in Las Vegas, last we heard. She never gave up the identity of Vicki's father. I was divorced and my son only muttered a few words to me when I called every month. Visiting me would be beneath him and I'd never been invited to visit him. Still, he seemed to be doing well, which I guessed I had to attribute to my ex.

The cumulus clouds in the east suddenly flashed repeatedly with electricity. Vicki exclaimed, "Whoa! I love this—look at those clouds, Tony. They look like the bottom of an egg carton. Man, I love storms." A deep rumble of thunder followed the flash and she looked back at me like an excited child. "This is awesome!"

"Always the adrenaline junkie. Might not be so awesome if we get pummeled by rock- sized hail."

"Quit being a fossil," she sighed. "Hell, they've used stones for massage. Mother Nature's power is a rush—just feel it!"

"I'd like to feel it from the safety of my home, with my good friend, Jack Pine, titrating ice-cold Dead Branch ale into my system."

With binoculars ground into the skin around my eyes, I watched the motorcycle that dropped the girl off do a U-turn, then cruise about 200 yards in the opposite direction she was walking. The biker was dressed completely in black and wore a black-tinted helmet. I was ready to set down my specs when I watched him slowly turn around. What do we have here? He stopped for a moment and reached into his vest. I zoomed into focus on his new distance. He was pulling out a gun. Shit!

"Vicki! Pull out on Veterans Drive!"

The motorcycle started back toward Raven.

Aware of my tone of urgency, Vicki didn't hesitate.

"Listen, this guy's coming back after our girl with a gun. If you want to bolt, just gun it and leave. I'd completely understand. This isn't what you signed up for."

Vicki did exactly what I would have done. She slowed the van to take away the shooter's angle and uniformly accelerated with the cycle as it approached, completely shielding the girl.

I directed, "Put me between the motorcycle and our street walker."

Our biker pulled alongside my decade-old, rusting Dodge Caravan and aimed the gun at the tinted window I sat behind.

I was ratcheted in place with tie straps, so I wasn't going anywhere. For the first time since I'd been in this chair, I realized I didn't want to die. I sat silently staring down the angry psychopath. I couldn't see his face and he couldn't see mine, but I knew I was facing off with a man completely void of morality. I missed that about the job. I taunted impotently, "You think that helmet's hot, imagine what it's going to be like for you when you get to hell."

He cruised alongside us for a moment, then, frustrated, returned the gun to his vest and gunned it. The Triumph accelerated like a rocket into hyperspace, leaving us in the dust.

Vicki stopped the van. "Damn, Tony! That was crazy! That's the biggest rush I've had since I quit using."

Oblivious to what had transpired, Raven strolled by and flipped us off, apparently thinking we were stalking her.

Vicki and I simultaneously busted out laughing. Vicki rolled down the window and yelled, "Love you, too! Just not the same way."

Raven ignored us and rushed, as best she could, toward the hotel. The wind was picking up and she was teetering on stiletto heels that looked like they didn't quite fit.

Vicki turned back to me, now more subdued. "I followed your directions, like you asked, but I don't want to see you put your life on the line again. Hannah and I need you."

The opportunity to save that young woman's life meant so much to me, I couldn't find the right words to thank her. Exhilarated, I blurted out, "I love you, Vicki! That was great driving. If you want the job, you are my driver for every mission from now on."

Vicki teased, "Wow! I got an 'I love you,' and I didn't even have to crawl into the back seat with you."

"Too late now. The moment's passed. We can call ourselves Ament Shileto Surveillance." "Nice acronym." Vicki exhaled a deep breath. "Now what?"

"Well, let's run him down."

Vicki gunned it and the van surged forward, gears slipping and the engine knocking. If not for my tie straps, I'd have tipped over. Vicki bellowed, "Fast and Furious—used van version!"

We both laughed, knowing we had as much chance of catching that motorcycle as a sloth had catching a bullet.

28

THEORY OF THE SEARCH FOR MEANING =
We discover meaning by doing a deed, encountering someone, or by the attitude we take toward unavoidable suffering. (Everything can be taken from a person but the last human freedom—to choose your attitude in any given set of circumstances.)

Viktor Frankl
Psychiatrist & Philosopher Austrian Holocaust Survivor, 1945

JON FREDERICK
9:05 PM, WEDNESDAY, JUNE 12, 2019 PAYNESVILLE INN
& SUITES, 700 DIECKMAN DRIVE, PAYNESVILLE

AFTER DISCUSSING WHAT had transpired with Tony, I called the Stearns County sheriff and he put some units on Highway 23, looking for our motorcyclist. Tony and Vicki sat in the back of the van, in the hotel parking lot, and kept monitoring visitors through the tinted windows. I couldn't afford to leave the hotel.

Raven spotted me as her mark immediately, reminding me that she'd gotten some good intel on my case. Still, she glanced around the lobby, likely looking for the presence of law enforcement, before approaching me. Raven clearly didn't even consider that sturdy, Native American Paula Fineday could be working with me.

I smiled congenially. "I'm Jon."

The concierge was aware of the sting, so he ignored my inviting the underage girl to my room.

As we walked the hall to my room, Raven attempted to be demure, "A romantic evening with a gentleman." This fell short for me, as she was just a child. She asked with affected interest, "So, what does a good man desire when he wants to be bad?"

"My fantasy is to be greeted at the door by a sensuously dressed woman." I opened the room door and stood in the entry, gesturing for her to go ahead of me. "So, get yourself ready."

"Sounds fantastic." Like a kitten in need of petting, she coquettishly leaned into me and purred, "But I need two hundred dollars to get in the mood."

"No problem." I slipped her two hundred-dollar bills.

As soon as she closed the door, I quickly opened the door to the adjoining room. My third colleague, Jada Anderson, joined me in the hall, carrying a bathrobe.

I knocked on the door and Raven opened it, in red lingerie, seductively offering, "Defile me."

I stepped aside and Jada was right on my heels. Raven's vacant eyes widened.

Jada raised a finger to her lips, wrapped Raven in a robe, and escorted her into the adjoining room.

With an RF detector in hand, I entered the room Raven had vacated and slid along the wall furthest from the bed. A hidden camera had been conspicuously placed by the red light on the bottom of the television, with a full view of the bed. I set the ice bucket in front of it. This camera wasn't of the quality Del used previously. It didn't sit right with me, so I continued along the wall. I discovered a much more sophisticated hidden lens by the thermostat. This was the exact lens Del had used in my room the last time. He had been here, but if Raven was working with Del, she wouldn't have the need for a second, cheaper camera.

When I returned to Jada's room, Raven was clinging tightly to Jada, her body vibrating with relief.

After they separated, Jada asked, "Why didn't you call?" "I don't have a phone," Raven offered, weakly.

Jada examined Raven's eyes as she patiently waited for her to continue. Raven pled, "It's different when you're homeless. I didn't have a place to go." I interrupted, "Where were you staying?"

Raven pulled the robe tightly around her, like a lifeline, and sat on the edge of the bed. "I don't know—in a shed in the middle of nowhere."

I crouched to look into her face. "Raven, I need you to be honest. We know you walked in on Veterans Road."

She tugged on her ragged, poorly chopped bangs. "Well, I didn't. I walked in on Cemetery Road. I got a motorcycle ride to Cemetery Road."

I quickly pulled up a map of Paynesville on my cell phone and zoomed in on Veterans Road. She may not have noticed that Cemetery Road turns into Veterans Road. "Where were you before then?"

With the hesitance of someone who generally didn't cooperate with law enforcement, she repeated, "Cemetery Road."

Jada sat by her on the bed and softly encouraged her. "You're not in trouble, Raven," she said. "They need to find the guy you were with."

Raven opened her fingers widely in front of her, as if she was tamping down her escalating agitation. "Before I started walking into Paynesville, we weren't on a road. It was more like a path."

Cemetery Road crossed a tarred path that ran south for thirty miles. The Glacial Lakes State Trail ran all the way to Willmar; it was the straightest shot out of Paynesville. I immediately discerned it was how Kaiko avoided the speed trap when he left Leda's home. He took his motorcycle down the tarred bike path. I turned to Raven and asked, "Who were you with?"

Indignant, Raven grabbed the remote off the nightstand and fired it into the wall with the velocity of a Michael Pineda rising fastball. It fractured and fell into pieces on the floor.

"I am so fucked!" she shrieked at us, her eyes wild. "Don't you get it? These guys are smart. They know everything you're doing. I'm so dead." She dropped on the edge of the bed, her fingers raking through her greasy black hair. "You just got me screwed. Guess I should've expected that— it's what happens to women like me, one way or another."

Toning it down, Jada calmly suggested, "Take a deep breath, Raven. You called me for help. Let me help." Jada carefully wrapped her perfectly manicured fingers around Raven's ravaged and ragged hands and nails.

Raven pulled her hands back as if she'd been bitten by a rattler. She glared at Jada and spat, "Everything's changed. I'm not saying another word." A quake of thunder shook the hotel. Raven's demeanor shriveled from obstinate to terrorized. She shrank into herself and her wild eyes skittered across the ceiling, as if she could somehow see the danger in the sky. It was a harsh reminder that Raven was just a child.

With a simple glance, Jada directed me to walk with her to the door. She inquired, "Can I talk to her alone? I might be able to turn her, if you just leave us for a bit. She may not have been an addict when she left Minneapolis, but she is one now."

"Meth is the common denominator for everyone but Todd in his murder investigation," I said. Meth had taken a harsh grip on our communities. Methamphetamine arrests had tripled since 2010. At the present time, there were more meth addicts than alcoholics in chemical dependency treatment in Minnesota.

Jada grimaced. "Is it okay if we order some food?" I nodded and left.

Tony was calling, so I responded, "Yes," as I departed.

He informed me, "Your assistant's arrived. She's sitting in the back of the lot." "My assistant?"

"Yeah, Maurice Strock's granddaughter. Mia, right?" "I didn't call her."

"East side of the hotel, last row."

"Thank you." I stepped out into the muggy night, my shirt immediately clinging to my skin. How was Mia going to explain this?

Mia was nervously checking her watch as I approached. She gasped when her eyes met mine through her open car window. I confronted her, "What are you doing here? I told you to take a couple days off."

Embarrassed, she struggled for words. "Del—Del told me you were meeting a sex worker here. I didn't want to believe him. Jon, what are you doing?"

Ignoring the inquiry, I asked, "Is Del coming?" Mia carefully considered her response. "Yes."

I tapped on her door as I contemplated my options. Not sure if she was an asset or a liability, I decided it was safer to leave her out of the loop for the time being. "Go home, Mia—just go home."

I called the Paynesville police chief, Mason McLean. Mason agreed to pick up his motorcycle and head south on the Glacial Lakes Trail. I noted the predicted storm and he scoffed, like I had, muttering that he'd believe it only when he saw it.

I wasn't one for passively waiting to hear back from him, so I told Mason I'd drive Highway 23 south to search for our biker friend. Even though the driver came in on a bike path, he may have left on the highway. Just the image of Mason made me smile. He had an untamed mop of hair, wild eyebrows, and a big, thick "stache" reminiscent of the Lorax from Dr. Seuss.

Mason said, "We don't have any reports of sex trafficking. I did, however, have a guy at a funeral in Hawick tell me that, when they went to the cemetery, he got a whiff of ammonia when the wind picked up. But even that seems kind of crazy. There aren't many meth labs around anymore. It's cheaper to have the meth brought in from Mexico."

"Tell me about Hawick." I could see on Google Maps that the Glacial Lakes Trail ran through it.

"Just across the Stearns County line in Kandiyohi County. Small town. Bunch of Norwegians. Has the same problems all poor rural areas struggle with: unsupervised kids occasionally ripping people off, some drug abuse, but mostly salt of the earth, decent people."

As I zoomed in on Hawick, I noticed Monson Lumber and remembered Zelly wearing her dad's Monson Lumber t-shirt the first time we met.

I called Paula and Tony and asked them to hang around the hotel in case Raven's ride returned, while I headed to Hawick.

I drove into town on 160th Street and, within a block, spotted a car with its lights on in front of the United Methodist church. Two groomsmen in matching tuxedos were leaning against a car talking.

Thunder reverberated like the upset stomach of an angry behemoth. I stopped and flashed my badge.

One quickly shared, "We were just picking up my car before heading to the dance. I left it here after the wedding

Mass. I wasn't sure if I'd left the windows down. Did we do something wrong?"

"You're fine."

Just then, Police Chief McLean's motorcycle pulled off of the Glacial Lakes Trail onto Twenty-Third Avenue, rumbling our way. I was about to ask a question when the information was volunteered.

The second man asked, "What is it with these chromosexuals taking their hogs down that bike path? That's the second one since we've been standing here."

I asked, "Did the first one head this direction, too?"

"No, just the opposite. He turned off the path, but took a right instead of a left. We could see its taillights."

The Google Map of Hawick indicated the road only went a short way in the other direction, and ironically turned into Hawick's Cemetery Road. Maybe Raven had been honest with me. She was on Cemetery Road in Hawick before she was on Cemetery Road in Paynesville. At this very rare moment, I was close to a killer, and about to get closer.

A deafening crack of thunder was immediately followed by a flash of lightning and the groomsmen departed quickly.

Before Mason was off his Harley, Del buzzed me. "What the hell's going down here? I'm at the Paynesville Hotel. Where you at?"

"How did you know something was happening at the hotel?"

"It's a long story." "Make it short."

Del groaned. "Okay, I have an agreement with the manager to call me when you rent a room there. We can talk about that another time—don't blame him. I've worked this area for decades. He knows he can trust me. You're new."

I wasn't happy about it, but said, "All right."

He paused and then, as if experiencing a catharsis said, "Son of a bitch, Jon, you set this up. I don't know why you needed this girl, but you wanted someone to talk about you being with a hooker so they'd offer her up. But why in God's name would you jeopardize your career like that?"

"The woman I picked up at the bar is my wife."

It was quiet for a moment. I wondered if he was going to reveal he videotaped us. He didn't.

Del burst into laughter. "You're a first-class ass! Where are you? Mia's here. She wants to know how she can help."

"If she insists on helping, tell her we could use another set of eyes looking for the man who brought Raven to town. Share the pictures we have of Kaiko Kane with her. Mason McLean and I are in Hawick and were going to walk Cemetery Road." We were headed into a potentially dangerous situation, so I could use another experienced investigator. "If you want to help us find the guy who dropped Raven off, come in with sirens off. We have reason to believe Kane may be here."

"I'll be right there."

As I turned to address Mason, a fat drop of rain splatted onto my hand, splashing on my cell phone screen. I quickly wiped it on my pants and deposited my phone safely into my pocket. Mason's belt vanished under cover of his belly. I knew Mason to be one of the most genuine, kindhearted people I'd ever met. He was abrasive to some, but never apologized for who he was. I glanced down at his red Converse sneakers, expecting nothing less. Long as I'd known Mason, this was his shoe of choice. He was ready to rock.

After explaining the situation to him, I asked, "Are you good to walk with me down Cemetery Road? I don't want to warn anyone we're coming. They're likely better armed than we are."

As the rain fell, everything around us was cloaked in a menacing green hue. Mason and I exchanged knowing glances, but didn't comment. We were in the game now. Weather be damned.

Mason was already wearing his bulletproof jacket. I pulled mine out of the trunk and put it on. He rose a bushy eyebrow. "You think I'm too fat to walk?"

"There are a variety of reasons people can't walk far at night."

Mason puffed up and rubbed his belly. "A good man builds a roof over his tools."

As we started walking, I commented, "Maybe that's where the term 'pole shed' came from."

We kept our flashlights off as we silently walked the dark, narrow road toward the cemetery by moonlight. The rain was coming down in earnest, now, and the periodic flashes of lightning, however dire, momentarily brightened our surroundings. We planned to use flashlights only as needed. The possibility that someone could be sighting us in on a night-vision scope made the walk even more harrowing. We said little, relying on our ears for clues. The killer would likely shoot me first, since Mason was a bigger and slower target. Mom used to say, "Night is the devil's playground." Not knowing what was lurking in the darkness was hair-raising. Bouts of unsettling thunder, ripping through the noise of the steady rain, compromised our senses further.

Finally, Mason pointed straight ahead. He spoke in hushed tones, swiping a meaty hand over his soaked and drooping brows and mustache. "With a graveyard here, a gravel pit behind it, and no houses close to either of them, this would be an easy place to hide a meth lab. We have to split up—there's too much area to cover. I'm going to head directly west through this field. You turn left at the gravel pit. If it's out here, it's west of us."

When I reached the cemetery, I stopped and considered the stories buried here. I was at death's door a year ago; walking by its backyard tonight was unsettling. There, but for the grace of God, go I. How many people buried here never knew their fate on their last day?

As I headed west, the musty smell of alfalfa helped me see Todd Hartford's murder in a different light . . .

29

THEORY OF MURDER AS A SITUATIONAL TRANSACTION =
Murder generally follows a sequence:
Victim offends killer; Killer issues threat;
Use of violence is forged in killer by victim's reaction; Battle ensues,
leaving victim dead.

David Luckenbill
American Assyriologist University of Chicago, 1977

JON FREDERICK
9:35 PM, WEDNESDAY, JUNE 12, 2019 CEMETERY ROAD,
HAWICK

THE DELUGE WAS relentless at this point, leaving us even more blunted from our surroundings. I headed west on a worn path just south of the gravel pit, slipping and sliding over the soaked earth. The ringers were off on our phones, but we agreed to buzz each other if we discovered suspicious activity. I kept my phone in my pocket against my leg, hoping I'd feel the vibrations, as I'd hear nothing over the din of the storm.

I saw a glimmer of light beyond the pit and committed to walking directly toward it. It may have just been a couple who pulled off onto a side road to park, but I was going to check it out. The alfalfa growing around me had matured and was about three feet high. As I waded through it, my pants became more sodden with every step. I felt like I was carrying additional weight. I entered a wooded area and dark shadows of trees hovered over me like gargoyles on the rooftop of a medieval mansion.

The sky nearly split open with a blast of thunder that rang violently through my bones. Staccato bursts of light danced above the dark branches. The short bursts of clarity helped me grasp my surroundings. The field was wending and I was approaching a grove of oak trees. A sudden movement to my left forced me to quickly jerk my body toward the sound. The bottom four vertebrae in my neck were fused, so I didn't turn easily. The culprit, a raccoon, scampered away. As my breathing tamed, I realized I'd drawn my gun.

With the next flash of the storm's fury, I could see in front of me the shadow of a sign nailed to a tree, about nine feet off the ground. I flashed my light on it briefly and saw the word "Firkinfest." Todd had told Zelly, "It must have been nailed up there by one of those big women who live here"— Norwegian Hawick women. Todd and Zelly had been here.

I shut my light off and called Del, shielding my phone with my body to keep my lifeline dry. "Have you ever heard of Firkinfest?"

"Yeah, there was a rumor online a few years ago that some high school students were having a big kegger in this area, but we never found it."

"Well, I think I found it . . ."

I directed Del to my location and told him I'd wait for him. I then called Mason and repeated the message.

As I took a few more steps toward the light, I realized it was coming from a small building hidden among some trees. I smelled phosphorous over the mossy scent of wet forest. It was a firkin meth lab. Todd was the one who put Leda and Zelly's lives in danger, simply by walking through dangerous territory. It had nothing to do with Leda's affairs.

Now being in a new county, I called the Kandiyohi County sheriff and requested backup. He warned me that, since we were in the midst of a storm and on the very edge of the county, it might be a half hour before help arrived.

Mason arrived drenched and heaving for air. We stood together in the dark, hunched over my cell phone, looking at the layout ahead of us. I pointed out, "When I look at Google Earth, it doesn't appear that there's a road to it. I'd bet it's powered by a generator."

Another roll of thunder rippled through the night, causing us to wait to continue talking. Mason pointed to the ponds close by and noted, "A water supply close. Do you think we should wait for Del?"

Del answered the question for us by pulling up on Cemetery Road. "I want to make sure we're all aware of each other's locations. I don't want to be shot in friendly fire."

Mason nodded. "I hear you."

Del came running toward us, panting as he approached. He'd donned a department-issue raincoat, but I didn't see any bulletproof gear under it.

When he reached us, I pointed ahead in the darkness. "Our lab is over there." I had to raise my voice over the rain. I gestured to his body. "Are you protected under that coat?"

Del caught his breath. "I'm good. Should I call for backup?"

"I already have." We all understood this could soon be a life-or-death situation.

The building's light went off and we were once again enveloped in blackness. I could just make out the dark shadows of my allies as we surged forward.

Mason signaled he would start off to the left of the building.

Del grabbed my arm and pulled me aside. "I videotaped you at the hotel. If anything happens to me, it's on a DVD in my glove compartment, in a case titled . . . And Justice for All. Just take it and destroy it. Sorry—I didn't know."

The video had served its purpose. I said, "You can make it up to me by getting us all out of here alive." I cautioned, "Don't shoot if you don't have to."

Del headed off to the right of the building and I went straight at it. I was hoping the door to the shed was right in front of me, as this would give me the greatest control of the situation. A flashlight shining inside the building helped guide me. At the same time, I heard a motorcycle starting up on the other side. At least two people were present.

As I got closer, I could see through a rain-streaked window. There was no door on my side of the shed. A tall, bearded man—the man the Rosses referred to as Paul Bunyan—was unloading kilos of meth from a metal cabinet. A Maglite rested on a tabletop as he frantically loaded package after package of meth into cardboard boxes. A padlock hung loosely from the door handle. He was packing up.

I could hear the motorcycle pulling away on the other side of the building. It sounded like it was plowing through a ditch. Dammit. Someone had warned them of our pending arrival. As encumbering as the storm was, I was at least grateful for its masking the sound of my approach.

Del and Mason were each working their way around the structure. This old farm building likely had only one entrance, so I needed to stay in place, in case Bunyan tried to exit the window by me.

I watched Del and Mason burst through the door.

Mason shouted, "Kneel on the floor and put your hands behind your head."

When the man hesitated, Del tased him and I watched the giant seizure to the floor. The hulking man immediately went into cardiac arrest.

I ran around the building. When I entered the doorway, Mason was on the floor with the man, trying to open his airway.

Del told me, "You're going to have to help him with CPR. I can't with my COPD."

I began the chest compressions while Mason did the breathing. The man regurgitated, as is typical, so we turned him sideways. Mason swiped his mouth out with a finger.

I couldn't help noticing the man had huge feet, easily a size fourteen. This wasn't the guy who left the boot impressions at the previous scenes.

Del knew we were both frustrated that he tased him so quickly. His excuse was, "We couldn't fight him. That goliath would have killed us."

Bunyan finally gasped a breath. His breathing was sporadic and weak, so Mason and I would have to stay close. I'd bet he had meth in his system. Methamphetamine use increased the risk of cardiac arrest. Being tased was more than his body could handle. I strained to listen over the angry storm, but there were still no sirens announcing much-needed reinforcements.

Del walked through the lab while calling for an ambulance. As he did so, he barked to deputies, "It's time to haul ass! We've got one suspect in cardiac arrest and another lingering around here somewhere . . ."

Once off the phone, Del told us, "It's a meth lab with two separate side rooms used for bedrooms. I walked by a tub with gallons of water against the side of the building that must have been used for washing and bathing. Did you hear that motorcycle stop after it got to the road? He's got it in take-off position and he's circling back on us."

The lumberjack was finally breathing regularly again.

"The only light in this hell hole is on us," Del pointed out. "I'm walking the perimeter outside. Mark my word, biker boy plans on picking us off, one by one."

Mason told me, "I need to find that water and rinse my mouth out."

That left me the only investigator in the building. The meth-maker continued to breathe, so I walked to the boxes stacked against the wall. They were filled with clear, four-pound bags of methamphetamine and the amount was enough to rival the September 2018 seizure in Minneapolis that confiscated 170 pounds. That stash was the largest seizure in Minnesota history, recording a street value of over seven million dollars. I should clarify that there was a large difference between the street value of these drugs and what they got for making the drug. Still, they would walk away with at least six figures of untaxed cash. The meth makers here may have had all their money tied up in product, which is why they were looking for cash from a home robbery or selling poor souls like Raven.

Mason returned, shaking rain from his head like a mangy dog. "They've got a hell of a generator out there. These boys knew what they were doing."

"Did you see Del?"

Mason nodded. "Yeah, he thought he heard a car and was going to check it out. I didn't hear it, but I'm having a hell of a time hearing anything through this storm." Mason looked down at our gasping suspect. "Del didn't have to tase this guy. Give the guy a couple minutes to think. Del's so damned impatient. Now he's out there in the dark, mumbling that the devil has us dead to rights."

Suddenly, a loud blast rang out.

Mason swore. "That was a gunshot. Who the hell did he shoot now?"

"I'll check it out."

Mason said, "I'll handcuff Sasquatch, here, to the cabinet and join you in a minute."

"Stay with this guy. Keep the phone line on so we can hear each other. Let me locate Del and then I'll call for you." I pointed to the window. "I'd stand with my back to the wall, next to that window, so you're out of sight and directly facing the door."

We heard one more shot. The deafening silence that followed roared in my ears. Even the storm had paused in trepidation. It felt like a kill shot.

I sprinted around the building. The night was black as pitch. I could hear someone racing away through the grass about fifty yards ahead of me. The runner was crouched and partially hidden in the alfalfa, making identification impossible.

I yelled, "Stop! Police!" Expecting gunfire, I ducked down into the alfalfa. When none came, I chased with the power of adrenaline surging through my system. I slid some, but made ground, until I heard what I discerned as either a guttural moan or a death rattle emerge from the weeds. The tragic reverberation cut through the night like a banshee's scream. I crouched and made my way to the sound, flashing my light for a moment to make out a body. The reflection off a badge stopped me in my tracks. Del lay dead with blood leaking from his stomach and forehead. The rain began pouring in earnest again, diluting his blood to a pinkish tinge. "Son of a bitch!" I bent down and said, "Del!" but of course there was no answer. "I'm sorry, Del."

I heard a car starting from over by the cemetery.

I bolted toward it. The killer was smart enough to leave the lights off, so I wouldn't be able to give a description of the taillights. I raised my gun—I wanted to fire, but I didn't. I believed Del's killer was fleeing, but I didn't know with absolute certainty. What if it was someone who heard the shots and now was just trying to get out of harm's way?

I immediately called for backup. "Officer down! A vehicle leaving the scene is heading east on Cemetery Road. We need that car stopped!" My car was more than a mile away.

Still, no sirens. One of the problems with rural Minnesota is the county deputies could be an hour away at any given time.

"So this is how it ends, Del." I prayed to God my children would never have the visit Del's daughter would get tomorrow.

Mason was soon at my side. Seeing an officer killed in the line of duty was heart- wrenching. It was a thankless job on most days, performed by people who just wanted to make the world better. The stakes were high and failure to read a situation correctly was lethal. I knelt in the mud by Del's body. He had his thorns, but deep in his heart, Del was a caring man. He had a daughter he loved, who was trying to help him.

Mason bent over with his hands on his knees to catch his breath and said, "Dammit! As much of a pain as he was, I liked Del." As Mason and I started back to the shed, he reminded me, "It could have just as easily been one of us."

And then we heard a shot from the lab shriek over the pounding rain.

Mason commented, "That was a rifle," clarifying that the first shots we heard were from a handgun. The long barrel of a rifle altered the sound enough to make it distinguishable.

Staying low in the weeds, I sprinted back to the lab. I hesitated a moment before entering, knowing a rifleman would be scoping in the entry. I kicked open the door and quickly sheltered my body with the outside wall. But there was no additional gunfire. As I cautiously entered, I heard the motorcycle starting up. Bunyan lay handcuffed to the cabinet with a gunshot wound in his chest; on the floor next to him lay a flat black Remington Model 783 bolt-action rifle. Del was right; the biker had come back after us. A rifle would be difficult to conceal on a motorcycle.

"Dammit!" When Mason entered I wanted to yell, I told you to stay! Instead I bit my lip. Motorcycle man must have realized he couldn't free Bunyan, so he executed him to keep him from talking. I pointed to the drug pile. "Two kilos of meth are gone."

Finally, sirens.

7:45 AM PIERZ

As was our routine, after I left a crime scene, Serena met me at the door with a pillowcase for my clothing. It took a bit longer than usual to peel the drenched fabric off of my body, but I stripped and went upstairs to shower. The sun was rising and I was dead tired. The kids weren't awake yet, so Serena crawled in bed with me, for my sake, knowing I slept better next to her.

She whispered, "I'm so sorry. I'm glad you're okay. I feel for Del's family."

I nodded. I felt so helpless. "It was a three-man operation. One's dead and two escaped. It was a disaster."

Serena pressed, "Did someone ever come back to the hotel for Raven?" "No."

"Don't you think that's odd?"

"There were obviously some hard feelings between the three people from the lab—one killed Chad. Chad Gnoh is the legal name of the guy we've been referring to as Paul Bunyan. Dan Moene's number was in the burner we found on Chad. And, by the way, Del told me the DVD he made of us was in his glove compartment, in a case titled . . . And Justice for All. But I searched his car and it wasn't there." I should never have involved Serena in this; she had the right to be frustrated with me, but she wasn't.

Serena knew me well enough to recognize my brain was fried. There would be no more talking. She kissed me and spooned against me, assuring me she loved me. While there was nothing that could alter my sadness, Serena's altruistic love was what I craved and needed.

30

SEXUAL THEORY =
*Sexuality in humans and animals is expressed through an impulse,
analogous to taking nourishment. Popular theory is the fable of
dividing the person into two halves—man and woman—who strive
to become reunited through love. It is surprising, then, to know
there are people who are attracted to the same sex, and that they
exist in considerable numbers. . . .*
*Conclusion: We cannot explain the origin of sexual attraction at
this time.*

Sigmund Freud
Austrian Psychologist & Neurologist, 1910

JON FREDERICK
4:25 PM, WEDNESDAY, JUNE 12, 2019 ASH AVENUE,
LASTRUP

I NEEDED TO TRACK down Leda Hartford. Del had taken on the task of making sure she was okay; now the task was mine. Del had failed to mention that Leda's new address was the same as my brother, Victor's. Leave it to my schizophrenic brother to have a woman, whose last two lovers were now dead, move in.

I cruised between "the two lakes of Lastrup" as I made my way to Vic's house. While many might have considered the one-acre Lastrup Lakes ponds, by definition, if the body of water had an aphotic zone, or an area where the sunlight didn't reach

the bottom, it was a lake. The Lastrup Lakers had been an ama-
teur baseball powerhouse for about fifty years. Lastrup was a
farming community that had produced an abundance of great
athletes. My favorite Lastrup tale was when a couple of young,
safety-oriented men painted a yellow crosswalk from the front
door of Tiny's Tavern to the front door of the town drunk across
the street. They probably shouldn't have painted over his car.

When I pulled in front of Vic's house, I could see my brother
and Leda sitting on the deck in the back, but they didn't notice
me. I walked around the side of the house and was about to
ask Vic what the hell he was doing, when my sadness for the
two lost lives gave me pause. I stopped just around the corner
and listened.

Leda: "Thank you for letting me detox here. I didn't have
any place to go. I hadn't realized how bad it got. It should only
be a couple more days."

Vic: "Stay as long as you want. It's nice to have the
company."

Leda: "I feel like it's not fair to you to keep others from
visiting, just to hide me out." Vic: "No worries. People don't
visit me. I can't tell my family you're staying with me—they're
going to assume we're having sex. My mom's a pretty hard-
core Christian."

Pause.

Leda: "Do you want to have sex?"

Vic: "Yeah, but no. I'd feel like I was taking advantage of
you and I want to help you out." Leda: "I can't be home alone
with that creep out there."

Vic: "Have you had a lot of sexual partners?" Pause.

Leda: "Yeah."

Vic: "You must be good at it."

Leda giggled: "That's not what I was expecting you to say. Sex
isn't like most things. The more partners you have, the worse you

are, because it's best with someone you have a strong, loving relationship with."

Vic laughed: "Then I must be really good at it."

Leda: "I'm not proud of having a lot of partners. I'm not proud of using drugs, either. What happened to me?"

Vic: "My dad says having a clear conscience is the sign of a bad memory."

I smiled at that. I felt like a voyeur, but couldn't find the right opening to announce my presence.

Vic: "Did you ever watch Sons of Anarchy?" Leda: "Sure."

Vic: "They always have sex with her standing, pinned up against the wall, facing it. If she's shorter, I'd have to bend my knees and then she'd have to move away from the wall to make room for my knees. And if she's tall, I'd have to jump."

This brought more snickering from Leda.

Vic: "Unless bikers only pick partners who are the same height." Leda sighed: "It doesn't really work."

Vic: "But in most shows, she's against the wall, facing him. I don't really want to be holding a woman up in the air the whole time we're making love, and I don't think my penis is strong enough to hold a woman in the air."

Leda's unadulterated laughter cut through the quiet afternoon. The mirth was so genuine, it was contagious.

Leda: "Forget the wall; the bed is the cat's meow. You make people smile. I've never met someone who was so nonjudgmental."

Vic: "Everybody needs help at some point and right now, I can help you." He paused, then continued, "I am judgmental. It cost me my relationship with the only woman I've loved. I struggled with the fact that she shot somebody. My brother, Jon, shot someone, too. I can't live with people who do that, even if it was justified. I know they're both great people. My paranoia starts doing weird things in my head and I wonder what else they could rationalize."

Leda: "Have you ever been raped?" Vic: "No."

Leda: "A man came into my home and raped me. Then he tried killing my daughter. Before that, I didn't think I could kill anyone, either. Now I'm not sure."

Vic: "There's still a big difference between not sure and actually killing someone."

I finally forced out a cough and stepped around the corner. "Hi Leda, Vic. I'm just here to make sure you're okay, Leda."

Vic nervously stood up.

"Thank you Vic, for helping Leda out." I couldn't help thinking this wasn't about Vic's mental illness. It was about my brother being a decent person. He took someone in who needed help, simply out of the goodness in his heart. I wasn't going to interfere.

It was hard to take Vic seriously at times, because of his shirts. He was wearing a white t- shirt with a red garbage truck that read: "Pierz Sanitation. Guaranteed Satisfaction or Double Your Garbage Back." It was all part of his desire to make people enjoy the moment.

I told Leda, "I want you to know Todd's death wasn't your fault. Todd and Zelly accidently walked by a meth lab when they were looking at hunting land. Todd may not have even realized it, but the meth makers decided they couldn't take the chance that he'd report it, so they killed him. And that's why they came after Zelly, too. I still need you to hide out. Based on the information I got from the lab, it appears Dan did some low-level dealing for these guys, to support his habit. The man who assaulted you knew you'd take meth from him, which he probably learned from Dan. He used with you so you wouldn't report the forced sex."

Leda went to Vic and hugged him for comfort.

"If you're okay with it, I'd like Zelly to stay with Marc for now. She's safe there." "Okay," she nodded warily and added, "but I have to visit her."

"My dad will take you to see her tomorrow."

"Is he okay with that? I don't want to put your family out further."

Vic smiled as he held her. "He's ex-military. He loves this kind of crap."

31

PYTHAGOREAN THEORUM =
*The square of the hypotenuse (the largest side) of a right triangle is
equal to the sum of the squares of the other two angles.*

Pythagoras Greek Philosopher, 500 B.C.

MIA STROCK
6:30 PM, THURSDAY, JUNE 13, 2019 PIERZ

THE MANHUNT FOR Kaiko Kane took place in central
Minnesota today, to no avail. Grandpa told me Sean
Reynolds was now at the scene and he was enraged over
the two deaths and no arrests. Realizing Jon had gotten
little sleep in the past couple days, Sean sent him home at
5:00. Even though the man had to be running on fumes, Jon
invited me over for dinner tonight. He told me he wanted to
make sure I was okay. I didn't need a babysitter. My guess
was Jon couldn't shut it off and needed to keep working.

I was sick from the deaths in Hawick. I didn't want Del
to die, but he basically killed a meth cooker—a crime not
punishable by death. Well, honestly, I didn't know exactly
who killed Chad Gnoh. All I knew was that Del sent him
into cardiac arrest and Chad was shot to death while handcuffed to a cabinet. It was easy to forget that this large,
red-haired man had people who cared about him, too. He
was just a college student trying to make some money. Now

tonight, I was supposed to enjoy an evening with Jon's family, knowing he was a cheating jerk?

I pulled into the driveway of Jon's rural home. I sat in the car trying to will myself to the door, but I just couldn't.

Oh crap! What was she doing here? That woman—that sex worker—was coming toward

my car.

She signaled for me to roll down the window.

I reluctantly complied and asked, "Why are you here?"

She laughed and said, "I'm Serena." As she beckoned me out of the car she smiled and said, "I love those Danskos."

Ignoring the comment, I said, "It doesn't bother you that he's married?"

She grinned conspiratorially. "It's a bit of a turn on."

"You're ruining his family! Jon has two young children."

She waved her hands in front of me and said, "Stop! I'm Serena, Jon's wife."

When it finally registered, I was furious. I stared at her, my boiling blood not reduced to a simmer by this revelation. What was wrong with these people? It was a cruel hoax!

She seemed to read my mind and said, "I'm so sorry, but we couldn't tell you. Stay here. Let me send Jon out."

Jon looked tired and appeared deep in thought as he sat on the porch. I joined him. "Is this some sort of hazing?"

He rubbed his forehead, "No, not at all. I was asked to find Raven. I did."

I hadn't considered that someone was out looking for that little whore.

Jon looked like he was going put his hand on my shoulder to comfort me, but thought better of it. "Since my first day on this case, I've believed somebody close to the investigation was bleeding out details. After Raven called for help, I asked Serena to help me start a rumor that I was looking for a sex worker, to see if my concerns were warranted." He gazed out over his yard. "They were."

He never told me that Raven had called for help. I offered, "I know for a fact Del spoke about it." Nervous and embarrassed over being played, I asked, "Was Sean the black man who delivered Serena?"

"Sean suggested we take advantage of the stereotype." Jon looked a bit sheepish as he shrugged. "I think he jumped at the opportunity to get his vintage muscle car out of storage."

I tried to shake the cobwebs loose. "Is Raven here?"

"No. She's locked down under armed guard. Raven's detoxing now. She is scared to death of the man who brought her to Paynesville—claims he can break into anywhere, so she'll never be safe."

A cute, dark-haired preschooler in a princess dress stepped out the door and said, "Dad, come in."

Jon introduced us. "Nora this is Mia, and Mia, here's Nora."

Nora said, "I'm four." She studied my face and, in a soft, angelic voice, offered, "I like your earrings."

Like her mother, the first thing she did was compliment me. No wonder Jon was protective of his family—they were gems. I told her, "I love your dress."

"It's an Anna dress, from Frozen."

Jon told Nora, "Give me a minute and then I'll come in and play the pushover game quick before we eat."

Nora brightened and ran back into the house. I had to ask, "The pushover game?"

"It's a fitting name for me as a father. I sit on the floor and declare, 'No one pushes me over.' Nora runs at me and knocks me over and then I chase her all over the house."

Jon studied me for a moment. "The man who died in the lab was Chad Gnoh. Ever heard of him?"

When I said nothing, he continued, "His father was from Singapore, but his mother was a red-headed American."

"You do know I've been in the United States my entire life, don't you?"

I could see his frustration when he added, "Chad went to Macalester College."

A deluge of thoughts flooded my brain as I struggled to offer a coherent response. "It's a big school."

"His cell phone had a number titled 'AIM.' He called it frequently."

My anxiety sky-rocketed and my mouth felt dry. "Do you think her name might be Aimey?"

His blue eyes pierced my soul as he silently studied me. At that moment, sound was frozen still outside his country home. What I would have given to simply hear a car drive by. His comfort, with prolonged periods of silence, was maddening. Finally, he shattered the silence. "Chad had a nine-millimeter handgun registered in this name, but it wasn't in the meth lab. Del was killed with a nine-millimeter."

The salivary glands in my mouth had effectively dried up. Fighting my xerostomia, I said, my voice cracking, "Why did Del kill Chad?"

"Del didn't kill Chad. Del was already dead when Chad was shot. I've been thinking about Pythagoras, a Greek philosopher and mathematician who was around about 500 years before Christ was born. These guys were serious about math. When he created the Pythagorean Theorum—A squared plus B squared equals C squared—he killed an ox to celebrate. When a man explained to his followers that the square root of two is an irrational number, they drowned the poor soul at sea."

Confused, I asked, "Irrational?"

"Followed by an infinite number of decimals. It bothered Pythagoras because, like me, he wanted clear answers." Jon leveled his gaze on me. "We've known there were three people involved, ever since the Ross break-in. Two were in the home when one called from the car. We now have two pieces to the triangle. A is a guy with a first-hand understanding of the criminal system. B is a Macalester student. So how do they combine to make C?"

"Maybe Del tased Chad to shut him up. And then the third guy takes care of Chad and Del to shut them both up. We both know there's no honor among criminals."

Jon focused on something in the distance as he spoke. "But here's where your theory falls apart. Del wasn't working with Raven. He only knew I was at the hotel because the manager told him. I think Del tased Chad quickly because Del wasn't particularly patient and he knew Chad would out-muscle Mason in a physical altercation. Del's health was terrible, so he wouldn't be of any help."

I was confused. "What was wrong with Del?"

"He was dying of chronic obstructive pulmonary disease."

It would have been nice if Jon would have shared some of this information with me. Maybe I could've saved a life. I realized I'd better exit this conversation before I said something I regretted. I wasn't in a talking mood. "Do you mind if I step inside?"

"Your internship is done. We found a Remington rifle in the meth lab, which I imagine will likely prove to be Todd Hartford's murder weapon. There are fingerprints on the barrel."

I understood. They were now looking for a cop killer and I would be a liability. I was ready to be done.

I left Jon sitting on the porch looking off into the wilderness that surrounded his yard.

An Adonis of a man—the Greek god of beauty and desire—was standing in the entry as I walked inside. With a half-smile, he saw through my sad eyes and said, "You look like you could use a hug."

I did. I melted into him as he wrapped his strong arms around me. For a moment I was at peace, and then a strong, dark-skinned woman grabbed my arm and yanked me back. Her features were Somali, but she wasn't in the garb; she was wearing a silky taupe blouse and perfectly fitted jeans that clung to her healthy hips. Her daring expression suggested that, beneath her pretty exterior were battle scars beyond my imagination.

She declared, "This is my man."

Adonis casually released me and said, "Hi . . . I'm Clay. This is Hani. And I am, apparently, her man."

Clay, Hani, and I ended up sitting uncomfortably together in the living room, while Jon burned up the little energy he had left chasing Nora around the house with his one-and-a-half-year- old son, Jackson, at his side. Serena and her parents put the finishing touches on our meal while Jon's brother, Victor, joined us.

Vic studied Clay and Hani, as if he was trying to work something out in his head. He finally said, "Christians say Jesus was the messenger. Muslims claim Muhammed was the messenger. The question I have is, did you get the message?" He looked from one to the other. "There's nothing about killing innocent people in the message from either."

Hani felt the need to clarify, "Jesus is a messenger in the Quran, also."

I threw in my two cents. "My problem with the Quran is that, if it's the word of God, how come God didn't correctly understand Christianity? Christians are accused of worshipping three Gods, but it's a monotheistic religion. The father, the son, and the holy spirit are one."

Vic contemplated, "Jon's a father and a son."

Hani explained, "The Quran was memorized by Muhammed and written down by people who listened to him throughout his life. The collection, which became the Quran, was compiled after Muhammed's death. It is Allah's word."

Vic managed to thwart a quarrel by interjecting, "If you believe in the internet, you almost have to believe in God. I mean, the argument is typically, how can God be ubiquitous? But the internet has proven a phenomenon could be everywhere at one time."

I liked this guy. I wasn't in an arguing mood. I added, "And can answer everyone's questions at one time."

Hani said to Clay, "I need to step out and pray."

She didn't seem right for Clay, so I made it a point to listen in as he softly teased, "Do you think God really cares how many times a day you pray, or in my religion, if you pray in a priest's house or your own house?"

Hani apparently had an answer for everything. "It's a moment of connecting in thought to Muslims throughout the world who are praying at this same time."

Vic irritatingly defended Hani, saying, "She's connecting with the collective unconscious.

Carl Jung wrote about this phenomenon in his theory of psychoanalysis."

Clay acquiesced, "I'm fine with it. I just think so much of religion is calisthenics, when it should be treating the person next to you decently."

Hani nodded in concession as Clay added, "Make sure you're facing east. You wouldn't want to get the angle wrong and miss Him."

Hani didn't have a "Chinaman's chance" with Clay. According to the saying, a Chinaman's chance was no chance. I had to smile over how we changed that stereotype. That might have been true a century ago, but that was before my Asian counterparts became the highest-income race in America.

I was single now so, after Hani departed, I wrote my phone number on a piece of paper and slipped it to Clay. He gave me a thousand-watt smile and tucked it away.

32

HAZARD + VULNERABILITY/CAPACITY TO HANDLE IT = *Disaster When a natural threat confronts the socially vulnerable, who already have a strained capacity to address it, disaster ensues.*

William Stephenson Physicist & Psychologist University of Missouri, 1953 (This formula is used by the International Federation of Red Cross)

MIA STROCK
11:35 PM, FRIDAY, JUNE 14, 2019 RAILROAD AVENUE, ALBANY

NOW THAT MY internship had ended, I was working as a quality assurance technician at Kraft Foods in Albany for the rest of summer break. The job paid sixteen dollars an hour and I supplemented my income with some side money.

Tonight, after work, I walked with some coworkers to Marcia's Bar for happy hour, and then a few of us decided to walk down to Shady's Tavern to listen to the Johnny Holm Band. It was nice to get out and dance a little. I met a guy. Not a get-rich-quick guy, like Hong Fa, but a disciplined country man who worked as a gunsmith in Albany. I smiled and considered, Maybe I can start over again.

While the rest of crew slid next door to Rookies Sports Bar, I decided I had enough and traipsed back to my car in the Kraft parking lot across the street. I was parked in the back lot, but I didn't mind the stroll under the stars on this warm June night. I missed Hong.

I wore a mid-length dress to show off my new shoes. My wedge espadrille sandals clicked on the street as I strolled into my new life.

I heard the thump of work boots behind me on the sidewalk. I turned and scanned the full parking lot, but saw no one. When I turned back and started walking, the thumping started again. I wished I hadn't had that last drink; I felt a little light-headed. I picked up the pace, shuffling through my purse for my car keys. If I'd have just gotten up when the alarm rang the first time this morning, I wouldn't have had to park in the back row.

As I cautiously stepped around the last row of cars, there stood Kaiko Kane—looking as ragged and horrifying as ever. I was alone, face to face, with pure evil. I shamelessly begged, "Don't hurt me."

I stood motionless as he stepped in closer and swept a strand of hair out of my face. I closed my eyes. Don't touch me.

Kaiko snarled, "You gave them Raven. Raven was mine."

"I thought we could use her," I pled, "to blackmail Jon."

He seized a handful of hair over my left ear and twisted it around his balled fist. I cried out involuntarily as I felt roots ripping. I gripped his hand, trying to hold it close to ease the strain on my scalp. He breathed sour funk on my skin as he yanked my face close to his. His lips curled into a mirthless smile and his voice was edged with the sharpness of a blade. "You know how far I'll go. I want the money. All of it. The only reason we have money is because of my sales on the side. I didn't mind splitting it when we were looking at a big payday, but now we know that payday's never coming. I want the money—Chad's third and your third. Where is the money?"

I sputtered, "It's here. I have a secure work locker I've stored it in."

I emitted a harrowing yelp as Kaiko viciously jerked me to the ground, then I was supine on the parking lot tar. The momentary relief I had when he let go of my hair was quickly replaced by the burning of my skin as my body scraped against the gravelly asphalt. In a fluid motion, he was on me and back in my face. "I don't believe you." He crawled between my legs and was grinding my backside raw.

I begged, "You don't want to do this. I'll get you the money. I swear, it's inside." I gasped, "We're in the middle of town!"

Kaiko's dark, reptilian eyes met mine. "This is overdue." I could feel him undoing his jeans. He said flatly, "You've got a debt to pay beyond the money."

I frantically strained against him, pleading, "I don't know what you're talking about. Please, let me get the money."

Kaiko reclaimed my hair in his fist and slammed the back of my head into the ground. I saw bright, white lights swirling in my vision; my fight effectively sailed away with them. He snarled, "Chad never should've had sex with my girl. It was your job to take care of his needs. Now, you're going to make that marker right."

"But it's not my fault," I said in desperation. I heard my underwear tear.

Kaiko spat out, "This is happening. It's a matter of if you're going to live through it." "Please don't kill me." I tried to allow my body to go pliant in resignation. "I'll do anything . . ."

And I did. It's funny what you remember. With my head turned sideways on the tar, I could still see the bar lights between tires.

Kaiko stood over me and smugly refastened his belt. "We all gotta do what we're good at.

Another woman and no complaints."

No one turns to the devil for empathy. I painfully turned on my side and slowly made my way to my feet, my skin seared with road rash. My ripped underwear fell to the ground and I mindlessly pushed my dress back down. Everything felt so unreal. I was standing only a few feet from the Lake Wobegon Trail, but a lifetime away from the gentle stories it possessed.

Kaiko slapped me out of my dazed state. "Pull yourself together and get the fucking money."

I started walking to the building and he snarled, "Do you have your key?"

As if on autopilot, I returned to find my purse had also fallen like trash to the tar. Kaiko leaned into my body and followed me into the plant. I didn't bother to argue. I remember walking to my locker and pulling out the duffel bag.

Kaiko snatched it out of my hand and rifled through the money. "Where's the rest of it?"

At that point, I was ready to say anything to get him to leave. I had spent six thousand dollars of the money furnishing my small rental home and paying off credit cards.

Kaiko pressed his body against mine. I tried to wrench away, because if sweat could smell like pure evil, his was it. "You are going to come with me and either produce that money, or I'm going to take it out in trade at fair market value—one hundred dollars a pop. You know you can't afford to turn me in." He smirked. "I left the rifle—it only has your fingerprints on it. They might not be in the system yet, but they'll fingerprint you faster than you can lie if I implicate you."

He intended to rape me sixty times. I couldn't survive it. It was time for me to do what I was good at. The lie emerged out of some dark, horrible place in my heart. "He had another woman. Chad gave the rest to her."

"I don't believe you." Kaiko pressed, "Name? Residence?"

It came out so easily. "Her name is Hani Egal. She lives in St. Cloud, but I don't know exactly where—on the east side— near Pantown. I swear, that's all I know." I prayed a malicious lie would be the end to this part of my life.

With a wicked glare of disbelief, Kaiko escorted me back outside. Was he going to kill me? Would I be writing my own suicide note? I was too destroyed to even beg. He had taken everything I had—my lover, my pride, my sexual intimacy, my money, and my empathy for others. There was nothing left of me.

Facing me, he placed a serrated hunting knife, with a cold steel talon on the end, to my neck. "You'd better be telling the truth, or I vow I'll hunt you down and devour that frail piece of ass that ambulates your conniving brain."

I didn't move. Without emotion, I told him, "I can't give you what I don't have." Kaiko scoffed, "Meth whore," and left.

I had now lost everything but my life. Looking back, I think I was in shock. In my disheveled dress and mindset, I walked one block east and sat in the darkness in front of Seven Dolors Catholic Church—an ominous, dark brick structure that was completely black at night. It had been years since I'd been to church. I hysterically tore off my sandals and threw them into the street. I'd never wear them again. I crawled onto the cool grass, lay back, and gazed at the stars. I had completely messed up my life and there was no going back. My mom and I must have self-destruct buttons that got triggered in adulthood.

I found myself glancing up at the church sign. The story goes that, when the church was being constructed, back in 1889, Simon Gretsch called for help from Our Lady of the Seven Sorrows when a bucket of cement slipped its pulley and hurled toward him in the bottom of the well he was digging. The rope tangled and the bucket's fall halted just before crushing him. Well, the bucket ravaged me tonight.

This was the bitter end to my story. I just needed to get home—to my gun. I gave myself an out. Maybe a shooting star would be a symbol of hope . . . but tonight, there were none. I guess even shooting stars are meteors that burn up as they enter the atmosphere. Like me, they become insignificant—nothing. "I pray to God my soul to take."

But this story wasn't just about me. A kind little girl lost her gentle father. Kaiko tried hunting down poor little Zelly like a swamp rat. And I wouldn't be the last woman Kaiko raped. I didn't want him to be part of another woman's story. If I was to have any hope of forgiveness, I needed to stop him. Enough was enough! I dug out my cell phone and dialed 911.

33

COULOMB'S LAW =
Like charges repel each other and unlike charges attract each other.
Similar charges can resist each other with repulsive forces, while
opposing charges can appeal to each other.

Charles-Augustin de Coulomb F
rench Engineer & Physicist, 1784

MIA STROCK
12:55 AM, FRIDAY, JUNE 14, 2019
ST. CLOUD HOSPITAL, 1406 6TH AVENUE NORTH, ST. CLOUD

I WAS ALL TUCKED in my bed on the third floor of the hospital, with an advocate from the sexual assault center sitting quietly by my side. I had no desire to see anyone I knew, because the first thing they'd ask is how I knew my rapist, and I wanted to be done lying. I was relieved my parents were vacationing in Texas.

The advocate answered a knock on the door and then stepped around the curtains with Jon Frederick.

I had been so focused on my searing pain and the misery I'd created for my family, I hadn't considered Jon would be talking to me before the night was over. I dismissed the advocate and Jon sat in a side chair next to my bed. Shame weighed on me like a lead blanket and I couldn't look him in the eye.

I had finally recovered from the shock of being raped, but my clarity and awareness also meant my pain had made its way to the front line. I had cranked my neck so hard during the assault, to avoid looking at Kaiko, I could only partially move it now without creating tears. It felt like he had taken coarse sandpaper to my groin, and the road rash that seared my ass was an immediate reminder of the violation every time I adjusted myself in that bed.

Jon took my hand and, with absolute sincerity, said, "I'm glad you survived this."

I couldn't stop my tears. I didn't know if I could bear his softhearted kindness. "Did they catch him?"

"No. The Albany police did a great job responding immediately to your call. They cut off the streets exiting Kraft and pulled over all the vehicles, but they didn't find him."

"I hope they shoot the bastard. How did he get away?"

Jon tried to make me feel better. "Even with everything you've been through, you're thinking like an investigator. How did he come and go from the lab?"

"I don't know. He was usually there when I arrived—" I stopped myself. Crap.

For the moment, Jon kindly ignored the fact that I had just incriminated myself. He asked, "What could you see right after the assault?"

I thought. "My car. The plant. That's it." "Nothing else?"

I recalled looking around after I finally got myself to stand up. "Well, just the Lake Wobegon Trail."

"Right." Jon continued, "And the meth lab was by . . . ?"

"The Glacial Lakes Trail." Both were tarred bike paths. He could move in and out quickly, while avoiding street cameras and squad cars. Embarrassed but resigned, I softly asked, "What made you think I was at the lab?"

"The puzzle pieces finally fit together for me. Remember the first time we met? I noticed the acid burn on your shoe."

"How did you know it was battery acid from a meth lab? It could have been sorbic acid from Kraft."

"I've done some research. You told me the shoes were new. Kraft stopped using sorbic acid last year. You were the person who drove Chad and his friend to the Ross home. It was your car on the recording. I have to admit, it was a clever way of erasing Owen Warner's videotape. Running into you outside of the hotel the night Del was killed removed my blinders. Serena suggested it was odd that no one showed up to pick up Raven. You did. Only you and Del knew of my encounters with Serena at the hotel. Del never called you and told you I was at the hotel. I checked his phone records. And then you wandered into the woods at Leda's home, looking for evidence. After a short search, you told me there was nothing of note, nothing to fear."

"There was nothing to fear at the Hartfords'."

"But the only way you could know that was by knowing where the meth lab was located. After I spoke to Del at the bar, I realized he never leaked that information. Throughout our conversation, Del made certain we weren't overheard." Jon watched me for a reaction, but I willed my face to show nothing. He continued to pound nails into my coffin. "And then, there's the name play. AIM is Mia backwards. Hong is Gnoh backwards. And Serena said that, when you two were visiting at our house, you referred to your ex as Hong Fa—which means 'red hair' in Chinese. You were just having too much fun with it."

I was suddenly very tired, but still wise enough to not admit anything. I asked, "So, now what?"

"I'm hoping you'll share everything you have so I can catch this guy. I know you went to college with Chad Gnoh. The officer who found you said she asked if your assailant was a stranger. You said he wasn't, but you wouldn't give up his name. Who is this third person, Mia? And why did he rape you?"

When I didn't respond, Jon pushed, "Please, just give me a name."

I so wanted to scream, Kaiko Kane! But my throat constricted my words; I couldn't. A little over an hour before, I was ready to purge my soul to get Kaiko convicted of rape. I could feel the dangerous web of self-protection settling over me again. He needed me to give up Kaiko, and that gave me leverage.

That name was my bargaining chip. I managed, "Not tonight."

Jon wasn't giving up. "Mia, if you turn your back on me, you're on your own. Sean will never agree to protect you until you cooperate. What's going to keep him from coming back?"

I'd never anticipated they'd get ahold of Chad's phone, but we had used burner phones, so I should have been safe. Mine was resting at the bottom of Lake Koronis, as I made sure to ditch it once everything imploded. "AIM" was probably a little obvious, but Jon's evidence was all circumstantial. I told him, "I didn't make the meth. I don't even use meth."

"But it was a pretty elaborate plan to get an internship through your grandpa to protect the lab. And shooting Todd would be easy for a former award-winning marksman like you."

I didn't respond. I was in serious trouble. A flashing light in my brain was warning, Don't admit anything. Everything I'd said so far could have been written off as the confused ramblings of a woman in trauma. The very essence of my soul suddenly darkened. I was completely alone now. I was an embarrassment to my family. If I admitted everything, it would slander Grandpa's name forever. It would be better for everybody if I disappeared.

Jon seemed to see through me. He asked, "Why do you think I'm here?" "Because you need information."

"Mia, you've made some serious mistakes, but I'm here because I believe there's a decent person in you, who can still turn it around. I wanted you to know I have hope for you, before you go to sleep tonight."

"Why did you invite me to your home if you already had suspicions?"

Jon tried to pacify me by saying, "I've known you, through your grandfather's stories, for years. You care—"

I cut him off. "You shared your suspicions with Serena and she needed to meet me. The two of you work as a team. You don't give a crap about me."

He gave me a you know better look. "I know anguish, Mia. God seems to help me at times when others abandon religion. Maybe it's because, rather than asking God to do magic tricks, I ask for self-understanding. A couple years ago, my daughter was sick. I was alone and filled with despair. It was the middle of the night and I couldn't get Nora to stop crying. Serena and I had separated. I had messed up at work. I felt so incompetent. And then I felt the presence of God."

"How? What happened?" I wasn't sure I was on board with his profession of faith, but he had my attention.

"Nora was only a little over a year old and I was trying to comfort her, silently pleading with her to stop crying. And then I saw her eyes pleading with me. I can't really explain it, otherthan a realization came over me that I needed to be strong." He shrugged, now lost in his experience. I felt some envy for his steadfast beliefs and was riveted, waiting for him to continue.

"My misery had turned my perspective inside out. I was praying for hope when it was my role to provide it. I needed to stop being so painfully self-absorbed. I thought I needed to be so many things, but I only needed to be one—a dad who offered hope to a child. If I could even distract her from her pain, I was the most important man in the world, doing the most important job in the world. In that moment, I was overwhelmed with God's love. I don't expect anyone to understand—religion is very personal to me. I asked for forgiveness for being stuck in my own pain. I didn't have to be anything and I was still worthy of love. I just needed to act like the person I wanted to be and God will love me."

He focused back on me and I was drawn into the sincerity of his faith. "That moment will come to you—maybe not tonight, but it will come—and you'll feel worthwhile again."

I felt a rush of heat—shame and my old friend, anxiety—burning through my skin, quickly followed by the chill of air against my anxious perspiration. I didn't know what to say. There was nothing I could say. His story deserved quiet reverence, even as my insides were turning hot circles.

Jon brushed the moisture off my brow. "I'm sorry you had to go through this, Mia. I'm going to let you sleep. You're facing a hard reality, so I'm going to end with a quote from Ida B. Wells: 'The way to right wrongs is to turn the light of truth upon them.'"

I reached over and squeezed his hand. He didn't have to be here. "Thank you." Jon said, "I'll stay here until you want me to leave."

I didn't want him to leave. He remained at my side, and I eventually fell asleep.

When I woke up, Jon was gone, but in his place sat Grandpa Maurice. He leaned over and kissed my forehead. I tried to turn away from him, my shame consuming me. Grandpa was the last person I wanted to see. A hand knobbed with age touched my cheek as he softly said, "Mia."

I fought through my self-disgust and looked into my grandpa's eyes.

He spoke with a sincerity that threatened all my defenses. "My girl, there is nothing you could do where I wouldn't love you. When I slip, I ask, 'What can I learn from this?' and then I move on."

"Grandpa," I choked out. "This is really bad. You can't let them take my DNA. Right now, they only have circumstantial evidence tying me to the lab."

He sat back in the bedside chair, bewildered. "How the hell did you get involved with a meth lab, Mia?"

My eyes burned with tears. "I loved Chad. He was this big, gentle lion. He convinced me he had one job to finish and he would never be involved in illegal drugs ever again. I didn't make the meth, or use it, but I'd spent a couple nights there with him. I thought I'd use any money made from it to help women like my mom."

Grandpa scolded, "You could never do enough to compensate for the damage done by producing meth in the first place. Did you ever consider all of the families you'd destroy?"

The tears spilled over and I told him, "I'm so sorry."

Sobs shook my body as I let everything go. Grandpa bent over the bed and hugged me, shushing and patiently waiting until I was cried out.

"I'm your grandpa first," he assured me. "I don't believe they have enough for a search warrant and they can't touch your medical records without a warrant. Did the BCA ask you to give a DNA sample?"

"No. I was just an intern, so I didn't have to. I've never been arrested and never offered it up on any ancestry sites.

Grandpa, you need to believe me. I didn't touch any of the meth, so they won't find my prints on any of it, but my DNA might be in the bed at the lab."

"If you're not in the system, there's nothing they can do with the DNA they found." Grandpa wiped away my tears. "We'll work through this."

He began to lay out a plan. "You're going to call Sean Reynolds in the morning and give him Kaiko Kane's name."

"What? How did you know?"

"I used to run the BCA. People are still willing to share information with me. They've had Kaiko's name for weeks and they found his prints in the meth lab. They need you to give up the name so it doesn't appear they're feeding you evidence. By going to Sean, they'll assume you don't trust Jon." His face looked a bit pinched when he added, "And we're going to need to undermine Jon to save your skin . . ."

I missed the old Chad. It started about us getting enough money so we could travel the world together. Instead, I watched Chad slowly drift away, with meth gradually taking priority over our relationship. Even at the end, if he would have just left when I called, he would be alive. Rather than listening to me, he was wasted out of his mind and determined to pack up all the meth before he left. Chad insisted Kaiko was "a necessary evil." I hated Kaiko for bringing that little whore to our lab. Kaiko's behavior brought in the BCA. If Chad and I would have taken on additional part-time work, we would be just as well off, financially, and we'd still be together. What was Chad thinking? Calm and composed men would approach us with reasonable and fair business deals for our mountain of meth? Possessing that much meth was a death wish.

34

THEORY OF PANDORA'S BOX =
In Greek mythology, Zeus gave Pandora a wedding gift of a beautiful jar, with instructions to not open it under any circumstances. Impelled by curiosity, Pandora opened it, and all the evil the jar contained escaped. She attempted to close the jar, but only Hope was sealed inside. For this reason, humans have been able to hold onto hope to survive wickedness.

Hesiod Greek poet, 700 BC

JON FREDERICK
12:00 PM, FRIDAY, JUNE 14, 2019 CEMETERY DRIVE, HAWICK

PANDORA'S BOX WAS opened and Kaiko Kane was still free. By noon, I was back at the crime scene. Dr. Amaya Ho was there with the BCA forensics team, helping process the evidence. She was talking to Faraja Oloo, a crime scene tech who had emigrated from Kenya to attend the University of Minnesota. Both wore their white, contamination-free coveralls, referred to as "bunny suits" by the techs.

They had taken a break and were conversing by Amaya's white van when I arrived. As I approached, I overheard Faraja stating she saw the problems between Somali and caucasian St. Cloud residents as inevitable.

Thinking of Clay's new partner, I asked, "Faraja, I'm sorry for inserting myself in this conversation, but why do you see the conflict as unresolvable?"

"Call me Fara." She nodded in greeting. "I was just saying it doesn't surprise me Somalis are struggling to get along with people in St. Cloud. They struggle getting along with people in Africa. I think it's because Somalia has never had a strong leader, so the Somalis, everywhere, seem to have a hard time taking advice from anyone."

Dr. Ho was respectfully steering clear of the topic. The corner of her mouth twitched almost imperceptibly; otherwise, her expression was impassive.

I wasn't well-versed on the issue, but responded, "I think it always comes down to individuals. I don't like being swept in with everything white guys have done."

Fara nodded respectfully, and then swept her hand from the gravel road to the field of alfalfa. "Any footprints or tire tracks were washed away by the rain."

I turned to Amaya. "You said you had something for me."

Dr. Ho was ready. "It's going to take time to process all of this evidence, but I wanted to tell you I've taken a look at some of the hairs I've found in the beds. There are three basic types of hair: European, Asian, and African. There was hair in both beds similar to Raven Lee's dyed hair, suggesting she was in both beds. There was additional hair in the redhead's bed, with which I'm familiar. It's Asian."

"Did you get DNA?"

"Yes, but it may be a month before we have the results."

"Please let me know when it comes in. As soon as I can get a search warrant, I'm going to have you looking for alfalfa in a car or on shoes."

Amaya bit her lip. "If the person claims to have been at another field, we can test the commonalities of pesticides used in the fields as compared to the sample. Can you give me an idea of the trail the killer took running away?"

"Not exactly, but generally."

"It may be a needle in a haystack, but plants, like people, have unique DNA. It's possible we could trace the leaves back to the exact point. But I need leaves, not seeds."

"Okay, why?"

"Leaves have the full DNA of the plant. Seeds contain elements from the plants it was cross-pollinated with." Dr. Ho continued, "I've examined Officer Walker. The first shot was fired into his stomach. Additionally, there was a circle of soot around the bullet hole in his forehead."

This meant the kill shot was pressed against his skull. It wasn't enough for the killer to shoot Del. Somebody had needed to shut him up, suggesting Del knew his killer.

35

HEISENBERG'S UNCERTAINTY PRINCIPLE =
*The location and velocity of an object
cannot be measured exactly, even in theory.*

*Werner Heisenberg German Physicist
Director of the Max Planck Institute for Astrophysics, 1929*

CLAY ROBERTS
5:35 PM, FRIDAY, JUNE 14, 2019 WILSON AVENUE
NORTHEAST, ST. CLOUD

HURRICANE HANI LANDED in my living room after finishing her workday at Target. She tossed her hijab on the table as she ranted and paced around. Hani crossed her arms. "Someone wrote on the wall of the women's bathroom at work, 'Hani gives head.' I think it was a woman from my neighborhood. They're all gossiping about my dad disowning me."

Trying to lighten her mood, I remarked, "That is bad. If you wanted to get the word out, it would be better on the wall in the men's room."

Clearly hurt, she flopped beside me and leaned back, socking me in the shoulder. "It's not funny."

"I'm sorry!" I threw my hands in the air in retreat. "People are just pullin' your chain. Did you report it?"

"Yes. They painted over it right away. But how many people saw it first?" "Why do you care?"

"I'm not a whore."

"My dad used to say, 'Those who matter don't mind; those who mind don't matter.'"

The pissed look she gave warned me this storm wasn't moving on any too soon. The benefit of not being married was I didn't have to stay here and listen. I stepped out to make a phone call and then returned to tell Hani, "I need to leave and take care of some business."

She wasn't happy. "Clay, where are you going? I never know where you are when you're
gone.

"I said that to Jon once, and he gave me some stupid physics theory about it." I had a stressful day of work, too. The wrong material came in on our house. The couple renting my Edina home called and jacked me up because they felt there was too much noise when someone walked across the floor upstairs. I dropped my worn body on the couch, giving my back a rest after a hard day's work.

Hani gave up on discovering my whereabouts. "It's frustrating when I could clearly help people and they avoid me because of my clothing."

"Well you've got to admit, most Somalis are hard to talk to." Shocked, she snarled, "I don't have to admit any such thing!"

I wasn't in the mood to argue. Our house was in Somaliville. I said hi to everyone—few responded, but almost every non-Somali did. That was just a reality.

As if she could read my mind, Hani took it down a notch. "They're not trying to be rude.
They're trying to respect their beliefs and their people."

I turned to her. "I don't get it. You're one of the nicest people I've ever met, but if I hadn't helped you out, I would never know that. From talking to you, it's like every Somali has a favor owed to somebody and it keeps them all tied together in poverty. No one emerges as a success. There's no room for individuality."

She considered this. "I think 'autonomy' is the word you're looking for. There's no room for self-rule. You take pride in independence. We take pride in humility. And you're assuming you found me. You know how many times I walked by this home before you noticed me?"

That brought a smile to my face. "If you want to get noticed, you can't hide under your bedding."

She finally smiled. "I'm sorry. My bad day isn't your fault. I have no desire to argue. Thank you for trying to make me feel better. I just want to curl up with you and watch another episode of The Marvelous Mrs. Maisel tonight."

I wished she would have said that before I made the phone call. I cleared my throat. "Don't you dare tell anyone I'm watching Maisel. I didn't expect to like it. But I have to meet with a customer tonight."

"How late are you going to be?"

I blew out a frustrated breath. "Hani, this is my job. I get offers because I'm willing to meet with customers after work hours."

"Okay, okay. I know. I just look forward to our time together. If you get home early enough, maybe we could make love."

She was worried I was going to cheat on her. I wasn't sure what to think about that . . .

9:45 PM
MELROSE BOWL AND SHIF'S BAR & GRILL 6TH
AVENUE SOUTHEAST, MELROSE

I opted to pass on the 100-ounce glass of tap beer they offer at Shif's Bar in Melrose. The ad said, "Are you tired of making trips to the bar?" Well, not so tired that I'd rather have an aquarium of beer in front of me. They were featuring Angel Seat Amber from Roundhouse Brewery. The "angel seat" is the raised observation seat in the caboose, where an engineer can look over the train for any overheating wheel bearings.

Maybe this cold amber would give me some perspective. I couldn't help wondering why Hani thought I was cheating. I was cheating, but how would she know that?

Mia Strock took a large swallow from her copper cup, then commented, "You know, it's not going to work with Hani. If you loved her, you wouldn't be here."

It was a safe bet that it wouldn't work. I mean, it never worked out for me. I just felt I was forced to have her move in, and I didn't like being forced to do anything. I simply said, "Yeah, maybe."

She looked a little smug, but didn't push it. After a pause, she asked, "Why is the emergency room at the St. Cloud Hospital always filled with Somalis with minor ailments? They need to learn how to use our health care system."

Now I was the spokesperson for Somalis? I sighed and said, "There are no medical offices near where they live. Just the hospital. All the health care centers are miles away in Sartell and Waite Park, and many don't have transportation."

"The two of you are oil and water. They just don't mix."

"Hani's kind and smart. It just takes a little time to get to know her."

I watched Mia pour down her drink like it was water. "She's Muslim, Clay. You're Christian. And that's it." She karate-chopped the air to make her point.

"Christian" and "Muslim" were just words. Would God define us by the categories humans put on us, or by our behavior? What if we behaved the same, but had been placed in different categories? Would any of our lives be less worthy?

Mia said, "Order me another Moscow mule."

I teased, "Is this drink named after a stubborn-ass traitor?"

The comment seemed to bother her. She asked, "What are you talking about?" "Nothing. I'm bombing as a comedian tonight."

Mia caught me watching her walk to the restroom and grinned over her shoulder back at me.

I tossed some bills on the bar. Hani was tender and caring. I was a better man when I was with her. Hani and I were both raised with lessons from the prophets Noah, Abraham, Moses, and Jesus. Hani just had one more prophet on her side—Muhammad.

A burly builder I'd known for years stepped over in Mia's absence. I smiled. "Hey, Kev, how goes the battle?"

"I'm a workin' fool. You?"

"Tryin' like the devil to find the Lord."

"So you've found yourself an Asian hottie. Or is it thottie now?" He chuckled. "I can't keep up. You should do her bronco style."

"Bronco style?"

"Yeah, you take her from behind, whisper another gal's name in her ear, and hang on until she bucks you off." Kev chortled at himself.

Oddly, the comment made me feel better about myself. It wasn't my humor anymore, and this was proof that I wasn't the man I used to be. I didn't respond. Honestly, I found myself wishing I was back home.

Kev asked, "Do you remember Molly Larson?"

Molly and I never dated, but I left Flicker's Bar with her half a dozen times. Flicker's, now Patrick's, was once the best place for me to be on a Saturday night. One morning, after a night with Molly, my dad asked, "How the hell did you manage to get a bare footprint on the windshield inside the truck?"

LYING CLOSE   233

I told him, "It wasn't mine." He smiled with pride and walked away.

Kevin brought me back to the moment. "I married her." And that's why I didn't kiss and tell. "Nice gal; friendly."

"She teaches catechism classes now. Molly's been good for me." "I've found a good one, too."

Kev watched Mia stumbling our way and screwed up his face in confusion. "Her?" I shook my head no.

Kev snorted, "Same old Clay!" He mockingly tipped a glass to me, chastising my dishonor. How easily I fell back into being what people hated about me—what I hated about me.

Kev shook his head with a huff of a chuckle. He was over talking about women. He asked, "Why the hell did you pull out of that Gull Lake contract? You had it! If you want to make money, you need to work with people who've got it, and it's stockpiled around Gull Lake."

"Yeah, I know. I may come to regret it. I've got something going here I can't leave right now."

Mia had returned and leaned into my shoulder as she slid on her barstool.

Kev smiled and then got to business. "Anyway, I came over because we could use a good carpenter with our project at the convention center. Think about it and let me know." He tipped his crusty John Deere cap and said, "I'll leave you two alone." He gave me that I know where this is headed wag of his eyebrows as he returned to his friends.

Not wanting to think about Kev, or Molly for that matter, and being too ignorant to talk about the motives of Somalis, I asked Mia, "Tell me about your parents. What did they do?"

"My real mother was a pianist."

"You mean not very smart?" Mia had just picked her mule off the bar and sipped it. She burst out laughing, spraying her drink on the bar before she could contain herself.

I needed to apologize. "I'm sorry. You meant unskilled labor. Hey, they deserve as much credit as anybody."

Mia was giggling so hard, she snorted. "A pianist, not a peon. She played piano." "Your mom had a penis—and played piano."

I thought Mia was going to die laughing. "Let's start over. My mom didn't have a penis. She played piano. Someone who plays piano is called a pianist. T at the end. P-i-a-n-i-s-t." Mia dragged the word out so I could hear every syllable.

"I didn't know that was a word. Sorry again. What did your dad do?" With devilish eyes, she said, "He was a trafficker."

Purposely avoiding my first thought, I clarified, "You mean road work?"

"Yeah, if you think of 'rode' like the past tense of 'ride'— to be on top of another and control her movement."

I took a sip of beer and waited for her to explain. I wasn't sure I cared enough to ask for more information.

Instead she asked, "How about your mom?"

"A magician. She vanished when I was thirteen." I could see my response made her feel we shared some kind of bond.

"And your dad?"

I grinned. "Construction. Taught me everything I know. How to build a house, how to demolish a relationship . . ."

When I pulled into Mia's driveway, she slurred, "Are you coming in?" "No, I don't think so."

Mia drunkenly dragged out the question, "Sooo, why . . . why did you invite me out for a drink?"

"I don't know. I need to sort out my thoughts."

Mia was trying to enunciate, but failing badly. She hiccupped and said, "It's just a hickup— a hook up. I'm not asking for a commitment. It's hard to be alone right now." She hiccupped again, and then mumbled, "Hard. Just fuckin' hard."

I waited, but she didn't get out. I wanted to go home. She wouldn't even remember our conversation tomorrow. Was I going to have to carry her in?

Mia coyly offered, "I have a porn video." She giggled. "A porn of your friends, Jon and Serena, if you want to watch it. Jon has a penis, but I don't know if he plays piano." She drunkenly guffawed, "Serena doesn't, though." She snorted as she added, "Play piano." Mia pointed a drunken finger at me and accused, "I saw the way you looked at her—forbidden fruit."

"How the hell?" I stopped. "I guess I could come in for a little . . ."

36

BIOGEOASTROMICAL THEORY OF NIGHT =
Night is our oldest haunting terror and is often described as a phenomenon to be fought rather than lived with. An effort should be made to understand how nighttime operates as an urban frontier.

Robert Shaw,
Urban Geographer Durham University, 2019

JON FREDERICK
SATURDAY, OCTOBER 3, 2020 ROUNDHOUSE BREWERY,
23836 SMILEY ROAD, NISSWA

I PASS ON THE Cinder Dick—an IPA named after a rail-road policeman—and go with the Boom Lake Lager. Serena is musing about karma and I reflect on how one night, June 14, 2019, ended for the major players in this story.

On an average night in the US, at 11:45 p.m.: 77% of Americans are sleeping;

14% are engaging in a leisurely activity, such as watching television; 3% are engaging in personal care, such as showering;

2% are at work;

1% are on the phone.

At 11:45 p.m. on June 14, sleep eluded all of us. As for the remaining categories, I guess it depends how you define leisure activity and personal care . . .

37

SUPPRESSION THEORY =
*Suppressing thoughts about the loss of a loved one increases
cortisol reactivity, which can lead to a variety of physical ailments;
however, reappraising the loss (or reframing) shows healthy
physiological adaptation to stress.*

Lydia Ross P
sychoneuroendocrinologist University of North Carolina, 2019

MIA STROCK
11:45 PM, FRIDAY, JUNE 14, 2019 RAILROAD AVENUE,
ALBANY

I FELL ASLEEP LEANING against Clay on the couch—
I woke up covered with a blanket, but alone. I groggily
double-checked the locks on the doors. I wedged chairs under
the doorknobs to make them harder to open, and set piles of
dishes below the windows so if anyone came in, I'd hear the
dishes clinking together.

I had two hard drinks to every one of Clay's beers, which
obviously didn't impress him. It was just so damn hard to fall
asleep with Kaiko still out there. I felt a sudden chill and icy
needles prickled across the back of my neck. Did Kaiko find
Hani tonight? I hoped not. Honestly, they all acted like they
didn't want to be here, anyway. Maybe she could be one more

martyr for the cause. With any luck, she'd kill him. It would be best for all of us.

I chastised myself for my behavior tonight. Grandpa said my mom had anxiety, too, but worked through it by avoiding looking at the audience when she played piano—and later by getting wasted out of her mind as a hooker. Tonight, I was a drunk, and I would've slept with Clay so as not to be alone. I was just like my mom. At least she got paid.

I set my gun by my nightstand. I should have discarded it by now. Instead, I'd held it every night since Chad died and, I had to admit, the grip was getting more comfortable in my hand. I scratched my temple with the muzzle of the gun. It could cost me my life. It could save my life. Either way, I wasn't ready to part with it . . .

38

SOCIAL DOMINANCE THEORY =
Inequality is maintained through force and legitimatizing myths held against subordinate groups. The belief of superiority enables one to feel justified in dictating others' behaviors.

Felicia Pratto Social Psychologist
University of Connecticut, 2011

KAIKO KANE
11:45 PM, FRIDAY, JUNE 14, 2019 ST. GERMAIN STREET, ST. CLOUD

I ENJOY THE SAMBUSA at the Somali Café—maybe a little too much cardamom, but I'd eat it again. People here treat me like I've got some contagious disease. No one here admits to knowing Hani Egal, but I don't believe them. A couple of these men seem to be itching for a fight, and they look strong enough to give more than I can handle. I just need to find the weakest in the pack. I wait for a young, scarecrow-lookin' man to leave, and follow him along his adventures in east St. Cloud. At almost midnight, he finally leaves a friend's home.

The dark, skinny man keeps looking back and picks up the pace. Maybe he has some sense of me in pursuit, but he has no idea what's about to rain down on his sorry ass. Every time he looks away, I quickly close the distance between us. When we finally reach a space where the street lights don't cover the area well, I tackle him from behind and press his face into the pavement.

He murmurs something indistinguishable, so I bark, "I know you speak English. I heard you speaking in the restaurant, so don't fuck with me. I want to know where Hani Egal lives. I know she lives in this neighborhood." Maybe he's even seen Chad with Hani. I taunt him, "She runs around with a big white guy. You guys must have some racist code against that. C'mon. Give her up."

He snivels, "I don't know her."

I pull out my blade and press the talon into his groin. "How 'bout I cut your dick off? I hear you people get off on mutilation."

His forehead is now slick with sweat, but he doesn't give up anything.

I gotta give this puny dude some credit, but he yips like a sorry dog when I grind the knife harder into his crotch. It's almost as if he's daring me to impale him. I consider it, but first, I need information.

"If you don't tell me, I'm going to cut you deep and let you bleed out. Then I'll pull what's left of your pants down and leave you lying here with a dildo shoved up your ass for your entire neighborhood to enjoy. And this will be how you'll always be remembered." It's easy to mess with people who are holier-than-thou about sex.

He squeaks out, "Okay, okay! She and the white guy have a house on Wilson Avenue Northeast, by Second Street. It's not on the corner, but it's the gray house. That's all I know."

I sheath the knife and stare down at him, all fetal on the ground, hands cupped pathetically around his junk.

"There, was that so hard?" I play nice for a minute and he peers up hopefully at me. "If you tell anyone I spoke to you, I will deliver on my promise. Now," I give him a swift kick in

the back to make my point. "Make yourself scarce, you sanc-
timonious bastard."

He rolls to his feet and, without looking at me, takes off
running.

I decide to spend the night sleeping with the degenerates under
the Mississippi bridge. I'll find Hani tomorrow. I want to get a
good look at the home's layout in daylight.

39

APPARATUS THEORY =
*A viewer of an event becomes a voyeur and can experience the
event on a deep level, as a reality, as if she were experiencing the
event herself. (A dominant theory in cinema in the 1970s.)*

Andy Warhol
American Artist New York, 1970

CLAY ROBERTS
11:45 PM, FRIDAY, JUNE 14, 2019 WILSON AVENUE
NORTHEAST, ST. CLOUD

I SAT AT THE end of the couch while Hani stretched out and rested her head on my lap. There was a note on the end table that read, ASTAGFURALLAH. I scissored it between my fingers and commented, "I'm not going to dare try to pronounce that."

Hani suggested, "Turn it over."

It read, I ask forgiveness of Allah.

Hani took a whiff of my shirt and chastised me, "You were with another woman." "Women build houses, too."

"Was it Mia?"

She was good. Trying to seem surprised, I asked, "Why would you think that?"

"I saw the way she looked at you." When I shrugged and didn't respond, she asked, "Do you want me to move out?"

"No." I don't think so.

Hani moaned through her tiredness and probably some frustration. She sat up to face me evenly. "Thank you for being honest. Do you want me to move into my own bedroom?"

I hesitated. "Maybe. But we need to finish one for you first. It's not permanent. I like sleeping with you, but I'm still adjusting. I've shared my bed with women, but never shared a house with one."

She deflated a little when she said, "Okay. But I don't get you, Clay. You're a quasi- Christian, but insistent I'm a certain way."

"That's not true. I want you to be whatever you want to be. I don't insist anything. I tell you what I can tolerate and if you don't like it, I'd understand if you leave, if that's what feels right for you. I know what I want. I'm more of a medium-rare Christian."

Hani squinted. "Medium rare?"

"Yeah. Think of it this way: when you see someone giving large amounts of time or money to help someone out, you think, 'well done!' That's not me. I'm not even a step below that, like your medium or average Christian. But a step below that is medium rare. I only go to church on the big days— JC's birthday, Cheesefare Sunday. I don't steal. I don't start fights, but I do finish them. I don't fool around with married women. I don't do drugs. I will always step in to help out an underdog."

I could see she was trying not to smile. "Cheesefare Sunday? I've never heard of it."

I tried to explain. "It's the last Sunday before Lent and it's all about forgiveness. My mom was a devout Orthodox Christian, so it was the last day we ate dairy products until Easter. Lent is about exercising discipline over the desires of the flesh."

"I'm impressed."

"Don't be. We gave up dairy to show we were devout and yet it was still okay for Mom to cheat on Dad. Mom always kind of misses the big picture. It's the feast of Saint Spyridon, my patron saint. He was a straw hat–wearin' shepherd."

Hani's frustration with me was replaced with interest. She suggested soothingly, "Tell me about him."

I regretted getting into this. "I remember the story because my mom and I were close when I was little. Spy—as I like to call him—converted a pagan by showing him that pottery consisted of three entities: fire, water, and clay."

"A metaphor for the Trinity," she said, nodding. "An entity can be comprised of three separate characteristics: the father, son, and holy spirit."

"My dad used to joke, 'Add a little firewater to Clay and he's a saint.'"

We sat in comfortable silence for a bit, but I knew I had to make it uncomfortable again. It was time for me to man up. "I met Mia Strock for a drink."

Hani asked warily, "Did you have sex with her?"

"No. Once I was there, I realized I just want to be with you." I took her hand. "I'm sorry.

I'm still sorting it all out."

She stroked my cheek. "Thank you for not sleeping with her." I could honestly say, "You're welcome."

"I like being here with you, Clay. By Islamic law, I cannot marry you, though, since you are not Muslim. If I was a man and you were a woman I could marry you, because it's assumed a woman takes the man's faith, and Christians and Jews are 'people of the book.' Here's the kicker— despite Islam's prohibition of women marrying outside their faith, about one in six Muslim women in the US are married to non-Muslims."

"Sooo . . . you can marry outside your religion?"

"Not through Islam. But that issue is basically moot, because I don't see a Muslim court granting me a divorce, especially when they hear I'm in love with a Christian. Legally, I am not married in the US, but I am married in my religion and that's what matters. I left my husband without a justifiable reason. So, here I am. I can't divorce. I can't marry. But I'm lonely, and I've found this gorgeous man."

"So your only option is sinning?"

Hani ran her hand through her thick hair. "Sins are forgiven, as long as they're not made public. Even though I am in your home, I never admit to anyone that we sleep together. This is why the writing on the bathroom wall was extra hurtful to me. It was probably written by someone of my faith."

I tried to wrap my head around this. This should've been my religion. "So basically, if you're a great liar, you're good."

"You're missing the point. When you sin, you don't make a spectacle of it."

"But your dad threw all of your clothes on the lawn and yelled in front of the neighbors."

Hani's posture collapsed in shame. She said, "That was my sin. He wanted everyone to know he is separate from my sin. My family is separate from my sin."

"There's no way out for you."

"Sometimes they will allow a divorce with khula." "Who?"

"It's payment to a husband for letting his wife go."

I straightened defiantly. "You do realize we put men in prison for buying teenagers. I'm not paying that sex-offending prick a cent."

Hani put a hand over one of mine, which had balled into a fist. "Calm down. I wouldn't ask you to."

Now frustrated, I asked, "Don't you get fed up with it all? They sold you. They humiliated you. For God's sake, they mutilated your body."

"The mutilation was done by fundamentalists, not true Muslims." With a sly grin she said, "And I have my own way of getting them back for it."

She wanted to change the topic, so I followed her lead. "Yeah? And what's that?"

"I will find a man and get so close to him that his pleasure will be my pleasure." She leaned into me and said in a soft, throaty whisper, "Every time I kiss him, it will by my kiss. Every time I touch him, it will be like he was touching me. Every time I put my lips on him—"

My testosterone skyrocketed.

And then she stood and walked toward our bedroom, declaring, "But not tonight."

40

THEORY OF KARMA =
Future consequences are inevitably shaped by our current behavior.
The idea was stated by Brahma Hindu priests in 700 BC in India,
and later restated in a letter from Paul the Apostle to the people of
Galatia as, "You reap what you sow."

Saint Paul
Saul of Tarsus Apostle & Theologian, 55

JON FREDERICK
11:45 PM, FRIDAY, JUNE 14, 2019 PIERZ

SERENA BROUGHT THE kids to her parents' for the night. Her parents were amazing. They made sure Nora and Jackson ate healthy, they learned about the farm, and they ended the evening under blankets on the deck, watching for bats and telling stories.

I massaged Serena's bare legs and vented my frustration over being unable to obtain a search warrant for Mia's home.

Serena leaned into me and brushed her soft, full lips against mine. "You've got a woman you can search right here, if you can take your mind off work for a minute."

I gently pulled her close and we kissed.

"You're giving me goose bumps." Her voice was changing to the voice. I looked into her eyes and watched her pupils dilate as her desire responded to mine.

"The best remedy is removing clothing."

Serena teased in a throaty voice, "That doesn't seem believable." "Time to test the hypothesis."

She smiled as we both pulled clothing off and discarded it without concern for its new resting place. I placed a blanket in front of the fireplace and Serena gracefully laid her bare, tanned body upon it. Her scintillating emerald eyes gazed love into mine without a spoken word. She was everything to me. Droplets of perspiration oiled our bodies and I experienced spine-tingling elation through the progressively deeper contact of our warm skin. Our movements began as smooth and pleasant as Beethoven's "Moonlight Sonata" and ended with the rapture of Nelhybel's "Festivo."

We lazily grinned at each other in exhausted ecstasy. You reap what you sow . . .

41

REACTION FORMATION THEORY =
*A defense mechanism in which anxiety-producing emotions are
replaced with the direct opposite. For example, a man who secretly
desires to dominate his partner might hate that aspect of himself, so
responds by continually submitting to her wishes.*

*Sigmund Freud
Austrian Psychologist & Neurologist, 1894*

SERENA FREDERICK
2:00 PM SATURDAY, JUNE 15, 2019 PIERZ

JON AND I were hosting a gathering of rancorous adver-
saries. Sean Reynolds, Jada Anderson, and Maurice Strock
were stopping over to discuss the prosecution of Mia Strock.
There were a fleet of resentments docked in the harbor among
this crew.

Maurice had raised Sean's ire by constantly checking in with
old compatriots on Sean's leadership of the BCA. Intended or
not, his scrutiny undermined Sean's credibility.

Maurice was angry at Jon for pushing for the prosecution
of Mia.

Jon was unhappy with Maurice, as he felt Maurice was
counseling Mia on obstructing his investigation.

Maurice lied to me last year, breaking my heart, until I
discovered the truth. Sean was experiencing an accelerating

burn of envy from Jada's need to continue to work with Jon. And I wasn't without my acrimony. A part of me I'd liked to have tamped down still simmered over Jon being present for the birth of Jada's son. So, if everyone walked away in one piece, that might be the best we could hope for. While I perceived the gathering as hell on earth, Jon viewed it as necessary, since he was beginning to question how far Sean would go to support him.

Sean and Jada sat next to each other, while Jon and I joined them on the patio. Sean verbally rubbed Jon's face in the dirt by reminding him, "People at the BCA aren't happy that you left a deputy and a suspect dead in Hawick. No more mistakes."

Maurice's arrival interrupted the lecture. He briefly looked over the four of us and said coldly, "The women have to go. They're not BCA staff."

Like girls assigned penance, Jada silently followed me into the house. I led her to our music room.

Her comment was kind. "Your house is beautiful, Serena. You had to be the one who decorated this."

"Thank you. Jon contributed."

Jada gave me a knowing grin. "Jon is a minimalist. Remember his apartment in Minneapolis? One decoration, of some sort, per room. They were nice, but it's like he knew he should decorate, got one thing, and was done. In the bedroom, he had that print of Frederic Church's 1874 painting, Twilight in the Tropics, with a light on it. It's a beautiful painting, but it was kind of like being in an art museum."

I remembered having that same thought myself, but really disliked the thought of Jada in his bedroom.

Jada was no fool; she quickly picked up on my reaction. She added, "You're good for him, Serena."

I shushed her and whispered, "We're good for each other."

I sat on the wooden floor below one of the open windows, where a gentle breeze blew through the screen. I patted a spot beside me under the windowsill, gesturing for Jada to sit. She complied, albeit awkwardly.

Once she settled in, I put my finger to my lips then pointed up toward the window. Jada beamed as she realized we'd be able to take in the entire conversation unnoticed. The men were sitting just outside the windows on our brick patio, in what sounded like a heated discussion.

Jon's tone was cooler than is typical. "We need to find Kaiko Kane. Mia is the one person who can tell us where to look. You've got to let us talk to her, before someone else is hurt."

Maurice countered, "Guarantee her full immunity and I'll bring her in today." Jon continued, "Mia used the internship you gave her to protect a meth lab." Maurice arrogantly retorted, "I didn't give her the internship, Sean did."

"Maurice," came Sean's voice, hard but controlled, "you promised her that internship. I agreed to make it happen."

Maurice pointed out, "But if you're going to bring her in for an interrogation, you're going to have to produce some evidence. Her request is not written anywhere, and I retired before Mia was offered the internship."

I looked over at Jada; she was steaming. Mia Strock had purposely waited to start her internship until Sean was the new supervisor, to avoid implicating her grandfather.

Incensed, she hissed, "I have to get Raven to admit she's seen Mia at the lab. Raven's declared she isn't saying anything about the case until Kaiko's in custody."

Sean took a shot at Maurice. "From looking through the records, it appears that back in the day, Mia's mother, Chang

Lu, was your informant. Isn't adopting your informant's daughter a bit of a bad boundary?"

Maurice must have paced in our direction, as we could now hear him clearly. The rising tension abated when his voice softened with sad resignation. "Chang Lu could bring a man to tears with her passion on the piano. And then, with the same intensity, she descended into drugs. I tried getting her out of that lifestyle, but she wasn't leaving. It's heartbreaking to see someone so smart and talented lose it all to heroin. She was selling herself to guys who weren't worthy of carrying her sheet music. Chang couldn't recover, and she finally asked me to take her daughter out of that lifestyle."

It was quiet for a moment as everyone processed his story. Maurice continued, "I thought I'd succeeded. The sad thing is it probably wasn't her mother that got Mia involved with drugs. My oldest grandson had an affinity for meth, but we finally got him clean and back out of it. Mia told me the other night that, even though she never used, he kind of normalized the idea of being around drugs for her. Mia fell in love with the wrong guy. I've met Chad. He was likable; he fooled me. Mia was too young to realize she was dating a psychopath."

I could feel the tension in Jon's voice when he interjected, "She didn't just lie for her lover.

Mia's a hunter—and maybe our shooter."

The insinuation agitated Maurice, as his voice got brassier. "I never considered, not even for a second, that Mia shot Todd Hartford. They have video of her on campus, at Macalester, at the exact time Todd was shot."

"Dr. Ho found hair from someone of Asian ancestry in Chad's bed at the meth lab," Jon shared. "We have DNA from the bed that's been sent to the lab. If it's hers, we're going to bring her in. Kaiko's a killer and a serial rapist. Mia can help us find him. There is no one else for us to talk to. We need Mia."

Maurice said, "We'll talk then. Mia's not speaking to anyone until she has immunity. I'm not letting her go to prison over falling in love with a con man. Do you have anything else?"

"Not at this time." Sean's voice was dripping with displeasure. And then he drew the line. "There will be no protection for Mia and no deal until she comes in and spills it all."

Maurice urged, "Give the girl a break. Mia's been raped. Let the poor girl heal."

After Maurice left, Jada and I joined the men. Jada went to sit by Sean. Sean reached over and took her hand.

The gesture seemed entirely for show and, at that moment, I realized Sean hated that he had come to desire Jada so intensely. In therapy Sean's behavior was referred to as a reaction formation. A public display of affection for a lover now resented. Few people engaging in the behavior realize how shallow it appears to everyone else. Jada compassionately complied.

Sean ordered, "We can't share any more information with Maurice. He still has friends at the BCA who are giving him details about our investigation."

After an awkward silence, I attempted to ease the tension by asking Jon, "How deep do you think Mia's involved?"

Jon turned to Sean, who granted his approval, commenting, "I know you're talking to Serena about the case, and Jada's involved, so we can speak freely here."

Jon revealed, "I think Mia told Kaiko I was spending time with Zelly. At the time, I thought Del was leaking information, but now I'm convinced it was Mia. Zelly's only alive today because of her own resourcefulness. And there were a lot of little things I wrote off as insignificant, until I considered Mia had been manipulating us from the onset. Mia found the bullet that killed Todd quickly, even though I mistakenly gave her the projectile trajectory for a full metal jacket. I'd bet she knew a soft-point bullet was used. They're more lethal, but they mushroom out quickly, so they don't travel nearly as far after hitting their target."

I pointed out, "But Maurice said Mia has an alibi."

Jon nodded, adding, "I think we still need to verify it. I believe Mia's task was to report my efforts to Chad. And she couldn't report on what I was doing if she was in the woods looking for a bullet. Then there's her erasing the tape of the car at the Ross home break-in. The lights flashed twice on the car when it shut off. That's a feature distinct to Toyotas, and Mia drives a Toyota Corolla. But I don't have the damn tape because Mia accidently set the tape by magnetized boxes at work, which erased it. It's not enough to arrest her, but it torments me."

In support of Jon, I quietly added, "I think Dan Moene's suicide letter was written by a woman."

Sean said, "But we're not going to get samples of Mia's writing without a search warrant. Even when we have the DNA, we still aren't going to be able to arrest her. Her DNA isn't in the system. I've already checked."

As a stay-at-home mom, sharing my thoughts with the BCA agents and an investigative news reporter was incredibly intimidating. I asked cautiously, "Maurice's oldest grandson is Mia's brother, right?"

Sean nodded.

Jon invited me to continue. "Where are you going with this?"

I felt the need to explain to Sean and Jada. "I'm a bit of a fanatic about words." I thought how to best lay this out. "It bothers me that Maurice said Mia learned about drugs from his oldest grandson, rather than from her brother."

Jada was interested. "And, you're implying?"

"I think Maurice is Mia's father. Couldn't you feel the longing in his heart when he spoke of Chang Lu?"

Jada pondered, "He did say he knew her before she was an informant."

"All of you deal with kids in terrible situations almost daily," I continued, "but he made Mia part of his family."

Sean leaned back as he contemplated it. "That's a compelling thought. We have Maurice's DNA, by his own command of all agents. If half of the DNA sample from the lab matches his, the person is his child."

"And, from the rest of that sample," Jon interjected, "we can determine sex, hair color, eye color, and even ancestry."

Sean smiled at Jon. "That would get you your search warrant."

Feeling energized, I proffered, "Let me talk to Kaiko's aunt. As a former victim of assault, I might be able to persuade her into giving up his location."

Surprised by my offer, Jon told me, "They live in Hawaii." Sean thought out loud. "I don't know."

"Sean, I like the idea," Jada said in support. "Serena might be your best shot. She pulled it off back when Jon opened his first murder book." It was a little weird having my husband's ex encouraging me to leave town.

Resigned to support Jada, Sean said, "Serena, if you'll go, I'll secure the funds. Paying for your expenses is a lot cheaper than sending an agent there . . ."

Jon hugged me as Sean and Jada drove away. "You don't have to go to Hawaii. You know I can't go with you. I have to be here, searching for Kaiko."

I was apprehensive about leaving, but it would only be for two days. I was always telling Jon I wanted the two of us to someday be an investigative team. I needed to act when the opportunities arose.

Jon kissed me and said, "We should start making up for that lost time together right now." As we hugged, I had a thought. "Jon, you have more than you shared . . ."

42

FERMAT'S THEORY OF REFLECTION =
Light changes course under water because it takes the quickest path.
In physics, the quickest and longest paths are the same (aberrations from the norm).

Pierre de Fermat
French Mathematician & Lawyer, 1662

HANI EGAL
10:30 PM, SUNDAY, JUNE 16, 2019 WILSON AVENUE
NORTHEAST, ST. CLOUD

THE HOME CLAY and I were working on was nice, even though Clay complained about all the things that needed repair. Our bedroom was like a hotel. We had the most comfortable bed I'd ever been in, and a walk-in shower—and they were new. Clay was polite and respected my thoughts on our home improvement project. That thought warmed me. It had become our home. I wished I trusted him. It was difficult being with a guy women ogle over. I was hoping trust would come with time. I appreciated that he asked me to go with him tonight for his business meeting. I'd hinted, but Clay still hadn't grasped that I couldn't go into a bar, and this was often where he landed after these meetings. Alcohol was forbidden, so I couldn't go to a place where people disobeyed God. To his credit, I'd never seen Clay intoxicated.

Another reason I wouldn't go was that I didn't want to cost him any business. I knew what many people thought of us in St. Cloud; not most, but many. In 2018, 88% of Somali households had at least one person working. We were younger than white Americans on average, so we had a lot of young mothers home with children. The average age for a white Minnesotan was forty-one. The average age for a Somali Minnesotan was twenty-two. We worked low-paying jobs that didn't allow us to break out of poverty. The average employed Somali earned $20,000 a year, in a state where the poverty line was an income of $25,000 or less. Nine out of every ten of us lived below the poverty line.

Despite our differences, the time Clay and I shared was weaving together commonalities that brought us closer every day. I'd come to realize it was a mistake for any group in America to remain homogeneous, as you risked missing the beauty of the blend. I could respect my culture without being imprisoned by it. I wished the rest of the world could have been as accepting of our differences as Clay and I. We laughed at our misunderstandings and we were happy together. We loved each other.

Muhammad warned that it was difficult for a person in love to refrain from sin. Allah gave us the ability to love, to use with our spouses. I was sold to a man as a child—my husband's ruthless nature couldn't sit well with Allah. If I went to the imam and requested a divorce, he would go to my husband, and my husband would demand my return. I'd rather go to hell than have that despicable man touch me again. I knew I wasn't a good Muslim, but I acted with love in my heart. I prayed this was what would truly matter. Muhammad said about his wife Khadijah, "She believed in me when people rejected me." I could say the same for Clay.

I wished Clay was home. I felt safe with him and it was hard for me to be alone. Somalia was still one of the most dangerous places on earth; people were advised to leave it, if they were able. But I'd heard of so many hate crimes here. Every other month, someone told me, "Go back to where you came from." I told them I came from East St. Germain Street in St. Cloud.

I had the sense that someone had been lingering outside our home since night had fallen. I was truly alone. My family had told me, "If you're with Clay, don't call." I shut the lights off so I could peer out the windows into the darkness. Did the bush just move? It was probably just the wind. For a moment, I thought I saw a shadow of a man emanating from the front porch light. I quickly stepped back. Was it just my eyes playing tricks on me? The shadow was gone when I looked again. I was creeping myself out. I so wanted to call Clay, but I didn't want to interrupt him, and I didn't want to appear weak. I could handle this. And why would someone rob our home? The objects of value we moved in—carpeting, beds, bathroom fixtures— weren't items burglars walked away with.

But I was alone, and black, and Muslim, and shunned by my family, in St. Cloud. Stop! I need to stop thinking like that! Our doors and windows had secure locks. Clay wanted me to feel safe. I still had some Somali friends who supported me, but they had their families to tend to. Okay, maybe watching something mindless and light, like Jane the Virgin, would distract me.

I took some deep breaths and was trying to relax on the couch when I heard Bang! Bang! Bang! It sounded like someone was pounding on an anvil with a steel mallet in our front yard. I peeked out the shade. What in Allah's name? There was a man standing under the street light in front of our house, hitting the metal lamp post with a hammer. He was not only staring at our house, his eyes were fixed on me.

My phone slipped out of my sweaty hand, but I immediately picked it up and dialed 911. "Help! You've got to get here as fast as you can. Wilson Avenue and Second Street, northeast St. Cloud. We're the gray, two-story house. Someone's standing in front of my house staring at me, pounding on the light post with a hammer. There's a second man sitting on the curb in front of him. Please hurry . . . Okay, I'll stay on the phone."

And then the man stopped hammering and started walking directly toward the house. I yelled, "He's coming to my house and he's still holding the hammer! Help!"

He was soon on the doorstep and started bludgeoning the door, trying to bust it open. I ran upstairs, quickly scanning the rooms for a safe place to hide. I slid into our bedroom closet. Clay had long raingear hanging in the closet, so I hid between it and my chadors, pulling the full-length dresses around me. Clay's hunting gear was on metal hangers that were strong enough to hang an animal. I could still hear the hammering, but to my great relief, I could also hear sirens closing in on our house.

Terrified, I whispered in the phone, "Please, get here." The dispatcher told me the officers were pulling up.

The police shouting outside, "Drop the weapon and put your hands in the air!" They repeated again, "Drop the weapon! Put your hands in the air!" I heard a scuffle on the porch and I worked my way out of the closet and down the steps. I looked out the window and the police had the man lying face-down on the ground.

I was still terrified, but felt I could breathe again. I stepped outside and an officer asked, "Ma'am, are you okay?"

"Yes, I believe so."

The operator ended the call.

He asked, "Do you know this man?"

I looked at the wild-haired man cuffed on the ground. "No."

"He's a homeless man," the second officer commented. "I've seen him on the bridge."

We were only a couple blocks away from the Mississippi River, and there were always homeless people milling around the bridge. I asked the man, "Why me?"

He smiled crazily, but didn't say a word. He looked drunk. The first officer asked, "Did he get into the house?"

"He never entered the house."

The officer walked me back to the front door. "The knob looks intact. He was so drunk he didn't do any serious damage."

There were dents in the doorframe, but the doorknob was fine.

The officer was kind and comforting. He sat with me on the front steps, while his partner stuffed the prowler into the back of their squad car. After I went over my statement with him a couple times, he asked, "Are you here by yourself?"

"Yes, but my man should be home soon." The officer suggested, "Call him."

"Okay . . ."

So, I called Clay. He was at Bad Habit Brewing in St. Joseph, about twenty miles away, but promised to immediately return home.

The officers left and I felt okay. I hadn't been imagining things.

After several minutes had passed and I was trying calm my nerves, I got a call back from the dispatcher. "I was just reviewing your call. What happened to the man sitting on the curb?"

Before I could process the question, a forearm hooked around my neck, constricting my throat. In my effort to hang on to the phone, I accidently ended the call.

I tried pulling his chokehold away from my neck, but he leaned back and squeezed so hard, he lifted me off my feet. I was getting dizzy and I couldn't breathe.

He grunted, "Where's the money?" I choked out, "Money?"

"I know Chad left you his money. I want it. All of it."

I tried to say I didn't know a Chad, but all that squeaked out was, "Know Chad." On the verge of passing out, I nodded like I knew what he was talking about.

He loosened his grip and my feet touched the floor once again. This man was a beast. His biceps constricted my airway like a giant anaconda.

I gasped for breath and told him, "I don't know a Chad, but I'll give you everything I have."

He started to squeeze again, but I turned my chin into the crook of his arm and dropped down, pushing his arm over my head. Almost on all fours, I scrambled in the only direction that allowed me to elude his grasp—upstairs. I immediately ran back to the closet. I slid into Clay's raincoat and gripped the hanger, pulling my legs up so I would be completely hidden in the coat.

His footsteps thumped a methodical death march up the steps. He was in no hurry. He had me.

And then the stomping stopped. With pained fingers, I held my breath as I waited for him to enter. What was he waiting for? Still blanketed in darkness, I finally peeked up through the neck of Clay's coat. The shadow of evil stood in the doorway. I quietly slipped back into my rabbit hole. Allah, I have indeed believed. Forgive me my sins and save me from the agony of fire.

The room brightened as he turned on the light. I could hear the dresser drawers being dumped. He was swearing as he threw items around. And then he stopped. The closet door slammed open violently and he shouted, "Where's the damn money?"

My stomach muscles were on fire from holding my legs up off the floor. My hands burned in pain as I continued to grasp the thin metal bar of the hanger as tightly as I could. My body was rebelling; I was slipping.

He pushed clothing around and nudged me, but didn't seem aware I was there. He stomped the wall behind me to make sure it was solid.

I pleaded with my body, Please hang on. My hold weakened and the metal seared across my fingers as I slid to the floor. If he was surprised by my body pouring out of racks of clothing, he didn't show it. The fury in his eyes was beyond anything I'd ever witnessed, even in Somalia.

He kicked me hard in the ribs, as if I was a sack of rubbish, and scoffed, "Look, desert rat, if you don't give me the money, I'll take you."

Defying him, I glared and said, "Allahu Akbar. Allah is greatest!"

To my great relief, Clay appeared, standing strong in the doorway. Before I could roll to my feet, Clay was on the man, thumping punches that sounded like the back of a cleaver pounding a steak. The brutal assault that followed was merciless. The intruder had no chance to counter the rapid-fire beating Clay was delivering. Clay had the man pinned against the wall and I could barely track the speed with which his fists were pummeling the man's torso and head. Each time the man tried to push himself off the wall, he was quickly slammed back into it. He flailed about wildly as Clay got ahold of his jacket and began slamming the man into the dresser.

I could hear sirens above the melee, followed by the screech of tires as squad cars slid into the driveway. I ran down the stairs to get help. I turned as I was descending to see the man buckled to his knees and drop to the floor. This threw Clay off for a moment, and the man made a break for the stairs, right on my heels. Clay was soon back on him and the two tumbled down the steps, nearly crashing into me.

I got to the door and flung it open, yelling, "Help!" Officers came running.

When they entered, Clay had the man back on his feet and was slamming him ruthlessly against the wall.

An officer ordered, "Let go!"

But Clay continued, his beautiful face twisted into a mask of rage. He pinned the man with his left hand and drove his right fist into the man's ribs.

Before I could reason with Clay, he pulled back to throw another punch, and the officer tased him. Clay's body arched violently with the impact and, now rendered powerless, he crumbled to the floor. He landed hard and curled on his side, his body looking like a broken doll.

I yelled, "No! Not him!"

The intruder took advantage of the confusion and bolted out the back door.

I pointed after him. "That's the burglar!" I dropped to my knees beside Clay, smoothing his hair off his forehead. His eyes were wild and his breathing heavy and rapid. His jaw was clenched so tightly, I was afraid he would break his teeth.

One officer pursued the man while the other stayed with us. Clay rolled onto his back and held his chest.

I asked, "Are you okay?"

He slowly sat up and nodded. "Yeah." I hugged him tight.

He whispered, "The thought of that man touching you, even making you fearful in our home, made me crazy. I'm dead serious—I was going to smash him through the wall."

Adrenaline was still racing through my body, too. I told him, "I saw a side of you tonight that scares me . . ."

Eventually, the officer returned alone. He couldn't find the man.

It was a long night, and finally all of the investigators, except for Jon Frederick, had gone. Clay and I went through the entire scenario one more time with Jon. I assured him I had never seen the man Jon referred to as Kaiko ever before.

Jon offered, "Do you two want to stay with Serena and me tonight? We have an extra bedroom. You can't stay here; it's going to be processed as a crime scene."

"Thank you," Clay said appreciatively. "Let me grab a few things first. We'll meet you there." Clay looked at the back door, "How the hell did he get in?"

"Kaiko has a blunt key. You can tap it into door locks and it opens the tumblers."

Clay told Jon, "So that's why you have the metal bars on the inside of your doors."

"Yes. It's a way to lock the doors that can't be manipulated by any type of technology. This was a well-thought-out break-in. Kaiko paid a homeless man to draw attention away from what he intended to do. When the police arrive, Hani walks out, so he knows she's home alone. While the focus is on the homeless man, he enters the back door." Jon looked at Clay, "But why would Kaiko think Hani had Chad's money?"

Clay was lost in thought, still pale from the ordeal. Deciding to rescue him, I told Jon, "Thank you. You and Serena have been so kind and respectful to me."

Jon replied, "When I'm at Catholic Mass and I look around, I see hard-working, salt of the earth people who go out of their way to be kind. Then I think about how the news only talks about slimy priests and their bad administration and it makes me angry. But then I realize this has got to be what it feels like to be Muslim in the US. So, I won't judge you by the slimeballs who claim to be Muslim, if you don't judge me by the slimeballs who claim to be Christian." He smiled kindly. "How you treat others is what matters." He receded into deep thought.

The pleasant twinkle had returned to Clay's eyes. Feigning exasperation, he said, "Jon, I know that look. What's on your mind?"

Jon's lips twitched into a half-smile and I could see this wasn't the first of such exchanges. "Fermat's theory of reflection. In physics, the quickest and longest paths are the same—aberrations of the norm. Maybe it's the same way with religion. At the extremes, you have the nonreligious and the overzealous hypocrites—the two groups most likely to be cruel."

Clay had a blank look on his face; I understood what he meant when he told me Jon would go to places he didn't understand.

I responded, "I think Allah loves us for the kind things we do, whatever uniform he wears."

43

THE RECALIBRATIONAL THEORY OF ANGER =
The function of anger is to recalibrate a relationship by an individual who places an inordinate priority on his own immediate welfare. Anger is a negotiative tactic by an aggressive individual, targeting someone viewed as potentially vulnerable. The tactic is intended to recalibrate the relationship between two people, raising the value of the aggressor. The tactic can range from withdrawal of love to violent aggression. The impact on the victim is seldom considered.

Aaron Sell
Center for Evolutionary Psychology University of California, 2011

CLAY ROBERTS
6:05 AM, MONDAY, JUNE 17, 2019 PIERZ

I FELT BAD THAT my anger scared Hani last night. Even when I was trying to do the right thing, I still disappointed people. She was still sleeping when I rolled over to answer my phone. Oh hell, it was Brooke Lange-- mom. It was as good a time as any to be tormented by her. Mom had friends in law enforcement, so I imagined she'd heard about the fiasco at my home last night.

I took it into the bathroom.

As usual, Mommie Dearest started out the conversation relatively kind. "Are you okay?" "Yeah. Unfortunately, the bastard got away. If they wouldn't have tased me, escape wouldn't have been an option for him." "Is our house okay?"

Mom had fronted me some of the money to buy the house. My initial intention was to turn it and pay her back with interest. "Our house is fine."

"They say you were living with a black Muslim." The rancor in her voice was the fruit of deeply rooted bitterness.

I retaliated, "You almost woke her up."

"Clay, are you kidding me? Get that queen of darkness out of my house." "It's my house. And anyway, we aren't there now."

Mom jibed, "It's not your house as long as I have money invested in it."

"I'll sell my home in Edina and get you your money."

"Even you aren't that idiotic! It will be worth a fortune in a couple years."

I didn't respond. I didn't want to have this conversation. Our discussions rarely left me feeling anything but angry and inadequate.

Performing as the serpentine hydra she was, she tried a new approach. "Clay, this isn't about the money. Why do you think she's with you?"

"We love each other," I said quietly. It was a thought I'd yet to share with Hani.

"Will she be the next Mia Khalifa?"

My blood boiled. "If you make another comment like that, I swear I will never speak to you again. I'm sure Hani has no idea who Mia Khalifa even is. It's a sin that I do. Khalifa may have born in Lebanon, but she was raised Christian. She was dressed in the hajib for porn just to sell more to Middle Eastern men." Mia Khalifa porn videos were some of the most popular videos online. I wasn't about that anymore. Porn clean for over a year.

"Clay, you don't know what love is. You have the Lange curse. We're beautiful, so people are attracted to us. They pretend to be what they're not, just to be with us, but their true colors eventually shine through. Your dad—"

I cut her off. "Don't you dare rip on Dad. He raised me when you bailed, Brooke." I couldn't help it. Every time she took things too far, I resorted to the dig.

"Oh, come on, Clay. Not that old song again. I hate when you do that. I am your mother." "That's been debatable."

"You need to check yourself; you're exactly like me. I left back then because I needed to be happy. You'd have done the same thing—I know you."

I prayed she was wrong. Please don't let me be like her. She mistook my silence for

agreement, so continued with her screwed-up rationale. "The Muslims are here to destroy Christianity."

"Hani came here as a child."

"The Quran tells them not to take Christians or Jews as friends. They've placed Christians in cages and burned them to death. Don't turn your back on us."

"The Old Testament condoned violence, too, but the best Christians I know say that doesn't make it okay. Jesus said it isn't okay."

"Clay, they're infiltrating our country to destroy Christianity. Imagine the power you give her. I'd bet she's smart. You were, at best, an average student. What do you honestly think you have to offer her? I'd bet she insists that you're just a passive little pet of hers. Am I right?" My silence cranked up her aggressiveness. Sensing victory, she twisted the knife, "They're laughing at you behind your back."

I rubbed my eyes. "Listen, the only other person I've felt this strongly about is married." "It would be easier for me to forgive you being with a married Christian than a Muslim.

For once in your life, just listen to me. Eternity is forever. Make the right decision."

Mama Lange made my head throb. Hani did say her initial attraction was to my looks. I threw on jeans and a t-shirt and made my way down the steps to the kitchen.

Serena was standing by the cupboard looking like an angel. The morning sun was shining through her thin pajamas, giving her skin a warm glow. Some couples allowed their partners a free pass if they got the chance to sleep with their favorite celebrity. I would take my free pass with Serena.

Surprised to see me, she said quietly, "I thought I'd sneak down and put some coffee on. I didn't expect you'd be up already. Jon's already left for work." She dumped a couple scoops of grounds into the filter, snapped it closed, and pressed the start button. She turned to me and said, "This case has been hard on him. He blames himself for failing to recognize Mia's betrayal sooner. Jon called Sean twice and asked him to transfer Mia, but he wouldn't. I don't know if that girl will ever be able to grasp the damage she's done. People are dead. Jon could lose his job."

Serena was such a sweetheart. It was hard to see her so tormented. "Jon's intensity must be hard on your relationship." I wondered if Serena had any idea of how beautiful she was-- dreamy green eyes and that perfect, round butt. Maybe she knew and that's why she was here, waiting for me.

She ignored my comment and asked, "Do you want me to make you some eggs? Otherwise, we have cereal." She smiled and said, "You are very kind to Hani. Jon shared with me that she's had more than her share of trauma. I appreciate that you made her feel comfortable here."

I'm not a terrible guy. Serena was finally seeing it. I stood up and closed the distance between us. I softly told her, "What I miss most is the opportunity to pleasure a woman."

Horrified, Serena clenched her fists and ordered, "Whatever you're thinking of saying next, don't. Don't you dare say another word. I'm the woman I am because of Jon."

"You were a caring and beautiful woman before the two of you got together. Jon had nothing to do with it."

"Then let me put it another way. If I was with you, I'd be the most intolerable bitch on earth, because I can't stand that you'd sell out your friends in a heartbeat. If you don't want this mug of hot tea tossed on you, get the hell out of my house."

As I waited for Hani in the truck, I beat myself up over my behavior. Why? I wanted Hani. Conversations with Mom made me crazy and I always responded by doing something insane. I self-destructed by annihilating my friendships and relationships. Why couldn't it be enough for Mom that I was happy?

I called Jon. "I need to tell you something. Hani had nothing to do with those meth dealers, but I think I know why Kaiko went after her. I went out with Mia the other night, and she hates Hani."

44

MIA STROCK
7:30 AM, MONDAY, JUNE 17, 2019 RAILROAD AVENUE,
ALBANY

I FELT LIKE A snowman, once built up with loving hands,
now abandoned and melting away. Last night, I found a
bottle of Jameson whiskey Chad had left at my place. I shed
a tear at the thought it would always be like this, then drank
half the bottle, straight. I woke up this morning with the worst
hangover of my life. A searing pain cut through my skull. I
couldn't even open my eyes. I felt like the entire Gopher football team had marched through my mouth in their stocking
feet. And my body hurt. Did someone shove a flaming torch
up my . . . an overpowering rancid, sweaty scent permeated the
room. I forced my eyes open.

No. It couldn't be. Kaiko Kane was lying in bed with me.
Please let this be a lucid night terror. I closed my eyes and
pinched my arm. When I reopened them, Kaiko's shit-eating

grin was undeniable. I was too drunk to block the doors last night, so my endless nightmare continued. Shame, guilt, trauma. Rinse and repeat.

Kaiko ruffled my hair like I was his pet. "Well, you got two hundred dollars more worked off your debt last night. Just fifty-seven more times."

I ran to the bathroom and threw up.

45

LEARNED HELPLESSNESS THEORY =
*When people are repeatedly subjected to an aversive stimulus they
cannot escape, they will eventually behave as if utterly helpless,
even after opportunities to escape become available.*

*Martin Seligman Psychology Professor
University of Pennsylvania, 1975*

KAIKO KANE
7:52 AM, MONDAY, JUNE 17, 2019 RAILROAD AVENUE, ALBANY

MIA STROCK PATHETICALLY turns into the fetal position. I slap her ass and tell her, "I'm showering. If you're making eggs, I'll have three. Some bacon or sausage would be good, too."

She doesn't move.

What am I going to do with this cowering courtesan? I've got the perfect fantasy woman right here—four of the top six categories on Pornhub last year were Asian, so it seems a shame to kill her. I could have use for her yet—and if she can fall for a big clumsy bruin like Chad, she can fall for me. Mia's a liar, but I get it. Sometimes it's the only way to get what you want.

With her back to me, I enter the bathroom and turn the shower on. I've got bruises all over my body from Mia sending

273

me on a wild goose chase after Hani Egal. That steroid of a man managed to land a few lucky punches. He's lucky the cops saved him.

I wince. It only hurts when I breathe. I traded some meth for some oxy. I take one, and I'll give a couple to my new lover.

I quietly reopen the door a fraction and wait for Mia to make her move. Where is she hiding that damn gun? She claims she ditched it, but I don't believe her. I went through her entire place last night. She doesn't move—she's too hungover. Talk about a woman on a downward slide. My old therapist called Mia's condition "learned helplessness." Once, when I infuriated the old man, he told me I acted like a parasite, moving from host to host. Everybody's cruel; Doc just expressed his disdain through words. And I don't care what anybody claims, we all take what we want. I'm just better at it.

I pour out a couple pills and shake Mia.

With eyes barely open, she whines, "What? I can't again. I'll end up in the hospital." "Hey, I've just got a couple of pain pills for you. They'll help you sleep."

She skeptically repeats, "I can't again. I'm torn up inside." "Don't worry about that."

"Just tell me if you're going to kill me. I'm not going to fight you. There's something I need to do first."

"I'm not going to kill you." I hold the pills closer to her eyes. "Look at them. They're oxys. Let me put you out of your misery for a bit. Sleep, my pretty girl." I brush her hair back. "Chill, baby. I understand." I nearly choke on the lie—like I would ever want to understand weakness like that. If I decide I need to have her again, I'll take some of her Vaseline and use a different portal after she passes out.

I think I'll stay here with my new friend for a bit. Mia knows I still have the draft of Dan's suicide letter she wrote, so she's screwed if she turns me in. I wheeled my motorcycle into her garage last night. While they're tearing apart St. Cloud looking for me, I'll be snug as a bug in a rug, right here in Albany.

I take a warm, relaxing shower.

46

IMPLOSION THEORY =
If explosions occur all around the main source,
it will reach critical mass and begin fission, which would ultimately
lead to mass destruction.

John von Neumann
Hungarian & American Physicist, 1932

CLAY ROBERTS
9:25 PM, MONDAY, JUNE 17, 2019 WILSON AVENUE
NORTHEAST, ST. CLOUD

WHEN I ENDED my workday, I rested my sore body on the couch. The combination of being tased and the few lucky punches the sawed-off Hawaiian landed bruised me some, but I had the satisfaction of knowing he was worse off.

Hani entered the room, but kept her distance.

I closed my eyes and dropped my head back. "What now—more messages on the wall at work?"

Hani studied me. "I know hate, Clay. Mia sent that man after me because you went out with her."

"I don't know anything about that, but I'm sorry if that's how it happened. Look, I've had a rough day." I looked her directly in the eyes and told her the truth. "I wasn't sure what I wanted when you first moved in, but I know now. I want you here. I want to be with you, and only you. Going out with Mia was a mistake."

"You lie so easily." Hani continued, "I heard what you said to Serena this morning. It's so humiliating to hear you tell her you don't feel you can pleasure me? It makes me feel like damaged goods. I've been ruminating about it all day. I need a little time to find a place, but I'll figure something out. I'd prefer if you didn't talk to me anymore."

"I'm so sorry. I was a damn fool this morning."

Hani shared painfully, "Do you have any idea what it's like to be betrayed by someone you love?"

I cringed everytime I think it. "I promise—it will never happen again."

"I gave up everything for you—my family, my friends— and you treat me like nothing.

What you've done to me was far worse than the attack." "I didn't ask you to give up anything."

"That just makes it worse. It's all on me, isn't it?" She continued, "You made such a big deal about me being married and then you hit on a married woman. How does that work?"

I leaned forward. "I've had this obsession with Serena forever. She was the one that got away. I'm getting strong feelings for you, so I had to make sure it was over with Serena. She slammed that door shut. Honestly, even if she would have opened it, I think I would have backed off. I want you!" I could see tears in Hani's eyes. "Hani, I'm ready to open my heart to you."

She stood strong. "On the day of resurrection, Allah will oppose a man who gave his word and betrayed it. Go to hell!"

"Is there a hell in Islam?" I realized immediately it was the wrong thing to say.

Hani wept as she offered, "It's where all non-believers go. It's not eternal if you can change, but I don't see you changing.

You're the same story, over and over again. And by the way, I don't go to places people frequent to drink."

I blew out a long breath. "I don't care about that. I went a year without drinking and I don't care if I've seen my last last call."

Hani glanced at me from the corner of her eye. "Why did you quit?"

"It's a long story. You could write a book about it. I know you don't think I've changed, but I have. Believe me, I wish I never would have said any of that."

"But you did. I'm not the door prize. I want to be the grand prize for somebody. Maybe I'm a hopeless romantic, but I pray I will be exactly what a man desires someday. You made me feel like trash. I know I'm damaged, but I don't need a man who reminds me of that."

I stood up and stepped toward her. "I'm the one who's damaged. I don't know why I did this. I feel so strongly for you. When it's all going too well, I always do something stupid. Believe me, I want to change. I know I can be the man I want to be, with you."

Hani slid away before I got to her, ran down the hall, and slammed the bedroom door behind her. I felt pained and sick.

I stood outside her door. "Hani, please talk to me. I'd do anything to make it up to you. I'm so sorry. Please."

"Just go away. Leave me alone. Don't talk to me. Give me that much respect, anyway." I bumped my head on her door. Another year, another burned bridge . . .

12:28 AM GENOLA GRAVEL PITS

I tore through the darkness of the Genola gravel pits, pushing my four-wheel-drive truck to the max. I hated myself. I had separated Hani from her family, shamed her in her religion, and now betrayed her. I slammed my brakes and threw the Chevy in park. I pounded the dash. I took one last, large swallow of the Maker's Mark bourbon, opened the window, and fired the bottle off into the pit. I leaned behind me and opened up the hidden compartment in my back seat where I kept my gun. Mom was right. There was no good reason someone would be with me. They went to bed with Brad Pitt, and woke up with me. An empty shell of a person. I destroyed people. It was time for that to end.

I shut all the lights off and opened the gun case. I could feel the tears stream. "Even though I walk through the valley of the shadow of death, I fear no evil, for you are with me; your rod and your staff, they comfort me . . ."

I sat motionless for a moment. I suddenly realized the gun case seemed light. I opened it to find a note that read, Someday you'll be forgiven for this. Where the hell was my gun? I flipped the note over.

The back side read:

Your life could be better, five years from now, than you ever imagined. You just need to get through tonight. Call me. I don't care what time it is.

Jon

So I did. Jon had no right to take my gun.

47

THEORY OF THE GOLDEN MEAN =
*All virtue is achieved by finding balance. This means that,
in order to find happiness, people should always strive for a balance
between two extremes.For example: Temperance is the midpoint
between overindulgence and insensitivity. A person should care
enough for others to give with a kind heart, but not give so much
that they're empty when their love is not reciprocated.*

Aristotle
Philosopher & Physicist, 300 BC

JON FREDERICK
9:28 AM, TUESDAY, JUNE 18, 2019
BCA EVIDENCE PROCESSING FACILITY, 11TH AVENUE
NORTH, ST. CLOUD

IT WAS A late night with Clay, but I got him safely back home. I had taken the gun out of his truck a year ago, anticipating he was much more likely to use it for self-destruction than for protection. It was a risk, but I ended up being right. There was so much hatred in his parents' divorce, I swore they'd both destroy Clay if it would simply prove the other failed. He insisted on spending the night at this father's, as he didn't want Hani to see him drunk. Clay agreed to get to therapy today and I made certain the session was set up. I told Clay's dad about how I found him. Informing family is a powerful anti-suicide tool. I picked Clay up before I left for work and handed him off to a deacon from the Church of St. Anthony in St. Cloud, who promised to deliver Clay to therapy, then spend the rest of the day with him. I reminded Clay we had a pact we made as abused children: No one would destroy us. He was back on board with it.

Dr. Ho had called me into the medical examiner's office. "Raven Lee's DNA was in both beds at the meth lab. And there was DNA from an Asian woman in Chad's bed, but no match in the CODIS for it."

As an afterthought, Amaya stated, "Don't send me any more emails about the alfalfa. As a matter of fact, call me from now on. My recent conversations with my boss suggest he is going through my emails. He's in a golf league with Maurice. Maybe I'm just being paranoid."

That would explain how Maurice seemed to be so on top of the investigation. After a moment of quiet reflection, I noticed an impish smile developing across Dr. Ho's face.

Like the cat that swallowed the canary, Amaya patiently held back her blue-ribbon news, waiting for me to ask.

"Do you have something else?"

Amaya replied, "Your beloved Serena gave you a gift. Maurice Strock is the father of the female who was in Chad Gnoh's bed. The DNA tells us she is a black-haired woman, of Asian ancestry. Half of our Asian woman's DNA is a match to Maurice Strock. Maurice is her father. And there is the evidence you need for your search warrant."

48

MIA STROCK
9:45 AM, TUESDAY, JUNE 18, 2019 NATURE ROAD, ROYALTON

GRANDPA MAURICE PICKED me up this morning and drove me to a farm in the country. I knew we were out in the sticks when we turned at a place called the 10 Spot Bar to get here. It was apparently "that one spot" on Highway 10 in this part of the state.

Hunched over, Grandpa lugged two large leather satchels with him. Uneasy and starting to feel unhinged, I followed him into the iron gray, weathered wooden shed. An old wooden chair and table waited for me inside.

My body felt used and abused and my head was pounding. I could feel my forehead prickling with hot beads of sweat. My system was on anxiety overload—I felt like I was going to have a heart attack as I sat on the hard wooden chair and watched him set up a polygraph machine. In other words, a lie detector test.

Maurice eyeballed me. "You look like death warmed over." "It's been a rough couple days."

Oblivious to the level of my pain and apprehension, Grandpa continued, "You know what I love about this place? No cell phone reception."

He wrapped the pneumograph tubes above and below my breasts as he instructed, "Mia, I need to know the exact truth in order to get you out of this mess. I get it. I'm family—it's hard to be honest with me. But there's a lot at stake here."

When he placed the galvanic skin response metal tabs on my fingers, I said, "You don't need to do this. I swear, Grandpa, I'll just be honest with you."

He placed the blood pressure cuff on me and tightened it, maybe a little more than necessary. He was trying so hard to be supportive, but I knew well what this was costing him. "If you're honest with me, this will be easy. When we're done, there'll be no more lies between us. We're too close to be lying to each other. You will need to respond 'yes' or 'no' to all of the questions. I'll be establishing a baseline with the first couple questions."

"But it's not going to work," I sputtered. "I'm too anxious."

Grandpa smiled. "I can adjust the machine. Honestly, it will make it easier to read. Is your name Mia Strock?"

"Yes." Red lines showed my blood pressure, two yellow lines monitored my breathing, and two green lines displayed my sweat on the computer screen.

"Do you identify as female?"

"Yes." The lines remained consistent. "Did you shoot Todd Hartford?"

Before I could say a word, the lines spiked crazily, like an out of control Etch A Sketch. I swallowed hard. "You said you told Jon I'm on camera at Macalester."

"I lied. You told me you were there, and I needed to buy some time until I had evidence to exonerate you. Now, I'm not sure I'll find that evidence." Grandpa was angry now. "You shot Todd. He was a great father with an ungrateful wife. He died for nothing, other than taking his daughter for a walk in the wilderness"

"Let me explain."

He stood and walked away from me.

I called after him, "Please listen. I shot at Todd. Zelly and Todd walked by the meth lab when they were hunting. Kaiko was convinced we needed to kill them. The three of us drove to their home. I told Kaiko if anybody was going to shoot Todd, I would. I took the rifle and—"

Grandpa indignantly turned back toward me, his eyes flaring.

My voice softened as I continued, "I fired a shot close to him," I emphasized, "but I deliberately missed him. You know how I can shoot. I could have killed him if I wanted to. After I fired the shot, Todd was spooked and we had to take off. I had hoped that would end any talk of killing him—but Kaiko apparently went back and shot him anyway."

Still troubled, Grandpa came back and sat by me. After making sure all of my biometric measurements were secure, he continued with the polygraph. "Did you kill Todd Hartford?"

"No."

He nodded with approval, as I explained, "Chad told me Kaiko wore gloves when he shot Todd, so only my prints would be on the rifle. But Chad wiped the rifle clean and then placed it on the table a couple months later, when Kaiko was high, knowing he would mindlessly move it, placing his prints on it. Then Chad put it away."

"The two of you really thought of everything." I knew better than to respond.

"Jon's brought up a number of ways you sabotaged the investigation. I've supervised him long enough to know he's not showing all of his cards. He has something big he's holding back and I need to know what it is."

"Grandpa, I helped with the investigation. I found the bullet from Kaiko's gun. I didn't cover up Todd's murder. I didn't want him killed. That's what got the BCA's attention."

Grandpa focused on the charts once again. "Did you shoot Del Walker?"

I didn't respond. I didn't need to. I could see the colored lines jumping on the screen. I finally shared, "It was dark. I thought he was Kaiko and he was going to kill me."

"You're lying."

"Okay, I'm sorry." I felt so weak and inept. Unable to maintain the levee, tears streamed over the damned. "I'm so sorry," I repeated.

It took me a couple minutes before I could gather my composure enough to speak again. "I had no idea who I'd run into, racing through the darkness and the storm to the meth lab. I was holding the gun because Kaiko scares me. I couldn't let him take me hostage. I didn't anticipate Del. He said, 'I just killed Bigfoot—that big red doofus in the lab.' I was so torn up, I fired the gun without even thinking about the ramifications. Imagine if someone bragged to you about killing Grandma, right in front of you, and there you stood with a loaded gun. I ran to Del and told him I was sorry, but when I saw he was gut-shot, I knew it was hopeless. Too many poisons were rushing into his system and we were too far away from a hospital.

You know as well as I do it's an incredibly painful way to die. So, I shot him in the head to put him out of his misery."

Grandpa took off his glasses and pinched the bridge of his nose. "Were you tested for gun residue?"

"No. I had the next two days off, so I stayed out of reach—except for eating a supper with Jon and Serena."

Grandpa looked so disappointed.

"Ask if I used the meth, or if I had any involvement of the production. You have to believe me, Grandpa, I didn't have anything to do with that."

"I believe you didn't have anything to do with the meth production." Grandpa shook his head. "What happened to you? You helped hide a meth lab and used the BCA to do it. You used me. You killed a law enforcement officer, Mia! Did it occur to you that he has a family?"

I was drowning in his disappointment and shame.

Grandpa put his glasses back on, but peered over the top of them at me. His sigh was as heavy as my heart. "Is there anything else I should know?"

"No."

He was still looking at the charts, which remained stable.

I slipped the tabs off my fingers and he helped me remove the blood pressure cuff.

Grandpa carefully put away the polygraph machine as I mopped the sweat off my face with the bottom of my shirt.

His warning was laced with sadness. "Mia, they're coming for you. Jon Frederick has obtained a search warrant for your home. Is there anything there that could implicate you?"

"No." I nervously took an inventory of my house and then it occurred to me. That damn sex tape of Jon and Serena was still in the DVD player. I took it from Del's car that night, because I was thinking I might be able to use it as blackmail if Jon got too close to discovering the truth. I could only hope Jon didn't know it was in Del's car. That DVD put me at the scene of Del's murder.

Grandpa stated, "That answer was too fast. Take your time and think about it. Where's the gun?"

At that time, the gun was in my locker at work. I chewed on my thumbnail, a long-abandoned response to anxiety, and appealed to his sympathy. "Kaiko broke into my home and raped me."

Taken aback, he softened. "After he raped you in Albany?"

"Yeah." I felt the anxious distress of a flashback for a moment, and then nervously focused on Grandpa.

A fiery anger burned in his eyes as he swore, "That son of bitch better hope he never crosses my path." He put his arm around me. "Are you okay?"

I nodded. My lips were tired of lying.

"You should stay with me. We'd love to have you."

"I need to keep my job. It's the only thing I have going right now. If I stop my routine, I'm afraid—" I didn't finish saying, I'd kill myself. I wanted Kaiko to return one more time. I had one last thing to do before I faced the fire.

I returned to the polygraph apparatus. "I think I'm best off not talking about the shooting of Del. I'll just act like I don't know anything about it, until you tell me different."

The battered chair scraped on the marred wooden floor as Grandpa sat close and told me, "It's time for me to be honest with you, Mia. You're my daughter. My DNA implicated you. The DNA test indicated that the woman who slept in Chad's bed had half of my DNA. They knew from the DNA she had Asian ancestry. It wasn't much of a stretch to suggest that I was your father, when my family adopted you . . ."

I stared at him, my mouth hanging open, trying to process this information. Like a lit fuse, my shock slowly sparked and burned its way to its destination: absolute outrage. He was no longer the hero who saved me from my addict mother. Instead, Maurice Strock was a coward father who left me with my addicted, prostitute mother for four years. And it was his fault they were searching my home. "You lied to me for over two decades!" I clasped my hands around the back of my neck and squeezed, as if I was holding my head from rocketing off my shoulders.

He looked down. "I'm sorry, Mia." He added, matter-of-factly, "There wasn't another way."

I thought about Grandma—or Stepmom, or whatever she was now. I loved Grandma. I would have never known that I was the result of Grandpa betraying her. She loved me and attended to me when I was sick. My earliest memories were of gardening with her.

I finally said, "Can I just go home?"

RAILROAD AVENUE, ALBANY

Squad cars were lined up behind Jon's unmarked Taurus in front of my home.

Grandpa, or Dad, I guess, pulled over and suggested, "It's better if you walk the rest of the way, like it's just a normal day. If they see you with me, they'll assume I'm prepping you so you can avoid prosecution."

Instead of saying, "You are," I nodded and stepped out. Before I shut the door, I asked, "How am I going to get my car back?"

"Give me some time to go over it before I return it. They're looking for alfalfa from the field where Del was shot. Do you have the clothes you were wearing that night?"

"They were hauled away with the garbage."

Maurice ran his hand over his thin, white hair. "Okay, good. Any evidence would be contaminated by now. How about the shoes?

"No, they're at the bottom of Lake Koronis. I ditched 'em before I drove home."

Investigators were going through every drawer and tapping the walls in my home to make sure there were no hidden panels. I watched a deputy pull out DVDs, one by one, making sure nothing was behind them. She opened each DVD case, looked inside, and then meticulously placed them back in their exact location.

I asked, "What are you looking for?"

The officer gave me a knowing smile, as if to say I had just confirmed she was on the right track.

Keeping my eye on her, I stepped to the side, so I could see into my open bedroom door.

Jon Frederick was sitting on my bed staring at a letter I had started writing to Grandpa. I remembered the letter. I didn't admit anything in it, so I should be okay. Still, his intense focus on it bothered me. What was he seeing? Finally, he took my scrawled thoughts and placed them into an evidence bag.

"What are you doing? It's just a letter to Grandpa."

His glare pierced through me. "What are you apologizing for?" "It's personal."

Jon sat quiet, waiting for me to fill in the empty space with words. I'd seen him do this too often to fall for it.

He asked, "Where's your car?" "I loaned it to a friend."

"I'll need your friend's name." "Not until I talk to an attorney."

I returned to watching the deputy rifle through my DVDs. She was getting to the end and looked frustrated. She finally finished and, as she stood up, asked me, "Do you have DVDs anywhere else in the house?"

"No."

She leaned into my space and pressed, "Are you sure?"

I pretended to be calm and collected as I said, "It's a small house. There aren't that many places to put things."

She backed off and I felt like I could finally breathe again.

Suddenly, an afterthought brought her back to my entertainment center. She powered on the DVD player.

A lump in my throat was nearly gagging me as I tried to swallow my anxiety.

Sensing my insecurity, she condescendingly glanced back as she hit the eject button. The tray opened.

It was empty. And then I realized the case for And Justice For All was gone, too. I had no idea what happened to that DVD, but for the moment, I was relieved. That perv, Kaiko, must have found it . . .

49

BLACK HOLE EVAPORATION THEORY =
*Quantum effects allow black holes to emit black-body radiation.
The electromagnetic radiation is produced as if emitted by a black
body, with a temperature inversely proportional to the mass of the
black hole. The black hole eventually evaporates.*

*Stephen Hawking Theoretical Physicist University of Cambridge,
1994*

SERENA FREDERICK
8:30 AM, TUESDAY, JUNE 18, 2019 WILSON AVENUE
NORTHEAST, ST. CLOUD

MY TRIP TO Hawaii was happening. My sister, Andi, offered to drive me to the airport, since Jon was now in constant demand in the search for Kaiko. I asked her to drive to a St. Cloud address on our way. When we pulled up in front of the home, we watched a Somali woman following her man down the sidewalk. We then passed a group of Somali women enjoying a conversation as they strolled down the concrete path.

Clay was out front, fixing the frame on his front door. I told Andi, "This won't be long."

Being his usual charming self, Clay invited me in.

I was impressed by his house. The kitchen was done in a soft orange, with seafoam green cabinets and wooden floors. It had a much homier feel than the medieval monstrosity he had built in Edina. "This is nice."

Clay gave me that grin. "I have to give Hani credit. She put colors together I wouldn't have considered, and I've got to admit, it looks good." His smile dissolved then, as he continued, "She once told me I turned our relationship into a black hole—sucked all the joy out of it."

"Do you want some Jon advice?"

"I doubt it. But I kind of owe it to him to listen. He might've saved my life. I honestly don't think I would've, but I'm not sure."

"Jon says the bigger the black hole, the colder, but even black holes eventually disappear."

Distressed, he glanced down. "I blew it. Hani was perfect for me. She even encouraged me to go to church—my church. Mom jacked me up and then I saw you, with heaven's glow lighting you all up—I lost my head for a minute. Hani heard our conversation and is done with me." He curiously glanced back up. "Why didn't you tell Jon what I'd said? I know you didn't. He'd been on me like sticky on ribs over it if you had."

"I wanted to give you the benefit of the doubt. Maybe I misunderstood and you were just venting."

He faced me directly and gave me a smarmy look. "Or maybe you understood and here you are."

The comment made my blood boil, but I remained focused on getting what I needed from him.

He quickly picked up on my consternation and waved me away. "Hey, I have no intention of anything. I've been insulting you for so long, it comes too easy." Clay rubbed his face. "I'm sorry. I always say the wrong thing. Let me make it clear. I want Hani. I miss her already."

"Then you need to let her know it, beyond a doubt. What's going on with you, Clay? You never gave up easily. A couple weeks ago, you were willing to fight her entire family; now you're just giving up."

He helplessly raised his palms. "I'm trying to be respectful." "You're disrespectful of me all the time."

"I'm sorry," Clay repeated. "I wish I could say that isn't true. Hani asked me not to talk to her." Dejected, he glanced across the floor, as if hoping to find something forever lost. Now ready for me to leave, he questioned, "Okay, if you're not here to jump my bones, why are you here?"

"I need a DVD."

"I don't have much for romance, but I've got a great collection of civil war movies and lots of action flicks." With a hint of nervousness, he walked me to his media center and opened up the DVD cabinet.

It didn't take me long to spot . . . And Justice for All. I opened it up to find the homemade DVD inside.

Taken aback by my glare, he asked, "How did you know?"

"Jon told me that Mia seemed surprised we didn't find the DVD in her home. When he mentioned that you had gone out with Mia, I wondered if somehow you'd ended up with it."

"Mia was drunk out of her mind when she offered to put it on. She passed out, so I just took it, assuming you didn't want it out there. Mia probably doesn't even remember telling me about it."

"Did you watch it?"

"Only a couple times."

I fumed. "Ass. Do you realize Jon was looking for this because it would have proved Mia killed Del? It was taken from Del's car that night, at the scene of the murder. Now there may be chain of evidence concerns."

Defensive, Clay said, "How the hell was I supposed to know that you were making porn videos to catch murderers? I was going to give it to Jon, but then, after the comment I made in your kitchen, I wasn't sure what to do with it."

Without saying another word, I let the door close behind me as I returned to Andi. "Let's go."

My sister started the car and asked, "What were you doing here?" I grumbled, "Picking up a homemade porn video."

Aghast, Andi questioned, "When did you start watching porn?"

My older sister was always excessively interested in my life, so I didn't mind making her work for information. "I didn't watch it. I'm in it."

"For God's sake, Serena, you made a porn video with Clay?" "Don't be ridiculous. I made the video with Jon."

"And you gave it to Clay?" She was lost in incredulity.

"No, Clay took it. Believe it or not, it might be used in the prosecution of a murder." Andi studied me in disbelief, then murmured, "Mom and Dad are going to love that." "Please don't say anything about it. It's a long story."

She slowly pulled the car away from the curb. "It's a long drive to the airport . . ."

11:15 AM, TUESDAY, JUNE 18, 2019
MINNEAPOLIS–ST. PAUL INTERNATIONAL AIRPORT, BLOOMINGTON

Getting through customs and to my gate was seamless. My experiences at MSP have been good and, as airports go, it was clean. Although the four-year-old licking the handrail as we went up the escalator was a little disgusting. My window seat helped distract the emptiness I felt from leaving my family. I'd always wanted to visit Hawaii, but never alone. It was hard enough to leave Jon, but leaving Nora and Jackson behind was decidedly worse. They were so dependent on me.

Jon had copied a letter Mia wrote to her grandfather for me. Allowing myself to finally look at it, I retrieved it from my bag:

Dearest Grandpa,

I am so sorry. I naively and blindly followed along, accepting a fantasy that no one would be hurt. You've always told me that allowing others to make decisions for you is still a decision. I have no excuse for behaving so recklessly.

The letter ended. There was no doubt in my mind, now, that Mia wrote Dan Moene's suicide letter. The ALIAS program would prove this. Mia, what have you done?

The flight was ten and a half hours. Jon arranged for me to be picked up at the Kona International Airport by a law enforcement officer who would transport me until I left the island.

8:30 AM, WEDNESDAY, JUNE 19, 2019 HAMANAMANA STREET, KALAOA, HAWAII

The officer drove me to the home of Iokua and Kai Kamaka in Kalaoa. It was a lot of K's, but that was Hawaii. Once the officer searched the home to make certain Kaiko Kane wasn't present, I was invited to enter.

Iokua had stocky, native Hawaiian features, while Kai appeared to have European ancestry. Even though Kai was a popular girl's name in Hawaii, its origin was Dutch, referring to a woman who lived by the sea. Iokua had powerful biceps like Kaiko, but they apparently weren't related. Kaiko's father, from my understanding, was only a sperm donor. I'd learned his mother was a heroin addict and Kaiko was passed around to relatives, until it was determined his mother would never be able to parent him. Kaiko spent years in juvenile placements before finally being taken in by his mother's sister, Kai Kamaka.

As we visited, Kai shared Kaiko's history of trouble in school, and eventual trouble for breaking into homes, before he finally left for California.

Iokua broke his silence. "The boy's no good. No discipline. He wanted to get rich selling weed in California. But now that the government's involved, it isn't as profitable."

Kai looked heartsick. "His mom overdosed in 2018; any restraint he once had vanished with her. His life has been a series of losses."

Iokua interjected, "You need to stop making excuses for that kid. At first, we thought it was just the troubled boys he hung around, but eventually we realized Kaiko was the trouble. His dad's entire family is a bunch of vultures, always scouring the earth for another carcass."

"But you still help him out."

Iokua clarified, "I don't." He gave his wife a weary glance.

Kai was plaintive. "Just to keep him off the streets. Every several months, he'll call and I'll send him a little so he can get a place."

"Where's the last place you sent him money?" Kai looked at her husband and didn't respond.

Finally, Iokua suggested, "Tell her. For God's sake, he's wanted for murder."

Kai said weakly, "He made me promise I'd never tell anyone his mailing address."

"Since he's been on the run," I shared, "we know he raped a young woman who was simply returning home from a night with friends. The investigators believe he will continue to assault women until he's arrested. I've been the victim of assault, myself, and I'd do anything to keep some poor soul from being violated like I was. Please help us."

Iokua grumbled to Kai, "You know how I feel about it." Sensing she was hurting, he tried to soften. "But you're going to do whatever you're going to do."

Kai got up and left the room.

Iokua apologized to me. "I'm sorry. This is how it always ends. Kai cries in shame and Kaiko isn't held accountable."

With tearful eyes, Kai returned with an envelope. She sat holding it in a tight grip. "I'm sorry, but I just can't give it to you. He's not a terrible boy. Situations just get out of hand for him and he never backs down. I was afraid he and Iokua were going to end up killing each other before he left."

I gazed helplessly at the envelope. The problem with not officially being in law enforcement was that I couldn't take that envelope from her. Kaiko charmed his aunt for favors and she mistook that charm for caring.

"He never apologizes for anything," Iokua muttered. "I was just trying to teach him some manners."

Kai shared, "He called a couple years ago and said something really bad happened. Someone was killed, but he didn't have anything to do with it. He was just there. I told him to go to the police, but he said he couldn't. He said the police did it."

This was a bit of a risk, but I didn't want to leave empty handed. I slowly got up and sat by her, putting my arm around her to comfort her.

"He specifically requested I only send money snail mail," Kai said, "so there wouldn't be any trace." She squeezed the envelope. "I'm sorry, but I just can't."

She didn't need to. I could now read the street address on the envelope in her hand: West Fifty-First Street and Washburn, Minneapolis.

Kai shared, "I promised him the money would be there tomorrow, but I haven't sent it. Iokua's right. At some point, I just have to admit I've failed. I didn't have the heart to tell Kaiko I hadn't mailed it."

I requested, "If he calls, please don't tell him that you spoke to me, or that you still haven't mailed the money."

Kai may have been naïve, but she wasn't stupid. Aware I'd read the address, she implored, "Don't kill him. You have to promise you're not going to kill him."

I responded carefully. "I promise the investigators will do everything in their power to avoid killing him."

Iokua broke his silence, uttering, "Pono."

Kai reached over and took his hand, sharing, "Pono is Hawaiian wisdom, referring to the feeling of contentment you have after doing what's right."

50

CALCULUS SQUEEZE THEORY =
*Describes the limit of function as compared to two other functions
that are easily computed. If a line is squeezed between two other
lines, it needs to be headed in the same direction. (In layman's
terms: If two police officers are escorting a wobbling drunk to a cell,
regardless of the path taken, the prisoner will end up in the cell.)*

*Archimedes of Syracuse
Greek Mathematician & Physicist, 242 BC*

MIA STROCK
6:30 PM, WEDNESDAY, JUNE 19, 2019 RAILROAD AVENUE,
ALBANY

WHEN I UNLOCKED my front door, the reek of Kaiko Kane permeated my home. The filthy libertine had eluded law enforcement, but still managed to find his way back to me. I had a feeling he'd be back. He had a good thing going here, why would he leave? I wasn't rushing off to call the police. I was hoping he'd return. Tonight, I was ending it.

I yelled, "Is spaghetti fine?"

Kaiko slithered around the corner. "Make sure there's enough meat in it. I can't stand the orange noodle foster home version." When I attempted to sneak by, he gripped my shoulders tightly, stopping me dead in my tracks. He smirked lasciviously. "We don't need to eat right away."

"I do. If I don't get something in my stomach, you're going to be holding a woman with the dry heaves."

Disgusted, he let me pass.

I washed my hands and got to work making his last supper.

When it was ready, Kaiko seated himself at the table, waiting like a king for me to deliver his plate.

The pasta was perfect al dente; the sauce was the best I could do with a jar I bought on sale, a pound of hamburger out of my freezer, and my spice options.

Kaiko skeptically looked over his plate and said, "I want to see you eat a forkful first."

I wrapped savory strands of noodles and sauce from his plate around my fork and took a large bite. "Mmm. I did good." If he thought I wouldn't kill myself to end his reign over me, he was a damned fool.

Relieved, he picked up his fork and began shoveling and slurping down the noodles. I had considered it, but I was afraid that, somehow, Kaiko would survive poisoning.

I watched him enjoying his meal as I loaded pans in the dishwasher. I bent down and felt under the dishwasher. There was my gun. After they had completed the extensive search of my home, I felt safe to bring it back home. I needed it. Kitchen work was beneath Kaiko, so he'd never find it here. I nervously wrapped my fingers around the pistol grip. I'd need to act quickly, with no self-doubt. Fire until it was empty. I'd save one. With a quick swoop, I pulled the gun free and began firing.

Instead of running, Kaiko walked directly toward me.

Click! Click! Click! I didn't need to fire a shot to know I was in trouble. The gun was too light. The bullets had been removed.

Kaiko's hand shot out and his fingers were around my throat, squeezing. He faced my dread with a smile. "You're mine. We're going to have a special night tonight. You've earned it . . ."

51

GERM THEORY =
*Secretions by a host organism (a person, for example)
can be contaminated by harmful microorganisms not visible
to the human eye.*

*Ibn Sina Persian Polymath & Physician, 1025
(Full name: Abu Ali al-Husayn, known as Avicenna in Latin and
the West) One of the great sages of Islamic medicine*

JON FREDERICK
8:48 PM, WEDNESDAY, JUNE 19, 2019
51ST STREET AND WASHBURN, FULTON AREA OF
MINNEAPOLIS

SERENA'S WORK IN Hawaii could bring an end to Kaiko's run and I was appreciative. I shared her information with my boss and Sean told me they'd have undercover surveillance in place by the mailboxes first thing in the morning, ensuring the trap would be set long before the mail arrived.

With Kaiko's ability to elude police, I thought I'd pay my family's former neighbor, Agnes Schraut, a visit. Agnes always had an eye on the goings-on in the neighborhood, like the Hunchback of Notre Dame, watching the world from her bell tower. Vic and I used to call her Quasimodo. Today, I had no doubt she could give us an extra set of eyes in the area.

Agnes was small but fiery; as a child, she scared the hell out of me—maybe she still did, a little. My dad used to shovel her sidewalk and mow her lawn, and it became my job when I was old enough. The rates never went up, as I got the same two dollars my dad received decades earlier. Money was never the issue. Her ratchety voice and surly demeanor effused the misery of being tangled in a barbed-wire fence to those unfortunate enough to be conversing with her. Fortunately, her flaming nature seemed to sanitize others from her, as it wasn't contagious. People walked away thinking, I don't want to be her.

Agnes answered the door of her small home and spat out, as if it was all one word, "Whatdoyouwant?"

Trying to be as polite as possible, I began, "I don't know if you remember me, but I'm Jon Frederick from Pierz. I used to shovel—"

She cut me off. "Is this going to be long? I don't have a lot of time left on this earth." "I'm asking for your help—"

Agnes interrupted again, "Thank me for paying your way through college."

I don't know that fifty-four dollars covered much of my college. Before I could say thank you, she was talking again.

"Does this have something to do with your retarded friend?"

Taken aback, I corrected her, "My brother, Vic, is mentally ill. He is an intelligent, caring man."

Dismissively waving her hand, she chided, "I know who Vic is. He's the only one in your family with any sense. I meant that Roberts boy."

I had to laugh at her insult to Clay. I guess if you define retardation as difficulty learning from experience, he would fit the definition. "No, this is about the rape that occurred in this neighborhood on the night of the Noor shooting."

"Can't help you. Finally, some excitement around here, and I spent the night in the hospital because I fell and thumped my noggin. If I have to bend down to pick anything up, I fall to the floor. How's that for a kick in the posterior? Then I can't get up, so I have to hit my medical alert bracelet and they send over this willowy Somali chick to come and peel me off the floor."

"Have you considered assisted living?"

"I don't qualify for anything," she scoffed. "If I just had someone to help me dress and bathe, I could stay living here." She stopped herself. "Are you interested? Pay's still the same."

I politely declined, "No, my work keeps me plenty busy."

"Jon-boy," she cackled as she belittled me, "you have no sense of humor. I am still a modest woman—even though I'm at that age where I don't have much to be modest about."

A teenaged Somali girl, donning a sorrel hijab and abaya, joined Agnes at the door. She nodded politely toward me, then addressed Agnes, placing a hand gently on the aged woman's rounded back. "Your bed is made and your clothes are put away. Is there anything else I can help you with?"

Agnes dismissed her, "Get back to school." I interrupted, "I'm Jon Frederick."

She softly shared, "I'm Nala." "How often are you here?"

Nala looked to Agnes for a nod of approval before responding, "Twenty hours a week, but it's not enough for Miz Schraut. Double that would be about right."

Agnes interjected in tones laced with her characteristic disapproval, "Her parents let her drop out of school to work here."

Humbled, Nala shared, "Not your worry. It beats being homeless in a Minnesota winter."

I took out a picture of Kaiko Kane and showed it to them. "Have either of you ever seen this man in the neighborhood?"

Nala shook her head. "No, I haven't." She shocked me by gently hugging Agnes and stating, "I need to get home. I can't be here tomorrow, but I'll be back in two days."

Agnes watched her leave, her expression showing a flash of softness before screwing back into her churlish demeanor. She complimented Nala in a manner that sounded like criticism. "That girl's a saint."

"Wali."

She scoffed, "Wally the beer man?" "No, "Wali is the Muslim word for saint."

"Are you crazy in the head? Always had those ramblings that nobody gives a damn about." Agnes carped, "She should be in school." She adjusted her glasses and reviewed the picture one more time. "That is a plug ugly mug." "Plug ugly" refers to the villainously unattractive, and is based on a Baltimore gang from the 1800s called the Plug Uglies.

She handed me the picture. "Okay. Don't let the door hit-cha where the lord splitcha." Agnes gripped the edge of her door and started closing it.

"He has Dutch ancestry, with some Pacific Islander features mixed in."

"So in other words, a mutt?" Agnes studied me for a moment and said, "Say, you're the guy who knocked up that Bell girl and left her with a couple of little bastards."

"No child is a bastard, but some adults are." She started, "I meant—"

I interjected, "I know what you meant. Serena and I are now married." "It's a little too late now," she groused.

"It's just too late for you. My family is doing fine." I wasn't sure how she was going to react. I wouldn't tolerate her insulting my children.

Agnes smiled slightly as she admonished me, "You don't have to be mean about it."

Trying to regain a kind composure, I offered, "Did I mention there's a ten thousand–dollar reward for information that leads to this guy's arrest?"

Agnes snatched the picture back from me in fingers aged and wrinkled to the point they resembled the feet of a frail bird. "Well, come in then, and have a seat."

I felt badly for Agnes, even if much of her misery was self-induced. Being alone can harden a person—even an already hard person.

Agnes took two of my cards. She placed one on her end table in the living room, where she sat watching TV by the light of a flowing river on a vintage Hamm's beer sign. The second was tucked away in a secret compartment in her pristine, classic Chanel quilted clutch. Agnes had an elevated chair that gave her full view of the street. She requested binoculars to use on her little perch, so I gave her my day- and night-vision goggles for the time being. I could trust Agnes. She was mean, but clearly took obsessively good care of her items. If she didn't give me anything in the next three days, I'd retrieve them.

Before I was out of her driveway, she called, "Do I still get the reward if I find him and one of your trigger-happy cops kills lizard-lips?"

"Yes."

52

DRIVE THEORY =
*Sadism is not restorative in intent. Dynamically, it entails the direct
expression of id-derived aggression.
Behaviorally, it is aggression for its own sake.*

Léopold Szondi
*Hungarian Psychiatrist, 1948 (Léopold Szondi was bought out
of the Bergen-Belsen concentration camp after 1,700 American
intellectuals paid a large ransom to Adolf Eichmann in 1944.)*

MIA STROCK
8:50 PM, WEDNESDAY, JUNE 19, 2019 RAILROAD
AVENUE, ALBANY

I WAS LYING IN my bed hoping my hell had momentarily
ended. After a dog-style pounding, I could finally drop my
pelvis to the bed and stretch out my legs. I peeled my face off
the mattress, where it had been pressed hard by Kaiko for the
last twenty minutes. It was all I could do to turn my head and
occasionally suck in a breath. My mind swirled, and I felt like
I was viewing the world from inside a plastic bubble, but the
oxys I'd taken were needed for my pain and to dissociate from
the assaults. A year ago, I was a promising forensics student
with a bright future. I used to think women who stayed in

abusive relationships were so pathetic. Now, I was far below them; they, at least, had some good days.

The blur of the human monster—the palena—was standing over the bed, still bare-chested, looking down on me. "What are you thinking?"

He pulled on his jeans and plunked down on the edge of the bed, stuffing his feet into his work boots. Through the fog in my brain, it registered I was looking at the boots—the super expensive, one-of-a-kind, but ordinary-looking stolen boots. Passing Kaiko on the street probably wouldn't cause anyone outright alarm, as he looked pretty ordinary, too. The true substance was under the outer layer.

"Why do you have to be so mean?"

"Everybody's mean," he sneered. "I killed a couple losers. You killed a cop. Leda Hartford's a whore. The county investigator was a drunk. The BCA investigator's got a hot wife and he's still sleeping with a hooker. The list goes on and on."

I was about to explain Jon was actually with this wife, but stopped when I realized he'd be furious for misinforming him. Pain radiated from my core; I didn't need any extra punishment. "What happens to me when these oxys wear off?"

Kaiko dismissed my concerns with hardened resolve. "You were going to kill me. What the hell did you expect?"

My vision was finally coming into focus. I tiredly looked up and said, "I could understand if you killed me, but to do this over and over . . ." I pulled my t-shirt off the floor and, after a brief glance at the bruises on my breasts, pulled it over my head.

Did something just bump against the house?

Kaiko heard it, too. He pulled the curtain away from the window and, satisfied we were alone, let it fall back. The corner toward me didn't close completely, so I still had a narrow view into my dark yard.

He ranted, "My mom never had consequences. I went from one dirtball relative to another—and they all hated me—while Mom just kept partying. So, I provide consequences to women who get wasted. Isn't it what they deserve?"

He was nuts. There's wasn't any point in arguing with him. "Why did you rape me the first time?"

He flexed his biceps, apparently thinking this was impressive. "You know why: because you deserved it." Kaiko leaned down. "Are we done fighting? I'll stop trying to kill you if you stop trying to kill me."

Feeling nauseated, I promised, "I'm done." Drained, I turned my head to the side. And then I saw the white hair. My grandfather was outside trying to get my attention. I didn't dare look at him—Kaiko would kill him. Grandpa Maurice's years of administrative work added no muscle to his thin frame. I spoke to Kaiko, so Grandpa would realize there was someone else in the room. "I may have given them Raven, but—" I cut myself off before adding, It was you they followed to the lab.

Kaiko knew exactly what I was about to say and was on the verge of exploding. I was back on eggshells. How do I dial this down? "Can I make you something to eat?" I heard Grandpa turning his key in the back door, so I sat up and raised my voice, "I think I have some ham in the freezer. I could make mashed potatoes with it."

But Kaiko heard exactly what I had, and bolted toward the back of my house. I quickly jerked my body out of bed to stop him, but fell painfully to the floor. The combination of the oxys and the brutal assault I'd experienced made walking damn near impossible. I yelled in desperation, "He's coming!"

Through the open bedroom door, I watched Kaiko slam the door on Grandpa as he entered, and Maurice's gun fell to the floor. Kaiko reached to the leather sheath on his belt for his knife, but Grandpa gripped Kaiko's wrist tightly before he could pull it out. They tumbled to the floor and Kaiko managed to roll on top of Grandpa. Grandpa was now lying on top of his gun, so he couldn't get to it.

I stumbled into the kitchen and jumped on Kaiko's back, covering his eyes with my hands, digging what was left of my bitten nails into his skin. It worked—for a second—until he elbowed me in the face.

Dazed, I dropped in a useless heap on the floor.

Grandpa angrily punched at Kaiko, which meant Kaiko's wrist was now free.

Kaiko unsheathed the blade and, with no hesitation, thrust it hard into Grandpa's ribs.

Grandpa gasped for breath, while Kaiko pulled the knife out and drew his arm back to slice into Grandpa again.

I screamed, now crawling toward them on all fours, "No! I'll go with you. Just stop. No more. Please, I beg you. I'll do anything you want, any time."

Kaiko's adrenaline was pumping and his eyes were vicious. He stood up and kicked Grandpa hard in the head, knocking him out cold. His eyes then fixed on me. "Get your ass dressed. We're leaving. If you're not ready in three minutes, I'm cutting his throat."

I retreated to the bedroom as quickly as I could to find my jeans. The phone Kaiko had taken from me was sitting on my dresser. I palmed it on my way by and dialed 911, then quickly slid it under the bed.

Kaiko entered the bedroom in time to catch me pulling my jeans up. "Any time, any place,
right?"

I nodded, fumbling to pull up my zipper and button my pants. Fear was quaking in violent tremors through my body now, making it difficult to function.

Kaiko asked, "Where's your phone?"

Afraid to make eye contact, I shrugged and focused on buttoning up the plaid shirt I threw over my t-shirt. "You took it."

He briefly glanced over the room and then gave up.

"We're going to hit a spot for old time's sake and then we're leaving Minnesota for good.

Out of state, out of mind."

I steadied my knocking knees and slipped my trembling feet into my Danskos, grateful for slip-ons. Kaiko grabbed me by the arm and forcefully dragged me toward the door. As we passed him, I looked longingly at Grandpa's still form on the floor, his lifeblood spilling onto the stupid rug I just had to have with meth money. Like me, it was now trashed. I could hear sirens headed toward my house as we drove away. God, please let Grandpa be okay . . .

53

BIG BANG THEORY =
The universe was created in a single moment from quark-guon
plasma as it cooled below two trillion degrees, creating a process
known as Big Bang nucleosynthesis. "It all started with a Big Bang."

Georges Lemaître
Belgian Catholic Priest, 1931

JON FREDERICK
10:23 PM, WEDNESDAY, JUNE 19, 2019
51ST STREET AND WASHBURN, FULTON AREA OF
MINNEAPOLIS

I WAS CRUISING I-94 east on my way to pick Serena up
at the airport when my phone buzzed. Sean announced,
"Maurice Strock was just discovered in bad shape at Mia's
house in Albany. He was stabbed and left for dead. The 911
call was made from Mia's phone, which was hidden under the
bed. Mia isn't around."

"Is her car there?" "No."

I pulled over and gathered my thoughts. "Okay, let's get
one of our ALPR cars cruising the Xerxes and Washburn area.
Maybe put a couple on I-94, north of Xerxes." An ALPR was an
Automated License Plate Reader. The high-speed cameras were
mounted on the front of some of our squad cars and the cameras
fed the data into a computer, where it was quickly processed. The

program had the potential to enable us to pinpoint the location of a car in seconds. I added, "Eventually, Kaiko's going to find his way to his mailbox on Washburn."

Serena's parents were watching our kids. Serena was in flight, so I couldn't explain my dilemma to her. I called her sister, Andi, and asked her to pick up Serena at the airport, so I could focus on bringing Kaiko in.

My phone buzzed again, and for the fourth time tonight, I could see on the caller ID it was Agnes. She may have proved to be more work than benefit. I hesitated before picking up, preparing myself to be polite, then reluctantly answered, "Hello, this is Jon."

"I've got your mongrel in the crosshairs of these specs. You know, I saw this deadpan dick in the neighborhood a couple years ago. He was a little fatter, then. He's arm-in-arm with some languid Wuhan wench. He's checking the bank of mailboxes." Pause. "Nothing. Now he's dragging the tart back to the alley."

I activated the lights on my unmarked car and sped toward Washburn Avenue. "Is the woman walking by her own will?"

"Sort of. She's a walking zombie. Probably got her out of one of those opiate huts. They're all named after silverware falling on the floor—ching, chang—"

I cut her off and called Sean back. I told him I was headed to the Fulton area of Minneapolis, and he promised to send backup.

I jerked to a stop at the corner of Washburn Avenue and Fifty-First Street. The first Minneapolis police officer to arrive was Bree Tosto. She pulled in behind my car and hopped out before her engine fully quieted. I directed, "Follow me," and we jogged toward the alley.

Bree confirmed, "You know where we are, don't you?" "Yes, I do."

"Is he obsessed with the Noor case?"

"I think Kaiko is the missing piece from the Noor case. He is the rapist who set that catastrophe in motion. I think he feels that nothing bad can happen to him here."

Bree unholstered her gun and gave it a brief check. "I suppose. He rapes a woman and then a police officer pulls up and shoots the only witness. He had to feel like it was time to buy a lottery ticket."

The dark alley was only about fifteen feet wide, with garages butted up to the edge of the road, making the scene claustrophobic. The only illumination came from a streetlamp on the opposite end, forcing us to walk a dark gauntlet.

Bree tapped my shoulder as we quietly crept into the alley. "You know, this is a nightmare. If either of us shoots anybody, we're the next ones down the road to prison. The people who determine our fate would love to send a white cop down the river, just to show they're open- minded, non-racist people."

"I know. Backup's on the way, but we can't afford to wait." I shushed her and, with stealth- like silence, rushed forward through the back street. We were almost on top of the assault before we were aware of it.

Bree flashed her light to illuminate a macabre scene with Mia, lying motionless on the pavement. With knife in hand, Kaiko tore open her shirt, launching buttons crazily in all directions. No one was rushing out to dial 911 on Mia's behalf tonight. Kaiko was hunched over her, working on unfastening her jeans.

I aimed my gun at Kaiko's head. "It's over. Drop the knife and get off of her."

He yanked a limp Mia to her feet and pressed the point of a knife against her throat, then slowly swiveled his head toward us.

Bree warned urgently, "Frederick! Do not shoot this man!"

Kaiko taunted Bree, "Jon Frederick's going to kill me. Shoot him! You've got a chance to save me—shoot him!"

He pressed Mia's head against his, keeping his head behind hers for protection, as he instructed, "If the two of you don't back off, I'm fucking slitting her throat. Back off!" Kaiko pulled her torso tight against his.

Mia was swaying and barely conscious; she was likely in shock.

Beads of sweat formed on my forehead. If I lowered my gun, he was going to cut her throat. His only escape was to force us both to try saving Mia. This was going to be over in seconds; Kaiko wasn't patient. The problem was handguns weren't that precise. Even shooting someone in the leg could be lethal if you hit their femoral artery. I crept to his right side, while Kaiko's gaze carefully followed me.

"What the fuck are you doing?" He pushed the knife a little deeper into Mia's throat to warn me.

Bree yelled again, "Don't shoot him!"

I saw Bree raising her hand toward her chest, so I directed her, "Keep that camera on!" The knife slid deeper into Mia's throat; blood was now leaking rivulets down her neck.

I fired a shot into Kaiko's leg and his knife-wielding hand pulled straight down, instinctively, to the wound. I rushed in and grabbed his wrist, pinning it to his back.

Bree brought his other hand to me and we cuffed his wrists together. An ambulance crew hurried in.

I yelled, "We need to wrap his leg."

A medic stepped in and I moved aside. Others tended to Mia.

The alley was soon flooded with officers and the darkness was now swirling with red and blue flashing lights. Mia and

Kaiko were loaded in ambulances and destined for separate hospitals.

Bree looked at me with relief, and whispered, "That was intense." She looked down the street, taking in the ghastly lightshow, and softly said, "I wasn't going to shut my camera off, by the way. The EMTs were coming down the alley to check out the scenario, and I was waving them back."

"Thank you, Bree." We both had adrenaline racing through our systems. Neither of us knew how to celebrate having a living victim and getting out of the volatile situation alive, so we smiled and awkwardly nodded. I said, "He was going to cut her throat. This man would kill anybody if it would benefit him. He eluded us in St. Cloud by throwing his victim into the river."

With her hand, Bree wiped sweat off her brow. She shared, "In the last couple months we've had officers who were fired for racist behavior reinstated by the union. People are angry. Every night, the tension out here gets heavier."

Bree and I were soon ordered to step aside and became silent observers of the crime scene techs. As a result of shooting Kaiko, I wouldn't be allowed to help with anything at the scene. The shooting would have to be justified before they'd even allow me to return to work.

After thirty minutes, an officer approached us. "Kaiko Kane is dead. He died on the way to the hospital."

I felt sick.

Bree kindly placed her hand on my shoulder to comfort me.

A second officer interjected, "I don't know that the initial report was accurate. Right now, we don't know."

54

QUANTUM THEORY =
*In the quantum world, a particle can be in two states at once,
because each particle is existing as a probability. Schrödinger
postulated that, if a cat was in a box with radiation that could kill
it, the cat is both alive and dead until the box is opened, and its
state is known.*

Erwin Schrödinger
Austrian Physicist, 1935

JON FREDERICK
9:30 PM THURSDAY, JUNE 20, 2019
BUREAU OF CRIMINAL APPREHENSION OFFICE
1430 MARYLAND AVENUE EAST, ST. PAUL

M Y MORNING WAS spent being grilled by Sean Reynolds, who was flanked by a group of hostile administrative staff, in the board room. My operating theory was to be honest and let the truth prevail. Looking back, I should've brought an attorney. The gist of the meeting was that I mishandled the situation in Hawick, and then I shot a minority while a cop was begging me not to. Kaiko wasn't dead, as far as I knew, but his health was in a precarious state. My shooting of Kaiko forced Sean to either support my decision or wash his hands of me. The first scenario had cost Maurice his job, so Sean was opting for the latter. I agreed that this investigation should have been handled better. But I didn't feel it should all fall on me. I was stuck between Maurice, who was obstructing the investigation, and Sean, who refused to allow us to surveil Mia—out of malice for Maurice. I was ultimately suspended, with pay, until the matter could be fully investigated.

I finally finished all of the paperwork necessary to close out my work and be out of the office for the duration of my suspension. I had a lot to think about. Fortunately, with paid leave, I could enjoy some time with my family before I needed to job hunt. I got the sense from Sean that my suspension wouldn't be ending soon.

Jada Anderson had asked to speak to me before I left for home. With the media frenzy this shooting had created, I couldn't afford to have our conversation occur any place where people could overhear it, so she met me at my car. Jada was holding her suit jacket partially over her head, to protect her from the showers, as she ran to my car. She folded it on her lap as she sat in the passenger seat. Her hair, which she usually wore in a braid or ponytail, was unrestrained and wildly frayed out.

I asked, "Tough day?"

She blotted her face with a sleeve and gave me a knowing smile. "Not as bad as yours. I shouldn't even be here. Sean would have an apoplectic seizure if he knew I was talking to you. They're locked in on making an example out of you for a number of reasons, the least of which is," she hesitated, "Sean thinks I spend too much time talking to you."

"Why do I need shielding? Kaiko would have killed Mia."

"Kaiko apparently has some slimy relatives who are anticipating a large payout. They have a big-money attorney who's threatening to start a race war if the BCA doesn't pay out. Sean wants to avoid race riots and he's getting a lot of pressure to have formal charges brought against you. They're saying you shot Kaiko in retaliation for his attack on Maurice and for Del's murder. You've lit the fuse on a powder keg, and I'm afraid innocent people are going to get hurt."

I watched raindrops spit cooly on the windshield, my heart heavy.

Jada continued, "Sean isn't completely off base here. Minneapolis is ripe for riots. The MPD has a dozen recent racial complaints they haven't even investigated."

I shared, "Between you and I, they've also received thousands of dollars of funding from the legislature for training in addressing racial issues better, and they haven't used any of it. I told a supervisor, if you have an incident, and people get wind of the fact that you've been warned and you didn't do a damn thing, people are going to lose it."

"What was his response?"

"We're too busy. We don't have time for training."

Jada sighed. "Well, you just created an incident, and we need to stomp out the fuse."

I didn't have an answer. Too many people's rights had been violated for too long. I didn't intend to stir this all up, but a vortex was forming.

Jada pondered, "Penny for your thoughts."

"Everyone who has ever lived has looked at these stars. Do you remember the Lillie Belle Allen case?"

"No. Should I?"

"Lillie Belle, like you, was an attractive African American woman who died on a night like tonight. A couple decades before we were born, a nicely dressed twenty-seven-year-old went to the grocery store with her parents in York, Pennsylvania. Lillie wasn't from the area, so she asked a police officer for directions and was mistakenly sent into a white neighborhood, where armed white gangs were walking the streets. She tried to turning her car around to leave, but her car stalled. When someone fired a shot at the car, she tried protecting her parents. She courageously got out, begging people not to shoot, and was shot dead. Over one hundred shots were fired into her car."

After a moment of silence for Lille Belle, I explained, "Lillie was killed in retaliation after a young black man shot a white police officer, Henry Schaad. Henry was newly married, simply riding in the back of vehicle cruising down the street. Henry was shot in retaliation after a black seventeen-year-old, Taka Sweeney, was shot in the back, walking down the railroad tracks in a white neighborhood. And Taka was shot in retaliation after a black child, who burned himself playing with lighter fluid, accused a white gang of burning him. This was later discovered to be a lie, made up by a boy trying to avoid discipline from his parents."

Jada stiffened. "That's the morbid scenario I'm trying to avoid. If you've ever read about the Red Summer of 1919, and the cruelty toward African Americans in the ensuing years, you'd understand why the boy's story was believable." Downcast, she asked, "How did the Belle situation end?"

"They managed to end the escalation by giving the white man who shot Lillie Belle, and the black man who shot the officer, the exact same sentences. It helped that people on both sides expressed remorse for the other, rather than making excuses for hate."

Jada's doe-like eyes met mine as she somberly said, "This could blow up on us."

The drizzle had now become a downpour, and paintball-sized tears pelted the windshield. I wasn't embarrassed to pray in front of Jada. She'd heard me pray before. I closed my eyes and launched a prayer into the night sky. "I'm sorry, Lillie Bell, that you had to suffer for all this senseless hate. You were just trying to be the voice of reason. Please help us find that voice."

"Amen." Jada asked sincerely, "What do you think about when people talk about white privilege?"

I carefully considered my answer before responding. "I get it. It's been unfair for a long time. And minorities have been targeted by the police. But it oversimplifies the problem. Most poor people in the US are white. My family worked day and night, but we lost our farm and everything we owned. The last few years on the farm, we'd look at the futures for our livestock and crops, and it was like we were getting robbed. My ancestors never owned slaves. They worked labor jobs, side by side with people of every nationality. When I graduated from high school, I had eighteen years dedicated to farming, knowing I could never be any more than farm labor—there was no way I'd ever have the capital to buy a farm. Many minorities have it bad and they need opportunities to be fair. But many white people have it bad, too, and need the opportunities to be equally fair. It bothers me that we have so many new billionaires while so many people, of all races, are stuck in poverty. Fighting among races takes us farther from solutions. It's not black people holding me down, and it's not white people like me holding you down. It's people with money, protecting their own."

While Jada quietly reflected on my thoughts, I added, "There is a reference from the Bible on Lillie Belle Allen's tombstone: 'Greater love has no one than this. That someone lay down her life for her friends.' I appreciate your help, Jada, but I want you to seriously mull this over. I don't want you to die for me."

Jada grasped my hand briefly. "Then we both need to be careful and work together."

55

MALICE AFORETHOUGHT THEORY =
Ironically, "malice aforethought" is a legal term suggesting that neither "malice" nor "aforethought" apply. Malice aforethought refers to a crime committed for no purpose other than to satisfy a grudge. The crime can be perpetrated without the slightest sense of ill will. For example, a man kills a woman to keep hidden a rumor that would disgrace him, without hatred for the intended target.

Rollin Perkins
Professor of Law University of Iowa, 1934

MIA STROCK
2:30 PM, FRIDAY, JUNE 21, 2019 UNIVERSITY OF
MINNESOTA MEDICAL CENTER
500 HARVARD STREET SOUTHEAST, MINNEAPOLIS

I WAS A COMPLETE mess. My head swirled with distressing drama and flashbacks. But Kaiko was damn near dead and that gave me hope. Overnight, a protest fueled by attorneys for his family emerged. It was amazing how many greedy relatives came out of the woodwork in a criminal's family when they believed a twenty million–dollar payout was possible. They were suggesting Jon was just another white cop who set out to shoot a minority. The Noor payout had painted law enforcement into a corner. I agreed to see Jada Anderson to give her my story. Jon saved my life. Ironically, I was the one person who might save his job.

Jada sat with her back to my hospital room door. She updated me, "Sean is initiating an investigation to determine if Jon's shooting of Kaiko Kane was justified. Jon thinks if he's honest, that will simply be enough, but it's getting so twisted, it will be hard for him to get justice. A statement from you, on his behalf, could help take some of the heat off. We've got people in power who think you can appease all of our past injustices by hanging a white law enforcement officer. I, like the vast majority of Americans, simply want justice, every time, regardless of race. No more cover-ups—honesty and justice."

I knew what she was saying was important, but I was distracted with regret for not having killed Kaiko myself. I was stuck in the moment of Grandpa's stabbing, replaying over and over what I should have done differently. My thoughts spewed from my mouth. "Why did I jump on Kaiko's back? I was in the kitchen. I should have grabbed a knife and ended him, right there."

Jada kindly reminded me, "You need to cut yourself some slack, girl. You had just been brutally raped and were under the influence of opioids. It had to hurt like hell just to move."

"I think I was afraid that, no matter what I did, Kaiko would win." I wasn't about to give myself a break. "If I would have ended it, Jon wouldn't be in this mess."

"Are you willing to make a statement in support of him?"

I nodded. "Of course I am. My statement should mean something. I have nothing to gain by supporting Jon. He was trying to get me charged with a crime. And Kaiko's not a minority, by the way. He has three white grandparents and one Hawaiian grandparent."

"Please don't make that argument," Jada interrupted. "Doing so would still imply race is a justifiable reason to shoot someone. Did you hear they found the gun that killed Del Walker in your car? Kaiko Kane's prints were on the gun."

That should've been good news, but all I could muster was, "I hadn't heard that." Had he smudged mine when he emptied my gun? My DNA would be on the barrel of the gun. I'd had it in my mouth. But, I guess with Kaiko's prints on the trigger, I'd still be okay.

A cameraman had set up on the window side of my bed, so he could get Jada in full view and both of us in shots when I was speaking. Jada had offered to have my hair and makeup fixed, but I declined. I felt so ugly inside, I didn't deserve any efforts to appear otherwise.

The camera began rolling and I started, "Kaiko Kane bragged of committing the most popular unsolved rape in the history of Minnesota. I had no idea it was the alley rape on Xerxes, until he brought me there and told me, 'I'm going to do you right here for old time's sake. This is one place where I can commit another rape and there is no way in hell anyone is stepping out to call the police. Your grandpa's buddies can find you right here.'" After I said it out loud, I realized he had planned to leave me for dead.

My hospital room door creaked open and, of all people, Sawyer Koep stood in the doorway. I had seen that arrogant prick on TV and wasn't surprised he was working with Kaiko's defense team. It was the perfect place for a hater.

Sawyer could just see the top of Jada's head over the back of her chair. He offered, "I'll catch you another time when you're not busy." He hadn't picked up on the cameraman beyond the foot of my bed, and he must have assumed the woman in the chair was just a friend. Sawyer jibed, "See ya, Blackface!"

For a moment, I was ashamed I'd have to take another trip down memory lane, with another African American, when I saw the force with which Jada rose from her chair.

The power Jada Anderson wielded as she turned toward Sawyer even scared me. "What did you just say?"

As recognition registered, Sawyer's smug expression dissolved into panic. He sputtered, "I—I wasn't talking to you."

Jada advanced toward him. "Were you talking to my cameraman? There are three people in this room, other than you, and two of them are African American."

"Believe me," Sawyer tried again, "I wouldn't have said it if I'd seen the camera—"

Jada cut him off. "You get your boss here immediately to apologize, or I'm leading with this clip on the news tonight." She turned to the cameraman, "Did you get it?"

"I sure did." He flashed an accomplished smile. "I never stopped recording. You're sitting in the chair, and this guy from Kleinfeld and Pritchard Attorneys walks in the room, in full view, calling you 'Blackface.'"

Sawyer whined, "Please, it was just a joke."

Jada smiled without mirth. "Then we can run it as a 'just for laughs' feature on the news. I'm sure it will be a big hit with all those working-class folks Bobby Kleinfeld stirred up to protest
. . ."

Within forty-five minutes, the stoic attorney Robert Kleinfeld was peering over his reading glasses in my hospital room, watching the recording of Sawyer standing in my doorway, sarcastically spouting, "See ya, Blackface," while both Jada and Sawyer were in full view facing the camera. The very same Sawyer Koep who was filmed standing at Kleinfeld's side, just hours earlier, as Kleinfeld spoke of the injustice wielded on Kaiko Kane.

Having no desire to exchange words with an attorney, I closed my eyes and pretended to be asleep.

Disgusted, Robert asked Jada, "What do you want?"

"I want you to look at the video from Officer Bree Tosto's body camera and read Jon Frederick's statement. Once you've done this, I want you to honestly state, in public," she emphasized, "that the shooting was justified."

Robert chuckled with arrogance. "It's malice aforethought. Sawyer was stupid, but there was no malice intended."

Jada declared, "We'll let our viewers be the judge of that." "What do you want?" he asked again.

"Hmmm . . ." I could tell by Jada's purr that she knew she had him over a barrel. "Justice, Robert. I want to see justice served, regardless of race or religion. Shouldn't we all want that?"

"This isn't about justice," he crowed sarcastically. "It's not even about guilt or innocence. It's about what you can prove. I've read the transcript—you've got a cop begging Jon not to shoot Kaiko Kane, and that means a colossal payout. She even warned Jon he could go to prison, and he shot Kaiko anyway. I'm ending Jon Frederick's career and providing Kaiko a proper defense."

Jada pointed out, "Well, I have proof that your paralegal is a racist prick. You can ruin the career of a good man to protect a cold-blooded killer; I can ruin your firm to protect a good man."

"I'm Kaiko Kane's defense attorney. I'm launching a defense."

Jada wasn't about to back down. "Well, I'm launching a defense, too. Yours is based on lies. Mine is based on truth. If I run this video on the news, your law firm will be . . . let's see . . . what's the word for it? Oh yes, blacklisted. Or would you prefer the term blackballed? If you haven't made a public statement in support of Jon Frederick within one week, I'm running this recording on the news."

56

LAW OF INERTIA =
An object in motion will remain in motion, unless it is acted on by an unbalanced force.

Isaac Newton
Physicist, Theologian, & Mathematician, 1705

JON FREDERICK
3:10 PM, SUNDAY, JUNE 23, 2019 MINNEAPOLIS 4TH
PRECINCT
1925 PLYMOUTH AVENUE NORTH

SERENA AND I sat at the kitchen table sharing an exchange of trepidation, which tasted a lot like tripe: chewy, rubbery dirt. I sent Nora and Jackson off with my parents to alleviate any distractions.

I handed Serena back our video in its And Justice for All case. "I'll let you destroy it." She
sighed. "You can't use it to prosecute Mia?"

"No. I could turn it over to the BCA, half a dozen people would view it, and then they'd tell me that, due to chain of evidence issues, we can't use it. We needed to find it in Mia's possession. Now, she can claim she never had it."

Serena snapped the DVD in half. "The fanatics on both sides are making me crazy. We've got people claiming you're a ruthless killer and others gift-wrapping ammo and placing it in our mailbox with notes that say, 'Keep up the good work.'"

"Holding up my shooting of Kaiko like a talisman does not help me. Jada suggested I speak to the crowd protesting the shooting in Minneapolis."

Serena scowled. "When did you start going to Jada before me?"

"I didn't. She called me with some inside information. They're not only going after my job, they may also send me to prison."

"That's crazy. You didn't do anything wrong."

"Sean said one of the Kane family attorneys accused me of shooting Kaiko because I was jealous of him dancing with you at the Red Carpet."

"That's not true—that never happened."

"Truth doesn't seem to be the priority. It's all about public perception and the Kane family is winning the propaganda war." I paused for a moment. "I shot a man, while an officer was begging me not to, and he may not survive."

"He had a heart attack."

"I know. But if it's determined I shot him criminally, and he dies of a heart attack as a result of being shot, I can still be charged with murder. Administration wants to avoid riots and come across as willing to punish a white cop. My shooting Kaiko has become about their lack of justice in the past."

"Punishing you doesn't fix that. Wouldn't it make more sense to improve police relations in African American communities?" Of course, she was pointing out the obvious.

"Yes, but that would be more work. It's so much easier to react rather than make useful changes. If we had a bunch of kids playing on a hill, and every day four slid down and were hurt, we'd build a hospital with all of the latest technology at the bottom of the hill, rather than simply questioning if they should be on the hill in the first place. Administration always just reacts. Anyway, Jada suggests that I have to get out in front of this. I have to try to win public opinion over. All they're hearing is the craziness being stirred up by money-hungry attorneys."

"What does Sean say?"

"He's ordered me not to speak."

"Then don't. You're going to end up getting shot." A sadness washed over Serena. "I can't risk losing you again."

I took her hand. "If I go to prison, I might as well be shot. I'm not walking away from Nora, or Jackson, or you, for years. I have to fight this."

The sorrow in my wife's eyes caused me physical pain. She finally said, "I can't support you on this. If you go, I'm not going with you." She urged, "Stay home and let Sean handle this."

"I'm sorry, but I can't. Sean's bailed on me." "I don't trust Jada."

I didn't have the heart to tell her I did. I loved Serena with all the warmth in my soul, but Jada had inside information I couldn't ignore.

As I left the house, Serena yelled after me, "I won't be there and I won't watch!" She was trying to shame me into staying. Honestly, it was my preference that Serena didn't attend. If some crackpot took a shot at me, as she feared, I didn't want her anywhere near me.

When I arrived at the Fourth Precinct in Minneapolis, Jada informed me, "I've got some good news for you. Robert Kleinfeld has stepped down as the attorney for Kaiko Kane's family."

Jada had informed me of the fiasco in Mia's hospital room, so I wasn't surprised. "How are people reacting?"

"They're accusing him of selling out." She reassured me, "It's going to take a series of things like this to turn the tide."

It was time for me to take a shot at being the unbalanced force to end the protesters' momentum.

As I made my way toward the front of the crowd, a young white girl stood by her mother, holding a banner that read, I thought you were here to protect us. An African American woman shared her frustration as I passed, saying, "We're the ones who come home to the empty bedrooms every night."

Even though my boss asked me not to, and Serena had begged me not to, I was speaking to the crowd. Jada was right. I needed to be assertive, or I'd become a victim of this dilemma. I was blessed to have a respected and honest reporter like Jada as a friend.

Before I stepped up to the podium, Jada straightened my collar and suggested, "Don't say anything about the attack on Maurice, or about Del's death. People will assume you shot Kaiko in retaliation."

"I won't. For one, I don't believe Kaiko killed Del." Perplexed, Jada questioned, "Who did?"

"Mia Strock."

Jada rubbed long fingers down her throat, clenching her fist when she reached her breastbone. "I was going to have her speak on your behalf."

"Mia's a wild card. I trust your judgment." I considered how Jada and I had both gone against our partners' wishes by taking my argument public.

Reading my mind, she commented, "I don't know if my relationship with Sean will survive this." She gazed out at the large number of people who had assembled and mindlessly added, "If it doesn't, it's on him."

Jada introduced me and, even though the crowd booed, they quieted to hear what I had to say.

I straightened my shoulders and began. "I am sorry for the heartache so many people have experienced as a result of mistakes made by armed officers. I'm not going to stand up here and try to defend every shooting, as I can't. I can say, however, that in the moment I shot Kaiko Kane, I thought it was the only way to save a young woman's life."

There were some discontented murmurs and more booing, but I could still be heard.

"The man I shot is going to be charged with murdering a caring father, who was killed only because he happened to be exploring the woods with his daughter, and they had unknowingly walked by a meth lab. Kaiko killed Todd Hartford, and tried killing Todd's nine-year-old daughter, to protect his lab. He was in the process of trying to rape a young woman when I confronted him. He was pushing a knife into her throat. He was going to cut her throat, which would have forced me and the other officer to attend to the victim and given Kaiko a chance to escape. On the video, you will hear an officer ask me not to shoot him. I believed if I shot him in the leg, he'd immediately react by pulling that hand toward the pain. This was not a shot that would have killed him, but any injury less severe wouldn't have been enough to keep him from killing her. I needed something fast and painful to stop him. It worked."

The crowd jeered.

Over their insults, I continued, "The officer with me had never met Kaiko Kane before that moment. I knew him from investigating his brutal crimes all summer. Kaiko had shoved another victim into the Mississippi River just a few weeks ago, so he could escape. I'm asking that you consider his history and watch the entire video, including the discussions between me and the other officer. We put our lives at risk to save a young woman. We were trying to put an end to the violence Kaiko perpetrated against her . . ." I was careful not to say others, as it would get twisted to suggest I was simply avenging the assault on my former boss. I ended with, "I'm asking that you support law enforcement so we can all work together to end violence."

Someone yelled, "You shot and killed a civilian just four years ago!" The booing began growing.

"I did. He was trying to kill someone. The man was shooting at her and I was fifty yards away. I'm not proud of it. I don't speak of it. It was the only way for me to save her. I assume that's what you would want me to do if it was your child, or sibling, or partner in danger."

Somebody threw a rock at me and, when I turned, I saw Serena had stepped on to the platform next to me. The rock missed us, and she placed her hand on my shoulder, indicating she had my back.

Jada stepped back on the podium and took the microphone with a purpose. "Do you have any idea of what a farce this is? A group of lawsuit-hungry fanatics are trying to tell you that this shooting, of a serial rapist, is equal to the injustices African Americans have experienced for decades. Don't you dare minimize our pain with this crap! We've had speakers take the podium and share tragedies of the killing of innocents. Jon Frederick shot a killer and a rapist, when the monster was about to end the life of one more victim. This is not the same story, so please listen."

Sensing her agitation, I wanted to intervene before she said something she regretted. Jada went out on a limb to help me and I didn't want her to have consequences for it. I took the microphone back and shared, "I know there have to be concessions to work through any social issue. Even though I honestly feel I did the only thing I could to save a life, out of respect for your concerns, I will stop carrying a gun. It doesn't mean I will never use a gun, but I won't routinely carry one. For example, if I'm called to a mass shooting, I'll bring a gun. But generally, I won't. In return, I ask that you support law enforcement. We are all on the same side. We all want this craziness to end."

The crowd was now quiet.

Serena wasn't surprised. I had already told her. She kissed my shoulder. It was a way to both get people to stop gifting me ammo and to end the insults that I was hiding behind my gun.

Mia Strock joined us on the stage. Both her presence and the large white bandage across her throat was a powerful reminder of the reality of Kaiko's assault. In a raspy voice, Mia forced out, "I'm alive today because of that shot. I keep hearing that Kaiko Kane's rights were violated. Don't I have a right to live? Don't I have a right to be protected by law enforcement, or is that right reserved for rapists and murders?"

She put her head down and wept as she leaned into me. I hugged her and we left the stage together. As far as I was concerned, it went better than I anticipated. No one apologized for the attempted stoning, but no one harassed us as we departed, either. Serena and I were allowed to walk away, hand in hand, with no further comments. It was done, and we'd just have to see how it played out.

Jada was an amazing friend. There was one more piece of this puzzle I needed to solve before I could walk away.

57

DEONTOLOGICAL THEORY =
The morality of an action should be based on whether that act, itself, is moral, rather than based on the consequences of the action. (In other words, the end doesn't justify the means, if the means are immoral.)

Immanuel Kant
Prussian Philosopher & Author of The Metaphysics of Morals, 1774

MIA STROCK
8:30 AM, MONDAY, JUNE 24, 2019 BCA HEADQUARTERS
1430 MARYLAND AVENUE EAST, ST. PAUL

M Y SILVER-HAIRED ATTORNEY, Kelly Ryan, sat in the conference room, gleaning information from the much-contested agreement she had hammered out with the BCA. Grandpa had selected my attorney for me, and I had no issue with her telling me to shut up and let her do the work. She promised me she'd make sure there were officers with Kaiko every second, so I wouldn't have to worry. This amused me, as anyone who believed I could ever stop worrying about Kaiko didn't know him.

Across the table, Sean Reynolds was calm, but clearly struggling to maintain his composure. Anger oozed out of every pore.

My attorney's grin was a bit snide when she slid her reading glasses off, telling Sean, "You finally have it worded correctly." Kelly turned to me. "They are granting you full immunity for your involvement in any crimes related to the shooting of Todd Hartford and any crimes addressed in this case after your internship with the BCA began, including the death of Dan Moene, the deaths of Chad Gnoh and Del Walker, and the operation of the methamphetamine lab, provided you honestly answer their questions to the best of your ability."

Sean glared at me. "You should be thankful Kaiko's alive. If Jon would've killed him, there'd be no deal."

His words felt like vile spit, but I signed the forms and the deal was done. I was free— right? I should have been relieved, but my stomach wasn't about to stop churning until I was out of here. Maybe it never would.

Ms. Ryan put her copy of the form away and I folded mine in front of me. She took the signed form from me and waved it in front of Sean. "And now, you, Mr. Reynolds, better make damn sure Kaiko Kane doesn't escape. Five years from now, they're not going to care if you liked the deal. They'll just know you signed it. Imagine the bomb that would drop on you if Kaiko disappears after you gave immunity to a woman who infiltrated the BCA. I'd have your agents babysitting him day and night, if I were you."

Sean left his copy resting on the table in front of him, as if he was too disgusted to touch it. He grumbled, "Maurice said we'll never regret this. I hope he's right."

All eyes turned to me. Parched with nerves, I longed to drink from the glass of water in front of me, but didn't trust my hand to get it to my mouth. I reluctantly began, "Chad Gnoh was my soulmate. We met at Macalester. Chad was a chemistry major; I was interested in forensics. We hit it off the first time we met. After we binged on the Netflix series Murder Mountain, he insisted we visit Humboldt County in California, to see where all the weed was grown. Chad told me he wanted to write a research paper on people who commit their lives to crime. So, we went to the taverns and talked to the trimmigrants." I inhaled and slowly breathed out, trying to obtain composure. I couldn't say maintain my composure, because I didn't think I'd ever had it. "The guys Chad sought out were the worst kinds of criminals, really dangerous men, so after a couple nights, I just stayed at the hotel while he did his research. Looking back, I think Chad knew what he wanted to do, even back then. They loved Chad. He was smart, and he was harmless."

"And this is where he met Kaiko." Sean sat back.

"Kaiko told Chad he had access to a stockpile of chemicals to make meth, if Chad could produce it for him. Kaiko loaded up the back of a truck with stolen chemicals and drove to Nebraska. Chad met him there, so they could ditch Kaiko's truck. They drove the motherlode of chemicals to an abandoned shed on property owned by Chad's uncle, in Stearns County. They were in production before I had any idea of what they were doing."

Sean confronted me. "When did you decide to infiltrate the BCA?"

Nervous tremors shook my fingers, so I clasped them tightly in my lap under the table. I was having a hard time maintaining eye contact with Sean, but I forged ahead. "I had been asking Grandpa for an internship with the BCA for years and he had agreed, but kept putting me off. When I finally discovered my fiancé was running a meth lab, I pushed Grandpa to make it happen. I didn't want Chad to end up in prison." I looked directly at Sean now. "I want to make it clear that I had nothing to do with the meth lab. I never used meth. I never produced meth. I never sold meth."

"But you protected a meth lab." He wasn't impressed. I didn't respond. Breathe in, breathe out.

Kelly placed her hand on my shoulder. "You're doing fine."
"I protected my lover. I would have done anything for him."
Sean bluntly asked, "Who killed Todd Hartford?"

"Kaiko Kane killed him after Todd and Giselle walked
by the meth lab. I asked him not to—I begged him. It was
unnecessary."

"Why didn't you go to the police?"

"I didn't know with certainty that he'd done it. I wasn't
with Kaiko when Todd was killed, or at the lab when Kaiko
returned. And Chad and Kaiko initially didn't say a word
about it. I know it sounds like I reason like a five-year-old,
but I told myself maybe it was an accident. I didn't want to
believe it."

Sean was relentless. "The ALIAS system indicates you
wrote Dan Moene's suicide letter." "When Jon Frederick convinced people Todd's death was not an accident," I said with a
sigh, "Kaiko wanted a fall guy. Dan was selling meth for him,
and had bragged to Kaiko that he was having an affair with
Todd's wife. Kaiko asked me to write a suicide letter and he'd
threaten Dan with it, so Dan wouldn't give him up. I had no
idea Kaiko was going to make him eat his gun."

Sean considered this. "And then you set up Giselle."

I adamantly denied this. "That's not true. I told Chad that
Jon was talking to Giselle, but I told him not to tell Kaiko."
With deep regret, I added, "But he must have, anyway. I am
so damn glad Zelly got away. You have to believe me. I never
thought he'd go after her."

"Was Kaiko Kane identified as one of the individuals living
within three blocks from where those boots were stolen?"

It wasn't easy to be honest to a tenacious and powerful
man who now looked like he could tear me apart with his bare
hands, but it was the agreement I made. "Yes. I knew where
Kaiko had lived, so I volunteered to work that block and the

blocks surrounding it. I made sure his name wasn't on the final list that went to Jon."

Sean commented, "Another crime—aiding and abetting a killer." My attorney reminded him, "Total immunity."

Sean's face didn't change, but his eyes flared with barely contained rage.

I closed my eyes, as I didn't want to see what my next statement was going to do to the already volcanic atmosphere. I willed myself the power to say it. "I shot Del Walker."

The dead silence that followed was anything but peaceful. The revelation stunned Sean. I opened an eye to see him turn to my attorney and crumple my copy of the agreement in his hand right front of me. "I thought you said there would be no surprises."

"It shouldn't be a surprise," Kelly remarked dryly. "This is what the lead investigator has been telling you all along."

Sean was now fuming. "You told me you lost faith in Jon. It's why you began reporting to me instead of him."

I stammered, "I—I was advised that the only way for me to get immunity was to undermine your confidence in Jon."

"Who told you that?"

Kelly intervened flatly, "That is privileged information."

Sean impatiently drummed his fingers on the table. "If Jon is charged with a crime, you will need to give up your source."

I nodded. I wanted to protect Grandpa as long as possible. "I never told Kaiko he was wearing a one-of-a-kind pair of boots, or that those boots put him at the scene of both Todd's murder and Dan's suicide. I found the bullet that killed Todd. I still helped with the investigation."

Sean was impervious. "If you hadn't helped some, Jon never would have trusted you. How did you get Dan to kill himself?"

"I only know what Kaiko told me after the fact. Dan was apparently falling apart. He was an addict. His fiancée left. Leda wasn't committing to him. Kaiko apparently told Dan if he didn't kill himself, Kaiko was going to kill him and then go rape Leda. Dan agreed to take his life, and Kaiko raped Leda anyway. That's the kind of guy Kaiko is."

An investigator entered the room and gestured to Sean to step out for a moment.

When he returned, Sean kicked the leg of the table so hard we all shook. "Kaiko Kane just died.

"I guess you will no longer need Mia's testimony," Kelly Ryan gloated. "It's been a pleasure doing business with you."

Worried, I asked, "What does this mean for me?"

"You are free," she said with a grin. "Your deal is set in stone."

I had been granted immunity for agreeing to testify, in a case they no longer needed to prosecute. I knew from Grandpa that Sean was pressured into making this deal by administrators, and he was now furious it had blown up on him.

Sean rubbed his face with both hands as he paced, before finally gathering his self-control. "Both your meth lab partners are dead. An investigator is dead. Jon is losing his job, and may be doing some jail time—all because you were able to manipulate him. Are you happy?"

I was miserable and needed to be brutally honest. "Don't put this on Jon—I manipulated you. Jon trusted your judgment. As I understand it, he asked you twice to remove me from the case, but you refused." I let it sink in, but before he could respond, I raved on, "I've been raped six times by a psychopath—fearing for my life every second—and my soulmate is dead, so don't think I haven't suffered. I still don't think I would've killed Del if he wouldn't have bragged about killing Chad. He called him 'Bigfoot,' like he was some kind of freak.

He crowed about killing the love of my life." I broke down crying and, like a small child, covered my head on the table.

Ms. Ryan sat uncomfortably frigid, waiting for me to pull myself together. Empathy wasn't her strong suit. I finally felt her hand on my back.

After Sean watched for several minutes, he sat in front of me and ordered, "Look up." When I didn't immediately respond, he raised his voice, "I said, look up!"

Kelly cautioned him, "Be respectful, Mr. Reynolds. Ms. Strock is not responsible for your investigator killing Kaiko, and it's not her fault you made this agreement. Mia's a victim here."

Sean toned it down. "Okay. This is how we proceed." He turned to me and said, "You don't do any interviews. None! We'll change Dan Moene's cause of death from suicide to homicide, for his family's sake. I'll announce we're closing the homicide investigations on Todd Harford, Del Walker, and Dan Moene, with Kaiko Kane's death."

By now, I was dissolving in tears. I forced out, "Okay. What happens to Jon?"

Sean narrowed his eyes, "You scapegoated him, why do you even care? Jon's my ticket out, too. After all," he picked up the crumpled agreement, "you can't talk about this case to anyone outside of the BCA. Jon's status has now been relegated to suspension without pay, the final step before termination. He disobeyed a direct order, and he shot and killed a man while an officer was pleading with him not to shoot him."

"I was there. Kaiko was going to kill me . . ."

58

THEORY OF POSITIVE PUNISHMENT =
Decreasing the likelihood of repeating undesirable behavior by introducing an unfavorable outcome.

Burrhus Frederic "B.F." Skinner
American Psychologist, Behaviorist, & Professor of Psychology Harvard University, 1970

JON FREDERICK
4:30 PM, TUESDAY, JUNE 25, 2019
FIRST STREET SOUTH, LAKE GEORGE, ST. CLOUD

I SAT ON A park bench at Lake George with Del's daughter, Katie, watching parents blowing bubbles to toddlers, kids running through the splash pad, and teens throwing Frisbees. I got a kinder, more pleasant view of life away from work. Katie had called me after she heard the investigation into her father's death had been closed, and I felt she deserved to know the truth. So, once again, I was defying Sean's order to avoid speaking about the case.

Katie looked troubled, so I asked, "Are you doing okay?"

"I thought it would be easier once Dad passed, but it's still hard. He was a good man, but few people got to know him like I knew him."

"That certainly is a credit to you, Katie." She quietly waited for answers. I didn't waste any time telling her, "I believe Mia

340

Strock killed your father, but she's been offered a deal where she can avoid being charged with murder for it."

Frustrated, Katie demanded, "How can she pull that off? For God's sake, she killed a law enforcement officer!"

"They gave her immunity for her testimony against Kaiko Kane, not realizing she killed Del. Kaiko's fingerprints are on the murder weapon. So, now they're just going to blame him. There are no witnesses and there is no direct evidence linking Mia to Del's death."

Katie studied me. "Then why do you believe Mia killed Dad?"

"Del didn't know Mia was in a relationship with one of the meth makers. None of us knew it, at the time. Del told Mia he was joining me in searching for the lab. When he told her where we were headed, she knew we'd find it. So, Mia left shortly after Del and called ahead to warn her partner, Chad, and his sidekick—Kaiko Kane. Del ended up tasing Chad, which sent him into cardiac arrest, but Mason McLean and I revived him. Del stepped out of the meth lab and found Mia hiding outside. He apparently made some comment to Mia that he may have killed 'Bigfoot,' not knowing this guy was Mia's lover. She was overcome with grief and shot him."

Katie pondered this. "Do you believe her?"

"Yes, I do. But unlike everybody else, I'm not so quick to forgive her. Your dad was a great investigator. He helped us shut down a lab that was producing millions of dollars' worth of methamphetamine."

"I can't let Mia walk away without consequences, even if she's the granddaughter of the head of the BCA."

I corrected her, "Former head of the BCA. I should point out that Mia's also been raped a half a dozen times by Kaiko since this all went down."

Taken aback, Katie said, "But she killed my dad."

"I know. If we open up this investigation, it will likely open up some criticism of Del. The plan right now is to award him the Medal of Honor and to have your family accept it for him."

"What do you think?"

"It's not my call, Katie." Mia deserved prison, but she didn't deserve to be raped. She took her time. "What do you think my dad would want?"

"I know what your dad would want, and it might surprise you."

"I doubt it," Katie laughed. "Dad would want severe consequences and he'd tell everyone so, even if it meant everybody in the community hated us for it."

I smiled. "Well, that's not the case. Del wanted to end his life closing up an investigation, so you and your children could be proud of him."

"I was always proud of him," Katie said, now fighting tears. "I know he ended up drinking too much, but even then, he'd call for a ride home, so he wouldn't be driving drunk."

My mind shouted at Del, What an unfair burden to put on your daughter.

She continued, "My kids are junior high, so it would be nice to have something positive about Dad I could experience with them." She hesitated. "There's been a lot of criticism about him, even though he was just doing his job."

"Del shared some with me. He would put his life on the line to save anyone."

Katie sighed. "Yeah, it was hard on his marriage and hard on me. It almost became easier when I found out he was dying."

I stood up. "Take your time and get back to me when you know what you decide. I promise to go back to the BCA and argue on your behalf." I firmly believed in fighting for victims, and Del's family ended up victims in all of this, too.

Katie was still processing. "My dad could be inappropriate at times with coworkers—not physically, but making stupid verbal comments he thought were funny. He'd try to justify it by adding, 'They know I'm old school,' when I'd give him hell. Do you think he ever made inappropriate comments to Mia Strock?"

I felt the situation called for brutal honesty. "My guess would be yes."

"Dad used to say Lady Justice wields a sword and the scales aren't balanced, so don't expect it to be fair or painless. But the good guys win often enough to make it worth it." She smiled slightly at the memory of her father's words. "Could you make Mia pay a price if the court doesn't?"

"I intend to." For her sake. "And I'm going to use something Del told me to do it. Your dad told me that he never believed the break-in at the Ross home was a robbery. The more I reflect on this case, the more I'm convinced he was right."

"Okay," she said with a nod. "I don't need time to think about it. If you can make sure Dad gets a very positive send-off, I'll sign off. Then I can focus on how great my dad was and be done with that betraying bitch who killed him."

When I returned to the parking lot, Sean was leaning on my car, arms crossed in exasperated vexation. As soon as he saw me, he pushed off the car and pointed directly at me and yelled, "You're fired! You were ordered not to talk to anyone, but you just can't stop yourself."

I was a bit taken aback, however, I felt I owed no apologies to him. "I got Katie to agree to not question who shot her father, provided Del is awarded the Medal of Honor. Paula Fineday is arranging this, so you don't have to do a thing—just let it happen."

Sean gave me a dismissive wave. I should have fired you right away. I'm trying to keep the twin cities from being burned to the ground."

"Another injustice will only postpone—and in the long run exacerbate—the problem."

Sean ignored my plea and ordered, "Stay away from Jada."

I understood what this was really about. "I have no interest in talking to Jada about anything but cases."

"Where were you the night Serena was in Hawaii?"

His unfounded jealousy was destroying a once-impressive man. As much as I respected Sean as an investigator and a friend, the insult of his implication was overpowering any allegiance I had felt toward him. I measured my words carefully, even as my own outrage was beginning a slow burn. "At home with my kids," I replied. "You're obviously following me, Sean. Check my phone records."

Sean reiterated, "You're done," and stalked toward his Lexus.

Something snapped in me. I yelled at his back, "Jada's just like you. She finds a story and runs with it, without feeling the need to explain her whereabouts to anybody. She expects people to trust her morality. You've got a good thing, Sean—don't destroy it."

Ignoring me, he slammed his door and drove off.

59

THEORY OF FORGIVENESS AS A HUMAN STRENGTH =
Transgressions and injury are inevitable in social interactions.
Forgiveness promotes healing by mending injuries and abandoning
the motivation to seek revenge. The process empowers the forgiver,
and the selfless act often motivates the offender to work toward
relationship harmony.

Michael McCullough
American Psychologist University of Miami, 2000

CLAY ROBERTS
5:00 PM, WEDNESDAY, JUNE 26, 2019 WILSON AVENUE
NORTHEAST, ST. CLOUD

I SAT ON THE steps of my house waiting for Hani to return. I had left work early, showered, and even set some flowers on the counter inside. It was weird to give someone flowers— here you go, watch 'em die. It seemed more like a threat, but Hani liked flowers and I wanted her to see I was well-intentioned. My therapist claimed it would serve me well to, for once, bring closure to a relationship.

Hani stepped out of her eight-year-old Fiesta, wearing a tan hijab and a faded black abaya. I wanted to believe she was mourning, too, but I was afraid that wasn't the case. Hani was one of those great American citizens who showed up to work, day after day, and gave it her best, no matter how difficult everyone else in the world acted. She would always have my respect.

She glanced at me curiously then smoothed her dress beneath her as she sat next to me. "Where have you been? You've been gone day and night."

"My friend, Kev, got me work at the convention center. They had a project deadline that required us to work every waking minute, so they gave us rooms in the hotel to crash in, the last couple nights. The endless hours gave me something to think about, instead of ruminating day and night about messing up the best relationship I've ever had."

She looked heartsick as she patiently waited for me to begin.

Option one was, Say what I want to say and hope for what I want to hear. "I don't want to be a terrible person. I've been one and it doesn't feel good. I want to be with you. You work like I do. You make me a better builder. You make me a better man. I'm a better Christian since we've been together. And working on this house with you has made me enjoy building again. But I can't be here and not be with you. I bought it to turn it, now I want it to be our home. I know you can't build a straight house on a crooked foundation, so help me fix my foundation and start over. I know I've acted like I don't respect you, but I do. Hani, I admire you."

I was hoping for an I love you, followed by a loving caress, but Hani didn't respond.

This brought me to option two: Say what you need to say and forgive her indifference. I started again, "I thought I was mad at you for not giving me another chance. But it turns out, I was just mad at me for blowing it. I wish it was just a matter of dusting myself off and moving on, but it's not that simple. I turned your life completely upside down. So, I'm learning to forgive you, and me, and everybody we seemed to interact with in the whole damn county, for ending us. And now I need to make amends to you. Everybody else can just—" it wasn't the right moment to swear, "just be the miserable people they are."

Hani finally spoke. "I don't understand you, Clay."

"I'm always punishing someone for my feelings," I tried to explain. "I wasn't sure if I wanted you to live with me, but in a hot minute, you were, and I resented not having time to think about it. So, I stepped out. I didn't have sex with Mia or anyone else. I just needed to talk."

"You could have talked to me."

"I know, I know, I know. Believe me, I've beat myself up over this." I thought some before going on. This wasn't easy for me. "I've had this urge for destructive revenge, every time I'm hurt." I waved my hand in the air. "And it always makes it worse. Jon's my best friend—and nothing could make him hate me more than hitting on Serena. And honestly, I don't have any interest in Serena anymore. I walked out their door wondering, 'Why did I just tear up my life?' I want women to leave me and men to kick my ass, like somehow that will prove my self-loathing was right all along."

Hani softly said, "Despised, but vindicated."

I wasn't sure what she meant, but she was probably right, so I said, "Yeah." I intently studied her mahogany eyes and admitted, "I love you, Hani. I don't want to be with anyone but you. I promise you, if you could consider giving me another chance, I'd make sure you never regretted it."

"Clay." She turned away as if to hide her pain. "I've been talking to someone else."

Of course she was. Wonderful! I'd blown it again. I stood up, "Okay. I've said what I needed to say, and that's that." I didn't want to cry in front of her, so I tried to avoid looking into her fawn eyes as I offered, "Don't be in any hurry to move out. Pay me what you can pay me for rent and I'll find another place to live. It's important to me, after all the damage I've done, to help you start over." I slowly stood and walked to my truck. Time for a long drive. I was done being self-destructive. I wasn't running. I just needed time to process all this.

"Stop!" Hani shouted, "Come back here!"

I turned. "What's the point? Hani, you are amazing. I truly believe that. But my soul can't to be comforted with words. Problems created by behavior can't be undone with words."

Hani responded with an unrestrained, compassionate smile, "I've been talking to a friend— about you. About the way we joke around and how you purposely misuse words."

With brutal honesty, I told her, "That's not on purpose."

She grinned. "It makes no difference. It's endearing. And then, every once in a while, you use a difficult word in exactly the right context."

I impishly grinned. "They all seem right when I say them."

Hani took hold of my hands and turned them upright, as if I was making an offering. She touched her heart, then gently placed her hand, upright, on mine. "You've taken me ricing by Mille Lacs, we've hiked Gooseberry Falls, picked mushrooms in the woods by Harding, and four- wheeled the Soo-line trail. We've even talked about tapping maples this fall and ice fishing. Do you know what my friend told me?"

I waited with eager anticipation.

"She said, 'You love Clay. Why are you fighting it?' And I realized I do. I've been waiting for the opportunity to tell you: I'm most alive, and happiest, and optimistic, when I'm with you."

Optimistic? I wasn't sure how I'd affected her eyesight, but the rest sounded perfect. I couldn't stop myself. "I love you, Hani! I—love—you."

60

ORTHODOX QUANTUM MECHANICS
THEORY OF COMPATIBILITY =
*Compatibility is the capacity for two systems to work together
without having to be altered to do so. When all material particles
in a component deform, translate, and rotate, they need to meet up
again, very much like the pieces of a jigsaw puzzle, and fit together.*

*Henry P. Stapp Theoretical Physics
University of California Berkeley, 2009*

SERENA FREDERICK
2:30 PM, JULY 4, 2019, INDEPENDENCE DAY PIERZ

JON WAS SUSPENDED without pay for saving a woman's life. Okay, he killed Kaiko, but if you were going to go around raping people, shouldn't you expect that someone might kill you for it? I know Jon didn't intentionally kill him, but I'd understand if he had. Jon insisted there was one more part of this puzzle he needed to solve before he could walk away. I needed to help him relax and let it go. There was no point in arguing with him over carrying a gun at work—Jon never liked carrying a gun. He didn't even wear a watch— no jewelry, other than his wedding band, not even tattoos. Honestly, I was surprised he carried it as long as he had.

I'd have liked for him to stay home for a bit, but having been raised in poverty, Jon simply couldn't go without providing his family an income. He anticipated he would need to find work with a road construction crew, due to limited employment opportunities in rural Minnesota.

Sean scapegoated Jon over jealousy of Jon's friendship with Jada. Jon was naïve about the impact his working with Jada had on others, including me. But I knew my husband, maybe better than he knew himself, and I loved him for being exactly the man he was. Together, we were a force to be reckoned with. I had told him that, one day, we'd be an investigative dynamic duo. He responded, "We already are," and pointed out that the checks go into our joint account.

Vic was outside playing some version of softball with Nora. Even though she was only four, Nora had no difficulty with frequently changing the rules, and Vic just good-naturedly went along with it.

I could see Vic and Nora in the backyard from our second-floor bedroom window. Jackson lay next to me on the bed, napping, while I considered planning something nice for Jon. He was such a good man. I flashed back to thirteen years ago.

2006
910 HENNEPIN AVENUE MINNEAPOLIS

I had gotten tickets for me and my sister, Andi, to see Jackson Browne at the Orpheum Theatre. We'd parked in a nearby ramp and were excitedly making our way down the bright lights of Hennepin Avenue, which featured a flashing squad car on every block to the venue, when we ran into Jon and Victor Frederick.

Jon and Vic were both strong, lanky farm boys. While Jon had a minimal-care, medium- length hairstyle, Vic had long, straight blond hair and lamb chop sideburns. I liked Jon, a lot, but hadn't seen him since we graduated from high school last spring.

The two of them were standing in front of the theatre, so, after smiles and greetings, I asked, "What are you doing here?"

Jon had a sweet, boyish grin. "We're waiting to go in, but it may be a while."

Vic interjected, "We just need to scope the place out and make sure it's safe, first."

With Vic's paranoia, Jon was the only one he trusted to take him off the farm. I admired the way Jon protectively cared for his brother. I imagined he'd bought both tickets with the hard- earned money he earned through physical labor.

"I've been looking forward to this concert for months." I beamed. "I've got tickets right up front, just above the pit, on the main floor. I got them online from a guy who had accepted a job in another city, so I got a great deal." Struggling to contain my excitement, and knowing they could be out here a while, I reached out and touched Jon's elbow. "We need to go, but it was nice seeing you both."

THIRTY MINUTES LATER

Frustrated, Andi and I had to push our way back through the crowd of people marching into the theatre. We bumped into Jon and Vic, who were now just entering.

Jon noted my expression immediately, and asked, "What's wrong?"

On the verge of crying, I lamented, "Of course the tickets were a great deal. They were fake." My voice trailed off as I said, "That scumbag ripped me off."

I wasn't in the mood to talk, so I started to step by when he called, "Serena, wait!" I didn't want to feel so inept in front of him but, to be polite, I stopped and listened.

Jon graciously offered, "You're in luck. I have two extra tickets, but they're up on the balcony. Clay told me to get two for him and then cancelled at the last minute. They're not near our seats, but you can have them if you want—free. They're useless to me now." He handed me the tickets. Before I could thank him, we had lost Jon and Vic in the crowd.

THURSDAY, JULY 4, 2019 PIERZ

Jackson was half awake and lazily clinging to me as his eyes slowly opened to his world. Vic and Nora sat by us at the kitchen table, enjoying some orange juice with a swirl of pomegranate poured into it. I was telling Vic we were all lucky to have enjoyed that great concert in 2006, which had ended with Browne's version of "Stay."

I said, "There are rumors that Jackson Browne may return to the Cities this fall. I'd love to find out where the two of you sat at that concert, and buy Jon those exact tickets for his birthday. That moment was significant to me." I didn't bother to explain that Andi was struggling at the time, and I'd spent money I didn't really have on those tickets to give her a night of reprieve from her problems.

Victor's long, bleach-blond hair had changed little over the years. He twirled a strand in his fingers as he laughed. "I was excited to hear we had better tickets than those balcony seats. But after Jon dragged me away from you, I realized there were no other tickets. I jacked him up, saying, 'We drove all the way down here for nothing!' He said, 'It wasn't nothing.' You know how he is. We got pizza and it wasn't long before we were laughing. He cranked up some rock music and we had a good trip back home."

I sighed. Of course there were no other tickets . . .

61

SCREW THEORY =
A powerful mathematical tool for the analysis of spatial mechanisms. Definition in complicated detail, for super-geeks: A screw consists of two three-dimensional vectors. A screw can be used to denote the position and orientation of a spatial vector, the linear velocity, and angular velocity of a rigid body. Therefore, the concept of a screw is convenient in kinematics (the mathematics involved in movement). Screw theory has become an important tool in robotics.

Sir Robert Ball
Professor of Applied Mathematics Dublin & Cambridge Universities, 1876

JON FREDERICK
6:45 PM, FRIDAY, JULY 5, 2019 WEST TWIN LAKE,
NISSWA

MIA STROCK ASKED me to meet her at a cabin on the Twin Lakes. When I arrived, the sun was setting in glorious hues of scarlet and amber, mirrored across the smooth lake surface. The air offered soul-cleansing peace and reminded me how pleasantly serene an evening on the lake could be. The warm Minnesota evening allowed Mia to be barefoot and comfortable in khaki shorts and a black t-shirt.

I joined her at the picnic table, which sat on the shore's edge. I asked her, "How did you manage to get a cabin on the 'Lake of Legends'?"

Mia was puzzled. "The Lake of Legends?"

"The rumor is that a former University of Minnesota professor bought all the land around the Twin Lakes, and doesn't allow anyone to access them, so they're loaded with large fish."

"Grandpa and I did catch some nice walleyes," she said with a smile. "Pan fried—there's nothing better!" She cocked her head toward me and added, "We have a bag of panfish filets for you. Grandpa says you like panfish with a cold beverage."

"I'll take them."

Mia meekly asked, "Even from a killer?"

"You were a killer. I'm kind of hoping you're not planning to continue to be one. How's Maurice's recovery going?"

Burdensome guilt emanated from her eyes. "Okay." "You saved his life."

Mia pointed out dejectedly, "After I put it in jeopardy."

"One day at a time, Mia. You did the best you could on that day. And that's what you do from now on."

As she peered out at the lake, I saw the surface tension of the water in her eyes had broken, sending a tear trickling down her cheek. Regaining her bearing, she posited, "I need to work out an agreement with you. Grandpa says you're relentless. You're never going to let this go— especially now that I've cost you your job." She gave me a sideways look. "His exact word was 'perspicacious.' I had to look it up. It means 'intense insight and understanding.'" Mia paused. "You lost your job for saving my life. The damage keeps on piling up, doesn't it? Grandpa has burned every bridge by defending me. I can't bring Del back. His family wants nothing from me. Hani wants nothing from me, obviously." She turned her palms up to emphasize, "There's nothing I can do."

I bit my lower lip, trying to make my anger productive. "I feel bad for the torture Kaiko put you through. Nobody deserves that. And I don't know exactly what fair is, but 'There's nothing I can do' is what people who are too lazy to honestly make amends say. Of course there are things you can do."

"Tell me and I'll do it. Grandpa says, just keep going to counseling. But counseling is just for me."

I stood up. "I'm going to have to walk to do this. Picnic tables are uncomfortable."

As she joined me, Mia blurted, "At first, I thought Chad was having an affair. I broke down and told him I didn't want to lose him. He told me he was planning for our future. It was such a relief to know he still loved me, I offered to help by getting in with the BCA. He didn't even have to ask. That's how much I loved him." She stopped to gaze at a loon calling out to her mate on the clear lake. "And then it all went to hell."

I stopped her. "Did you help with Dan's suicide? The ALIAS program indicated you wrote the letter."

"No. Kaiko made some money for us, selling meth on the side. He told us the investigators would eventually question Dan, so he asked me to write a suicide letter to scare Dan. Kaiko told me he'd present it to Dan as Dan's fate if he ever ratted Kaiko out. That's why I was so sick to discover Dan's body. At that moment, I realized I was screwed. Kaiko had that suicide letter I wrote, so I had no way out. And Kaiko brought that damn teenage sex worker to the lab. When I discovered both he and Chad were having sex with her, I began crumbling. I wasn't sleeping. I started drinking heavily. I wanted to walk away, but I was in too deep. And I was still naïve enough to believe this could end with no one else getting hurt."

"You killed Del."

She stopped and looked directly at me. "I did. This weighs so heavily on me I've thought about killing myself. But even that's too self-centered. It solves nothing." She paused, but held eye contact. "You were exactly right. Once Del told me you guys were searching near Hawick, I knew you were going to find the lab. So, I called Chad and told him to get the hell out. I didn't go there with intention of killing anyone. I intended to hide and see what transpired, but Del found me. When he told me, 'Damn, I killed Bigfoot,' I shot him. I regretted it immediately after, but there was no going back. Del was thunderstruck, so I ran to him and tried to apologize. But he saw right through me and said, 'You're the traitor.' He was gut-shot and was dying. When I put my gun to his head, he looked at me with regretful resignation, but he didn't fight it. I finished him. I tell myself that I took him out of his painful misery, but the truth is, I didn't want him telling anybody about me before he died."

Sticking true to form, I walked in silence waiting for her to finish her thoughts. Mia pulled out her same argument. "He told me he killed my lover—"

"Del tased Chad," I corrected her. "He didn't kill Chad. Kaiko returned and shot him."

Mia sullenly agreed with a nod. She stared out at the lonely loon floating on an abandoned lake. Her mate hadn't responded to the call. "It never occurred to us that Kaiko may have planned to kill us both, once the meth was made. I'd bet it was that psycho's plan from the very beginning."

I told her, "It was kind of you to speak on my behalf."

"Not really. Grandpa made me. I wanted to hide, but he told me I had to show up. He said when people saw me on TV, all bandaged up, I'd get my immunity. It worked." She sighed. "And he's back to Grandpa, again. Dad is the man who raised me."

We continued walking. "Why did you have to punish Hani?"

"It was something I came up with in the spur of the moment, to keep Kaiko from killing me. And for a minute, I had a crush on Clay."

"It would have been nice to warn her. I asked you to go home twice on the day you shot Del."

Downcast, Mia replied, "I wasn't thinking clearly."

"And then you wanted to punish Raven for being with Chad."

"I wanted her punished," she agreed, "but I had nothing to do with Kaiko's decision to try to shoot her. I only found out about that later from Grandpa. Kaiko's the one who sent me to pick her up. I went because I didn't trust Raven alone with Chad."

As we entered a small clearing, we came upon Jasper and Brenna Ross sitting on the shore. Bewildered, Mia stopped in her tracks. "What are they doing here?"

Jasper hopped to his feet, yelling at Mia, "What the hell is wrong with you? You were going to let that psychopath rape Brenna? For what? What did Brenna ever do to you?"

Mia hissed, "So you would know what it's like to be burned, like you burned me."

Brenna moved to Jasper's side and studied Mia. "He was going to rape me in front of my son."

Mia feebly countered, "Your son wasn't supposed to be home."

Brenna was typically poised, but couldn't contain herself. She marched hard toward Mia, saying, "Screw you, you self-absorbed—" We had all braced for her rant to continue for some time, and justifiably so. But, as quickly as her rant started, it ended. Composed, she turned to me, "Thank you, Jon, for solving this." Brenna turned back to Mia and said, "You are not worth my energy or my time." She briskly marched away.

Brenna Ross was a classy woman. Jasper quickly pursued her.

Browbeaten, Mia responded, "Screw me. If she meant literally, the damage has already been done."

My obsessive brain recalled screw theory is a kinesthetic math theory, so in a sense it was literal. But I wisely chose to keep that to myself.

Mia turned to me. "How did you know my affair was with Jasper?"

"You worked for Kraft. Jasper was a financial planner for Ore-Ida, owned by Kraft. You wouldn't go after Jasper for revenge—you still loved him. You wanted to take away what he desired. The same way you directed your anger at Hani, because you liked Clay, and the way you directed your anger at Raven, because Chad had sex with her. You should have been angry at Jasper, and Chad, and Clay. You'd think with the manner your mom died, you'd be mad at men, but you want to punish women. Hell, you even tried to set up Leda Hartford."

"I haven't forgiven Mom for leaving me. That's what my therapist says." She slumped, defeated. "How did you put it together?"

"There was only one attempted break-in. If it was about the money, there would have been others. Del was the one who put the bug in my ear that maybe the Ross incident wasn't supposed to be a robbery. So, I went back to the timeline. Brenna always came home from work on Fridays and napped. Jasper always worked late. This was a carry-over from his work at Kraft. The woman Jasper had the affair with at Kraft probably knew the pattern. Someone wanted Brenna to suffer; however, everybody who knows Brenna loves her. It had to be someone who only knew Jasper."

We walked back toward Mia's home; she was silent while I ticked off my process. "You told me, the last you heard, he was involved with a married woman. He was. But by some blessed chance, on the day you set Brenna up, Jasper decided to pick up their son and they came home early. That's the wonderful thing about human behavior. You can predict it most of the time, but never one hundred percent of the time."

"So, now what? You know I have immunity." Her attempt to grasp for safety made me kind of sad for her.

I contradicted her, "Actually, you don't. Not for this. You were granted immunity for any involvement in Todd Hartford's murder and any crimes that occurred after you started your internship. The attempted assault on Brenna, which you orchestrated, occurred before you started your internship."

As she registered this information, Mia began to panic. "I can't go to court! O.J. Simpson went to prison for nine years for stealing back his own clothes, because everyone knew he got away with murder." She stopped abruptly and implored, "Imagine the sentence I'm going to get for setting up a rape, from a judge who knows I got away with killing a cop."

I felt for her, but was without pity in this moment. I continued matter-of-factly, "Maurice is going to tell you your attorney could get you acquitted. But I'm not interested in a trial or in having you serve prison time. It's about making amends. You're going to be offered a guilty plea, and you'll be given ten years' probation, with no prison time, provided you comply with the requested community service."

Mia's labored breathing was like that of a child on the verge of crying. "So, how do I make amends? Can I even make amends? Prison doesn't scare me as much as facing hell. Please tell me there's some hope."

"I've got a challenging way for you to make amends, if you're up for it. You have a debt to Somalis for sending Kaiko after Hani, and you have a debt to humanity, in general. I know an elderly woman named Agnes Schraut who needs help on a daily basis. She's mean-spirited, and she has a teenaged Somali aide who dropped out of school to help her. I want you to live with Agnes and be her aide. You can draw twenty hours' pay each week as a personal care attendant, but I want you to donate the entire amount to the Somali girl's family so she can return to high school. I understand you will need to find other work, too, but that will have to be around Agnes's schedule. Helping Agnes and Nala is a lot more productive than prison time."

The offer seemed to bring Mia peace. "If you can make this happen, I'm signing on. I don't care what Grandpa says. When can I start?"

After I drove about ten miles south toward home on Highway 25, I pulled over to the side of the road. I picked up the bag of fish fillets Mia had given me and walked to an open field. I wanted Mia to have this legal charge to force her to make atonement for her conduct and to prevent her from ever having the opportunity to work for law enforcement in the future. I dumped the fish in the dirt and headed back to my car. Would I eventually trust Mia enough to take food from her? Maybe, but it was still too early.

When I reached my car, I turned to watch eagles descending on the fish. I loved the return of eagles to central Minnesota. Hopefully, they wouldn't be lying dead when I drove by the field tomorrow.

62

THEORY OF JEALOUSY =
*Jealousy is the wrecking ball that destroys love, under the pretense
of preserving it.*

*Frank Weber
American Psychologist & Author, 2020*

JON FREDERICK
10:05 PM, FRIDAY, JULY 26, 2019 PIERZ

SERENA AND I sat watching Jada on Eyewitness News, discussing my suspension from the BCA.

Serena thought out loud, "Sean once exuded class. He falls deeply in love and becomes possessive, suspicious, and petty. It's insane. Jada loves him. I hope he can work through this. It's sad."

"He has exactly what he desires, but he doesn't trust it. Jealousy is the leading cause of spousal homicide worldwide."

"Sean will walk away," Serena reassured me, "but it's asinine."

On television, Jada was on the street in Minneapolis asking people's opinions about the shooting of Kaiko Kane. Most believed the shooting was justified. We both smiled as she approached Agnes Schraut.

Jada stated, "Agnes, I understand that you were the one who saw Kaiko Kane on the street that night and called the police."

Agnes smiled; she didn't trust anyone enough to share that she received $10,000 for it.

Jada continued, "What are your thoughts of Jon Frederick being suspended for shooting Kaiko Kane?"

Agnes's entire face scrunched into wrinkles of disgust. "What a crock of crap. If I would have had a gun, I would have shot the bastard myself. What would you do if some guy kept returning to your neighborhood to rape women?"

Ignoring the question, Jada asked, "Did you hear that the police officer with Jon told him not to shoot Kaiko?"

Agnes spat, "Yeah, that cop's what we used to call a 'sugar tit'—someone who always wants to pacify everyone, rather than having the matzah to take care of it herself. They suspended a cop for using a gun—a gun we gave him to use for that very purpose. It's like suspending a taxi driver for giving rides. It makes no sense."

And there was Mia in the background, patiently waiting for Agnes. Mia was her new personal care attendant.

And by the way, the eagles were still alive.

Jada thanked Agnes and cut away to the next story. Serena laughed. "Sugar tit?"

"My grandma still uses the word for a pacifier. Before they had pacifiers, they used to roll a dishtowel into a nipple and dip it in honey or sugar to soothe babies."

"We definitely have to visit Agnes and bring her a gift, now that she's defending you. It amazes me she was so kind to the young Somali woman helping her."

"Agnes was kind to my mom, too. I think if you're willing to suffer through a hundred days of insults with her, you turn the page and she becomes your greatest ally. Mia handles her surprisingly well."

Serena smiled warmly. "It doesn't surprise me. Mia wants to be helpful. She just naïvely blinded herself to all of cruel the complications that would ensue from her lover's plan. Sometimes, I worry Hani may see Clay with those same rose-colored glasses. But maybe Hani's the one who will change Clay."

63

JON FREDERICK
7:30 PM, SATURDAY, JULY 27, 2019 PIERZ

IN THE LATE afternoon, I crawled up on the roof by our music room and nailed two two-by- fours to the roof, with the ends hanging over the eve of our patio. Serena and the kids curiously looked on.

Serena silently observed, patiently cognizant the story would be revealed soon enough. She gave me a great deal of latitude with my odd projects, knowing I would have shared any permanent changes to our home ahead of time.

Nora couldn't contain her curiosity. "Dad, what are you doing? Why is there a hook at the end of the boards?"

"I have something in the trunk of my car that we're going to attach to these hooks."

Nora rubbed the itch off her nose with the back of her hand, and then pointed to our outdoor furniture. "But the couch is right below it."

I crawled off the roof and Nora helped me retrieve a large mosquito net from the trunk of my car. We unfolded it, and I attached it to the hooks so the thin, translucent net draped over our couch completely. I told her, "Now you and Jackson have to pick out some books. When the sun sets, we're going to sit out here reading by flashlight, and none of the mosquitos will be able to touch us."

Nora sprinted to the house to load her arms with books, with Jackson in pursuit.

Serena softly said, "I have a feeling that something's going to occur under that mosquito net before the night's over that has nothing to do with reading."

"Stargazing."

She teased, "You or me?" "Both—at some point." "Great expectations."

"I meant we'd both be lying next to each other looking up at the stars before the night's over. But I'm open to other inter-pretations . . ."

11:33 PM

Serena nuzzled into me. "I miss you. We need to find you something other than road construction, so you're not gone so much of the week." She teased, "We could do this more often." The moonlight shimmered off her emerald eyes as she searched mine and asked, "What are you thinking?"

The long week of physical labor was starting to take its toll, but I didn't want the night to end. I shared, "Even if it didn't save my job, I'm glad I spoke out. It deflated the stories Kaiko's crazy relatives were telling, and people began to con-sider reason."

Serena kissed my forehead. "I'm glad you spoke out, too—now that you lived through it. It was scary, though. I love having you right here, at home."

My phone buzzed, ending its silent rest on the edge of the dark fire pit. Seeing it was Forensic Pathologist Faraja Oloo, I answered. With Serena snuggled into my side and the kids safely resting in their beds, Fara's news couldn't be the worst news. I placed her call on speaker.

Fara shared, "I'm sorry for calling you so late, but I felt it was important. I'm at the lab finalizing my report on the autopsy on Kaiko Kane. I've been consulting on my findings with Dr. Ho. When I reviewed everything with her tonight, she suggested I call you immediately, before this becomes public information."

I said nothing, bracing myself for whatever she was delivering. As she paused, I heard the rustle of papers in the background, while my insides expressed a similar cacophony.

Without looking at me, Serena grasped my hand and held it tight in hers.

Fara revealed, "Amaya interviewed the officers who rode along with Kaiko in the ambulance. They noticed something didn't seem right."

I tensed. "What happened?"

"The paramedic was afraid Kaiko's heart rate was a little too fast. He was healthy, so he would have been fine if the medic would have just let it go; however, the medic was worried about ventricular tachycardia, so he was given permission to administer lidocaine hydrochloride. In the cramped quarters of the ambulance, he grabbed a syringe of lidocaine hydrochloride, in concentrated form." She paused and the implications of this began to take shape in my brain. "The concentrated form has to be diluted in saline," she clarified, "and titrated into the vein very slowly. That undiluted injection sent Kaiko into cardiac arrest. It's a miracle they revived him at all, but Kaiko never fully recovered from it. This is what ultimately killed him."

Serena and I finally dared to look at each other; her eyes were wide and hopeful. I asked Fara, "Why didn't the hospital report it?" Relief shot through my veins like adrenaline. I felt vindicated. Serena stayed silent and sturdy, ever my rock.

Fara explained, "They tried covering it up. The medic claimed he didn't realize he made a mistake, and the hospital was reluctant to investigate. After all, the publicity generated around you covered for them. But your good friend, Dr. Ho, suggested I complete an extensive tox screen." She paused. "Kaiko died from a heart attack, induced by an overdose of lidocaine hydrochloride."

My mind quickly began calculating what this meant for me. My road construction days were over. Serena was on the edge of the couch now, looking at me with suppressed excitement. I asked, "So, what happens now?"

"We'll do a press release tomorrow."

Serena whispered to me, "Give Jada the exclusive. She deserves it." I passed the suggestion on.

I hadn't killed Kaiko. This meant no criminal charges—I would be exonerated. I would need to thank Amaya.

Serena smiled through tears of joy. "You and I, my man, are going to celebrate. We should get a hotel room, and let my parents enjoy a night with the kids. I'm thinking the Travail tasting menu, maybe a good band at a small venue."

I kissed her. "Thank you."

Serena's body suddenly tensed, "There are eyes watching us."

I turned my phone light on and aimed it in the direction of the blue, glowing eyes. Three deer stood at the edge of our yard.

Serena laughed with relief. "You and your crazy ideas."

I teased, "Are you worried they've been traumatized by what they've seen?"

She laughed softly. "If they start acting it out, we might hear about it from hunters. 'Deer only seem to do this around the Fredericks.'" She pulled the blanket around herself and headed toward the house. "Time for a comfortable bed, in our safe and secure home."

I gave the stars a last glance before heading in. These stars witnessed Del Walker's murder and the murder of Lillie Belle Allen. But tonight, they witnessed unbridled passion and altruistic love.

John 15:13: "Greater love has no one than this. That someone lay down their life for their friends." Serena stood in front of the inflamed crowd next to me, as stones were cast my direction. If someone comes to your side when people are casting stones, you know you're with someone capable of the greatest love.

My love for Serena is no less.

ABOUT THE AUTHOR

FRANK F. WEBER is a forensic psychologist specializing in homicide, sexual assault and domestic abuse cases. He uses his unique understanding of how predator's think, knowledge of victim trauma, expert testimony, in his true crime thrillers. He has profiled cold case homicides and narrated an investigative show on the Oxygen channel.

MURDER BOOK

murder book (n): the twenty-first century term for a cold case where a homicide is suspected. Jon Frederick spent his adolescence protecting his mentally ill brother and worrying about his parents' farm as it headed toward bankruptcy. So when Mandy Baker, the alluring new girl in town, pursued him, he was easily enamored. But on the day he ended their tryst, Mandy vanished. There is no doubt in the small Minnesota town of Pierz that the flirtatious girl is dead, and there is little doubt that Jon got away with murder. A decade later, Jon is made an investigator with the Bureau of Criminal Apprehension. While investigating a case near his hometown, Jon quietly reopens the murder book on Mandy Baker and begins to see commonalities between Mandy's disappearance and his new case. Digging up the past raises intriguing possibilities with an old friend, Serena Bell—but also forces them to work through old betrayals. As the investigation intensifies, Jon realizes he has crossed paths with the killer before. *Murder Book* was a 2018 Midwest Book Award Finalist in three categories.

THE I-94 MURDERS

A tryst of bondage. A lover's murder. Investigator Jon Frederick returns in a search to uncover the identity of a killer creeping through communities along I-94 in Minnesota, targeting couples who store their fetish photos online. The killer taunts Jon with hidden messages embedded in local media that lead him to Sonia, a young woman with a terrible secret. A fast-paced thriller based on the profile of a true-life serial murderer, The I-94 Murders guides the reader with an insider's light along the dark road of the killer. "Like being privy to both sides of a taut and terrifying game of cat-n-mouse. Frank Weber nailed it again!"~ Timya S. Owen-President of the Twin Cities Chapter of Sisters in Crime. *The I-94 Murders* is a 2019 MIPA Book Award winner for Best Romance.

LAST CALL

Audrey Evans, 19, disappears in the dead of an arctic winter night after leaving a convenience store in Brainerd, Minnesota. Investigator Jon Frederick is called in and is not about to let Audrey end up one of the 40,000 missing women in the U.S. In Jon's personal life, a deceptive past lover jars his intense relationship with Serena and sets in motion a pending tragedy. The explosive situation is amped up further after Jon's name is used to solicit a woman, and one last call detonates it all. Referencing actual Minnesota crime cases, this spine-tingling thriller tests an investigator's tender compassion and the gritty resilience of a soft spoken young woman. *Last Call* is the 2020 MIPA Book Award winner for Best Romance.

LYING CLOSE

A hunting accident, a rural home break in, and the disappearance of a teen, all occur in a 30 mile stretch of rural Minnesota. Jon Frederick realizes they are all symptoms of a larger problem. Lying Close also involves a relationship between a white rural Christian, and a Somali Muslim woman in St. Cloud. It's hard to believe in 2020 that there are still young people in the United States who can't tell their parents who they're dating because of hate. *Lying Close* is a thrilling mystery, with a forbidden love affair.

BURNING BRIDGES

Harper Rowe defies her mother's last wish to search for her biological father, only to find she's opened a door better left shut. What happened to Billy Blaze? Based on a true story, this thriller contains his actual criminal history. A true crime novel loaded with unsavory characters, dangerous situations and the reality of the underground drug world in St. Cloud. The story takes you on a ride with surprising twists from Bemidji to St. Cloud, Minnesota, in the midst of the Covid era and the Minneapolis riots.

Purchase the books and receive them in the mail with no shipping fee from: **frankweberauthor.com**